Their Language is the Sun

Their Language is the Sun

A Novel of 1966

CHRISTOPHER WARD

The Minos Press

Published by The Minos Press, Cambridge, 2025

www.minospress.co.uk

ISBN: 978-1-7396322-3-6

For my dearest departed love
and for the children who inspired this book

Comrades to whom our thoughts return
Brothers for whom our hearts yearn
When words are over;
Remember that in each direction
Love outside our own election
Holds us in unseen connection:
O trust that ever.

WH Auden

THE MAIN CHARACTERS

The Big Five – Older children who are to leave Park House for Binstead soon

Gloriana	Red-haired reader and thinker and poet. She narrates part of the story
Patch, Patrick	Red-faced, well-padded boy. Leader amongst the children. Chief of the Elecs, the children whose chairs are powered by electric batteries
Mick	Big, russet-haired, freckled boy. Chief of the Mecs, the children in manual chairs
Greg	Strong, dreamy, a philosopher among thousands, pop song artist
Helen	Raven-haired beauty girl. Her hormones are raging

Other important children

Robbie	Older boy already transferred to Binstead. Budding lawyer
Kevin	Harpo-haired, potty-mouthed. He has sticks and National Health specs
Dan	Haemophiliac, the only bigger child who can run about. He can bash you but you can't bash him

The young women, the nurses

Lizzie	Nurse with a gratey Essex accent, a nice figure, and wild black hair

Debbie	Tall handsome nurse with a golden mane. Best friend of Flick
Flick	Skinny petite nurse with close-cropped black hair. Best friend of Debbie
Angela	Blonde nurse, country girl from Suffolk

The lads

Richard	Boy volunteering before he goes to university
Pete	Muscly young handyman with a 42 inch chest

The main grown-ups

Jane Ratcliffe	BA SRN. Acting Warden of *Park House, Home for the Less Able Young*
Mr. Salter	The sallow Bin Man. Head of *Binstead Asylum for Incurables*
Mr. MacAskill	Head teacher in the school. Something happened to him in Africa
Miss Payne	Possibly tarty swimming teacher
Mrs. Noble	Warden of Park House. On a sabbatical in California

The animals

Bertie	A greasy mongrel
The birds	Tropical birds – a turaco, parakeets, a pair of Guinea fowl

PART ONE: JUNE 1966

1

This is the day our doom begins. This is the day the Bin Man comes for Robbie.

At first the Vehicle of Doom is a tiny dot far off. It looks like a black ant, and for a long minute it stays that way.

I sign to little Harpo-haired Kevin who is standing grumpily at the window beside me.

'Fuck me, it's the Bin Man,' he mutters.

He knows what he has to do. Off he stumbles on his sticks, zig zag, zig zag and only once falling over before he gets to the door. From there he starts bawling in his thick Cumbrian accent,

'Fuckin' Bin Man cum for Robbie, innit.'

There's a low moan from the gang who are massed in the Great Hall. I hear Patch calling out in his piping voice, 'Right mates, let's get this over with', and they all move out. I can hear the buzz of the electric chariots and in a few moments there is Patch, hugely plump and red, whizzing out in his silver and vermilion Armstead 302 at the head of his posse in their motorized chairs, the ones we call the Elecs because their chairs are powered by electric batteries. Behind them, all the Mecs in their manual chairs throng out. Big russet Mick leads the Mecs, shouting *Gangway, gangway!*

Lizzie and Debbie, my special nurses, are already out there taking five in the afternoon sun. I can see them loafing against the ivy-covered bit at the front of the House, next to the big front door that we never use. Handsome Debbie's got her red mini-skirt on, which in my view is a bit of a mistake for a big girl like her. Lizzie is in her old jumper and jeans, which look okay, because with Lizzie it's her figure you notice anyway. She's smoking, lolling by the tarnished old brass plaque that says *Park House, A Home for The Less Able Young*. She's got her hand cupped round the fag to hide it from the Rat but I can see the little wisps of smoke curling up behind her. Then she puts her hand to her lips and takes a huge puff, wretched girl.

Now I can see the black ant moving from the gates along the drive towards the copse. The Vehicle of Doom starts to climb the rise and then it disappears amongst the trees.

The big front door swings open and out steps the Rat herself — Miss Jane Ratcliffe BA SRN. She shouldn't be coming out that way! Only Mrs. Noble, our Warden, comes out that way, and the Rat is only Acting Warden whilst Ma Noble's away on her sabbatical.

And yes, the Rat's in full regalia, plaid skirt, buttoned up blouse, cardy, thousand denier stockings, steel tipped brogues. She turns her basilisk eye on Lizzie who has just adeptly flicked her gasper into the nearby drain. Smoke continues to rise from it. However, it seems the Rat is too worked up about Robbie's transfer to bother about that.

The Rat barks something out to my two girls. She obviously wants them to stem the tide of Elecs and Mecs and Walkers that is now surging across the gravel towards the narrow neck where the drive which leads from the gates swings round to enter the big gravelled parking area in front of the House.

Lizzie and Debbie shake their heads. They say something to the Rat and head off towards the Great Hall. I think they may be coming to get me, so that I can see whether Robbie escapes his Doom again.

Patch and the Elecs and Mick and the Mecs are now

massed in the narrow neck of the turn below the parking area. Their chairs are all mixed up together in a solid wedge. They fill the drive five chairs across and ten deep. Patch's idea must be to stop the Vehicle of Doom from getting to the House.

Big, slow, dreamy Greg wheels his manual chair across the gravel towards them. Alongside him is Bertie, our old mongrel who turned up last year and who has sort of attached himself to Mick and Greg. Bertie is black and white and greasy. He has no status, he's not an official pet or anything. As usual, he is swivelling his bulgy eyes from side to side, on the look-out. I can see the whites. He has the guarded look of a dog living on the edge.

Greg and Bertie are the last to join the gang in the narrow neck, apart from a couple of little Walkers who are chucking gravel at each other. They're so young they think this is a picnic or something.

Jane Ratcliffe BA SRN is now plodding towards the gang. Her heavy shoes sink into the thick gravel and she makes slow going. However, her bulby piano leg calves work mightily and at last she makes it to the lawn. She skirts the phalanx of Mecs and Elecs and steps onto the drive in front of them.

Meanwhile the Vehicle of Doom pokes its ugly bull nose out of the copse. I can hear the crashing of the gears. It's an attempt at a tricky change down from second to first.

The Vehicle chugs along until the driver can be plainly seen behind the steering wheel, framed in the windscreen — and yes! — it's none other than the Bin Man himself, Mr. Salter, Warden of the Bin.

Negotiating around a pothole in the drive, Mr. Salter seems to get his double declutch sequencing wrong again. There is an excruciating grinding sound of metal tortured to the limits of endurance. The Vehicle of Doom stops right there, about a hundred yards from where Patch and the gleaming chariots of the Elecs are massed, all mixed up with the sturdy bodies of the manual chairs and their strong armed, big shouldered Mec riders.

Dreamy Greg has now wheeled through the gang and joined Mick and Patch at the front. He sits there impassive in his outsize mechanical chair, resting his massive head on one fist, bearing himself like a philosopher amongst thousands.

I wonder, does Greg actually know that we Big Five are also headed for the Bin next year? That one of these days Mr. Salter will be coming for us – for Mick and me and Helen and Patch and for dreamy old Greg himself. Or maybe not for Patch... ah well.

And where exactly is my beautiful Helen today? Still in bed, perhaps, which is one way of dealing with the rage of teenage hormones, I suppose.

Little Kevin, his Harpo hair glistening in the sun like a Brillo pad, is doing a sort of war dance with his sticks on the grass beside the gang until he tumbles over and goes down heavily in a frenzy of waving sticks and *fuckin' this* and *fuckin' that*. I can easily hear him even from my window.

Lizzie and Debbie put their heads round my door.

'Gloriana darling, do you want to come and see the fun?' Lizzie asks, although she doesn't need to ask. Of course I want to see what happens, even though it won't be fun. So I nod and they start shoving and tugging on my big bed to roll me out. It's heavy going but Debbie's a well-built girl and Lizzie's a tough little Tomboy at heart. They get me out of my room with only modest damage to the door frame. As I go, I can see through the window that the Rat has reached the gang and is confronting them, bravely in my view as they look a fearsome lot, all in a wedge like that.

Lizzie and Debbie whizz me across the Great Hall, scraping the big black and white tiles, but they've been scraped for centuries, so we don't care. The two girls are as keen as I am to get out and see if Robbie can escape his Doom again. Lizzie's running ahead, pulling and steering with one arm. She glances back at me. The effort is putting a bit of colour in her pretty pale face and it suits her. When she sees me looking at her, she does a pantomime of panting and sticks out her tongue.

'Oi,' Debbie calls out as we veer into the crap old Thirties sideboard that's stood empty along the wall of the Great Hall since forever. Debbie is doing the heavy pushing but she's not out of breath at all. I can see her lovely steady face above me. She glances down and makes a little pouty kiss at me.

And wow, now we're out and the girls are rushing me through the thick, resisting gravel. They keep up the momentum until we're about halfway and then my wheels get stuck and the girls start effing and blinding good-naturedly as they yank me along towards where the Rat is now haranguing the gang.

'Move back! Move back!' she's shouting in her corncrake voice. She grabs at a manual chair and by prodigious effort manages to heave it off the drive onto the grass. However, it's just a Littley, about seven the kid is, and as soon as the Rat's back is turned the boy slips his chair back onto the drive.

Lizzie's labouring now, and even Debbie's beginning to flag. This gravel's literally about a foot deep and we get stuck in one especially arduous bit. Lizzie does some more mock panting pantomime hanging over the end of the bed. Her pretty face is quite pink with it all. Debbie says, 'Shall we just watch from here, darling?' As we have a perfect side-on view of Patch, Mick and the gang, and of the Rat, and also of Mr. Salter the Bin Man who has now clambered out of the Vehicle of Doom, given it an ill-humoured kick with his over-sized foot, and started to trudge menacingly towards the gang – it's a yes. I can see everything and hear everything from here.

As Mr. Salter moves slowly and heavily towards the Rat and Patch's posse, I see that the general atmos of menace which goes with him is made up of certain particulars. There is the thin greying hair combed across his balding pate and brilliantined into place. There is the skull-like visage, with the hollow eyes and sunken cheeks the colour and texture of bruised fruit. There is the cadaverous and lanky figure clothed in an ill-fitting suit from a ten-pound tailor, badly rumpled at the crutch and bagging at the knees. And the outsize black shoes that convey his huge plates of meat step by menacing step across the distance that separates the Vehicle of Doom from Patch's posse.

Mr. Salter strides up to where the Rat is hopelessly struggling with the chair of another little Mec. Patch, Mick and the gang look on, motionless and silent. Patch has been pursuing his political studies recently, reading up on Gandhi and the methods of passive resistance.

Salter wisely ignores all this and gets straight to the heart of the matter.

'Who's in charge here?' he asks brusquely, peering at the Rat.

'Err,' says the Rat. Salter's mouth contracts inwards as if he is sucking something bitter up a clogged straw.

'And who might you be?' he asks in rude voice.

'Erm... Miss Ratcliffe, Jane Ratcliffe. Erm... how do you do.' She holds out her hand towards Mr. Salter who ignores it, so she draws it back again. 'I'm... erm... standing in, as it were.'

'Ah, Lady Bunfunkington's off on her jaunt to California already is she?'

'Lady...? Oh! Mrs. Noble, you mean. Yes, yes, that's right. She's off on her sabbatical. I'm standing in.'

'Well, where's the prisoner then?'

'Erm... prisoner...?'

'Ah, I see... Not to worry, just a manner of speaking. It's... err...' Mr. Salter consults a clipboard. 'Robert Willis. Transfer to Binstead. I've come for him meself, so let's be having him.'

'Err, yes, err...'

Wow! In all this menagerie, the Rat has completely forgotten the Main Idea – that Robbie's supposed to be here to surrender to Mr. Salter and be carted off to Binstead. The Rat scans the gang, presumably hoping against hope that Robbie is hidden amongst the throng. But of course he isn't.

The Rat looks about in a satisfyingly hopeless way. She spots Lizzie and Debbie lounging over the end of my bed. Lizzie has even managed to light a Woodbine. She ducks down every so often for a quick puff.

'Elizabeth, Deborah, where is Robert? Can you go and fetch him here please. Mr. Salter has come to make his transfer.'

The girls look up.

'Sorry, Miss Ratcliffe,' Debbie says quite politely. She's the better brought up of the two.

'What do you mean, *Sorry*, Deborah? Please go and find Robert and bring him here at once. Mr. Salter's waiting.'

'Oh, right.'

Debbie gives her little red skirt a tug. She crunches off across the gravel and disappears inside.

The Rat tries to engage Mr. Salter in a conversation about the weather. His dead eyes rest scornfully on her for a moment and then he turns and walks right up to the gang who are still crammed into the narrow neck of the drive. He scans the crowd for a minute. Nobody says anything. A couple of Littleys start to cry but Patch glances round at them and they hush up.

'You,' Mr. Salter says, looking at Patch.

Patch lets his little piggy eyes rest on Mr. Salter for a moment.

'Yes, you, the fat red one in the Armsworth 302.'

There's a faint murmur of surprise. Mr. Salter may not have been to charm school but he knows his electric chariots, it seems. However, nobody considers this a plus point and the gang at once resume their sullen look.

'Yes, you, fat boy. You look like a ringleader, so get this lot cleared out of my road. I've got to get me van up.'

I am watching the Rat's face during this sally and it's conflict I see battling there. And I know what it is. The Rat's new to management. It's only her second week in charge. She wants to do well. There is a situation. She wants to learn from Mr. Salter how to handle it. She's watching him eagerly for tips. And yet...

I can't help smiling. The problem is – when Mr. Salter speaks, his voice is, well, not to put too fine a point on it – rather *common*. Agh agh aiee, as the Treens in Mick's *Eagle* comic cry.

Meanwhile, Patch is still posing as Gandhi. His piggy eyes drop down, he's not engaging. His plump lips are a scornful slot between the great red dewlaps of his cheeks. His regal scorn is strengthened by his kit. He's got on a bright red shirt, buttoned up tight. You can see the coils of kingly fat rolling down his Michelin-man body. Nobody budges an inch.

'Bugger this,' Mr. Salter says and stumps off back towards the Vehicle of Doom. The Rat stands looking shocked beyond belief, presumably by Mr. Salter's fruity language. She is making motions with her hands as though she were washing them extremely thoroughly, just like in those *Instructions to Nurses for Proper Hand-Washing* that no one at the House in living memory ever took a jot of notice of.

Debbie now saunters out through the doors of the Great Hall. She has been inside an implausibly short time of about two minutes max. As she comes towards Lizzie and me, she swirls her lovely long blonde hair unconcernedly. The sunlight catches it and for a second it shines like shot silk. She looks as though she hasn't a care in the world.

But here is the Rat scurrying over, smoothing her plaid skirt with her meaty-looking hands.

'Well?' she asks, 'well?' Behind her lamp-like specs, the Rat looks the polar opposite of Debbie i.e. incredibly stressed.

'Oh, yes, Robbie,' Debbie says in her nice drawl. 'No, I couldn't find him. Sorry.'

'But you must, you must.'

Debbie offers nothing further, but gives her hair another swirl. At the other end of my bed, Lizzie is looking shifty. The colour's gone from her pretty face now and she's crinkling up her nose. From where she's got her hands out of sight below the level of the bed, wisps of blue smoke curl up and drift into the blue empyrean of the perfect afternoon sky.

The Rat gives Lizzie a suspicious look but her mind is grappling with the higher concern.

'I need to know where Robert is,' she says in a peevish way, as though this all had to do with her and her authority.

Which, Jane Ratcliffe, it definitely has not. Don't you see it's about a larger thing altogether? That it's about the Doom of Robbie, my soulmate, my brother?

Just at this moment up pops real trouble. This is in the shape of Dan, our one and only Big Walker. He's a haemophiliac, which is rotten for him, but also rotten for us as it means he can run about and bash kids up and you can never ever bash him back, even if you could catch him which you can't because he's a Walker and he can run very fast. If you bashed him, he'd bleed to death or something. Dan has impunity. He's as pretty as a stoat and twice as nasty.

It's just as I am reflecting on Robbie my soulmate and the Rat is having a pet and looking daggers at Lizzie that this Dan wanders round from the hydrangea lawn where's he's probably been pulling the legs off beetles. He scrunches over the gravel towards us.

'Lookin' fer Robbie?' he asks nonchalantly. He's got this way of speaking where he keeps his teeth closed, so you can see his verminous little incisors when he talks.

'Oh, yes, Daniel, yes' cries the Rat, like he'd just delivered her from lions or some such. And the little stoat says, 'OK, I'll fetch him. I know just where's he's hid his self.'

Ratcliffe! You can't let him get away with that, surely!

But she does. She positively beams. She lets Dan say OK and she isn't going to dock him sixpence off his pocket money, like she does everybody else in her recently-declared War on OK!

Lizzie is taken up with surreptitiously stepping on her cigarette butt, so she apparently misses this corrupt exchange and the flagrant breach of the rule of law under which we sometimes imagine we are living. But Debbie and I give each other horrified looks. Debbie is a big, placid, lovely girl who is rarely disturbed but now her lips part and her eyes narrow and her brow furrows. It seems Robbie's really for it now.

I wonder briefly if russet Mick the Mec couldn't go after Dan and give him a good kicking before he can get to Robbie. When he wants to, Mick can move like lightning in his new tungsten Lavington Mechanical. However, Dan has already sprinted round the corner of the Great Hall and soon he can be seen running at top speed up the path to the Tower. Which, of course, must be where Robbie has hidden himself.

It seems Robbie's running out of options. He's tried a chicken pox scare which bought him a couple of weeks, and he got Kevin to stamp on his specs, which was worth another week. Today, it seems all he's got left open to him is hiding in the Tower. In his chair and with his abbreviated legs he wouldn't have been able to get any further.

There is a sudden roar and we look towards the Vehicle of Doom, which has been revived by Mr. Salter's attentions. Mr. Salter has been bending over, cranking the thing for the last five minutes. Now he straightens up, withdraws the starting handle, and climbs into the cab. He gives the monster full throttle. Clouds of blue smoke drift across the lawn towards the hydrangeas.

There is a bout of grinding of recalcitrant gears and crashing of the dicky clutch and then the Vehicle of Doom lurches forward and heads towards Patch and his posse. Mr. Salter, framed in the windscreen, is the picture of vengeance. As the Vehicle picks up speed, some of the Littleys cry out, and young Kevin shouts,

'Fuck me, he's going to run us over.' He scoots onto the grass where he at once tumbles down.

'Steady,' Patch says in his high-pitched voice. It's the first time he's spoken.

It turns out that it's not Patch and the posse that is under threat but little Kevin sprawling on the lawn. Mr. Salter has rumbled almost up to Patch's front line which holds steady, but then he gives an almighty yank on the steering wheel and the Vehicle mounts the bank onto the lawn and rattles on in the direction of the hydrangeas. Kevin can be seen letting out some expletives but these are lost to the deafening thrum of the Vehicle of Doom's tappets.

Fortunately Mr. Salter, alerted by the sun caught on Kevin's round National Health specs, spots the little kid thrashing on the ground and swings the Vehicle of Doom aside. He regains the courtyard in front of the House by way of the hydrangea bed. The Rat covers her eyes as the Vehicle ploughs through a Prize Blue. The damage is fortunately minor and can no doubt be repaired in a season or two, as can the deep tracks scoured by the Vehicle in the prized sward of the lawn.

Mr. Salter manoeuvres the Vehicle off the lawn behind Patch's posse. He then speeds up across the gravel and swings the vehicle around in a handbrake turn and brings it to a halt.

'Yah! Yah!'

Dan is screaming from the path below the Tower as he trundles poor Robbie down towards the waiting parties. Robbie is gripping on to the armrests of his chair for dear life as Dan careers along the path and shoves poor Robbie across the thick gravel. Dan pulls up breathless, his stoat-like charms temporarily obscured by a patina of sweat and a bright puce colouring to his cheeks.

'Found him in the Tower, din I?' Dan looks to Mr. Salter eager for praise or points or something but he quickly discovers the low esteem in which the victor holds the Quisling. Mr. Salter pushes Dan aside and grasps the handles of Robbie's chair and begins to wheel Robbie towards the Vehicle of Doom. Robbie's dear face is pale but he looks determined.

Meanwhile, Patch is backing everyone out of the neck of the drive onto the courtyard. He orders the Walkers out first and they jump to it, then the Mecs, and at last his Elecs who manoeuvre their heavy chairs laboriously to turn in the narrow space. It takes a minute or two but by the time Mr. Salter has wheeled Robbie up to the Vehicle of Doom, the whole posse is massed there.

The dog Bertie is just finishing a careful round of peeing on each of the tyres of the Vehicle of Doom in turn. Mr. Salter kicks Bertie, which draws a gasp of disapproval from everyone except the Rat.

Mr. Salter opens the door of the Vehicle and everyone presses forward to peer inside to see the famous Straps. And yes, they're there alright, thick leather thongs to hold down the reluctant. Which would include anybody in their right mind headed for The Bin.

Ah Robbie, my reader, my brother, my love.

Mr. Salter leans inside the Vehicle and starts ferreting around. I can see he is unclasping the thongs, readying everything to accommodate Robbie's rather unorthodox anatomy.

While Mr. Salter is rummaging, I look at Robbie. He spots me and smiles and gives me a gay little wave. Seeing this, Patch calls out in his piping voce,

'Hurrah for Robbie!'

Everybody starts shouting that and Robbie looks really pleased at the send-off.

Mr. Salter straightens up and turns round.

'So,' he says to the Rat who is standing nearby shifting her weight nervously from foot to foot on the gravel, 'so, who's going to pop him in then?'

The Rat looks round for Debbie who's good at heavy lifting but she and Lizzie, anticipating this demand, have adroitly dropped down on their hands and knees behind my bed where they are nicely out of sight.

'You'd better do it then,' Mr. Salter says, pointing rudely to the Rat.

'Oh, no,' she says quickly, 'oh no, I couldn't do that.'

Mr. Salter looks scornful.

'Righty ho then,' he says. 'If you want a job done properly...'

He leans over Robbie's chair and after a bit of experimenting, he gets one arm round Robbie's thin shoulders and the other under Robbie's bum and hoists him up.

In Mr. Salter's arms, with his little body and his big black specs, Robbie looks like a ventriloquist's dummy. He looks like Archie Andrews.

Mr. Salter steps towards the Vehicle of Doom. As he does so, Robbie leans towards him, into his neck. He looks like he's going to give him a nuzzle or even a kiss. But it's not a kiss because Mr. Salter does a leap and a stagger and lets out a kind of scream and he throws Robbie face down on the seat of the Vehicle and starts to hit him on the bottom with his hand, whack whack whack. As he does this, we all see a big red mark on Mr. Salter's neck where Robbie has bitten him.

After about three or four of these blows, Mr. Salter pauses. He puts his knee on Robbie's back to pin him down and starts rummaging in the Vehicle. After a moment he pulls out a cane.

'Right, you little cunt,' he cries and raises the cane.

A great cry of No! goes up, within which even the Rat's voice can be heard. No!

Mr. Salter pays no attention but takes a couple of not very well aimed cuts at Robbie's bottom. One of these lands on the door frame of the Vehicle and the other on the back of the seat. And then as Mr. Salter is preparing to correct his stroke and make sure that his third cut lands on target, several things happen.

First, Robbie rolls off the seat. He slithers to the ground and flails about waving his arms and his little legs and shouting,

'I'll sue, I'll sue!'

Bertie rushes up and starts to lick Robbie's face.

And then an unknown youth, a walking biped youth, tall, mildly pimpled, with floppy brown hair and not very impressive physique, dashes up the drive where he has been progressing at an accelerating pace towards this unusual scene.

The youth cries, 'Stop that! Stop that at once!' He grabs the cane from Mr. Salter's hand and smartly snaps it across his knee.

For a moment there is absolute silence and then everybody except for Mr. Salter and the Rat begins to clap and cheer.

The New Man has arrived.

2

At tea time, views in the Nurses' Lounge are sharply divided.

Big Debbie is not unkind. She is on the sofa, sitting with her cuppa in a queenly way. With her free hand, she pulls her red mini-skirt down over her big round thighs and says that frankly the New Man looks a bit of a weed. Settling down next to her with an iced fancy, her best friend, the skinny elegant Flick, backs her up, even though she hasn't seen the New Man yet.

Lizzie's inclinations are more liberal. She saw the look on the Rat's face when the New Man snapped old Salter's cane. Not that it had stopped Robbie being carted off to Binstead, but at least Robbie and the New Man had given Mr. Salter and the Rat what for first.

'Where is he anyway? He hasn't come for his tea or anything. And he's down to take swimming.'

'Probably having a quick J Arthur in his room,' Flick says. She doesn't think that much of men.

Lizzie decides she'll take the New Man up his tea and have a proper look at him. She makes up a tray with a cup of milky tea and two lumps, a toasted tea cake and a couple of iced fancies. She heads out under the appraising eye of the other nurses. Flick gives her a scornful look.

Sadly, just outside the New Man's room there's a difficult little staircase and Lizzie trips. She plunges forward and the lukewarm milky tea spills down her front, making a big wet panel on her green jumper.

'Bleedin' hell,' she cries, shooting forward into the New

Man's room. Although it's broad daylight and the sun is shining, the curtains are drawn tight. The sunlight poking through a chink in the curtains falls directly onto the principal object in the room, a narrow bed and on it the New Man stretched out quite naked. As Lizzie crashes into the bed, spilling the rest of the tea and the iced fancies over him, he leaps up and lets out a surprisingly high-pitched scream.

Lizzie grabs the rumpled sheet from the bed and begins mopping at her sodden jumper which is now clinging to her front. She feels the New Man's eyes upon her and glances at him. He is up against the wall, looking terrified. His body is hairless apart from the sprawling locks on his head and the dark fuzz around his strangely pointy willy.

''allo,' Lizzie says. She puts on her Essex accent because she has heard the New Man is posh, or posh-ish anyway. 'I see you're in your birthday suit.'

'Hallo.'

Lizzie feels disappointed. Nude against the wall, he now looks soft and daft.

'Sorry about that,' she says. 'I thought I'd bring you a nice cuppa and some cake and have a butchers at the same time.'

'You certainly did that,' he says. At which, Lizzie softens her scornful look very slightly and gives a short laugh.

'By the way, I'm....'

'I know who you are,' she says, 'you're the New Man. We all seen you just now. That was fab, what you did.'

The New Man grunts. In the half-darkness, Lizzie can't see his look. She tosses down the sheet, which now has a brownish patch on it.

She takes a step back towards the door. She is looking at his smooth shiny chest. Still up against the wall, he passes his hand through his floppy brown hair.

'Well, I'd better be off then. Don't forget you're down for swimming after tea.'

But as Lizzie turns to leave, a crowd of the other nurses turns up at the door. They push in. Lizzie is carried along before them almost up to where the New Man is standing. The girls all stare at him and burst out laughing.

'Blimey,' skinny Flick says.

'We came to see what you're up to, Lizzie. We heard the horrible screams. What's that all down your front?'

'Aw, shut it, Debbie. An' I can see your knickers.'

Debbie pulls her red mini-skirt down a fraction.

'The New Man hasn't been here five minutes and you...'

Debbie says 'New Man' in a humorous, mocking way, and all the girls laugh. They all go on staring at him. He crosses his hands over his private parts.

'New *Boy*, more like.'

'An' he's got a name, thank you very much, Richard, innit?'

The New Man, Richard, nods in a dejected way, looking down at his feet.

'Cat got your tongue, cat got your tongue,' a couple of the girls chant.

'Oh, bugger off, you lot. Leave the poor kid alone. Here.' Lizzie picks up the soggy sheet and hands it to Richard who swiftly wraps it round his waist.

'Hallo, what have we here?' Debbie is remorseless. She is holding up a book she has grabbed from the bedside table.

'*Nausea. Nausea* by Jean... Paul... Sarter.'

'It's quite philosophical actually,' Richard blurts out unwisely.

'*Come off it.* Is it a man called Jean, or a woman called Paul? Either way, they make me sick.'

The girls all laugh and cast jeering eyes on Richard, who

has shifted to the corner of the room, as far as he can get from the crowd. He moves uneasily from foot to foot.

'And what's all this?' Skinny Flick is now yanking a strange contraption of steel tubes and springs out from behind the scratched old wardrobe.

Bullworker, she reads out, looking at the tubes.

'F off, Flick,' Lizzie says in an exasperated voice, glancing at Richard who is still in the corner sporting the stained sheet like a fakir. She sees now the faintest of manly shadows across his gleaming chest. He looks so young. She feels a new surge of sympathy for him. Now she wants to protect him, like a pet or a bratty little brother.

'*Bullworker,*' Flick reads out again. It's written on the tubes. '*Bullworker puts bands of steel around chest and biceps.*'

The girls all laugh mockingly and Richard colours up.

'Come on,' Lizzie says firmly, 'leave him alone. He's just a kid. Anyway, we gotta get the children ready for swimming.'

The girls begin to amble out, making a selection of further sarcastic and filthy remarks on the New Man and swivelling their eyes up and down his body in a taunting way.

Lizzie stays till last. When the others have left, she picks up the broken cup and saucer from the bed and retrieves the teacake and the iced fancies from the floor.

'Sorry about that,' she says in a matter-of-fact manner. 'They don't mean no harm.'

Richard wants to say he's been to boarding school and after that no initiation rites could possibly faze him. But he's not sure Lizzie would understand. And anyway, it's not quite true. He's never been through it with girls before.

3

Gloriana looks forward to the joy of the pool.

Now Robbie's gone, I feel like dying. But I'm putting it off for the next hour at least. The Rat can kill me then. But first, it's sacrament time. First, it's bathing in the pool.

I'm sliding in. I let the warm smooth waters fold around my limbs. My cares and limits float away. Yes, really. In the pool, I always think and say that I am the *unbound, unbounded being that was intended all along.*

It's like that miracle pool in the Bible that the Rat's always banging on about — Siloam or Bethesda or whatever. The halt and the lame are ranged round on loungers. The surface of the water gets troubled, they make a dash for it, and first one in gets healed.

So far, this hasn't happened at Park House but we live in hope.

And boy oh boy, do we need hope. Robbie's been carted off in straps to Binstead. Next year us Big Five are going to be carted off in straps too. And Binstead's a lifetime sentence. So, yes, sacraments are spot on just now. Miracles are most welcome.

I'm slipping in. Aaaah, the first moment is the best. It is as warm as warm. I slide in. In a moment, I'm floating free, free from my shackles. No longer a sad struggling animal of earth. I'm a creature of the Vendian deep. The amphibian balance is reversed, tilted back to water. My old soul regains its primal element.

I float and float and the water laves me. I'm back in amniotic fluid, back when I had a mother, back before I shot out into this world of difficulties.

I dream I'm in that other pool, Bethesda or whatever. The waters ripple, I am made whole.

Tarty Miss Payne presides over our swimming. Actually, it may be that Miss Payne is not really a tart, she just looks like one, the way her rather pitted skin is so pasted up. She slaps on powder inches thick and then daubs these big bright roundels of rouge on her cheeks, and lipsticks her rather bulging-out lips into a violent red gash. Underneath I think her hair is probably a sort of mousy brown but she heaps on loads of henna, not very expertly, so it comes out bright orange, with some reddy-goldy streaks running through it here and there.

On balance, overall, looked at from an independent point of view, you would say definitely she **is** a tart, but then there's no doubt she has a soft heart beneath the powder. As our judicious leader Patch always points out, you have to look at the context. There is no real evidence of tarty ways. Miss Payne does after all have a 'steady' boyfriend, name of Ray, in nearby Billericay. Ray is a used car dealer. He must be very attracted by her stunning athlete's figure (for a woman of forty odd). So, on balance, we think she's tarty, but not actually a tart.

Miss Payne flaunts her lovely figure around in tight blue overalls, or sometimes, for swimming, she may slip into a tight black one-piece bathing suit which shows off her small hard breasts. We generally assume that she can swim, although she has never yet been seen in the water. I don't think her caked-on make-up would survive.

And wow! The New Man, the Richard, is on swimming duty. When he shows up, I am already in, floating lazily on my Lilo. Big, lovely Debbie and her special friend Flick – skinny, sardonic Flick of the close-cropped black hair – they are on either side of me, treading water, making sure I don't flip over. Debbie looks so strong and magnificent in her pink two piece which shimmers and refracts in the water. She and skinny Flick (who is in a stylish turquoise one piece) chat across me comfortably about Cliff Richard (a wimp) and Dusty Springfield (adorable). They start singing *You don't have to say you love me, just because you do*, but then Debbie laughs so much they have to stop.

I thrust the Rat and Sallow Salter from my mind and lie there in the water's embrace, lazily watching Richard. His somewhat stringy form is not escaping the connoisseurial scrutiny of Miss Payne. In fact, he is obliged to parade back and forth before her expert gaze in his old school trunks (a washed-out navy blue with some merit badge stitched on – from here it looks like a curvetting dolphin, I wonder what feats he did for that). He has to trog past la Payne not once but seven times as he delivers the boys to the water, running them along the poolside and past Miss Payne's painted face and discriminating eye to where the ramp slopes down. This is a set-up which allows us to slip straight into the pool. As he brings Mick past, I hear Miss Payne say, 'Richard, hold the fort. I've just got to pop out a mo.'

Richard nips out and immediately comes back carrying little Harpo-haired Kevin — he is the last. Richard walks right down the ramp into the pool with him. Kevin's frail little body starts thrashing furiously, much as it does on land, only without the sticks. 'Concentrate,' Richard says patiently, 'focus. Legs one after the other.' He tries briefly to teach the boy the back crawl, but skinny Kevin only flails and thrashes about like a stifled haddock, and in the end Richard just holds him and lets him flail.

Our great red leader, Patch, is sitting quietly on the pool side, resting his head on the stick of his Armsworth 302. He can't come in these days but he is keeping an eye on his people.

As I watch him, I see his tranquillity suddenly drain away. His head turns. Alarm comes into his red features. Helen, dear Helen, has apparently had enough of spending her teenage years in bed. In fact, she's not only decided to get up, she's decided to come swimming. She is swaying with her lilting gait down the poolside in a clinging yellow one piece swimsuit. She looks lovely, with her smooth olive skin, her long glossy black hair, her delicate face.

She walks along the poolside, her eyes cast down. At first I think the swimsuit has some special properties but then I realize it's just that I haven't spotted how Helen has been developing fast under the cast-offs and shapeless hand-me-downs we children usually get to wear. I see in a flash how curvy she's become. Suddenly she looks like a woman, all the basic ratios are there, and she's got a general overall sheen of something that's quite new. I glance at Richard and see him registering all this too. Then he shuts his eyes and jerks his head away.

He turns Kevin round, so that they no longer face Helen, who is now above them, at Richard's back. Kevin stops flailing and says, 'I'm fuckin' worn out, mate. Get me out of here.'

But before Richard can steer the little kid to the ramp and haul him out, something smacks into the water just beside us and in the great geyser of water that shoots up, there is

Helen, shrieking.

'What the fuck!' Kevin screams.

Helen is thrashing about strangely. She is in the deeper bit, the six foot deep end. She disappears for a moment and there is a strange, shocked pause in which everybody stares at where she went down and is waiting for her to emerge at the other end after three deft strokes. But she doesn't come up and after an eternal moment which lasts precisely about one second, Debbie calls out to Richard 'She can't swim!', and in the same moment Patch is heading for the big red ALARM button on the wall.

As the scream of the alarm goes up, Richard heaves Kevin onto the side of the pool, with the kid bawling *Fuck you, Richard, you motherfucker!* The water cascades off the little boy's skeletal body. But by then, Richard is down at the bottom of the pool scooping Helen up back to the surface and holding her head high, his panicked legs scissoring through the water, thrusting them both towards the ramp.

You can see she is a dead weight but he manages to drag her up far enough so that she is out of the water above the waist. Her body lies there quite inert, nothing about her seems to be moving.

'She's fuckin' dead, mate,' Kevin shouts gleefully. 'You've fuckin' killed Helen!' Some other kids are screaming. Richard dithers, although he must know each moment counts. But does anyone know what to do? Debbie, who is still supporting me, shouts out 'Holger Nielsen, Richard!', and he calls back in a panicky voice 'Is that on the back or the front?' What on earth did he get that merit badge for? Flick, who is on my other side, yells 'Try mouth to mouth!' and you can see Richard looking at Helen and wondering, for example, what if the lungs are full of water? Should he use mouth to nose? We all know these are the questions but the answers seem to be lacking.

Meanwhile, there is no sign of breathing from Helen's newly prominent bosom. The top third or so of her smooth round breasts lies outside the fringe of her yellow costume.

Still Richard dithers, and Kevin, who has grabbed his sticks, scoots over enthusiastically, shouting 'She's kicked the fuckin bucket, mate', and all the other children are shouting and crying.

But then there is the lithe Miss Payne in her tight hugging crimplene gymnastics suit shoving Richard sideways with such force that he falls back heavily into the pool, banging his shoulder against the side. Miss Payne then drags Helen right up the ramp and flips her onto her front and lays the head on the arms which in an instant she gets neatly folded. Then Miss Payne is drawing the arms forward and pressing on Helen's back in simple harmonic motion and generally Holger-Nielsening the girl back from her watery stupor, whilst giving Kevin a deft clip around the ear when he dares to breathe 'She's fuckin dead, in't she?'

And when Helen is quite restored to the land of the living and decently covered in a slightly grubby towel that Mick contributes from the floor of the boys' changing room, and after practically everyone in the entire House has rushed down to gawp and crowd around her, and after one of the little girls who has been reading up on these things has asked her if she has seen the rainbow bridge and were all our pets really waiting for us there, we all get changed and Helen is whisked off to bed and a supper of hot buttered toast soldiers and sweet milky tea, lucky fish! Then Debbie and Flick wheel me back up and as we pass the boys' lats, there is Miss Payne who has cornered Richard. She is pushing him up against the wall with her small hard breasts in the lead and saying,

'I'm going to have to report this, you know, regs and that. And what were you up to there, anyway, my boy? Eh? Eh?'

4

I lie looking through my huge sash window. It's late in the afternoon now and the sun is laying tall shadows across the park. A wave of starlings coils around the ancient lime tree and rockets out of sight, heading for the upper air. I'm tired out after swimming and all the drama of Helen. And I'm sad because this is the time when Robbie used to come and read to me. Every day he came, and we read and we read and we read. That's how we got our education, nothing to do with raffia in school and Mr. MacAskill's stupid antics.

But guess what? Who should walk in but the New Man himself, Richard.

He must have already have heard things about me as he looks quite terrified and very young. I soften my look accordingly, and when he glances at me, I have a very docile, biddable appearance.

Unexpectedly he says,

'Hallo, Bernini girl.'

And then, even more unexpectedly, he adds,

'You're really pretty. And you have such lovely red hair.'

Wow! That is nice of him, and I feel a quick surge of affection.

'One of the nurses — Lizzie is it? – said you might like me to read to you.'

I smile and sign to him YES! But already he has turned to my bookshelf. From behind he looks too thin and his white nylon shirt hangs a little loose on him. As he lifts his right arm to run his finger along the paperbacks that make up my library, I catch a whiff of his nylon-extruded sweat. This boy needs work. He raises his hand to touch the books on the top shelf and his hair flops back.

I look at his hands as he runs his finger along. I see now that they are small deft clever scholar's hands. This gives me great confidence. But I can tell from the slight hunch of his shoulders and a certain quality of his silence that he is disappointed with my little collection. Not surprising really, they are just kids' books, and then only ones approved by the Rat. It's dear Robbie who had all the good books.

Richard taps at the top of a book and it falls into his hand. Interesting choice, Richard.

NOT!

The Naughtiest Girl in the School. Prig's book. You can tell, because it's actually the Ratcliffe's favourite. The one and only time (thank God!) she read to me, the loathsome creature read five chapters of *The Naughtiest Girl* which is a story of one child's Manichean struggle with evil and of her eventual salvation through works. After an hour of this, even la Ratcliffe noticed that I had dozed off, or was pretending to, so she borrowed *The Naughtiest Girl* to finish it off by herself. And as malevolent luck would have it, she actually returned the accursed thing.

I watch Richard closely as he reads, which he does well. He reads the chapter where the Naughtiest Girl is digging for redemption in the School Kitchen Garden under the eye of the priestly Older Boy, Edward. By prodigious effort, she digs up the entire potato bed in record time and then sedulously cleans off her spade and the big nearly new fork and hangs the gleaming tools on their proper pegs in the potting shed.

Later, the Satan-Nemesis figure creeps in and soils the tools. Sadly, the Satan-Nemesis figure is a flat character whose potential interest is never sufficiently developed by Blyton – I always wonder whether Enid really knows how to portray pure pointless evil. Anyway, the Naughtiest Girl is blamed but she is not punished, it is worse than that. The priestly Edward lays his disappointed eye frequently upon her, which stings her more cruelly than any punishment. She feels the monkey bites of shame so dreadfully that it actually makes her Naughty again, which in my view is the only realistic bit in the entire book.

I watch Richard's face whilst he reads out this cack. There is a light brush of fuzz above his upper lip where a moustache might go, and also fuzz on the bit between his cheeks and his ear and down to his chin. All this gives him an engagingly coltish look but sadly not one that will hack it with our girls.

Just as we get to a modestly interesting bit in *The Naughtiest Girl*, the bit where Enid is going to explain to what depths of irredeemable naughtiness the Girl will now sink, Richard snaps the book shut.

'So, what do you think her chances are?' he asks.

Whatever does he mean? Her chances of turning into a first-rate little hypocrite like, apparently, everyone else in the school? Her chances of emerging morally unscathed from such an unsuitable education in all the vices of conformity and lack of imagination?

I suddenly have a horrible thought. The Naughtiest Girl indeed. Surely Richard's not attached to such life-denying tales of regret and absolution?

I give him my questioning look. Very fortunately he now says,

'I mean, I suppose life's not much like that really? Shall we go on with it another time? Or something a bit grainier? I'll look something out for you.'

I mouth *Yes* and he smiles.

Just then Lizzie and Debbie rush in. Lizzie says,

'Rat's called an Emergency House Assembly. Got to get you down to the Great Hall.'

Richard says 'Cheerio, Bernini girl.' Lizzie gives him a funny look and out he goes.

5

I suppose we're going to get a wigging from the Rat. Who cares? Now Robbie's gone, I don't, not particularly.

Lizzie and Debbie heave me down to the Great Hall. They are prattling on about *Ready Steady Go!* but as I don't know anything about *Ready Steady Go!* I am left thinking about Robbie, my brother, my soulmate. Dear Robbie had all the best books. Debbie and Lizzie used to get them for him and he kept them under his bed, away from the Rat's prying eye. She only found them when they packed up his things for his move to the Bin. What's all this? she said, poking at *Of Mice and Men* with her meaty digit. Sod off, you old cow, Robbie said back – he was past caring by then. He always had this exaggerated sense of fairness which was bound to make him cross. After all, nobody said life was fair.

Robbie's thing was he was always answering back. He'd ask *Why?* He'd always say *But you said...* Gosh, he could have been a lawyer, couldn't he? He'd have loved that. But apparently not possible. There was trouble with his legs and so it was Binstead for him, no ifs, no buts, no *Why*, no *But you said...* Watch repair, I think he's going to be doing.

Because that's how it goes. There aren't any lawyers amongst our leavers. We do raffia and crayoning in class. We learn nothing, we know nothing. And then it's banged up in Binstead and throw away the key.

But as for me, as for us, us Big Five due to go next year, I refuse, I absolutely so completely utterly refuse to let Binstead happen to us.

So Richard... I'm choosing you. Today I choose you as my champion. Because if we're ever going to dodge Binstead, we need a thinking, walking, talking guy to do things for us.

So, Richard, get the silly initiation rites with our nurses over with. And when we're free, maybe we'll go and rescue Robbie.

But something bad is about to happen, something really really bad.

Big russet Mick the Mec is heading down to the stables. Mick's the senior Mec, burly sandy-haired freckly Mick, ox-strong, straight-talking Mick, orphaned of both parents, Mick with his practical bent and his love of woodwork.

Mick's trying to put Robbie's carting off and Mr. Salter and the Doom of Binstead out of his mind completely. He knows this is an ostrich policy. He knows a plan is needed. But even though Mick thinks a plan is a good idea and it might even help, he doesn't want to think about it right at this minute. He will think about all that later. Just now he wants to be alone to think about a Great Event that is happening at that very moment not very far away, which will never ever happen again in his entire whole lifetime, maybe never again in the entire history of the world for ever and ever. Something he would die to see or hear or just be some tiny fractional little part connected to somehow anyhow. For Mick's mind is hovering over triumphs, or at least the prospect of them, the triumphs about to be played out before hundreds of millions on a soggy pitch where the ball comes off very quick and an Englishman's foot flies like lightning to connect.

Today is the very first game of the World Cup in London,

and England are going to win it. Says Mick.

Mick bowls across the cobbles to the low stone building that used to be the stables of Park House. Inside, he is surprised to find Pete, Park House's muscly young handyman.

Pete has been off on a week's leave, 'seeing to his girlfriend Jackie' as he has advertised far and wide, especially to the open-mouthed nurses. He is back earlier than expected.

'Everything OK?' Mick asks solicitously. He loves Pete, because Pete is a physical, practical bloke who says what he thinks. It's Pete who has said to Mick not to worry about Binstead, not yet anyway. Pete always says *It's amazing how many problems in life go away if you do absolutely nothing about them.*

Pete and Mick have been making a huge bird cage down in the stables. Pete's idea is to put in a heater and get some tropical birds as fun for the kids. The cage is half done. Rolls of wire and sawn up lengths of four-by-two are lying about everywhere. But for once Pete is not working on the cage. He is bending over the work bench, concentrating on something else.

'Yeah, yeah,' he says absently, avoiding Mick's question. Because things had not actually gone all that well with Jackie.

'Whatcha doing?' Mick asks, at the risk of annoying Pete, who is in fact doing something intricate with a soldering iron.

'Transistor radio. For Gloriana. Six transistors and a diode. Little cracker.'

Mick's heart leaps.

'Can we try it out?' he asks.

Pete nods and deftly slots the bits together and wiggles at the dial and as if by miracle it is the England against

Uruguay game with which the World Cup kicks off. They hear through the crackles Her Majesty the Queen, who is standing all alone in the middle of the vast pitch at Wembley and saying,

I welcome all our visitors and feel sure we shall be seeing some fine football.

Pete snorts. Because Pete is eighteen, old enough to remember the humiliation of England the last time, in '62. His parents actually had a telly even back then and he saw with his own eyes the Brazilians shaft England in the quarter finals. With their thick bags flapping around their knees, our boys had trudged morosely off the field into the tunnel looking like Eighth Army Tommies after an especially brutal pounding by Rommel. At the other end the Brazilians had been samba-ing away, their gleaming thighs dancing gracefully in their sexy little white shorts, the dusky girls hanging off them adoringly.

'Nah,' Pete said, 'don't get your hopes up, lad. The only time we'll get the World Cup is when some stupid dog finds it under a hedge.'

Which was where Pickles the black and white mongrel had recently found the trophy after it was stolen from an exhibition.

Pete's low expectations turn out to be correct in this first game. England plod to a dismal, goalless draw. Even though Kenneth Wolstenholme, the BBC's urbane commentator, says quite justly that the Uruguayans were playing with ten full backs and a goalie, our boys are just lacklustre. Pete is vehement in his scorn.

'Blimey! Win the World Cup? That lot? Fifteen corners and sixteen shots at goal, and they couldn't slot a single one. Might as well throw in the towel right now.'

Mick says nothing but he secretly keeps an optimistic

flame burning in his heart.

Just then, little Harpo-haired Kevin pegs in.

'The Rat's only fuckin' called a emergency thingy in the Great Hall,' he says frothily.

'Payback time,' Mick mutters.

6

Eeny meeny miny mo
Sit the baby on the po

When Debbie and Lizzie heave me into the Great Hall, there's a great hullaballoo going on. The Hall's a ginormous room, the full height of the house and the length of a fleet of buses. It must have been a glory in some ancient period like a century ago or something. Now us lot are here it's looking a bit chipped and chapped. The nymphs on the ceiling have suffered particularly badly. The boys are always aiming their catapults at the softer parts of these sportive girls.

'Where to, darling?' Debbie asks and I indicate my usual place, so they park me up beside the battered old Thirties sideboard that's been dumped along the end wall.

'Showin' off your fuckin' fanny again, Debbie?'

It's little Cumberland Kevin who's been popped up on the sideboard. Kevin's only about ten but he has somehow acquired a big vocabulary.

Debbie gives her red mini-skirt a token tug but it stays right up at the top of her thighs.

'You can just shut your cake hole, young Kevin,' Lizzie says and gives him a light slap on the wrist. Kevin turns his pale face to her. With his billowing curls he really does look like Harpo Marx. His National Health specs glint in the evening sun that's streaming in through the vast old windows of the Hall.

'Fuck off, Lizzie,' he says, but you can tell from the way

he says it that he means Sorry, as he really likes Debbie and Lizzie. He starts drumming with his sticks on the fruit patterns that have been carved into the fully fashioned doors of the old pearwood sideboard.

When he's done
Wipe his bum

Debbie pats my hand and Lizzie arranges my hair a bit and strokes it. They hang about, loafing over the end of my bed. They want to see the fireworks when the Rat comes in.

You could say that the mayhem going on is probably not what the Rat has in mind for her 'Emergency Assembly'. But Patch is in charge here and he's not intent on showing the Rat any particular respect.

Just now he's sitting like a lord in his gleaming Armstead 302. Patch is our leader and every day he looks more the part. He's like a big red pasha now. This last year his conditions have crowded in on him and he has swollen hugely and become all fiery-looking. Patch in shades of red, our Great Elec, Patch who quells unrest with a word, who heals with a touch, who inspirits us by his swagger and bravado.

But also Patch... and here the thought tails off... Patch who is mortal, very mortal, mortal wasting Patch, Patch of limited perspectives, wasted Patch of already so little strength, Patch who's going to have to live out his story by the age of sixteen, who has his own particular Doom hurtling towards him. Patch who can never ever escape his Doom – unless it's into his own myth.

Patch is actually counting out players for British Bulldogs. There are about twenty children huddled in a circle around his flowing red bulk, boys and girls together and all sizes. There are some of the really little kids, seven, eight, nine years old, and it's Mecs and Elecs and Walkers all together, because Patch always makes the games for everyone (with the one exception of the stoat-like Dan).

Tell his mummy what he's DONE

Out goes a little kid, a sandy haired boy who can't be more than eight. He looks relieved.

Patch is counting them out one by one. This always takes the hugest length of time. Of course it would be quicker to count them in, just choose one Bulldog straight away, but that's not how the children like to do it. The counting out's almost better than the game itself. The children cry out excitedly *Dip!* and Patch rattles off the counting-out rhyme, pointing with his finger and turning his big Armsworth 302 around inside the circle.

Red, white and blue
The cat's got the flu

Just then, Mick speeds over in his tungsten Lavington Mechanical and says to Patch,
'She's on her way.'
At once our cheerful mood drains away. We all fall silent.

You can hear her coming from far off. The clack clack of her specially strengthened steel tipped brogues goes before her. Then in she strides — The Rat — Miss Jane Ratcliffe BA SRN.

She's still sporting her signature kit. There's the cable-knit woolly cardigan, heavy, hideous. It's that off-beige colour called taupe. The cardy is pulled well down over the habitual thick skirt which is patterned with an obscure and very dark tartan in sombre browns and greys. She looks very sombre, very taupe, all over.

Her lamp-like specs, set above the tightened lozenge of her mouth, survey us sternly. She spots Richard standing awkwardly at the back and gives him a grim nod.

The Littleys gather in front, a fringe of mechanical chairs and one or two unsteady walkers. Kevin is still up on the crap old Thirties sideboard. Mick and Greg herd the bigger Mecs into a loose formation. The Elecs buzz over to join Patch, who is positioned off to the side.

We put on our usual front of guarded nonchalance. But even this seeps away when the Rat begins to speak.

She swivels her sturdy frame to address us. She notices that Helen is not there.

'Where is that girl?' she asks.

Nobody offers any information. The Rat gives a peevish *Tsk*, and slides her heavy spectacles back up her prominent nose with a single finger. Then she starts.

'First, let me say how disgracefully you all behaved when Mr. Salter came to collect Robert. You brought shame on yourselves and on Park House…'

She pauses, presumably to let the shamefulness sink in. In the silence, Patch can be distinctly heard to say 'Poo'. Probably wisely, the Rat ignores this. She continues,

'I considered what punishment would be appropriate. I thought of simply cancelling swimming. But after long re-flection I have decided that would not be fair to the younger children who, after all, have been misled. And by whom…?'

Does this require an answer? Nobody makes any sugges-tions and the Rat continues.

'I will tell you by whom. It is by you older children, you five older children who might have been expected to know better.'

'Yeah yeah,' Patch says.

'I'll ignore that rudeness, Patrick. But that's exactly the kind of behaviour that has led me to make my decision.'

The Rat's nose is a shiny one and at this point she has to pause to push her great giglamps back up again. As the specs are restored to their place, her eyes swell to a horrid size behind the huge thick lenses.

'A decision that I have not taken lightly, as it is in a way an admission that we have failed here at Park House.'

'Oh, get on with it,' Patch says.

'So I have decided that you older children will be transferred to Binstead early.'

Agh-agh-aieee! Binstead! Early transfer!

She peers at us, presumably to make sure we have taken in this news.

'I have managed…' – she pauses with the exasperated air of one delivering great benefits to her people but only after a tough struggle – '… I mean I was able to have a word with Mr. Salter before he left and he has very kindly agreed, on a quite exceptional basis you will understand, to accept you for early transfer. At the end of this term. That's a matter of weeks. He has even agreed to motor over from Binstead again in the coming days to give you five your Pre-Transfer Evaluation.'

Agggh! Pre-Transfer Evaluation! Agh-agh-aieee!

'Wossat?'

'What is what, Patrick? Do you mean Pre-Transfer Evaluation? Mr. Salter has to… umm… as I understand it, I think he has to evaluate your condition, so to speak… your capabilities and so on and so forth… This will not be easy for me, of course. It will no doubt require quite a bit of extra paperwork.'

'Poo,' Patch says.

'Yes,' says the Rat, 'and once you five have had your Pre-Transfer Evaluation, then you'll be leaving us for Binstead.'

How she manages to convey the capital E on *Evaluation* is a wonder but she pulls it off. And now it is the turn of Richard. She turns her stupendous gaze on him.

'As for you, young man, kindly come and see me. To-morrow morning, *first thing.*'

Richard reddens and looks shamefully guilty. And then out goes the Rat, or nearly, because she has another thought and turns back.

'And if I see that filthy mongrel that was hanging around this afternoon here again, I will have it put down. Is that clear?'

At this, some of the Littleys start to cry. The Rat strides off and the clack-clack of her shoes gradually recedes down the corridor.

I look at Patch beside me and he looks at me from his little currant eyes.

We signal to each other *Resist*. RESIST!

7

Next morning, Lizzie comes in at seven to give me my embrocated rub. She opens the tall shutters. Sunlight pours in and floods the room. Whilst Lizzie massages in my oils, I lie like a sleeping princess waiting for my prince to release me. Vaguely, very vaguely, Richard comes in to this, but I edge the thought away.

Lizzie smooths me all over from the big bottle of lavender water we keep by the bed. She brushes my hair, singing softly *Rapunzel, Rapunzel, let down your red hair*. As she is dressing me, she says, 'Oh, postcard. It's from Robbie at the Bin.'

She says it lightly. She has no idea. She holds it up. It's a picture of Binstead. I can't bear to look. He's drawn a stupid little stick figure of himself gesturing from a slit-like window high up in a tower and he's written some stupid stupid words on the back.

Richard is nervously trailing through corridors, hunting for Miss Ratcliffe's office when Lizzie bumps into him.

Richard is very aware that this is the girl who yesterday has seen him quite nude. Lizzie says nothing about this. She is, nonetheless, carrying in the not quite serious sector of her soul – a large, actually dominant sector of hers – an image of his smooth chest and his curiously pointy willy.

'You look dead scared,' she says.

Richard says he's on his way to see Miss Ratcliffe.

'Cor. I know what you need,' she says and takes him by the hand.

They come out into a small and dismal courtyard that is squeezed between two wings of the house. Although the sky is certainly blue high up and sun is shining somewhere – Richard remembers seeing it earlier on – the yard is sunless and quite cold. Lizzie shivers in her green jumper. Richard notices that it is the same jumper she had on when she burst into his room and that it has a big dark patch across the front. Clearly, Lizzie has not bothered to wash it. He feels this must be evidence of something but before he has time to think about it he sees Lizzie looking at him in a challenging way.

'Ciggies?' she asks.

Richard has no cigarettes, of course, and Lizzie gives him a sidelong look, rolling her eyes, a motion which looks moderately contemptuous to Richard.

'You smoke OP, then?' she says, holding out a brown packet of tiny cigarettes that she has fished out after some intriguing ferreting under her jumper.

'Ummm…' Richard briefly reviews the cigarette brands he knows – Embassy, Kensitas, Capstan, Woodbines. As he takes one of the little cigarettes, the strange thing is, he sees the brown packet is clearly labelled *Players Number 10*.

'OP?'

'Other People's, you nana. You never done this before, have you? Well, never mind. Here, these are matches, you rub one along that black bit on the side and…'

'Alright, alright.'

Richard discovers there are a fair number of humiliations along the road to lighting a cigarette. A quick breeze springs out of the funnel of the bleak walls and blows out his first two tries, and Lizzie makes a grab to get the matches back, which he clumsily evades. However, the intimate sensation of having this little fight with a real live girl instantly cancels out any shaming effect of his keckhandedness. His third try flares in his cupped hands for just long enough for Lizzie to duck her head winningly and get a flame on one corner of the top of her cigarette which she then keeps going by means of several convulsive puffs. He likes the intimacy of her bowed head bent over his cupped hands. She has wavy black hair which is incredibly tousled. It makes her look like a wild creature.

The cigarette burns a bit unevenly at first, down one side, but she passes it to Richard who awkwardly slots his own fresh cigarette between his lips and experimentally wiggles it up and down.

'Blimey, light the effing thing,' Lizzie cries and grabs Richard's unlit cigarette from his lips, sticks it between her own, takes back her own fag from which she then lights Richard's. After contemplating both cigarettes for a second, one in either hand, she passes the unevenly burning half-smoked one to Richard.

'Here. Won't make no difference to you. I mean as a virgin smoker, like. Now get that down you, it'll do you good.'

Richard takes the cigarette. There is a dab of red on it from Lizzie's lipstick. He feels he is entering some exciting dangerous zone. He takes a drag and is in the middle of his first smoker's cough when a sash window just next to them is thrown up with some emphasis.

'Elizabeth and – you, erm, Richard – kindly put out those cigarettes and see me at once.'

'Blimey, it's the Rat,' Lizzie breathes with a careless air that to Richard looks slightly put on.

The bespectacled face of Miss Jane Ratcliffe BA SRN regards them hostilely for a moment and then the window is forcefully closed again.

As a recently demobbed schoolboy, Richard is used to all

forms of authority and, liking a quiet life, generally finds it convenient to buckle under, so he throws down his cigarette on the gravel and steps on it.

'What you do that for?' Lizzie says, narrowing her eyes. A tiny bit of colour has sprung up in her otherwise pallid, almost pasty face. This makes her look somehow roused, but Richard has no idea whether she is angry or what, and he looks at her for more information. It turns out to be a simple thing and he thinks this is something he has learned about her. She says crossly,

'You're such a nit, Richard. That's a waste of a perfectly good ciggy.'

She moves away from the window, down the side of the house, walking close to the sunless wall. She stops for a minute, leaning against the stonework which looks damp, in fact looks like it's been damp since the place was built. Lizzie curls her hand round her cigarette and brings it up towards her face. She takes a long drag and her fingers linger on her lips. It's like a rite, or a sacrament. Or a sex act.

Lizzie flings the cigarette away across the gravel. Sparks fly off it and a tiny wisp of smoke rises straight up towards the heavens.

Jane Ratcliffe kicks off the interview in a robust fashion.

'What in Heaven's name did you two think you were up to there?'

Lizzie and Richard are on the threadbare Axminster carpet in the Warden's office which Jane is occupying while Mrs. Noble the Warden is away on sabbatical in California. Lizzie and Richard don't sit down. In fact, in this segment of the office the only chair is the one behind the desk, and Jane Ratcliffe has chosen to stand during the interview. She is about five nine, Richard guesses, and is quite broad and sturdy looking in an unathletic way.

Lizzie makes an irritated movement as though she were going to answer Jane's absurd question, but she evidently thinks better of it as she says nothing. They both stand and look at Miss Ratcliffe, waiting for her next sally.

The main feature in Ratcliffe's bland and otherwise featureless face is the pair of huge spectacles which dilate her eyes to the size of small saucers. The overall effect is a peevish cross look presumably compensated by extra-power binocular vision. She peers at them through these tremendous magnifiers.

'Elizabeth, you know the rules. No smoking in house or garden. I'm docking you five shillings off this week.'

'Oh no, Miss Ratcliffe, I need the money. I'm really skint.'

'Well, then you can cut down on smoking and whatever other little treats you may be spending your money on, can't you.'

Lizzie's lips wrinkle dangerously. Richard thinks she's going to spit at Miss Ratcliffe. But she apparently masters this elemental urge and says,

'OK.'

'Elizabeth.'

'Sorry.'

'I'll be lenient this time but do remember, sixpence docked off for every time you use that – Americanism. Now, be off with you.'

Richard thinks of trying to leave as well but Jane Ratcliffe flaps her hand at him in a *stay behind and see me* sort of motion he is familiar with from his school.

'Well, young man, this has been a bad start, a bad start indeed. Your behaviour yesterday was, well, inexcusable. You brought disgrace on Park House... and...'

Richard guesses that he has also brought shame on Miss

Ratcliffe. However, she doesn't actually say this. Instead, she says she will be lenient, just this once, but that it will basically be curtains if anything further untoward takes place.

Richard nods humbly. He has the distinct feeling he really is back at school, and in a way he is, as Miss Ratcliffe now starts to explain.

'Setting that aside, let me welcome you here – a home and school for the… ah, less able… where the first things we teach are morals and cleanliness and order…'

A grey light that is slanting in from the window at right angles to where Miss Ratcliffe is standing gives her face an unhealthy leaden look. Words continue to fly out in Richard's direction from her unadorned lips. One or two penetrate slightly. *Dystrophy*, for example. He idly tries to parse *dystrophy* from its Greek-sounding bits (Richard has until recently been studying dead languages). And *spina bifida* should be Latin, shouldn't it, although not mentioned in Virgil as far he knows. But actually, Richard's mind is not particularly engaging with Miss Ratcliffe's speech. Instead, he is looking out of the window, through which he can see the courtyard where he has just smoked his first cigarette and, if the truth be known, just shared his first semi-intimate moment with a real girl. Looking up a bit he can see a sort of buttress and then a small oblong of chalky blue sky across which an aeroplane is lazily crawling.

It appears that Miss Ratcliffe is still talking. His attention is drawn to this fact by a gurgling cough she gives and he manages to pick up on the very end of what she seems to have been saying, which runs,

'… so you see, young man, you mustn't imagine these children have any choices, and they should be under no illusions either. Their lives will be hard, very hard, and we must bring them up that way...'

'What way?'

'We must bring them up hard. You'll see that really is the kindest way. We must prepare them for their future life. For Binstead.'

Richard looks away from Jane Ratcliffe's face which has become oddly animated during this speech. He has found it rather depressing, although he supposes Miss Ratcliffe must know what she's talking about. Instead, he thinks of Lizzie holding the cigarette in her coiled hand and drawing smoke into her lungs, and of the red from her lips on his one, the one she gave him. He is greatly regretting having put his foot on it.

'Oh, and yes, one other thing. This is a moral home. We don't allow any... goings on, as it were. This is of the utmost importance. Uprightness is everything. The last New Man... well...'

Jane Ratcliffe's voice trails off and she dismisses Richard with a wave of her hand.

'Who? Him? *Him*? Come off it, Gloriana.'

Patch practically spits this out, he is so scornful.

But Patch, we are so in need. We lie here inert, just waiting. And for what? Why, for Binstead.

'Nah,' says Patch in a dismissive voice. 'Nah, these toffs just like to wank.'

'Not that last one,' slow heavy Greg puts in.

The funny thing with Greg is, you never quite know if he's with it or not. Greg the Mec, slow, ponderous, powerful, silent Greg, 'still waters' dreamy Greg, who intones as he advances oh so slowly towards you, powerfully wheeling his massive manual chair – **I got a pop group**. Beautiful fancy. Still, it **is** 1966 – the times are a-changing, dearest

Greg.

Greg's dressed in his usual kit. He wears the same thing every single day, his pink tie-dye shirt with its massive floppy collar, the natty waistcoat with the pearl buttons. And every day his shirt is freshly laundered by someone no one except Greg knows who. It's the Miracle of Park House.

As I say, you never quite know if old Greg's with it or not. For instance, here he's right on the ball. It's absolutely true. The last New Man got shunted out sharpish under a large black cloud. He tried to jump on Helen. We're Not Supposed to Talk About It, so of course we do.

And where is Helen now anyway? Because Patch has called a meeting of the Big Five. Patch snorts and narrows his eyes to little dots.

'Mick, go an' get Helen out of her kip,' Patch says in his squeaky voice, and Mick bowls out in his tungsten Lavington.

We Big Five have been together at Park House since the Year Dot, since our parents kicked the bucket or otherwise renounced us – Helen, the three boys – Mick, Greg, our mighty, beloved, doomed Patch… and ME – Gloriana Gillespie!

What can I say about me? I lie here stretched out in various postures, watching, listening, reading, imagining. A thousand thoughts cram my mind. I see everything, I feel everything, I remember everything. I long for life. I long to escape. I long to be free. And I wrestle with the terrible awful truth that I have my limitations. *I can never ever be a waitress.*

Patch buzzes up to me. I can feel his hot stale breath on my face.

'Really, Gloriana?' he says. 'The New Man? Really?'

I sign to him *YES. We need a clever fellow. We need someone who can think. And we need him NOW. Patch, the Doom of Binstead is on us. The end of term! Weeks away! We have to act.*

Patch raises an eyebrow. Now darling Robbie's gone, Patch is the only person in the entire place who knows my language.

Ten minutes later Mick scoots back in.

'She says she's never going to get up ever again,' Mick reports.

He looks downcast. I know exactly why. It's because he's sweet on Helen. He's always had a soft spot for her and now she's fifteen she's becoming quite gorgeous. She could be a model, like lovely Jean Shrimpton. Already, like a model, she knows not to say too much, because her voice is like a little child's sing-song, up and down, sweet nothings.

Dear Helen doesn't clock everything that's going on but we always help her. But now this lying in bed day in, day out – I don't get it. She used to be so bright and chirpy. It's just since the last New Man left that's she's become dull and leaden.

For sure Helen knows about Binstead, and she knows that Sallow Salter is Mr. Big over there, the Warden of Binstead and that one day soon – very soon now after the Rat's latest outburst – it's going to be us he's coming for in the Vehicle of Doom. But, Helen, it's not lying in bed day in day out with a pillow over your head that's going to make Binstead go away.

'So,' Mick says in his truculent way, 'what's the plan, Patch?'

Patch slowly turns his fiery face on Mick.

'I'm thinking about it. Gloriana thinks we should get the New Man to help. Wossname, Richard, innit?'

'He's great,' Greg puts in. Greg has been hugely impressed by the New Man breaking the cane.

'But first,' Patch says, changing the subject, 'what shall we do about that cunt Dan? That's a evil thing he's done to old Robbie.'

Mick agrees.

'Let's give him a kicking he'll remember,' he says.

8

May I, composed
Of Eros and of dust,
Beleaguered by negation and despair,
Show an affirming flame.

Richard has been reading poetry to me. He shuts the book up and puts it on my bedside table where I can look at it at night.

'For next time, beauty girl' he says and I flash him a confirming smile. Then he puts his hand on mine and says,

'What is this all about, Gloriana? What's the problem with this Binstead place? I mean, I suppose you've got to go somewhere.'

Richard! For Heaven's sake!

I indicate my mantelpiece. He goes over and starts examining the tiles on either side of the grate.

'Pretty,' he says. 'Dutch, I suppose.'

After a few moments admiring the dirty old tiles, he straightens up and finally spots Robbie's postcard on the mantelpiece.

'May I?' he asks. He picks up the postcard and peers at it.

'Hmmm,' he says, and then, 'so what's all this about, Gloriana? What's this dump? Who's the little stick figure?'

He looks on the back, where Robbie has scrawled in his untidy hand 'Abandon hope...'

'Hmph. *Lasciate ogni speranza...* what on earth?'

Well, Richard, if you'd pay attention, if you'd watch me,

if you'd learn my language instead of showing off in Latin or whatever that was supposed to be, then maybe I could explain. Look – helpfully it even says on the front

BINSTEAD ASYLUM FOR INCURABLES

Yes, Richard, it's a picture of The Bin itself. See that shoddy-built workhouse in maroonish London brick? That sad and pompous edifice where all sides face north and the damp flows in on a daily basis. That's Binstead alright.

Need I say more? Binstead's like the Bates Motel. You check in, you don't check out. Sallow Salter, Warden of Binstead Asylum for Incurables, comes for you. He straps you into the Vehicle of Doom, off you go, and that's it, curtains. Doom. And now we Big Five have got an early ticket. In a few weeks, at the end of term, we'll be strapped up and packed off to that black hole to live out our stingey lives in 'care'. Then the damp will seep into us as well and rot us to the core.

See, Richard, see how Robbie has helpfully drawn a little arrow pointing to that slit-like window. That's his dormitory. And, Richard, look at that stick figure gesturing **Get me out of here**. That's dear Robbie himself. My brother. My love.

And the point? You saw the point. You saw Sallow Salter come for him, cane raised. You saw Salter pop him in the Vehicle of Doom and strap him up tight. You saw him carted off to Binstead. Now he's checked in and he'll never check out. Binstead's a true branch of the Bates Motel chain. Slow or fast, it kills you…

Richard, pay attention. I'm signing to you. Learn my language, please. Come on, Richard, you're a scholar. It's not that hard.

'Hmm,' he says after a bit. 'So this is where you're headed, is it? Doesn't look too promising. Basically, not too happy about that one.'

Richard, I do believe you're beginning to get it.

I sign to him *'Then help us.'* It's a simple sign and I give him my plaintive look but he just frowns and says 'Hmph'.

And then, quite unexpectedly, he says,

'Of course, I know Binstead. We used to pass it in the coach on our way to play Epsom. What a dump.'

He peers at Robbie's postcard again.

'Must have been a workhouse, I suppose. You can always tell when a building has been sad. Can't you just feel the saturated old walls seeping misery still?'

He pauses and then goes on,

'Surely we can do better than that.'

Yes, Richard, we really can do better than that.

He puts Robbie's postcard back on the mantelpiece and bends down to look at the tiles again. After a minute, he comes over and touches my brow with his scholar's hand. It feels cool and dry.

He turns to leave. At that moment, the sun comes out from behind the clouds and bathes my bed in golden light. I know then that Richard's going to help us. He's going to be my Champion and set me free.

I lie content, turned to the sun, turned to my Great Mother, originator of all this life which seethes around me.

Like a lemur, I turn up my palms and drink in the rays.

Patch is counting out for Chain He when all of a sudden, in runs Dan. He starts striding up and down the Great Hall.

'OK, Greg,' Patch calls out in his high-pitched voice.

Dan thinks he's invulnerable because he's a haemo. He thinks he's not going to get the kicking he so deserves.

He even seems unaware that Greg is rolling steadily towards him. The little stoat keeps hopping between the big black and white tiles in some complicated pattern of his own. He's deliberately landing on the lines. Typical. He knows perfectly well the lines are unlucky. It's just a provocation. He's asking for bad luck. And it's heading his way because Greg, four-square in his chair, heavy and slow, is right behind him now.

Too late Dan sees the danger. Dreamy Greg is on him. He grabs Dan by the boy's skinny forearm. Greg's hand is so huge it goes right round Dan's stick-like arm and then some. He grips Dan's arm with all his strength. Dan squeals and writhes like a girl but he can't break free. He has to mind his frail skin anyway. The tiniest lesion and he could be laid up for weeks.

'Let me go, you cunt,' he screams. He makes his free hand into a fist that he can use without abrading his skin and he starts to rain blows down on Greg. He doesn't harm himself that way, but then he doesn't seem to be harming Greg much either.

'Fuckin' give 'im what for, Greg,' Kevin calls out happily. He's perched up on the crap old sideboard next to me.

'Right, mate,' Patch calls out in his high-pitched voice.

Dan sticks out his tongue at Patch, big mistake, and he shouts out 'Shut your gob, Patch'. Why he does this is not clear, as it is sure to make Patch angry. Anyway, Dan is really in for it now. Yet he doesn't seem to care. Of course, he believes that Greg will never give him the clobbering he deserves. He thinks that a Mec will never clobber a haemo. He twists this way and that but he can't get free, and Greg just holds on to him, waiting for Patch to buzz over.

'Fuckin' nose picker,' Kevin calls out gruffly from his perch beside me. He waves his head about from side to side so his Harpo Marx curls shimmy. 'Give the motherfucker a good kickin'!' he adds for good measure.

I have a brilliant view of all this, parked up by the sideboard next to Kevin. I watch Patch making his way over at the carelessly stately speed he always uses when he's bent on the administration of justice. As Patch comes nearer, Dan begins to look nervous and he wriggles a bit harder. At the same time he is bashing away with odd glancing blows that make no impression on dreamy Greg's great helmet of a head. Greg just holds on and tightens his grip a little more. Dan is really squealing now, and it's looking like the tears are about to spurt out as they usually do with him.

'That's it, pipe the fuckin' eye,' little Kevin calls out happily, drumming with his sticks against the scarred old sideboard.

'LET ME GO, DOMEHEAD!'

That does it. Patch speeds up. His cheeks are puffed out and getting redder, sure sign of his anger. His face takes on a grimmer look. Justice must be meted before things fall apart. He comes up to where Dan is writhing.

'That's a clear abuse,' he says, 'that is, what you said to old Greg here, that... word you used... a fit Walker like you with all your advantages...'

Patch pauses.

'... Greg what never did anyone no harm, Greg what 'as 'is dreams and so on...'

Patch pauses again. The pauses are almost longer than the words he speaks.

'... and yet, we could 'ave forgiven that, misplaced sense o' fun an' all that. But... the other day with Robbie... that's a evil evil thing you done.'

Patch's face seems to swell even larger and become even redder.

'What you done the other day... **that** we cannot forgive.'

Dan looks really scared now.

'So... you'd be none the worse for a good kicking...'

'But you can't do that, Patch, you know you can't.'

'Oh, can't I? Well, yes I can. Old Mick here'll do you a good kicking any time, won't you Mick?'

Mick nods vigorously. Patch regards the terrified, squirming Dan for a long minute. All the children gathered round are hushed with excitement. Is the stoat-like Dan finally going to get the kicking he deserves? Even Kevin says nothing. He is goggling with his mouth open.

Patch turns his head away and then, not looking at Dan, he says at last,

'So, here's what I'll do, matey. Here's what I can do for you. I'm gonna be lenient. I'm gonna suspend your kicking. I'm giving you two weeks Coventry. You be on your best behaviour during that time or you'll get the kicking. Understood?'

'Oh yes, Patch.'

'An' count yerself lucky.'

'Oh yes, Patch.'

Greg releases Dan. All the children turn away, talking amongst themselves but not one more word is said to the stoat-like Dan, the Outcast for a Fortnight.

As the summer evening closes in, the nurses wash the weary children and pop on their pyjamas or their nighties. They make them brush their teeth or brush them for them according to the case. Then they put the children down in their comfortable beds.

Skinny Flick, an elegant item in her smart page boy cut and her super clean starched cotton drill tunic and trousers, is doing Girls Nightly Medicine as she always does. She volunteered for this when she arrived at Park House last year. It seemed the closest thing to the real work of healing which Flick believes is her vocation. She chose to do the girls rather than the boys because girls are, in Flick's view, so much nicer than boys, and girls always seem to be in second place at Park House. Flick continually wants to give her own sex a boost.

She trundles the medicine trolley along the corridor. Outside Big Girls Dorm she pauses and looks at the mass of pills and potions. She holds one up. It is a large transparent glass bottle which holds the thick white emulsion that is Helen's new tonic.

'Helen, dearest, sit up.'

Flick takes special care of Helen. She thinks she's lovely and vulnerable and she wants to really look after her.

However, nothing of Helen can be seen at present. After the incident at the pool, she has taken to her bed again. She is lying with the covers pulled right up and her head is buried under her pillow.

'Come, my baby, come on, it's time for your meddies.'

A faint groan comes from under the pillow.

'There's your pills and a new emulsion, darling. You know you love emulsion.'

Helen stirs and turns on her back, still under the covers, but she slides the pillow back so that her mouth and chin are visible.

Flick sighs and says, 'Open wide.' Helen parts her rather full lips and Flick slips the first of the pills in. Because Helen cannot swallow the pill dry, Flick tries to give her a drink of water, but it spills over Helen's cheek. Flick dabs it dry with her very clean handkerchief and then strokes Helen's throat like she does with her golden labrador Rusty at home. Sure enough Helen gives a gulp and down goes the pill. Two more pills follow in the same way and then Flick takes the big glass bottle from her trolley.

'Right, open really really wide.'

Flick slips the big tablespoon into Helen's yawning mouth and the thick white emulsion slides off. Helen's tongue deftly licks off what is left on the spoon.

'Nice, little one?'

'Nnn. Tastes funny,' Helen murmurs, pulling the pillow back over her head and turning on her side.

Big Debbie, Flick's friend, comes by. She has just finished Boys Medicine. Tonight, she's wearing her comfortable old pink pants.

'What's this potion, then?' Debbie picks up the bottle of emulsion. 'Why's it got no label on it?'

'Helen's emulsion. The Rat mixed it up for her. She says it's a tonic.'

'Looks pretty dodgy to me.'

Flick changes the subject.

'You look comfy,' she says, gazing at Debbie's pink pants.

'Do they make my bum look big?'

'Mm. Coffee?'

They go off arm in arm.

Powerful, gentle Greg's job is done. He has helped Patch to punish Dan and he is very happy about that. His waistcoat is folded, his pink tie-dye whisked off to the wash by the hand that cares for him so that it will be ready clean for the morrow.

Greg falls asleep. Soon he starts a dream. He always dreams and thinks this may be the most important part of his day. Sometimes he tries to work out what his dreams mean, and sometimes he just enjoys them. Often, he goes over them in the morning, and he is always keen to get to bed or even just to nod off, so that he can have a dream.

Tonight, his dream lasts either about a minute or an hour or more. It goes like this:

I go in to 'ozzie. It's nice and cool. People come and shake my hand. One man talks funny. There is a show. A thin girl sings. She has a mask on. We all clap. We sit around a table. We are all looking for a job. There is a hard test. I sing. They choose me. Just me.

For Greg, the feeling of this dream is good. When he goes over it, he is pleased that he should be in such a pleasant place and amongst such nice people. He considers that he is indeed taking a tough test, and he believes it is a good sign that he sings and is selected.

9

*B*echuanaland Conference sign report providing for the country to become an independent republic of Botswana on September 30th, 1966.

Patch, who is reading the *Daily Express*, is positively exploding.

'MacAskill!' he cries, 'MacAskill, look at this. Even bleedin' Bechuanaland now. They're really scrapin' the barrel what to throw out. I mean, MacAskill, what you lot done really? Chucked it all away.'

Mr. MacAskill, our headmaster, is the frizzy-haired man with a face the colour of mahogany who is at present preparing raffia for the girls. Mr. MacAskill's dark complexion is actually a very deep suntan, because he has Spent a Lifetime in Africa.

'Mmmm' he murmurs in his preoccupied way. But all the same, his face takes on a stricken look and he starts mumbling,

'Chucked what away, Patrick?'

Mr. MacAskill's hand goes up and rubs at his grey, metallic-looking hair which always stands up like wire wool. He is a very old man, fiftyish, sixtyish, unimaginably old and past it anyway. He seems suddenly more confused than usual.

'The whole lot,' Patch says unhelpfully. "ere, toffee nose, open me Elizabethan.'

The second part of this speech is addressed in peremptory fashion to Richard who in addition to being my Champion is actually supposed to be teaching us in our pathetic little 'school'. Richard, who has been listening to a litany from Greg about his pop band and his pop song, looks up. He sees that Patch is gesturing towards the bookcase and he quickly spots *Stanley Gibbons Elizabethan Stamp Catalogue 1961.*

'Alright, mate, now turn up Bechuanaland… now just look at that, MacAskill, look at them lovely definitives. Real stamps, they are. An' look at the Queen – lovely young woman, an' queenly an' that. Now what? Botswana. **Botswana!** Republic! They'll be chopping off the Queen's head an' havin' labels instead of proper stamps, pretty little labels with flowers an' wotnot on to sell to little girls that don't know what a real stamp is.'

Patch glares at Mr. MacAskill as though he is somehow personally responsible for the Bechuanaland Conference. As though he is already preparing a new issue of *sans culottes* republican labels that will use the blood of empire loyalists instead of more conventional adhesive.

'Now, mate, lemme see the Index page – that's right, page eleven, fanks. There!' and Patch begins to read out in his squeaky voice 'Aden, Aden Protectorate, Antigua, Ascension, Australia, Bahamas, Barbados, Basutoland, Bechuanaland, Bermuda, British Guiana, British Honduras, British Solomon Islands, Brunei…'

During this recital, Patch's face has swelled and reddened with his emotion. He stares truculently at Mr. MacAskill. It's like he's the schoolmaster and poor old Mr. MacAskill is the erring schoolboy.

Mr. MacAskill's sunburned face takes on a more than usual woebegone sagging almost angry look to it. He fiddles with the cuffs of his super-shabby tweed jacket which is just as much a give-away as his face. You can carbon-date him by it, really – to The Thirties (for both MacAskill and jacket). Three decades of bodily secretions and pipe tobacco have worked themselves into the stuff of the jacket without benefit of dry cleaning, and also into the crevices of Mr. MacAskill's swarthy face. It's like Mr. MacAskill's life has somehow slowed down, maybe it's even stopped. The buzz is **Something Happened to Mr. MacAskill In Africa**. Lord knows what, but there's definitely a tinge of obscure tragedy that clings to him.

'An' that's just the As and the Bs. You know how many countries and whatnot there are in that *Elizabethan Catalogue*, and it's only 1961, five years old, I mean how many colonies and stuff, all British? **One hundred and three**. One hundred and bleedin' three countries and stuff, and five years ago they was all ours. Now what we got left? Bleedin' Cayman Islands and effing Gibraltar.'

'Well, times change, Patch, we had to let them go.'

'Pffff,' Patch snorts. 'Shouldn't have taken them in the first place then. You was supposed to civilize them. Now look.'

'Err... I suppose they... umm... wanted to be free.'

'Really? *Really*? That's a surprise. Most people prefer bein' told what to do, so they don't 'ave to think too much. Especially when they're bein' told what to do by toffee-noses like you and this bloke' – here Patch gestures rudely at Richard. 'Isn't that what you're for, governing the Empire an' that? I mean, you're not much good at anything else, are you?'

Richard is standing by Patch still. He's looking a bit puzzled and uncomfortable. I expect he's surprised by Patch's conservative views. And I'm sure that in toff schools like the one Richard's probably been to the boys don't lecture the masters like Patch is now doing to Mr. MacAskill.

'Maybe,' Mr. MacAskill says, in an attempt at a diplomatic outcome, 'maybe it's better for people to govern themselves badly than for philosopher kings to govern them well.'

Which is quite a thought. But Patch is not having any of it.

'Come off it, MacAskill. You lot have just given up, haven't you?'

'Times change. We must change with them.'

Another thought. But Patch dismisses this one out of hand.

'Bollocks,' he says derisively and turns to Richard.

'Nah, come on, yer toffee-nosed git, close up me Elizabethan Catalogue.'

Soon afterwards, Mr. MacAskill, looking a little fatigued, says,

'Right ho, children, Richard's going to take over now.'

Oh, no. I can't believe it. Mr. MacAskill going to 'slip out'. This is definitely not right. Patch, stop him. You have the power.

But Patch is probably intrigued to see what Richard does, so he nods at Mr. MacAskill who is already heading for the exit. At least Mr. MacAskill has the decency to look a little guilty.

As Mr. MacAskill slopes out of the door, Richard calls out plaintively,

'But what shall I teach them? Where's the lesson plan?'

Patch laughs.

'Use your nous, my boy,' Mr. MacAskill's voice comes back to us as he heads off down the corridor. 'Tell them about… Vietnam… or test them on their tables… or…'

***

70

The Dog opens at 11 and Joe MacAskill is right on time. He orders a large whisky and a pint of bitter to wash it down.

Patch's critique has touched him to the quick, like a mine running under his existence, where it joins a hundred other mines that he has been constructing for himself. For MacAskill has been an Empire man, through and through, practically all his grown-up life. Out to Africa in '34 when he was in his early twenties and, barring his spell in the Forces in the War, that had been it, his life for three entire decades.

'*What?*' his college chum Tommy had cried when he said he was joining the Colonial Service. It really had seemed second rate next to the professions or the home civil service, or even third rate after the great prize of the Indian service. But old Burdett, his tutor, had said in his ponderous, kindly way 'You know, MacAskill, Africa offers more opportunity for doing great and permanent good than any department in England.'

On the way out, the flying boat put down on the Nile at Cairo. In the hotel, he danced with Margot Paget, the daughter of the Under-Secretary for Finance in the British administration there. Margot had shining lovely arms, so MacAskill delayed his departure. They walked by moonlight on the banks of the Nile, and there she broke down his resolve not to propose to a girl until his career was established. A year later, on his first leave, they married and she joined him, his precious catch and prize, up-country in his round mud hut.

All this was really odd. As an undergraduate he had no notion of serving the Empire, in fact very little notion of Empire at all. But then old Burdett had broached the subject over sherry. There had been a dinner with a mandarin called Sir Ralph Furse from the Colonial Office, and the offer had been made.

'I am not qualified,' he said. 'What do I know of the Dark Continent?'

But Furse smiled comfortably and stretched out his arm across the polished mahogany between the nuts in their silver and the claret in its crystal, and put his hand on MacAskill's forearm.

'But why me?'

'Our methods are mole-like, quiet, persistent and indirect. We look for – oh, what? – good family, I suppose, the better Public Schools, adequate mental equipment...'

'Just adequate?' MacAskill could still recall his pique.

'Generally, you see, the spectacled chap is not considered suitable. Then... good judgment, good sportsmanship, understanding of human nature, character...'

'My goodness. How can you gauge all that?'

'Simple. A man looks you in the eye, he shakes your hand, these things.'

'But I know nothing of Africa.'

'You're a Greats man, aren't you, MacAskill? The study of the eternal problems of thought and conduct? And we have much on our side. Above all there is our mission, and the faith, brains and guts of picked Englishmen.'

At first, in the small round hut which shuddered in the wind and was infested with biting insects, MacAskill kept the faith and used his brains, and endured his guts' constant revolt.

He even managed to look on the Governor as a philosopher king, or at least as a higher grade of prefect. For a spell he truly believed that the Platonic virtues of loyalty, courage, responsibility and truthfulness really did equip the Englishman to rule.

Margot came out. He played polo, cricket. There were

mixed doubles at tennis. They drank large gins. He learned forestry and road construction. He was absolute ruler over a hundred thousand souls. He was just in his doings. He admired the simplicity of it. He went up in the Service. Margot and he moved into a big house with servants.

But along the way, disillusioning cracks began to show themselves. A gold discovery was excised from the native reserves although he had been promised this would not be so. In some local elections his police were mobilized to push through the government's candidate. Meanwhile, Margot smiled pluckily but faded at an accelerated pace. The worst came during the War. MacAskill was called up. Singapore fell and much of Asia, and the whole Empire, not just MacAskill's bit, looked suddenly decrepit, untenable. Natives' loyalty began to appear ill-advised.

When MacAskill returned after VE Day, the 'deep-voiced, broad-fronted dreamer musing on Empire' had become in his eyes a folly. The natives rebelled, and he had a grudging sympathy for them. He read a bit of Sartre, a bit of Camus, a smattering of Fanon. He heard about the fellow Mannoni in Madagascar who got sick of the whole colonial project and went back to France and founded the discipline of ethno-psychiatry. MacAskill almost did come to believe, as he had taxed Patch in class, that it was better for people to govern themselves badly than it was for philosopher kings to govern them well. Somehow, these thoughts had got out, and he was moved into a desk job under the eye of the Governor's ADC. Margot suffered a terrible demotion in the pecking order of wives. She grew embittered and faded faster still. The end of Empire was accelerating toward them anyway, but for MacAskill and Margot it came a little sooner, in one disastrous night.

MacAskill signals to the landlord of The Dog and orders

another large whisky and another pint of bitter.

'Kevin?'

Kevin at first just stares at Richard through his round National Health specs. There is a very long pause indeed, and then he says very deliberately in his Northern accent,

'Yan pimp's pimp
Tan pimps are dick
Tethera pimps are bumfit
Methera pimps are gigert'

It goes on like this for a while. Richard has made the mistake of starting his arithmetic lesson by asking Kevin to say his five times table. Eventually Kevin stops, having presumably reached twelve times five. He gives Richard a challenging look. Patch says helpfully,

'Don't bother about 'im, mate. He's from Cumberland.'

Richard's eye roves around the room for inspiration and falls on a rather weather-beaten Map of the World on the wall. There is a line in red crayon erratically extending from the south west of England to a dot in the middle of the Atlantic Ocean.

'Gosh, what's all that about?' he says.

'Chichester,' Patch says. '37 south 12 west.'

Patch scoots his big Armsworth 302 over to the map. He raises his sharp button eyes and scrutinizes it with care. It is the kind of map the conservative Patch really likes. In fact, this old stuff, old maps and other old things that Mr. MacAskill gets out of the cupboard are the things Patch likes best. Now he says in his high-pitched voice,

'South south west of Tristan da Cunha. Nice map. Nice and pink.'

Richard peers at the map. It really is a map of an older time, even pre-war, perhaps. After all, most of these places have shown Britain the door in recent years, haven't they? Richard looks puzzled and Patch says impatiently,

'Francis Chichester. Plymouth boy, you know, like me. Sailing single-handed round the world. We're following 'im on the map.'

There is a rare hint of respect from Patch in this remark.

In desperation, Richard pulls down a battered old Puffin book from the shelf and says he's going to read to us. He holds up the book – it is called *Tales from Troy* – and he asks 'OK?' Big russet Mick groans and yawns theatrically and says 'Can't we get a telly?' and Kevin says 'Shouldn't say OK. That'll be fuckin' sixpence.' But then Patch says 'Give the toff a chance' and we all settle down and listen. Sort of.

Sort of, because it turns out to be really *Boy's Own* stuff about valour and battles and honour and kings and heroes and horrid deaths. The girls mostly just get on with their raffia but the boys get hooked. Mick listens quietly for a change and Kevin keeps nodding his head and making little slashing motions with his sticks as the Greeks pile into the Trojans. I can see Patch looking intently at Richard the whole time and when Richard reads out about the chariots Patch has the especially perky look that he gets when he's excited:

Hector harnessed the brazenfoot horses to his chariot, swift fliers with manes of golden hair; he clothed himself in gold, and caught up the whip of wrought gold and mounted the car...

All at once, Patch calls out,

'Stop! Stop right there!'

Richard looks up.

'Wossat you just read?'

'What?'

'That bit about *gods love* and stuff...'

'Whom the gods love, dies young, you mean?'

Patch nods and Richard mutters something strange.

'Wossat?' Patch cries sharply.

Richard says the same thing again, and this time I pick it up.

Hon hoi theoi philousin, neos apothneiskei

'Crikey,' Patch cries. His button eyes have widened. He seems genuinely amazed. 'Is that Latin or something?'

'Nearly. Greek.'

'Cripes.'

It turns out that Greek is amongst the dead languages Richard has studied at toff school.

Patch is now gazing at Richard with something that looks almost like respect. This is unprecedented. Patch lowers his voice and Richard moves closer to hear him.

'Right, mate,' he says, 'that's it.'

'Ah.'

Patch pauses. His great round red face is glowing even brighter.

'Yup, that's it. I wanna go with them Trojans. Actually I want us to *be* Trojans. Noble warriors and that...'

'I... I don't think... I mean, I don't understand...'

Patch ignores Richard and goes on.

'... yup, brave noble warriors. And like, you know, sort of include everyone. Not all warriors, course, but everybody something, all together, all in it together. An' the girls and the little kids too. Like how old 'Ector is wiv that white-armed Andromache and their kid... wossname...'

'Astyanax.'

'Yup, whatever.'

'But how...?'

'Here's how, mate. And you're gonna help us, right?'

Richard looks super-perplexed by all this. But, Richard, can't you see? Think! Patch has got the short straw. If he's lucky he's got just months to live out his story. *Whom the gods love, dies young.* Doesn't this just fit his case? And Trojans, battling Trojans... can't you see? Don't you get it? Can't this be Patch's own particular myth?

10

Flick is an ambitious and intelligent girl. She will soon be eighteen, when she wants to apply to train as a real nurse, an SRN. With this in mind, Flick is trying to cultivate Miss Ratcliffe as she will need Jane's support when she applies for her nursing training.

Flick is naturally interested in medicines, and at present she is interested in Helen's new medicine in particular. She wants to know what it is and what it's for. So when she spotted Miss Ratcliffe that morning in the Sluice, she went in after her. For some reason, Jane was scrubbing out bedpans.

'Lizzie's already done that.'

'Not even barely adequately.'

Jane Ratcliffe scrubbed on, dousing the pans with quantities of bleach.

'I wanted to ask about Helen's emulsion…'

'Yes?' Jane put a bedpan aside to drain and grasped another.

'I mean, what is it? What's it for?'

'Tonic. It's a tonic. A cod liver oil emulsion with some sugar and vanilla.'

'But why does she have to take it? It doesn't seem to be doing her any good.'

'Doctor's orders.'

'But she's still refusing to get out of bed.'

Jane Ratcliffe scrubbed on and said nothing.

'And she keeps saying it tastes funny.'

'Felicity, if you wish to become a nurse, you must learn to follow instructions. As I said, it's doctor's orders. Now kindly excuse me. I must get on.'

And Jane seized another bedpan, which to Flick's eyes looked already gleaming with cleanliness.

After tea, Patch summons everyone to the Great Hall. He's got on his bright red shirt. He looks huge and red and kingly. His face is puffed and red.

'From now on,' he says, cruising up and down in front of the crowd in his gleaming silver and vermilion Armstead 302, 'from now on, we are all Trojans.'

He explains. He is King Priam. His special crew – the short-straw Elecs – are the noble Trojan elders. The others are all dubbed noble Trojan warriors, boys and girls alike. Each has their role. There is the cavalry – solid reliable Mick and dreamy Greg and the other heavy Mecs. And then the light-armed skirmishing troops, and the heralds and what not which is mostly the few Walkers we have and the lighter Mecs. And they're all – every one of them – Patch insists – they're **all** nobles.

And dear beautiful Helen is in it too. Flick has persuaded her to get out of bed for this. Of course, she gets the part of Helen whose face launched a thousand ships.

Dodgy, pretty Dan wanders in. Everyone turns away. He starts pleading with Patch to be let off the rest of his Coventry for good behaviour. He wants to be a Trojan.

Patch looks scornfully at him and says,

'Bugger off. You're a god.'

Dan looks puzzled by this but pleased. Of course, he believes he's a god because he is powerful over the others like a god on account of his running. He wanders away and loiters by the crap old sideboard, grinning.

Patch doesn't mention to Dan what is obvious to all of us, that Dan is actually god-like not because of running but because he is unreliable and arbitrary in his judgements. And also that he has special blood like a god, and he can hit you but you may not hit him, which also seems to Patch a god-like characteristic.

Patch tells everyone to form up according to their role – elders, cavalry, light-armed troops, heralds and what-not. Bertie sidles up between Mick and Greg. Mick stops and pats the dog's head, releasing a frowsty miasma that quickly spreads. As Mick pats him, Bertie loses his guarded look and squirms with pleasure. His tail thumps on the tiles. Bertie is in love with Mick. He's also in love with Greg. He is in love with both of these beefy boys. He cares nothing for us girls.

'We're gonna practice our anthem,' Patch says. 'C'mon over here, Richard.'

Richard, who has been hovering modestly by the piano, walks over.

'Just listen to this,' Patch says, and Richard intones in a monotonous nasal voice,

Hon ho theoi philousin

Patch says,

'Come on, the elders, you gotta repeat that.'

After a few goes they more or less get it. Then Patch says,

'Now the rest of you lot do the other bit.'

Richard shouts out at the top of his lungs,

NEOS APOTHNEISKEI!

'Fuckin' stupid,' Kevin mutters but Patch gives him a look and he shuts up straightaway.

Richard starts them all going with it and soon most of them have got the hang of it, Greg and Mick in particular. During this, Dan hangs around by the sideboard, looking sarky. Patch buzzes over to him and mutters something which the rest of us can't hear, and after that Dan wanders out.

In a few minutes, Patch marches them off round the Great Hall, himself in the lead. The elders chant their bit *Hon ho theoi* and the rest shout back.

NEOS APOTHNEISKEI!

The new Trojans enter into the spirit of it and start rushing back and forth. There is a great clashing and screaming. Patch looks on benignly. The noise is unbelievable.

And then in comes the Rat. She comes in clapping her hands together and shouting above the racket of the children,

'That's ENOUGH! Whatever is going on here?'

She's wearing her signature taupe jumper and dingy tartan skirt again.

The little kids freeze. I can see some trembling lips. As the Rat is up the other end of the Great Hall shouting at the little kids, Mick starts to wheel himself quietly towards the passageway leading to his dorm. Bertie slopes alongside him, but they never reach the passageway as the Rat barks out,

'Michael!'

Mick pulls up abruptly and does one of his fancy pirouettes, wheeling around to face the Rat. He sits up very straight in his chair. This might just pass for old-fashioned courtesy but it is actually, as we all well know, including the Rat, a subtler form of insolence. Slowly Mick turns up his big freckly face on which the russet stubble can clearly be seen springing out. He regards the Rat steadily.

'Yes, Miss Ratcliffe?'

'How many times have I told you that disgusting old mongrel is not allowed in here? I am sure it has fleas. They'll get on the children. I'm going to have it put down.'

But Bertie has wisely already made himself scarce, so his putting down has to be deferred.

The Rat moves on, striding diagonally across the Great Hall, stepping thoughtlessly on lines or not, so no luck for her. She disappears towards her office. The horrid clack-clack of her steel-tipped shoes gradually recedes.

The Trojans sit quietly pondering. I look at Patch who is conferring with his elders. This Trojan thing is such a grand idea. If you must live out your story by the age of sixteen, latest, which is the case for Patch and all the Elecs, all his new-dubbed Trojan elders, it might as well be a big story lived out with maximum honour, which, when you think of it, is actually quite Homeric.

11

Lizzie holds up the letter.

'He sent it to me, dunno why.'

Lizzie, don't you know the Rat checks our post? Not that we ever get any anyway.

'Lemme see if anyone's still up.'

Lizzie waltzes off and nabs the only kid she can find. It's little Harpo-haired Kevin who was skulking near the Sluice in the hope of an extra half an hour before bed. She gets him by the ear and brings him in. He wobbles horribly on his sticks, his baggy jeans are practically down round his ankles.

'Fuckin' cunt,' he says to Lizzie amiably and she smiles sweetly at him.

Kevin settles on the chair beside my bed. He opens the letter and holds it up for me to read.

'From fuckin' Robbie, innit?' he says. 'Poor sod.'

Fearful, I start to read.

> The Bin
> Binstead Village
> Surrey-on-the-Styx
> Hell

Day 8 of the 12,410 days of the rest of my life in The Bin

Dear Gloriana, dear Patch,

You're going to ask me how I got 12,410. Well, I asked Sallow Salter if I could see my file and he said No, but I got it from his secretary, a nice lady called Dawn with bazookas the size of large melons. *Life expectancy < 50 years* it said, so I've got 34 years max to go, which is 34 x 365 = 12,410 days. As I've been in The Bin 8 days already, that's 12,410 – 8 = 12,402 days to go. Here's one of them (yesterday, Day 7):

A DAY IN THE LIFE OF ROBERT WILLIS: DAY 7 of 12,410

7 a.m. Wake to the bell. Gripping feeling of dread. Why? Nothing special. Just my usual *fin de siècle ennui angst*. Trev the Dorm Boss draws back the curtains. I look out on a high brick wall. No sun in sight. No sky either.

7.30 a.m. The nice male nurse called Steve who is from Trinidad helps me put on my clothes. I say 'my clothes', but they're not actually mine. I put on underwear which comes from a big wicker basket in the middle of the lino. Today the vest is too big and the pants are too small. Yesterday it was the other way round. Steve brings me a shirt and trousers from the communal wardrobe out on the landing. He chooses these carefully every Monday, and I wear the same ones every day for a week. Does that make them mine?

8.00 a.m. Breakfast. We're the first shift – it's us Handicapped and the Loopy Ladies. There are about three more sittings after us. We chuck food about.

8.30 a.m. Workshop. We Watch Repairers are up one end. The other end it's the Blind Weavers. Ted's on my bench, he's a bifida, quite nice. We chat off and on but there's nothing much to talk about. I repair three Timexes, a gold fob watch, and some little kid's alarm clock where the rocking cockerel bit has dropped off. I do a good job. Ron, our foreman, says so. I feel a faint pride.

12.30 p.m. Lunch. Sad slop, greasy meat, huge, steaming boiled potatoes that burn the roof off my mouth, and those baked beans that look like the cooks have cut their fingernails into them. There's a sponge shaped like the long cylinder they cook it in, with a scarlet sauce poured all over it. They call it Dead Man's Arm. Gripping feeling of dread.

1.30-2.30 p.m. Quiet time. Play draughts with Ted in the Rec Room. I win all three games and he gets cross.

3-6 p.m. Free (after a fashion). It's a half holiday. But we can't go out anywhere. There's no transport. Apparently we go out once a month. I mooch about the grounds, which are OK. There's a copse with a couple of paths I can get my chair along. There's a dead mouse on the path. I'd like to bury it but I can't reach it. I hear but don't see a woodpecker. Then it starts to rain and I head back. Gripping feeling of dread. Gathered in the porch sheltering from the shower is a gaggle of the Loopy Ladies. They are all chattering like geese. They're in their forties and fifties, mostly. I already recognize Mary and Anne and Sheila and Martha. They're going out shopping. Three nice girls from the Grammar School have come up to escort them.

One of the Loopy Ladies gives me a toothy smile. It's a particularly frumpy one with her green coat tied round with string. She's called Norma, I know. I smile back. There are hundreds of these Loopy Ladies here but actually they don't seem particularly bonkers to me. I wonder about Norma.

'Hallo, beautiful,' I say.

'Hallo, handsome,' she says back.

'What you in for then,' I say conversationally. It's our standard joke. I don't for a minute expect her to answer but she does. She bends over me and whispers,

'I was wayward.'

I pretend to look puzzled, so she whispers again,

'I had a baby.'

Illegitimate, she means of course. That's what most of them are in for. Having bastards. It's a threat to society, you understand. Mr. Salter gave us a lecture on it when we arrived. We're not to speak to these ladies, he said. They are marked by promiscuity and feckless breeding, he said.

'I held my daughter for a week and then she was gone.'

My heart cries out. I look at the pretty girls from the Grammar who are chatting so nicely to Mary and Anne and Sheila and Martha. But Norma is still pursuing her tale.

'I was unclean. That's why they make me do the laundry.'

This is getting really distressing but just then what should heave into view but the yellowish visage of Sallow Salter himself, the Embodiment of Evil. He has a sharp word with the nice girls from the Grammar and tells them to get on with it. The Loopy Ladies form into a sort of loose crocodile two and three abreast and go off into the rain holding hands. As she steps off the porch,

Norma gives me another toothy smile and says 'I so enjoyed our little chat, Robbie.'

But already Salter has grasped the handles of my chair. He whisks me round and wheels me inside. In the hall he pauses and comes round to face me. He pushes his horrid greasy face at me. I can see the hair up his big nozzies. It's a forest in there.

'Willis, I expressly forbade you to talk to those women.'

'I don't see why I shouldn't,' I answer back riskily. His brow creases up with anger. He looks like he wants to hit me but he doesn't.

'Because they are emotionally disturbed,' he says too loudly. 'Because they are feeble minded. Because they tend to restless and aggressive behaviour. If I catch you at it again, it'll be the Bulb for you.'

Gripping feeling of dread. The Bulb at the Bin is an enema. According to Ted, they do a special milky one with a gigantic bulb syringe. Ted's had it a couple of times and he says it's not a nice experience.

I become angry myself. I say,

'You give me an enema and I'll sue.'

Salter just laughs a nasty laugh and says,

'You're so full of shit, Willis, you really need one.'

I turn my chair around, and there through the open door I spot Norma disappearing out of the gate. She turns for a moment and when she sees me she gives a cheery wave.

6-8 p.m. Supper, change for bed.

8 p.m. Dorm locked. Lights out but I read by my bedside light. This is tolerated. I'm reading *A Day in the Life*

of Ivan Denisovich.

10 p.m. I put out my light. I lie down to sleep and I think about Norma. I decide I will ask her if she would like to leave. If she says yes, I will help her. Legally.

END OF DAY 7/12,410. 12,403 TO GO.

So you see, I'm OK. I'm not dying. I haven't been pathologized as an imbecile, or discredited as a sexual deviant. They haven't done a leucotomy on me or put me in a deep insulin coma or given me Largactil or clapped on the headphones for a good old dose of ECT. If I play up, they're not giving me the needle or pumping me full of Paraldehyde. I'm not being prescribed the destruction of the posteromedial hypothalamic nuclei. I'm not being put in a straitjacket or given cold water baths or being slapped with cold wet towels. I haven't even had the Bulb yet.

No, I'm not dying at all. It just feels like I'm already dead.

The thing is, do I want to live in a world where having a baby is a crime and disability is a threat? And where the only pleasure I'll ever get is when Big Bev sticks the Bulb up my bum. Actually, the short answer is No. What I really want is to live in a world where I own my underwear.

Hey, my friends, I need something. Can you get one of the nurses or somebody – or that new New Man – to buy this book and send it to me in a different dust jacket (Salter checks our mail)? It's called The *Regulation of Asylums: Theory, Practice and Case Law* by J. Wilfred Gwilliam.

Abyssinia!
            Yr very dearest friend,
                R. Herbert Willis

'Herbert,' Patch says when he reads the letter. 'Ha, he never let on about that. Now, who can we get to send 'im 'is book?'

Who indeed?

Dressed in her spotless cotton drill tunic and trousers, Flick is doing her rounds with Girls Nightly Medicine.

She is still really puzzled by Helen's emulsion. So she looks up and down the corridor. Seeing no one, she quickly unscrews the bottle and takes a good swig.

Bleaugh! It's certainly a sickly emulsion. But Helen is right, there is a slight bitter taste to it, which lingers on the palate long after the medicine has gone down.

Later, in the room Debbie and Flick share, big lavish Debbie murmurs,

'Nighties Off?'

Flick, who is already in her bed, replies,

'Don't be so bloody coy, Debs. Anyway, I'm wearing pyjamas, in case you hadn't noticed. And no, since you ask, definitely Nighties On tonight. I feel really odd.'

12

ext day is Jane Ratcliffe's half day. Park House breathes relief while the Acting Warden steps out for her solitary constitutional in the ancient beechwood that lies nearby. She keeps carefully to the dry path, avoiding scuffing up any of the fallen leaves for fear of setting off her chest – although she has brought her inhaler just in case.

Jane's mind is in turmoil. She has so longed for this chance to run Park House, to show her love for the children and to guide them aright.

But already, after, what was it, just two weeks after Mrs. Noble left for California, already everything is going wrong, so horribly wrong. The dreadful scuffle over Robert's transfer, and the quite awful behaviour of the New Man, the Richard, and the general slackness and smoking and that sly Elizabeth. Even Deborah, of whom she had such hopes, was not being exactly helpful.

And now the girl Helen and that incident at the pool.

Thank the Lord that she has been able to arrange that early transfer for the troublesome older children. The sooner they're off to Binstead the better.

Jane walks carefully on the dry path, keeping her eyes down to look out for roots that she might stumble on. Everywhere to either side of the path a litter of last year's leaves lies like souls waiting to be incorporated back into the soil where they will feed the trees that bore them. Reflecting on this old endless cycle gives Jane no perceptible satisfaction, rather the opposite, all that annual repetition, the rising of the sap, the reproduction, the generation of souls all so thrusting up and all cut down and all withered in their turn. What is the point of it all, what is the *point*?

She stops to listen for birds, but there don't seem to be any, only a faint rushing sound as the breeze stirs the tops of the trees and, very far off, a car horn.

Everywhere these days there is such a dreadful *lightness*, which Jane sees as wicked. These young people don't seem to realize that life's not for giggling and pop music and watching empty programmes on the television and ruining your health with cigarettes. They have to understand that life is for work and love, and really when you came to it, they were the same thing. For no reason at all, people made of this such a complicated almost insoluble question.

Jane stops again to listen. She has been hoping to hear a yellowhammer, as she knows they are nesting here this year. This time she does hear sounds but not of a yellowhammer. Someone is walking, not far away. She hears a twig snap and leaves are scuffed and someone coughs just once. It sounds like a man.

And the children, the little children. Jane knows that children live in the present, unthinking, especially the children at Park House whose future is so scant. Each day they must struggle in their short, difficult, painful lives. It is her job to care for them, and to guard against their darker potentials which are always menacing to emerge, the lying, the stealing, the levity, the cruelty. She wants to keep them from the awful mixed-ness of life until their little unspotted souls can pass over to the other side, where they will be freed from their cumbersome bodies and be glad at last. Like Jesus the children suffer, and like the women who cared for Jesus, Jane wants to affirm the children's humanity with acts of love before it is too late.

These are some of Jane Ratcliffe's thoughts. She believes her motives are good. But it all comes out wrong, so wrong. When she takes a good hard look at herself, the person that is revealed to her is not the person she means to be. When she wants to show her love, her absolute love for the children, they call her a silly old moo. When she wants to steer the young people out of their culpable lightness into a deeper vein of moral seriousness, they call her the C word (cow) – or worse, the B word (bitch). Once she was quite sure, Elizabeth's lips had even framed another C word, but she wasn't going to think that, even of Elizabeth.

And now this Richard. Jane has chosen him rather than the other one the charity had suggested because he sounded serious with his Latin and Greek A levels and he has been to quite a good school.

It was so necessary to have a decent young man after the horrible debacle of the last one who had been caught making up to Helen. The worst of it had been that Helen had, well, responded to the boy's disgusting behaviour. It seemed that her nature was, well, not to mince words... of a *filthy* kind... Thank goodness it hadn't gone any further. Jane had caught it just in time and sent the dirty boy packing. He'd been off the premises the same day and good riddance.

But now Helen was becoming a problem again. Miss Payne had reported that incident at the pool. The girl's filthy instincts were, it was clear, coming to the fore again. The sooner she could be sent to Binstead the better, even before the others. In fact, right away if possible. Jane presumed that an adult institution would have ways of dealing with natures like Helen's...

Already, Jane has phoned through to Mr. Salter who had so much more experience. Sadly he had no room right away for the girl but he had recommended a good sedative which the doctor had, after some quite unnecessary hesitation, prescribed. Taken in an emulsion, it was apparently hardly noticeable, Mr. Salter had said. Jane has high hopes that it will work wonders and keep the girl's base instincts in check.

Jane sighs and walks around a pile of leaves which have blown across her path. Then, through the grey trunks of the beeches which are attractively spotted with silver and green, she sees him. He is in a car coat and a cloth cap, walking towards her on the path between the trees, a hundred yards away.

She looks for the dog, she feels safe when there is a dog, a man with a dog is safe enough. But there is no dog that she can see, only the man in his car coat. A shot of panic explodes inside her. He is coming on and she can see now that he is middle-aged, the silvery hair a bit too long and splaying out on either side of the cap. He is fiddling with the bottom of his car coat, where the zip joins, below the waist. Jane doesn't like this gesture at all and glances nervously around her. She is alone in the beechwood and the man is coming on, now whistling tunelessly. His head is slightly bowed so she can see the check pattern on the top of his cap.

Jane has schooled herself to treat every stranger as if he were at least an angel, if not the risen Christ. But now she finds she cannot breathe, her heart is thumping uncontrollably inside her. When the man is still ten yards from her, he looks up and nods. In seconds they will meet.

Abruptly, Jane turns off the path and walks as fast as she can between the trees. By good chance there are none of the fallen branches or clumps of brambles which encumber the wood elsewhere. She presses on through the leaves which here have drifted quite thickly, up to her ankles in some places. Beneath the layer of dry brown leaves there is a further underlay of wet soggy leaves from previous seasons. Heading uphill, she has to scuff through this dense mat of leaves. All the time she does not dare to look back to see if the man is following her.

After a minute she reaches a slight rise where there is a clearing in the wood. Several stumps show that the clearing is quite recent, but already brambles have covered most of the area.

She turns and looks back. She is panting hard. Through the complicated pattern of the trees, she glimpses the man, trudging on along the path, his eyes once more bent downwards.

What if he had been an angel or the risen Christ?

She feels it then, the familiar tightening. Tiny spores of mould from the dead leaves have entered her lungs which are beginning to contract dangerously. She scrabbles in her bag for her inhaler.

13

Patch finishes counting out. He leaves the children to play Chain He and scoots over to where we are, up by the piano, me and Mick and Richard. Richard is teaching Mick to play *Heart & Soul*. He says anyone can play it and Mick is testing this theory to the limit.

'OK, Mick,' Patch says in his piping voice, 'me an' the toff are gonna 'ave a word in private.'

Mick takes the hint and wheels away to join in Chain He.

Richard looks enquiringly at Patch. For a while, Patch says nothing. I can feel the heat burning off him. Kilocalories are steaming off his plump red cheeks and off his Michelin-man body.

'Gimme me a choc, mate,' Patch eventually says. Richard's brow wrinkles.

'Gimme a bourbon cream.'

'Where are they?'

'In me bag, you silly git.'

Richard glances around and spots the old school satchel that is strapped to the back of Patch's big Armsworth 302. The leather of the satchel is scuffed and scratched. Richard opens it and all three of us peer inside. There is a box of Cadbury's Milk Tray. There is also a turquoise-coloured booklet.

Richard pulls out the Milk Tray, consults the orientation chart and selects the bourbon cream. Patch opens his mouth and Richard pops the choc in.

'Lovely. Gorgeous.' Patch smacks his lips as he revolves the chocolate around his mouth. When he is finished, he says,

'Wipe me gob, mate.' Richard fishes out his handkerchief and does the job. Then he slides the Milk Tray back into the saddle bag. Patch and I watch closely. Sure enough, Richard has to move the turquoise booklet slightly and he gives a little start as he spots the title. *A Doctor's Marital Guide for Patients: Combined Regular and Rhythm Edition.*

'Now, gimme a Turkish Delight.' Richard pulls out the Milk Tray again, picks out the chocolate and slots it into Patch's capacious mouth. I can see Richard wangling another quick look at the *Doctor's Marital Guide.*

'To me,' Patch now says, talking through the chocolate and settling down for the interview in his own peculiar style, 'to me, you're a toffee-nosed git. Probably a wanker too, I shouldn't wonder.'

Richard says nothing. Clearly he is stuck for a reply to this statement of Patch's. In fact, he looks like he is not at all sure where the conversation is heading. Patch's little grey button eyes are scanning Richard's face again.

'C'm 'ere, mate.' Richard bends close to the furnace of Patch's face which seems to be burning brighter now he's been stoked up with chocs. 'C'm 'ere, closer.' I see Richard recoiling slightly as he gets a whiff of Turkish Delight mixed in with Patch's none too sweet breath. But then Patch says,

'Wanna borrow me *Marital Guide*, mate?'

'Erm...'

'Thing is, I can lend it to you. But first you gotta get rid of the Rat.'

'Goodness.'

Patch leaves a decent pause and then looks inquiringly at Richard.

'Well?'

'I... ummm... no, I couldn't possibly do that.'

Patch looks scornful.

'Course you could, mate,' he says. 'Oh… and you gotta learn Gloriana's language.'

Wow. That is really nice of Patch. I need someone to talk to now that Robbie's gone. Of course, Patch himself has always known my language but his interests are completely different from mine. If Richard learns my language, we can talk about books and stuff.

Richard does some frowning and wrinkling and screwing up and he gives a little tug at his floppy locks. Then he finally grasps what Patch means. He turns to me and says 'You mean learn to sign?' and I bestow my most gracious smile on him. Like a child he can't help smiling back.

'Not a problem,' he says unexpectedly. 'If I can learn the paradigm of *luo* at the age of eight, I can probably pick up a smattering of sign language.'

'Yeah, yeah,' Patch says, but I understand at once that, as a posh boy, Richard doesn't mean a smattering. He means that he will do it the toff way, pretend not to be studying at all and then suddenly mastering it completely. Which is fine by me. Patch grunts in a half-satisfied way.

Richard looks like he wants to say something.

'Umm.'

'Yes?' Patch says magisterially.

Clearly, Richard is keen to continue the conversation. He casts a sidelong glance at Patch's saddlebag where the turquoise cover of *A Doctor's Marital Guide for Patients: Combined Regular and Rhythm Edition* is still in plain view.

'Erm…'

'And there is another thing you gotta do. You gotta buy this book…'

Patch opens his plump hand and there folded up is a bit of paper on which Mick has copied out the title of the book

Robbie asked for – *The Regulation of Asylums: Theory, Practice and Case Law by J. Wilfred Gwilliam*. Richard screws up his face and tugs at his hair, and this screwing up and tugging continues when Patch explains that Richard then has to find a dust jacket from another book of the same size and put it onto J. Wilfred Gwilliam's oeuvre and post it off to Robbie.

Eventually Richard says yes. He agrees to go into town on his first day off, buy the book, get a dust jacket off some other less inflammatory text, and post the thing off to Robbie at Binstead.

'Erm...' Richard's eye is resting again on the turquoise-coloured booklet in Patch's saddlebag.

'Yes? You want to borrow me *Marital Guide*?'

'Umm.'

'Like I told you, you can borrow it when you've helped us get rid of the Rat.'

'Umm.'

'Look, mate, it's not that hard. Here's what you do...'

Richard is in his room. It is after supper where the nurses have been chatting among themselves, mostly about *Juke Box Jury*, which Richard is sadly not very up on, being keener on Puccini and Sibelius, at least until now. He is going to have a good read this evening of the book he has just borrowed from Gloriana. But first things first. He will look into *Teach Yourself British Standard Sign Language* later. Because first he has decided to move the girl friend question decisively forward.

Richard has come to believe that if he is to get anywhere with Lizzie who is probably older than he is and he supposes light years ahead of him in 'experience', he needs to get a Forty Inch Chest. So he gets his Bullworker from behind the wardrobe. He has invested 7/6d down on this capital item, and he is committed to sending off weekly postal orders for 2/3d for the next twelve months. Where the money is to come from is a secondary question which he has put off till later. First he wants results.

The Bullworker has green handles at either end of two long shiny tubes, one of which slides into the other against a strenuously resisting spring. The booklet, admittedly poorly translated from the Japanese, shows how, if you grasp the green handles and compress the tubes one into the other, you will quickly build (1) chest muscles of steel (2) piston-like arms (3) shoulder muscles like legs of mutton, and by extension (4) a body girls cannot keep their eyes and hands off.

For maximum effect and as shown in the booklet, Richard takes off all his clothes except his underpants and stands in front of the mirror. Posture erect, shoulders back, head upright, all as shown in the text, he begins to squeeze. The first try he gets the one tube halfway into the other before the strenuously resisting bit springs back. The second try he cannot get it in quite so far, and then he falls into a rhythm of about one third in, hold it for a second or two, then ease it out.

He looks in the mirror and sees no difference from his weedy 'schoolboy' look. He perseveres, panting lightly. He feels a pain in his shoulder and also after a while feels, and notices in the mirror, a thickening down below.

He is thinking of Lizzie.

He closes his eyes.

She is not so very beautiful or even particularly pretty. She is certainly not well spoken. His mother would have a thing or two to say about her, not that he is thinking of taking her to see his mother. She dresses in any old thing. She does not correspond at any point to his dreams which are of sulky brown girls – Lizzie has a pasty pale complexion which sometimes looks blotchy when she is cross or otherwise moved. Richard also dreams of girls with gleaming blonde hair to their waist – Lizzie has that mop of unruly black hair.

Yet yet yet. Despite all these unideal features, despite all these lapses and clearly substandard aspects, it is Lizzie who dances before Richard's eyes as he slides in and out until he reaches one hundred and ninety-eight times. Two to go. By now his head is hammering, his shoulders are numb from pain, sweat is spilling into his eyes.

It is about to end in the most delightful way when there is a rapping at the door and it is thrown open.

Richard recognizes the young handyman, Pete was it?

'Blimey, mate. Cor. Blimey. Still... whatever turns you on. Comin' for a pint?'

Flick is on her rounds for Girls Nightly Medicine.

There is a conflict in her slim breast about Helen's emulsion. She wants to do the right thing, but just now she is not sure what that is. On one side is Jane Ratcliffe, an SRN and the Acting Warden, who has put out this emulsion for Helen 'on doctor's orders'. Flick's grasp of medical ethics is that she should do what the doctor says. This is what Jane Ratcliffe had said in the Sluice, too. And Flick certainly wants to keep on the right side of Miss Ratcliffe. She has just received the forms to fill in to apply to become a student nurse.

Yet the emulsion seems all wrong. Judging by the effect it had the other night when she took a swig herself, Flick has come to believe that the emulsion has been made up with drugs just to keep Helen quiet. Hadn't she herself felt really woozy the other night and not at all up to things?

In fact, thinking it over, Flick has concluded there is no healing about this medicine at all, and it is not, in Flick's view, the work of the healer to suppress Helen's natural tendencies, even if they are inconvenient.

So Flick makes up her mind. She takes the large emulsion bottle and pours out Helen's nightly ration. Then she slips into the Girls' Toilets and tips the ration down the sink.

Back at the medicine trolley, she puts a firm tick against Helen's name, to show that she has dispensed the medicine.

'That thing you had there, that whatsit, you don't need that.'

'It's to get a Forty Inch Chest,' Richard says humbly.

'Pah, what's that for?'

'Forty Inch Chest? It's to stop the fellow with all the muscles kicking sand in your face.'

Pete laughs briefly. His forty two inch chest seems to Richard to swell even broader.

'Nah, don't need that.'

This is contrary to everything Richard had understood up to now.

'Look, Rich, you're not a very physical sort of bloke, are you? Never will be. But, see, there's birds... some birds, anyway, they go for you educated toff types... more the speccy type of birds, of course... but then when they whip the specs off, cor. No, you know what you got to do, mate?'

Richard looks as meek as he can.

'... you just gotta get the chatting up bit right. And you gotta get a budget. You have to take her out to the pub and buy her a Snowball...'

Pete is Richard's new best friend. They have been in The Dog for two hours. While they drank their first pint, Pete had kicked off with some general abuse which had increased rapidly in tempo when Richard made an unforced error in admitting he has not yet had sex, although, as he added, he 'really intended to quite soon.'

'Christ Almighty, where do they get you children from?'

'Why, have you?'

'Me? Me? Course. With me an' my girlfriend Jackie it was up them stairs and the shithouse door never stopped. That is, until her old man caught us.'

'And... other girls, I mean, before?'

'Course. Loads.'

Pete drank deep of his pint, studying Richard over the rim.

'I know what your problem is, though, Richard. It's your Mummy Darling, isn't it? You posh types just want to marry Mummy, don't you? Admit it, don't you?'

But it turns out that in spite of Pete's filthy language and dirty mind, he really is Richard's best friend. This feeling grows on Richard during their second and third pints. What is thrilling is Pete's utter indifference to the sort of thing Richard is used to talking about – such as, Marxism as a new way of looking at the world based on evidence, for instance, or the inevitable collapse and extinction of our sun in some distant astronomical time, to take another recent example. Pete's own special topics – sex, smokes, drinks, cars – really are thrilling. However, there seems to be a lot to learn if you want to keep up and make it in this new world that is opening up.

'Got to get a girlfriend, Richard,' Pete repeats several times and the more times he said it, the more Richard agrees with him.

'You can have any of them you like,' Pete says loftily. 'Except Angela, of course.'

Pete seems to be fixated on a nurse called Angela Cudmore. This is a rustic girl with a sizable bust, thick skeins of blonde hair and a queer peasanty Suffolk accent. Angela is not particularly popular and she keeps herself pretty much to herself. Richard has overheard Lizzie calling her 'an idle thickie'.

Pete bangs on about this skulking busty creature for quite a spell as he has every right to do as he has bought all the rounds so far, Richard not having a bean. Pete has, it seems, walked out with Angela a couple of times and he now starts on a rather detailed account of his partial explorations of her upper erogenous zones. The report on his attempts to move to the lower ones is, however, quite a bit shorter and bleaker.

At length, as they broach their fourth pint, Pete says,

'So, who you got your eye on, then, young Richard?'

'Oh, you know...'

'Come on, spit it out.'

Oh, well... Lizzie, for example...'

Pete laughs at this point, nastily in Richard's view.

'Good luck to you there, mate,' he says cryptically. 'Good luck with that one, I say. Now, who's your back up?'

'Back up?'

'Yeah, got to have a backup.'

'Ummm... Debbie?'

Pete laughs more loudly and, in Richard's opinion, even more nastily.

'Cor, you don't 'alf pick 'em. Debbie! Ha! Well the best of British with that one too. Cor.'

Pete laughs a bit more. Richard thinks he looks like a horse. His upper jaw is definitely projecting beyond the lower, just like a horse, and the laugh has a stupid whinnying sound to it.

But still, Pete is his best friend. There on the scrubbed wooden table in front of him, next to the damp rings of his four previous pints now stands his fifth Pete-bought pint, and beside it, in the ashtray which implausibly asserts *Guinness is Good for You*, smoke is rising from the lengthening ash on his seventh or eighth Pete-proffered ciggy. Richard smiles weakly.

Thinking about it later, Richard wasn't entirely sure how the session actually ended. At some stage, he seemed to be making his way alone across a very large and sloping field which was shared by numerous bulky black cows with well-developed territorial instincts. The cows loomed up from time to time out of the darkness as he wended diagonally down the field.

The lights of Park House could be dimly seen, like valves on an old wireless. He had nearly made it to a gate which a handy burst of moonlight from between two clouds now revealed, when a cow nudged him from behind and he fell in a large cowpat.

As he stumbled through the gate and closed it carefully, he felt a presence at his knee and a loud snuffling. Putting his hand down, he felt what was evidently the head of a dog which from the greasy feel of it he concluded must be the noisome Bertie. Bertie trailed him towards the House, inhaling in an unnecessarily exaggerated fashion the odour of the cow pat, most of which Richard could now feel clinging to his trousers.

The French windows were mercifully not locked, and no one was about. He moved quickly across the Great Hall and slipped down the corridor and up the stairs to his room.

When Richard fell into his room, full of ales and reeking of cowpat, Helen was in his bed. At first, she came across a little blurred but even with his freight of pints Richard could not mistake who it was. Her raven hair streamed on the pillow like a comet's tail. She was sleeping, or pretending to sleep.

Richard's first foggy thought concerned certain stains on the sheets. But then the second was how – well – *lovely* she looked. Her face was in profile and her eyes were shut and he saw her good Roman nose and the black eyelashes falling impossibly long, and her lips slightly parted, and for exactly a single nanosecond he felt impossible desire leaping up, and then the iron gate of every prohibition he knew came slamming down.

He said, 'Helen, you've got to go.'

She shammed sleep a bit more but he could see her eyelids fluttering. Her mouth looked like it was muttering *No*. Then suddenly she sat up, displaying a beautiful pair of the first naked breasts Richard had seen since his mother put him on formula at the age of two months.

He crashed out of the room and then hissed back through the crack.

'Get up. Put your clothes on.'

He peeped through the crack to make sure she was indeed putting her kit back on. She was. He glimpsed the lovely bosom disappearing under a shapeless shift with a big floral print that looked like it was a hand-me-down from the Ratcliffe herself.

At last she came out. She was crying. She ducked up at him and kissed him, a little sideways, on the lips. Then she zigzagged her way up the nurses' corridor.

Her head was hung down. Her tears fell on the ragged carpet. She did not notice the one in the shadows who had been watching, who had seen the kiss. But then Jane Ratcliffe was taking good care to keep herself hidden amongst the mops and brooms.

14

Morning roll call comes up one short. It is soon discovered to be Greg, big slow contemplative Greg. A hue and cry goes up and Jane Ratcliffe orders a search of the grounds.

Everyone else claims they are busy, so the task falls to Richard. He seeks out Lizzie. He has unaccountably got into the habit of trusting her advice.

'Greg AWOL again?' she says carelessly, but Richard presses her.

'Shouldn't the police be told?' Today Lizzie is wearing a skirt, a blue cotton one which, while quite rumpled and far from new, has the advantage of ending several inches above her knees.

'Shouldn't there be helicopters?' Richard asks, admiring her pretty legs. But the questions fall flat. She just says,

'Lord, no. He'll turn up. He always does. Try the Tower.'

Then she skips away before he can pump her for better tips. His eye follows her. In his view, the interview has not been wasted.

It is a morning of cold and occasional rain. Gusts of wind are blowing in off the marshes to the east as Richard sets out for the Tower. He has seen this edifice, which stands on a hill behind the House, but he has not yet been there. First, he walks through the gardens behind the House. Here there are Italian terraces whose charm is losing ground to the return of rebellious nature. The flagstones are awry and split with the movement of the protesting earth beneath.

The detailing of the balustrades is horribly chipped and eaten up by lichen. There are huge hydrangeas shaking their pale blue flowers in the wind. Richard carefully climbs the wide stone steps, which are uneven and green, and made slicker by the recent rain.

Going carefully, his head bowed, he nearly bumps into the girl who is coming down with more assured tread. She pauses just beside him on the step. It is none other than the busty blonde-maned rustic Angela Cudmore, favoured of Pete. For the first time Richard is seeing her close up. Her cheeks are red, her profuse golden hair tumbles over her shoulders and down her back. Her bosom is startlingly large, straining against the buttons of her gingham blouse.

Richard inwardly admits to a grudging admiration for Pete's readiness to take on such ripeness. He thinks Angela's exuberance is attractive and repellent in equal measure.

Angela Cudmore says nothing, just gives him a slow look. He sees she is carrying a bag.

'Seen Greg?'

'Why?'

'Because he's missing.'

'Ah.'

Beyond Angela's shoulder, Richard sees white and grey clouds moving fast towards them across a dark copse. The tops of the trees sway and shake in the gathering wind. Angela glances round at this looming weather and then without a further word walks off, stepping in a competent way down the bumpy treads.

Richard carries on up, cautiously, and soon the Tower reveals itself. It is triangular, with turrets at the corners and narrow slits for windows.

The rain now starts up quite hard and Richard dashes for

the Tower. It has heavy wooden doors. These yield to his shove and he tumbles inside. It smells of bats. A dismal light filters in through the window slits and his eyes adjust to the penumbral gloom.

The floor is in fact covered with bat litter, mixed in amongst the dust and chips of fallen stucco. From the dark corners there is the sound of rustling, scurrying creatures. A shaft of pale grey light picks out, in the very centre of the room, a massive statue, twice life size. It is of some bod dressed in the kit of an antique Roman general.

Suddenly, through the half open door, two skinny cats dash in like wraiths and scoot for the corners.

A deep melancholy voice says Richard's name. He looks round the back of the toga-ed general, whose name he now reads chiselled on the plinth – *Sir Roper Smytheson, Saviour of the Indies*. Parked up against Sir Roper's sandalled foot is Greg, in his chair. The silver stars on his waistcoat gleam dully in the grey light. He looks in sombre mood. Open on his lap there is an exercise book, and in his hand a pencil.

'Hallo. We were... sort of looking for you...'

At this juncture there is a huge commotion in the corner as the skinny cats dart to and fro harrying the rustling, scurrying creatures, which turn out to be some very agile mice. The cats drive them hither and thither. And then in lumbers Bertie. The dog shakes the rain off his greasy coat, barks gruffly, twice, and sets about chasing the cats around the room. After a couple of turns the cats give up and shoot out of the door where the rain can now be seen falling in torrents. The mice hurry off and disappear. Bertie comes and sits down next to Greg, panting hard, his pink tongue lolling awkwardly.

'Richard,' Greg says in his slow way, 'I'm writing a pop song.'

'Gosh.'

'Would you like to see it?'

Greg hands the exercise book to Richard. Resting the book on the big toe of the Saviour of the Indies which is illuminated by a thin dash of ash-grey light, Richard looks at Greg's song. The book is rather tattered, with leaves of rough paper. Across the two pages in the middle of the book, Greg has pencilled in a series of lines and squiggles. Although they make no sense to Richard, he thinks they might be runes or possibly Linear B.

'The words *and* the music,' Greg says slowly and firmly, which seems to Richard to confirm they really are runes.

'Gosh,' Richard says, putting the exercise book back in Greg's lap.

The boy says nothing and doesn't move.

'Gosh,' Richard says again, 'that's well… quite something.'

Richard looks around for inspiration. What more can he say to the boy? His eye falls on the side of Sir Roper's plinth that is just behind Greg. Here there is more informative text about the Saviour of the Indies.

DISCIPLINE ESTABLISHED
FORTRESSES PROTECTED
SETTLEMENTS EXTENDED
ARMIES DEFEATED
PEACE CONCLUDED IN THE CARNATIC

Finding nothing relevant in this and vaguely troubled by the scansion of that last line, Richard puts his hand on Greg's arm, to show solidarity at least.

'Now, Greg, do you want to come back with me? Looks like the rain's stopping.'

'Not yet, Richard.'

'Oh.'

'Angela'll come for me later.'

'Oh, gosh, Angela… she's looking after you then?'

'She's from Bungay.'

'Oh, yes, right…'

'I'm from Bungay. We're from Bungay.'

Richard bends down and hugs the boy briefly. Then he leaves. Bertie is sitting alongside Greg, watching out for cats.

'Dear Gloriana, we need to have a little chat.'

My eyes are on the light beyond the window. I am searching for the sun in the damp fog that seeped into the park when the rain cleared and which still lies heavy on the landscape at this mid-morning hour. I scan the big lime tree which is stirring uncertainly in the faint breeze, reaching for the light. A clutch of heedless birds flutters in and out of the dense foliage. I dream I am a bird, fluttering up. I do not listen to the Ratcliffe. She says again,

'Dear Gloriana, we need to have a little chat.'

Finally I glance at her. Actually, this is hard to avoid as she has now positioned herself between me and my window. Typical. I see that her mouth has pursed to a prune-like *moue*.

'I mean, dear Gloriana…'

Dear Gloriana! Good God, I'm not her dear.

'… as you know, Mr. Salter has kindly agreed to bring forward your transfer for the end of this term…'

My eyes are on the Rat. Her back is to the bright window. Her face is in the shadow. Always in the shadow.

'He'll be motoring over from Binstead soon for your Evaluation. You must begin to prepare yourself as best you can...'

For what? The Last Rites?

Help, help! I feel so alone, so unprotected. What can I do? It's the Bin, the Bates Motel. You check in, you don't check out!

But now like an angel here is Richard suddenly bursting in, all fresh youth. He apologizes for lateness. The Ratcliffe, it seems, has agreed he can sit in, or maybe he is just barging in. Who cares? I say Big Kudos to Richard.

Cleverly, he draws up a chair sideways on to both me and the Rat, as though he might join either side of the argument. Ratcliffe looks neutral about this. I don't think she expects any danger from Richard's quarter. We shall see about that.

There is fuzz on Richard's face, above his upper lip and down his cheeks. Oh Lord, he has forgotten to shave again. He looks like a peach with all that fuzz. Can a peach take on the determined prune of the Ratcliffe's tight-set mouth?

My clever boy, my champion. Well, so I hope. But I have a doomy sense that I may still be headed for Binstead, have been ever since that nameless mum dumped me on the doorstep in a wicker shopping basket without a note. But Binstead! Bastard, bin, abandon – place of abandonment. Robbie's missive was definitely not encouraging, more like a drowner's cry for help. Really, you check in to Binstead, you don't check out.

I must pay attention. Richard has started to say something, albeit in the high pitched, rather weedy voice which seems to come on him at moments when he is a bit nervous.

'I mean,' he is saying and his voice is wobbling, 'I mean, couldn't Gloriana do better than that. I mean better than just, well – nothing much at all...'

The Ratcliffe comes back on cue. She has been pondering

this problem of the vegetable life.

'It's not nothing at all, dear Richard' (stop saying **dear**, Ratcliffe. We're not your dears.). 'There'll be activities. A spiritual life. She has a soul, you know.'

The soul is the Ratcliffe's ace and she slaps it down.

Richard's hand moves uncertainly up to his cheek and he rubs at the fuzz. There is some throat clearing and he tries to lower his voice as he says,

'Gloriana's super bright.'

Now that's a trump of some kind, isn't it?

But Ratcliffe doesn't at first cotton on. I think it is Richard's voice which deceives her about his seriousness. Try as he may, it keeps riding up and quivering around his unprepossessing higher registers, almost girly. How he must hate that.

Still, I believe he could still take the trick. Because he is not going to engage on the soul question, thank goodness. As if to emphasize his position, he gets up and moves his chair over by my bed. He sits about where my middle is, so that he can look out with me at the misty park. The muffled light shines on us, the Ratcliffe is in the shadows. This move makes Ratcliffe quite uncomfortable and she starts glancing from me to Richard and back again. She is trying to read what is happening.

Actually, nobody really knows. It is a decisive moment but what the decision is to be is far from clear. Quite unknown at that instant, in fact.

However, some faint meteorological adjustments are taking place outside, and Richard and I let our eyes rest for a moment on the thinning mist and on the watered sun which is now filling the park with pale yellow light.

Richard glances at me. I have put on a new expression and I sign to him Resist! Resist!

The Rat spots this and says 'What's that? What are you signing there?'

But guess what? Richard ghosts the faintest little motion with his hand which looks like a Yes. In fact it's definitely a yes. Richard is learning my language.

'I think,' he says, still looking at me and not at the Ratcliffe's flinty phizz, and his voice finding a middle register that if not exactly authoritative is at least not quite so weedy, 'I think that Gloriana could go to university.'

Wow! My face quickens with an instant joy.

I am looking at the Ratcliffe's stunned expression. This sally has knocked her sideways. The notion that anybody from Park House could go to university has struck her with the force of a completely novel idea (me too, but never mind about that). Then the Ratcliffe's shock gives way to some complex workings, and she moves a fraction in her chair. Her lips lose their lozenge tightness and part ever so slightly.

In a moment, she has clearly reflected enough to see that she can't oppose on principle this alternative way of letting in the light, so she says,

'But how?'

Coming from Ratcliffe, that's practically a yes.

'We can find a way, Miss Ratcliffe,' Richard says quickly. Rightly he sees this is not a time for mere details. In fact he has an extra trick up his sleeve, and it's the way ordinary people use an old saw to round off difficult conversations. With a dab of genius, he says,

'Where there's a will, there's a way.'

Which, amazingly really, does take the trick, because the Ratcliffe can only nod and say 'Well, we'll have to think about it, won't we.'

She gets up, smoothes out her tweed skirt as best that

reluctant material will allow and leaves the room, and I am pretty sure that is a tail I see hanging between her piano legs.

I am all smiles, and my eyes adore Richard. I sign Thank you, thank you, and he says out loud, marvellously, ridiculously,

'Think nothing of it.'

15

In the Great Hall, the noble Trojan elders advance.
Their king is ahead of them on his gleaming vermilion and silver Armsworth 302, his huge red face puffed out in pride, his eyes bright with triumphs. The light from the dusty chandelier falls coruscating on the polished chrome of the Armsworth's footplate. Behind come the four noble elders in line abreast, they've dressed to the right and their distances are impeccable. They flow forward chanting:

Hon hoi theoi philousin....

The noble Trojan warriors, girls and boys alike, are lined up on either side. They shout back:

NEOS APOTHNESKEI

Patch and the noble elders arrive at the chipped old pear-wood sideboard. There Helen is perched, dressed as usual in her old yellow frock rather than as the disputed princess of Troy. And yet she looks sufficiently dazzling. The troop nod to her and wheel and turn about and head for the piano, still chanting. The noble warriors, boys and girls together, shout back their antiphony.

Richard is sitting at the piano, watching all this. As he runs his hand idly up and down the frayed tapestry cover of the piano stool, he feels a light touch on his shoulder. He knows at once without even looking up that it is Lizzie. She and Debbie have just brought Gloriana in. He has been willing her to come over – and brilliantly here she is. He turns and looks up at her. She looks frankly pretty fagged out. There are dark smudges under her eyes. Her skin is all pasty and blotchy and a small red pimple has sprung up on her right cheek since he last saw her this close. He thinks she looks terrible, but somehow she doesn't.

'Woss all this then?' she demands in the grating Essex voice she steps up for certain occasions.

'Trojans.'

Lizzie bursts out laughing.

'An' that... chantin'... woss all that about?'

She has to shout this as the lively Trojans are delivering another round of their ditty at increased volume.

NEOS APOTHNESKEI

'Woss that mean then, Richard?'

'Whom the gods love, dies young.'

Lizzie is looking around the room in a puzzled way, as though she doesn't quite get the Trojan business. All at once her body gives a little spasm and her eyes widen and then quickly narrow. Her face takes on a fretful look.

'What's up, Lizzie?' Richard asks but she says nothing, just pats him on the shoulder and skips away and runs back to Gloriana.

Lizzie and Debbie have brought me in to watch the Trojans, which is super. My heart rapidly becomes light. Patch has found his heroic, emboldening myth. He has listened rapt to Richard's reading of *Tales from Troy* – Trojans who went down battling, Trojans who fixed their myth forever and scattered seeds that fell far and wide. And not just in Rome. I bet that Dido had a daughter. Before she, you know...

While Greeks, seedy old Greeks... Richard told us the Agamemnon character came back to a domestic because his wife was having an affair, and she topped him. And then her son and daughter did her in. And then **they** came to a nasty end, pursued by Furies...

But Trojans! Hector was a hero, Richard said, when Achilles was hiding among women.

So yes, my heart is light for Patch, and he is so serene. But...

BUT!

Dear Lizzie runs over to me and seizes my hand and presses it. Her dear pale face has become very white as though she has been struck by an electric terror. Every hackle of her simple spirit is aroused.

'Look, darling, look there,' she murmurs.

And I look and see his sallow face. He is looking round the room. Sizing us up, I know, because he glances at me and then away, and then he stares at dreamy Greg who is sitting up stock still and looking rather august and stately, and then I see another watcher in the shadows pointing at each of us in turn, pointing and then moving on, now at big battling Mick whose unshaved stubble makes him look like Desperate Dan, and then at my lovely lovely Helen. She looks beautiful, perched on the old Thirties sideboard, bowing her head with such grace to the homage of the Trojans.

Now the finger points at Patch, who is giving a short oration on the new dispensations for the governance of Troy. The sallow face withdraws into the shadows, no doubt asking a question. The answer is probably a No, and his respondent in the shadows is certainly the Rat because I can make out the metalled tips of her shoes glinting dully in the gloom.

The sallow face reappears, looks at Patch again, moves slightly from side to side in what is clearly a shake of the head, sweeps the hall with jaundiced eye, and slips back into the shadows and away.

Lizzie is at my side. She is holding my hand. There is

nothing to say, so she says nothing, like the sensible girl she is. Because we know who is sallow face and jaundiced eye. We know because he came for Robbie. It's Sallow Salter.

'Tea, Mr. Salter?'

'No, I think not, thank you muchly. Shall we get on with it? It's a bit of a drive I've got back to Binstead.'

'Well, yes, of course, I quite understand. So nasty these long drives. Here's the listing for the end of term transfers. I've completed it as best I could. It's my first year, of course. Mrs. Noble usually does it but she's... you know...'

'Yes, of course. Still off in America, isn't she?'

'And, Mr. Salter...'

'Yes, dear?'

'... I cannot thank you enough for agreeing to take these five early.'

Park House Leavers Pre-Transfer Evaluation Summer Term 1966

Name	Sex	Age next birthday	Status	Capabilities	Outlook
Gloriana Gillespie	Girl	16	Spastic tetraplegia. Dumb. Constant bed care required.	None	MTP/LTP (?)
Gregory Smith	Boy	16	Hydrocephalus. Mechanical wheel-chair.	None	STP/(MTP?)
Helen Scandizzi	Girl	16	Mental limitations. Partial spina bifida. Ambulant with limi-tations.	Highly limited. Possible do-mestic work (e.g. cleaner)	LTP
Michael Norris	Boy	16	Spina bifida. Mechanical wheel-chair or crutch ambulant.	Highly limited. Possible un-skilled manual work.	LTP

Patrick Beer	Boy	16	Muscular dystrophy. Electric-powered wheelchair.	None	

Even to Jane Ratcliffe the Pre-Transfer Evaluation seemed a bit of a bald statement. But of course, you had to fill it in conscientiously. It was for the children's own good. No point fabricating fanciful little stories like that wretched Richard, filling poor Gloriana's head with idle fancies. University, indeed! Salmon will walk in the street first! After all, life itself is no bed of roses (although wouldn't a bed of roses be rather uncomfortable? She'd pricked herself very badly indeed last year when she'd tried to prune her mother's big old Victorian climber...).

Mr. Salter studied the form closely.

'Now this Eyetie girl here... this Helen Whats-it... is that the one that... ummm...? Did you...?'

'Yes, I got it made up. But it doesn't seem to be working as it should. There have been... ummm... incidents...'

'Oh?' Mr. Salter sounded interested.

'Yes, incidents, Mr. Salter.'

'Well, if it gets too bad and you want me to take her pdq, give me a bell. Things are a bit tight just now but I could see what I could do.'

'Thank you, Mr. Salter, thank you so much.'

'Now I hope none of these new lot are trouble-makers. As it is, I've my hands full with that Willis you sent. Proper little so-and-so. He's been bothering the Loopy Ladies...'

'The *what*?'

'Oops. No, he's been working up one of our ladies, Norma by name, one of our feeble minded out-of-wedlocks. He's got it into his head that we're keeping her against her will as it were. He was talking about trying to get her a

Review...'

'My goodness. Well, it's true he was always intrigued by the law. Such a pity he couldn't have taken it somewhere, but of course in his condition...'

'Well, I doubt it will go any further but if it does I'll put Norma into Specials for a week, just in case she's tempted. That should focus her mind, if you get my drift...'

Jane Ratcliffe was astonished to hear this and she wondered what exactly Specials were. She opened her mouth to ask but already Mr. Salter had turned back to the Leavers Evaluation.

'Now here...' Mr. Salter tapped his forefinger three times on the schedule, on the last box. It seemed even to Jane, so respectful of hierarchies – and Mr. Salter was after all the senior man – a somewhat peremptory gesture, and the off-colour impression that it made was all the darker because she saw the yellow staining on the finger. Mr. Salter was a smoker!

His finger stayed resting on the last box, the box where her Parker ball-point which her mother had given her for her last birthday had remained poised when she was completing the form.

'Err, you haven't fulled out this box here.' *Fulled*? And Mr. Salter's accent!

'Patrick Beer, Outlook? MTP? LTP? Medium term patient? Longer term patient?'

Mr. Salter really was not quite... well... not quite.

'What do you think we should put, Mr. Salter?'

'Come on, love.' *Love!* Mr. Salter was definitely Not Quite. But then his job was hard. Running Binstead was no cake walk. He deserved her respect.

'Well, actually... frankly, Mr. Salter... you saw him... Patrick, the overweight boy with the high colouring... the one in the electric wheelchair...'

'Oh, yes, of course. The Armstead 302. Nice little runner, that.'

'It's dystrophy, you see... late Stage Four... highly degenerative... running into Stage Five...'

'Oh, OK, righty-ho, I get you now.' Mr. Salter's thin yellowish face showed nothing. 'I'll just pop him down as... Have you got a pen? Nice one, ta.'

Mr. Salter took Jane's Parker in his nicotiney fingers and wrote firmly **NONE** in the last box, in block capitals. It was, Jane noticed, a rather uneducated hand.

PART TWO: JULY 1966

16

~~Dear Mrs. Noble,~~
~~Your creature Ratcliffe is a hard and vengeful woman and~~
~~must be replaced at once. Otherwise...~~

~~Dear Mrs. Noble,~~
~~I am so sorry to trouble you when I know you must be so busy~~
~~but I felt that I must bring to your attention a problem that has~~
~~arisen at the House. Miss Ratcliffe...~~

Dear Mrs. Noble,
I write on behalf of the children of the House who are more
and more miserable. I am afraid to say that some of Miss
Ratcliffe's initiatives have reduced the small happinesses the children enjoy. Miss Ratcliffe has recently brought forward the
transfer of the five oldest children to an adult institution, which
could perhaps be a little early for their stage of development.
Also, there are ideas that perhaps the leavers could do better
than simply go on to spend a lifetime in care.
　Please excuse the temerity of this letter but I thought I should
pass on these messages from the children.
　Yours sincerely,
　　R.

'Alright,' Patch said shortly. 'Better than the other ones
anyway.'

'Ermm.' The turquoise booklet was sticking prominently
out of Patch's saddlebag.

'Results first, mate,' Patch said. 'Good what you said to
the Rat, though, about Gloriana and college an' that. Now
we gotta think of somethin' for the others.'

Patch buzzed away. Richard went up to his room and began a fair copy of his letter.

***

'Look,' Richard says. 'I think this'll do the trick.'

He is holding out this really tattered old paperback. I look at it doubtfully.

PELICAN BOOKS

READING FOR PROFIT

BY

MONTGOMERY BELGION

Lately British Prisoner of War No. 182

The front cover is actually hanging off. Richard says he unearthed it in the second-hand bookshop in town, although it is so dog-eared and tattered it looks like it has been through many more hands than two and most of them rather grubby ones at that. Apparently, anyway, according to Richard, this Montgomery Belgion, Lately British Prisoner of War No. 182, sets out the books which Every Educated Person Should Read (or at least all the books old Montgomery Belgion could remember in the Oflag where he was banged up at the time and where he delivered these lectures to his fellow PoWs).

Crikey. Is this really Richard's way of defeating the Sallow Man? Is Monty Belgion going to get me into university?

I sign to Richard *Is this going to work?* but he doesn't

notice. He is too busy riffing through the shabby little book. While he is doing this, I look at the picture of Monty on the back cover. He has a sharp nose and thick black eyebrows that sort of lower over his eyes. I can't read much of the write-up about him as Richard keeps jiggling the book about but I do spot that he 'prefers his authors dead', which sounds a bit ominous. And there's no mention of university that I can see. If Monty didn't even go himself, a fat lot of use he's going to be.

'Ha,' Richard says suddenly. 'Ha!'

I look inquiring.

'So, Gloriana, listen to this. *We read primarily in order to be moved.*'

Richard stops and gives me a significant look. So far, I'm not very moved. I feel quite static in fact. I sign *So what*? He tries again.

'*The quality of our emotion is the measure of the quality of our literature.*'

I sign, *Vague, Monty, extremely vague. There must be more to it than that.*

This time Richard is focussing on me. I sign again and he gets it. Or at least he laughs.

'Hang on, Gloriana, let's just see... *the question is...* wait for it... the question is *Are the symptoms of literature actually present?*'

Which are? What *are* they, Richard?

He laughs again. At least he can follow me, even if we're getting strictly nowhere. He keeps flipping through. There's a long irritating pause. At last he says,

'Ah, here we are. *Must be well-written... be absorbing, admirably ordered and proportioned to best effect... possess humanity... must be endowed with significance...*'

We think about this for a little bit and then Richard

proposes we start reading some stuff to see if we will be moved. We will detect whether the Symptoms of Literature are present.

'So,' he says, 'Monty suggests starting with Shakespeare. Look, I've brought the Sonnets.'

Richard settles down to read. I settle down to detect the Symptoms of Literature.

Richard is wandering along with his head still full of sonnets when he bumps into Lizzie. She is carrying a huge pile of clean white towels, huge enough that the pile comes above her head. She has to walk half-sideways to see where she is going.

'Bloody laundry duty,' she says, bumping companionably against him. 'I'm just a bleedin' skivvy. Here, gimme a hand.' With this she shoves the bulk of the towels into Richard's arms.

'Where to?' he asks.

'Timbuktu. No, laundry closet, you nana.'

They walk side by side across the Great Hall. Lizzie doesn't seem to use any scent but there is always something attractive going on in the air around her. Richard has a go at returning the companionable bump but she says 'Oi' and skips ahead.

In the laundry closet, Lizzie reaches up and starts to put the towels on a high shelf. Over the pile in his own arms, Richard watches her from behind. She deftly tamps the towels in with the smooth round edge of the fold facing out. With her arms up like that, she looks very sturdy and confident. Her old green jumper rides up above her jeans about four inches and he can see the small of her back, the soft pink indent where it goes in, and her narrow waist and just the beginning of a delectable curve. He is tempted to throw the towels down and make a surge, but she whips round and looks him in the face, straight in the eye.

'Richard,' she says, 'don't get no ideas now' – she is hamming up her gratey Essex accent again but he can't tell if she means that as a distancing thing or the opposite – for him it's definitely the opposite. There is something sexy about the rasping edge of it.

'What?' he says, pretending to be puzzled, and feeling bleak.

'What? You know what. You was lookin' at me.'

'Well?'

'You got a dangerous look, matey. Don't think I don't know. Here, gimme them other towels.'

He leaves the laundry closet. Lizzie follows him out and puts her arm through his.

'You're just a kid, Richard. I'm nineteen. Anyway, I already…'

Lizzie thinks better of whatever she was going to say. Instead, she gives Richard a shove.

'Get yourself a nice little girl, Rich.'

***

The Bin
Binstead Village
Surrey-on-the-Styx
Hell

Day 15 of the 12,410 days of the rest of my life in The Bin

Dearest sister and brother,

Thank you sooooooooooooooo much for the *Regulation of Asylums: Theory, Practice and Case Law*. It came so beautifully disguised in a jacket of *The Little Man* by Ruby M.

Ayres that I almost threw it out in disgust. But fortunately I didn't – and now I am in love with J. Wilfred Gwilliam. I want to be him. I too am going to write a book of four hundred pages that is so cool in its arguments, so measured in its summations, so just in its judgements. Then between the coolness and the measuredness and the justness of my text, I will show my love and my humanity just like JWG. Like him, I will write at the very front, just after my imposing title set in heavy Copperplate Gothic, a light and airy sans serif dedication to *My Dear Soft Wife*. In that sudden flash, you see all the man. I don't know yet what my Dear Soft Wife will be called but JWG's was called Agnes May. She kept him, he says in this love letter of a dedication, *from Hours of Vinous Discussion at the Reform Club*. This will be my world when all is well with me.

And you know what? I read J. Wilfred's oeuvre all evening and far into the night. And already I have learned more than enough for my purpose. Which is – to request a Clinical Review Board for Miss Norma Winifred Cummings.

Norma has agreed to cooperate. It took her a very long time to grasp what I meant, which is OK because she came here when she was still fifteen and now she's forty-five. When she started at the Bin she was younger than those nice girls from the Grammar, now she looks like a granny. She's been here a lifetime.

She owns one frock which she wears when the Governors come, twice a year. Otherwise it's hand-me-downs from the Rotary pot luck, every Monday. She has no clue whatever about the world. She came in here before Munich, before Hitler's War. Of that War, she seems to remember nothing, except one story about when she was in the copse at night. They'd gone to listen to night-ingales, she said. 'But then they came roaring above us and we couldn't hear the birds anymore.' I couldn't make head or tail of this but the old charge nurse who was listening told me it had been Lancaster bombers heading for Dresden. The nightingales left, she said, and didn't come back. After that, Norma doesn't remember very much. She has a vague idea about the Queen. I think they hired a telly for the Coronation and for Winston Churchill's funeral last year.

She keeps saying *I was unclean. That's why they make me do the laundry.* This one compelling lie they've been telling her for thirty years paralyses her whole being.

I said to her, 'There's no connection, Norma. Laundry's just a job.' But she wasn't having that.

'It can't be,' she said. 'If it was a job, I'd get paid for it.'

Anyway, we managed to have a long talk, Norma and I, and in the end she agreed I could make up a case for her. She said she wasn't really clear what I was on about, but she trusted me.

I bowled round to the Office straightaway. By my good luck, Sallow Salter was out and friendly Dawn, the nice lady with the big bazookas, was alone there. She looked stunning. Her brown hair was piled up in a massive beehive. She had on pink lipstick and matching shocking pink nail vanish, and a beautiful jumper in a very pale pastel blue. It was a really tight fit, I wonder she could breathe. I complimented her madly on all this get-up. I said it's a bit like pearls before swine, meaning Yellow Dog Salter, and she laughed and said it definitely wasn't for him.

Anyway, I chatted her up a bit and sure enough I

found beneath the big bazookas a beating heart of gold. She whipped open a filing cabinet, her fingers flicked deftly, and in a few moments she came up with a very thin, dark green file: **NORMA WINIFRED CUMMINGS**. Inside was just a single sheet of pale yellow paper marked *Carbon 3: patient's record.*

Norma Winifred Cummings: d.o.b. December 9th, 1921
Admitted: June 1st, 1937 (15 yrs 5 months)
Diagnosis: Feeble-minded (COW – IBM – USA)
Review date: N/A

'I s'pose,' Dawn said, 'you'll be wanting to know what all that means.'

She looked in a little manual she had on her desk.

'COW *Child out of wedlock.* IBM *Intercourse before marriage.* USA *Under-age sexual activity.*'

'Blimey,' I said, 'that's really feeble-minded.'

Dawn stared at me for a moment and then burst out laughing.

'I got married in my eighth month,' she said. 'On my sixteenth birthday.'

She asked me what I had in mind and I told her.

She laughed again.

'The best of British. That'd really put old Salter's nose out of joint.'

I thanked her and turned my chair round to leave.

'But you know, Robbie,' she said, 'once these people have got you, there's not much you can do.'

So with J. Wilfred Gwilliam's magnum opus in my head, and with his love for his Dear Soft Wife Agnes May in my heart, I am preparing Norma's case for the Clinical

Review Board. And, dear G, dear P, her sponsor will be none other than –

Yrs truly,

Robert 'Perry Mason' Willis

17

'Forking mummy crap bollocks.'

Mick is raging. Patch waits patiently, resting his flowing chin on the stick of his Armstead 302 and keeping his eye on the distraught Mick. Richard hangs back, fingering the letter he has just read out.

Mick wheels himself up and down – they are in the stables, where the big cage for the tropical birds is almost finished – shouting 'Mother? Mother! I don't have any mother!' It could pass as Victorian melodrama. Then he calls to Bertie and wheels himself abruptly away to his work bench, his big freckly face full of scorn. Richard goes after him, but the boy is already sawing up bits of four-by-four with savage cuts.

Richard reads through the letter again to himself, noting idly that it is written on Basildon Bond, the same small blue notepaper his mother used.

2, Hawthorn Road,
Hammersmith

Dear Miss Ratcliffe,

I hope that you will excuse me for writing 'out of the blue'. I enquired of your head office and they very kindly suggested that I write directly to you.

I am the mother of a boy who is staying in your 'home'. His name is Michael Norris. He was born at a time when I was unmarried and I had, of course, to give him up. After a number of years of marriage, I am now alone and quite 'comfortably off'. I would like to meet Michael and to ask him whether he might wish to come to live with me.

I know that this may come as a surprise to you and to Michael. I hope that you will pardon my intrusion. I look forward to hearing from you in due course.

Yours truly,

Araminta Cavendish (Mrs.)

Araminta's hand was upright, rounded and precise.

''s a chance for you, Mick,' Patch says and buzzes off. Richard goes with him.

Bertie looks longingly after them. He knows it's tea time. But he stays with Mick who is still fiercely sawing up wood.

On the face of it, the Sluice was not an ideal place for asking a girl out. Yet, if you discounted the bins heavy with soiled smalls and the saccharine pong, you could see why it might work. It was a narrow chamber, a bit of a squeeze even for two, and in its own peculiar way it was quite intimate. You had to face forward, so some of the awkward things that might come up when broaching a shift of the paradigm – towards asking a girl out, for example – you didn't have to worry about, like what sort of look on the face (cocky, alluring, imperious, bland, shy, etcetera), the cast of the eyes (how much eye contact, how much fluttering and glancing), how much sincerity etc. etc. And at the limit, if the approach was clearly failing, you could pretend you were just there to wash out your knickers or Y-Fronts, according to the case.

At least that was what flashed through Richard's calculating mind when he spotted Debbie heaving a pile of dirties into the Sluice. Because if not Lizzie, then Debbie. He had to get on with the girl friend question.

He nipped in after her. For once she was not laughing at private jokes with Flick.

Debbie looked up in surprise, blinking in the neon light which now emphasized her smooth complexion and glinted off her prominent shiny nose. Her gleaming gold hair was gathered back into a ponytail, held by what looked like a couple of rubber bands. She gave Richard a quick inconsequential smile, nodding her head. Her lips just parted as she bestowed the smile and he saw there was a tiny gap between her front teeth, and the palest little blonde fuzz on her upper lip. She looked at him questioningly.

There was a pause. His eye dropped to her bosom. She was wearing a rather ugly – albeit tight-fitting – top with too many thin hoops in garish colours running around it. The top, which emphasized her rather impressive embonpoint, was tucked into her habitual baggy but serviceable pink slacks. The slacks' elasticated waist delineated the halfway mark of what appeared to Richard as Debbie's desirable, if rather daunting, body.

'Ye-es,' she said in an assumed jokey voice. 'Come to muck in?'

'Actually...' Richard hesitated. Debbie was already reaching for the bleach. Before she could wield that pungent dampener, he blurted, 'Actually, I wonder if you'd like to come out. With me, I mean.'

Debbie started, dropped the bleach in the Sluice and whirled round. He saw at once that she was laughing, in a grunty, suppressed kind of way.

'Sorry, sorry, sorry,' she said, visibly trying to get a grip on herself. Her eyes were creased up so he could hardly see her pupils at all.

She took a step towards him and put her hand on his arm, a motion that seemed to fall between emotional steadying, although of whom was left open, and a hint of complicity.

'I thought you knew,' she said, and then she drew him towards her with an extension of the steadying, complicit motion, and breathed something in his ear. This process of whispering brought her body rather excitingly right up against Richard's. Her warm breath tickling his ear and the faint scent of lotion that she gave off set a whole range of conjectures going in his mind. What if he overrode her objections and seized her round the half-way mark?

But the action lagged behind the thought. The hot susurrus in his ear ended. Her perfumed breath floated away. She dropped his arm and made a showy little skip back to her end of the Sluice where she seized the bleach bottle from the plughole and held it up like a challenge.

'Ah...' What with the hot breath and Debbie's exciting closeness, he sadly hadn't caught a word of what she had actually been saying. But she waved him away with the bleach bottle, smiling resplendently. As he sloped off, she called after him,

'Please don't tell. The Rat wouldn't understand.'

Yes, OK, he thought. But *what*?

To Richard's profound consternation, this episode was all round the nurses' common room within minutes, and when Lizzie, who had it direct from Debbie without the imaginative embellishments of the common room, told Gloriana, they couldn't at first stop laughing. When they did, however, Gloriana eyed Lizzie, who divined instantly what the girl was thinking and said,

'No way José. I'm not into kindergarteners.'

But Gloriana just smiled.

***

Later that day, the children greeted their tea with cries of distress and chucked the burned rissoles about.

The problem was in the kitchens. One of the two old cooks who struggled in the steam-bath heat of the House kitchens, a Mrs. Pettigrew, always referred as Old Pettigrew, took her venerable Morris Minor to Snells Garage to have her wheels balanced. It was all the rage that year. Snells' man Withers, a dreamy countryman whose mind was going over for the umpteenth time an incident fifty years before in his childhood with Veronica the vicar's daughter, forgot to tighten the nuts that held Old Pettigrew's wheels on. The Morris Minor ended in the ditch and Old Pettigrew in the hospital.

Crisis broke out. The other beldame cook, always referred to as Young Win although she was actually older than Old Pettigrew, was prone to panic attacks. Without the steadying influence of Old Pettigrew, Young Win went to pieces. Even Win's famous jellies with their suspended fruits started coming up all runny.

But what to do? Jane Ratcliffe had no idea.

But Patch had.

After tea, Richard joins the cross and hungry Trojans in the Great Hall. The kids are scooting round in a messy, raucous game. It's a complex house rules version of Chain He. Richard watches this mayhem from his seat at the scratched old grand piano. Kevin and Greg are not taking part in the game tonight. Kevin clambers onto the piano stool beside Richard and begins bashing furiously at the keys. Greg wheels himself up behind Richard. He wears, as he does every day, his pink tie-dyed shirt and his little black waistcoat with its silver stars. Richard knows that someone washes out the shirt every night and dries it over the huge kitchen range, and then presses it early each morning before Greg gets up. But who this angel is, no one except Greg has the foggiest idea.

'I got a group, Richard,' Greg says. 'I got a pop group. An' I wrote a pop song.'

'I know,' Richard says, too enthusiastically. Then, because he feels bad at patronizing the boy, he says,

'Come and play, Greg, come and sit here.' Richard moves across and tugs at Kevin who is too taken up with bashing the keys to say anything and Greg levers his body onto the piano stool on the other side of Kevin.

Helen is out of bed again today. She is sitting on an old horsehair sofa which is up against the wall. She is pulling out the errant stuffing which lies in piles around her. The boys bash away and don't notice Helen coming over with her strange lilting gait until she is right there next to them.

'Fuck off, you cunt,' Kevin says mildly, but Greg puts his hand on Kevin's shoulder and the little boy shuts up.

Meanwhile Helen is trying to squeeze onto the stool next to Richard.

'Be my love,' she says in her childlike voice, 'Richard, be my love.'

Richard looks aghast.

Be my love, for no one else can end this yearning... she sings softly. *Just fill my arms, the way you've filled my dreams.*

'Fuck off,' Kevin says, and then adds helpfully, 'This wanker doesn't know fuckin' Mario Lanza. He only knows fuckin' *Heart & Soul*.'

Helen tries to push onto the stool again, so there's nothing for it but for Richard to budge up and let her in.

Kevin starts playing his own Cumberland version of *Heart & Soul*. Greg joins in, and so does Richard. There they are, four of them crammed on the piano stool, Richard

pounding at the bass end and Kevin and Greg fighting fren-
ziedly at the treble. All the time, Richard feels Helen's soft
body which she is pushing up against his side.

Eventually, after seventeen reprises, Kevin just starts to
bash at the keyboard with his fists. Greg takes him by the
wrists to stop him. The music peters out. Helen slides off the
stool and she jumps up and grasps Richard from behind
around his waist and hugs him. Through his shirt he can
feel her breasts against his back.

Mercifully, Debbie dashes up and grabs Helen by the
hand.

'Come on, you lot. I've found some old cake.' She herds
the three children away from the piano.

A chain of Trojans seven abreast sweeps down the Great
Hall. The children who have not yet been tigged scream and
flee before the wave.

Something nudges Richard's elbow and there, resting on
the stick of his gleaming Armsworth 302, is Patch, his big
face peering up like a great red moon.

'I seen you with Helen just now, mate. Bit drastic that.
Don't be a stupid git now.'

Richard smiles vaguely.

'She needs to be kept busy, mate.'

'Busy with what?'

'Well...' – Patch's fleshy face screws up into a big red
mask – 'well, you know she's an Eyetie...'

Richard shakes his head.

'Yup. Dad was a PoW. 's got a Mr. Whippy van in Bog-
nor. Mum's a corker. Seen her last Speech Day. Bit on the
plump side, Italian like, but – cor!'

'So?'

'Well, Eyeties like to cook, don't they?'

'So?'

'Oh, come on, you stupid git. An' by the way, mate, about the Trojans…'

Richard waits.

'Yup, what're we goin' to do next?'

'Like what?'

'Like what do we Trojans actually do? Like, what does King Priam actually do, rulin' an' that? And what's it like living in Troy with the War an' all that? And how do the Trojans beat the Greeks…?'

'Do they?'

'I dunno. Maybe. An' what happens after the War…'

'Hmmm.'

'You know what, mate, you should write us a play.'

Patch drops this one and leaves it flopping. He starts to back his chair away. The interview is apparently at an end. Richard says quickly,

'Ummm, Patch…'

'Yup?'

'That book… the one in your…'

Patch's currant eyes rest on Richard for a long moment, and then he says,

'You mean me *Marital Guide*?'

'Yes. I mean… what's it for?'

'For? What do you think it's for, toffee nose? Bleedin' sex education, that's what.'

'But why have you got it?'

Patch looks super-scornful.

''cos I'm in charge of it, that's why. I let 'em see it when they're sixteen. Little treat for their birthdays, like. Prepare them for leavin' and life an' all that.'

'But why you? Shouldn't the school, or the House…'

Patch laughs, a short, contemptuous laugh.

'Come off it, mate, are you nuts or what? Who you got in

mind? Ratcliffe the Iron Maiden? Or poor old drunken angry Mr. MacAskill? Givin' sex education? Ha!'

Patch turns his chair and prepares to move off.

'Ummm…'

Patch turns back again. His face performs a sort of smile within his massive cheeks and his eyes become bright and fractionally larger.

'You had any reply yet from Ma Noble yet?'

Richard shook his head.

'Tell you what, mate. You promise to write us a nice play an' you can have a quick dekko at me *Marital Guide*. Just for a bit, mind. I got four kids comin' up to sixteen.'

Patch gives his Armstead 302 a half turn. The saddle bag is open. Richard slides his hand in, whips out the booklet and slips it in his pocket.

Only at that moment does he see that Lizzie and Debbie have wheeled Gloriana in and all three of them are eyeing him with interest.

18

Oh, alright, I'll meet the old bag,' Mick says to Richard.

Patch has been on at him for days.

'It'd be at least one of us out of the Bin,' Patch kept saying. 'At least one of us.'

Actually, Mick's heart isn't in it. What did he want with a mummy? He'd grown up with his mates, Greg and Patch, and old Gloriana – and Helen. He loves them. He doesn't love any mummy.

After all, she could hardly have loved him. This mummy had taken one look at him and turned away. Where had the old bat been all these years when he might have needed her? Every minute of every day for the last fifteen and a half years she could have come to him, she could have loved him. But no, nothing. Just self, self, self.

It was too late for mummy love now. He'd rather go to Binstead than sit with some old biddy drinking tea.

'On one condition, though...'

'What's that, then?'

'We get a telly.'

'Mmmm, not so sure about that...'

'Well, take it or leave it. Do you want to hear a joke?' Mick goes on without waiting for an answer, 'So King Arthur goes away and he puts this chastity belt on Guinevere. She says how do I do a wee, so Arthur makes a hole and he puts a little guillotine on it just in case. When he comes back, he lines up all the knights and says Now get your willies out. And Sir Galahad's has got chopped off, and Sir Percival's is all 'orrible and mashed up, and all the 'ole 'undred of them the same. Except Sir Lancelot whose willy is all nice and shiny and pink, and King Arthur says Sir Lancelot, faithful servant, name your prize, and Sir Lancelot says *Agh-agh-agh*.'

It isn't from mummy-need that Mick says he'll meet the old bag. It's because Patch keeps banging on about it and Mick wants him to stop. It's out of curiosity. It's because it's an outing. And it's because, if they got a telly, he would get to watch England win the World Cup, and that would be sooooooooooooooo worth it.

Richard fingers his Homer. He is in fact supposed to read the entire *Iliad* in Greek and half the *Odyssey* as well before he goes up to university, but he has recently decided not to do that. Greek stuff doesn't seem all that important these days. His old red Homer that was only a month ago practically his life's companion now looks like a fusty school book, which is what it has been all along.

Richard leafs through his *Iliad*. One thing soon becomes clear – there aren't many laughs, other than some snide stuff in Book Ten about how non-U it is to wear a ferret skin cap. The rest of it is along the lines of,

> The Trojans now stormed the ships like flesh-eating lions. Hector raged like a fire on the mountain working destruction in the deep recesses of the woods.

Hmm, hard to stage that one. Perhaps a scene where heroes converse about heroic values. He spots a conversation between Hector and Achilles.

> Friendship between us is impossible and there will be no

truce of any kind till one of us has fallen and glutted the stubborn god of battle with his blood.

Was the tone right? It seemed, well, remorseless. Perhaps a pathetic scene might be better. He remembers Achilles slaughters Hector. Maybe here noble pity would enter in.

Thus Hector's head was tumbled in the dust. Achilles refused to wash the clotted gore from his own body. He addressed Hector's corpse: 'I wish I could summon up the appetite to carve and eat you raw. At any rate, nobody is going to keep the dogs from you.'

Richard tosses the *Iliad* aside. He decides to go and look for Pete and see if he wants to go up to The Dog.

Richard looks in the staff dining room for Pete, but the only person in there is Lizzie, who looks even more fagged out than usual.

'Woss this rubbish?' she says crossly when she sees him and throws down her spoon. Lizzie is broad in her compassion but she likes her hot food. Richard can only agree with her. Everybody today has been complaining about Young Win's calamitous spotted dick.

Richard mentions Patch's thought about Helen, and Lizzie leaps up from the table.

'C'mon, Richard, I can't stand this crap scoff any longer.'

Miss Ratcliffe addressed herself to the large black telephone on her desk.

'Binstead 301,' she said, and after a minute she heard Mr. Salter's secretary answering. She was put through with satisfactory promptness.

'Yes, love. Problem?'

'Perhaps, Mr. Salter. How are you, by the way? Yes, I do need your advice, or even your help.'

'Yes, dear, Salter is willing. Fire away.'

'Well, you may remember the girl Helen, Helen Scandizzi...'

'Umm. Oh yes, the frisky Eyetie. Pretty little thing. She's the one you asked me about. Still dosing her up like I said, are you?'

Since Mr. Salter's visit, Jane Ratcliffe's mind had been pondering the problem of Helen. On this topic, her thoughts about Helen and Helen's future had gone off on quite another track from those of Patch and Richard and Lizzie. The child's grotesquely swelling bosom and curving fecund hips, the almost obscene way she walked, swaying from side to side in clear invitation, that little girl's voice she put on, the glances she cast at anything in trousers... it was all just a come-on to, well, to filthy venery.

If the girl was allowed to carry on like this, she'd be in pup in a month or two and joining the other immoral creatures at that new council home for fallen women. 'Unmarried mothers' they called them – ha. Misnomers all. 'Unmarried' was a virtue, a spotless virgin state. And 'motherhood' was a privilege and the purpose of the holy state of matrimony. 'Unmarried mothers' – it was, it was... it was a... 'contradiction in terms' seemed too weak a... just sluts, really...

'Ye-es, Miss Ratcliffe, Jane if I may? Are you still there?'

'Oh, yes, Mr. Salter, woolgathering, I'm so sorry...'

'Terence, please, Jane. Do call me Terence. Or Terry, if you like...'

'Oh, yes, well, Terence... it's all rather delicate, you see...'

'Mmm, yes, what's up?'

Jane began to sketch a portrait of Helen as a girl subject to urges which could no longer be contained by the frail measures available at Park House. The more robust disciplines of an adult institution seemed essential, she concluded.

'Oh, righty ho,' Terry Salter said reassuringly. 'Sex rears its ugly head. Don't worry, love, we know exactly how to deal with that at Binstead.'

'Errr... may I ask how?'

'Best not, dearie. Don't ask, don't tell, I always say.'

'I mean, you won't... tamper with her, as it were...?''

There was what sounded like a guffaw from Mr. Salter's end.

'Stone the crows, Janey my dear, you've got an imagination and no mistake.'

Jane knew this to be untrue but she let it pass. She said,

'You see, Mr. Salter... Terence... I'm afraid of something blowing up, not to mince words too finely. I was wondering, might there be a possibility of a more immediate transfer, even before the end of term?'

'So you want to get shot of the little flirt a.s.a.p.?'

'Not to put too fine a point on it.'

'Okey dokey. I'll do my best. I'll need to juggle things around this end.'

'Well, thank you so much... Terence.'

'Not at all, Jane. It's between professionals. I'll bell you if I can find a slot for the little madam.'

When Richard and Lizzie knocked at her door, Jane Ratcliffe had just hung up the phone. And now here were this wretched pair saying that Helen could take over the cooking! Really!

Jane thought quickly. She wasn't about to let on that Helen was to be transferred early. Better 'play along' as it were.

'Yes,' she said, 'yes, that is a good idea. I will explain to Young Win. Both of those women should have retired years ago anyway. In fact, I will go to see her right away.'

Jane felt that a little disingenuousness could be excused in so delicate a matter.

'Oh, and…'

'Yes? What is it?'

Richard said hesitantly that a television might perhaps be a great help to the children's education, so many school's programmes on these days, so much that can be learned about the world…

Jane pondered a moment. She was in fact a little concerned about Mr. MacAskill's rather erratic behaviour and perhaps some televisual education might not be such a bad idea. And so, to Richard's surprise, she agreed.

'But only rented,' she said quickly. 'Park House is not made of money.'

A massive thumping was coming from the kitchen.

Thwack!

The heavy meat cleaver came down on the prone chicken and cleft it along its entire back bone.

Crack!

The breastbone split from behind, and Helen's hands flattened the bird.

She flipped the carcass over, then grasped the heavy chopping knife and severed the joints of the wings and legs, taking care not to detach them. These, too, she flattened, pressing with her palms on the cool meat.

Then she turned the carcass breast down again and

began to pound with the big meat pounder. The blows rained on the bird. At last, satisfied, she patted the cool surface of the meat again. It was a loving touch.

Now she took a handful of black peppercorns. Her mother had told her, 'In our family we have small hands – *piccole manine* – and if we need a tablespoon of a dry ingredient, we may use our small hands instead.'

She lightly crunched the peppercorns in her hand and sniffed them. She thought she could smell the hot shore from which they came. She turned away and sneezed into her apron.

She tossed the peppercorns onto a clean white napkin and folded it, then reached for the heavy hammer she had borrowed from Pete. She began to smash down rhythmically as her mother had showed her, chanting her song: *a-mo-re, a-mo-re, a-mo-re!*

When the peppercorns were cracked, she set them aside. She got out the deep brown dish she had decided to use and she scooped up the flattened chicken in both hands and laid it in the deep dish. Then she took the larger part of the cracked peppercorns and began to rub them over the cool glistening blue-pink flesh of the chicken. She rubbed until the surface of the flesh was black. She halved four lemons and squeezed them out on the glass lemon squeezer and poured the juice over the surface of the chicken. Then she took the tin of extra virgin olive oil that Flick had bought for her in town, and she tipped in just the right amount, the amount her mother had showed her.

She put the deep brown dish on the side counter. It was beautiful. She set about her other kitchen tasks, and she prepared the vegetables. Every fifteen minutes she returned to the dish to turn the chicken and to baste it in the oil and lemon juice.

Lunch was at one. She knew that *pollo alla diavola alla Romana* must be served up the minute it is ready, so at exactly a quarter past twelve she began to heat the big cast iron skillet. On the dot of half past, she sprinkled the chicken with a pinch of the sea salt Flick had got her. Then she picked up the bird in her palms and laid it, flesh side down, in the pan.

She watched it cook until she could see the flesh browning, then she basted it with the oil and lemon and turned it over. She watched and turned the bird again, and then again. She took a fork and pushed it against the thigh. It felt very tender. It was ready. She lifted it and laid it on a porcelain dish she had found at the back of the cupboard and which she had warmed in the Number Five Oven of the vast range.

She took the cracked pepper she had reserved and sprinkled it on. It was time to serve her lover.

19

Sunshine is my drug. Wheel me out, Lizzie. Wheel me out, Debbie.

It has been a perfect summer's day, a day of perfect balance. The faintest breeze wafts from the west. Silver grey clouds drift high in the azure sky.

So after tea, Lizzie and Debbie push me out. They make a token fuss, of course, but Pete and Mick have fitted me new, bigger wheels with hard rubber tyres and my girls roll me as smoothly as silk across the grass which is all tufty and brilliant green. We pass by the outsized hydrangeas whose pompons are swollen to fantastic size, and then past the royal scarlet and imperial purple of the bending fuchsia. They pop me under the great lime tree which is loud with bees.

The afternoon is warm and like an embrace. Clouds of small off-white butterflies dance here and there in the golden light, feeding on everything they find delicious. Unhurried swallows cruise the air.

I'm talking to a little off-white butterfly here. She has perched on my chest, as though for a chat. Hallo. Do you think I am a big flower? Do you think I'm St Francis?

And suddenly here is Richard running across the lawn, book in hand and crying,

Out on the lawn I lie in bed!

What, Richard? You look a little odd, wearing that old Aertex short-sleeved shirt that's a bit too small for you. Your arms look like sticks. And your floppy brown hair is getting too long, it's flying out. And – oh, no – you've put on

151

KHAKI SHORTS.

Seriously, Richard, do you want a girl friend or not? I'm not going in to bat for you with my girls if you go on like this. Because shapely though you may think your thighs to be, *Girls Don't Go out With Boys Who Wear Khaki Shorts!* Not never nohow. Full stop.

But Richard apparently doesn't know or doesn't care. He settles on my bed and rubs his tummy. He says he has had an excellent lunch. Then he starts declaiming from his book:

> *Out on the lawn I lie in bed*
> *Vega conspicuous overhead*
> *In the windless nights of June.*
> *Lucky, this point in time and space*
> *Is chosen as my working-place.*

Which is nice. But I really have to look askance at those shorts. He notices my look and gives them a swift tug, but that makes them no more proper. And now here is Lizzie coming back with my drink. She is springing across the turf like a young dryad. Richard leaps up and enthusiastically but probably unwisely declaims:

> *Ah! The sexy airs of summer*
> *The bathing hours and the bare arms*

To which Lizzie, who is actually wearing her green jumper and her old jeans, elegantly replies,

'Oh, come off it, Richard. And what the heck are you wearing?'

At last, they go off, not exactly arm in arm. In fact there is a measurable distance between them that is not just feet and inches, but they look OK, they look not like probables but at least like possibles. And as I learn from the late-night sporting news on the transistor radio Pete gave me, sometimes, quite often, the Possibles actually beat the Probables.

But doff the shorts, Richard.

And so I'm left to think about the day. The momentous day. About King Patch's notion.

Richard was taking us for Art. On the blackboard he had written the Trojans' motto in Greek characters, with some half-moons that he called rough and smooth breathings, which sounded seductive in a way. *Whom the gods love, dies young.*

Hon hoi theoi philousin, neos apothneiskei

Of course, Richard only appeared to be taking us for art. Really, as usual, it was Patch who had decided it, Patch who was in charge, and Richard just a sort of helper really. Patch wanted big splashy colourful placards that his four Trojan elders could sport on their electric chariots. And he wanted an extra big kingly sort of one for himself, to fit on his massive shiny Armsworth 302.

Pete and Mick had run up some blanks from three-ply offcuts they had down in the old stables, leftovers from their tropical bird cage. Today was the day for us to do the lettering. All the Trojans who could hold a brush were bent over their desks copying from the blackboard, first in pencil, then inking in the motto with bold black calligraphic strokes. Patch was cruising round from desk to desk, encouraging and spotting errors. The four elders looked on keenly, like pondering savants.

'Nah, smooth breathing, Kevin,' Patch said. 'Other way round.'

For once, Kevin said nothing. He rubbed out his pencil mark and did the half-moon on *apothneiskei* the other way round.

As he went around, Patch's eye darted from time to time to the Chichester map with its great swathes of pink. The pin that marks the solo mariner's progress is moving perceptibly across the Indian Ocean now, past pink Mauritius, between pink Seychelles and pink Maldives, heading for the pink isosceles of India and its pink pendant tear, Ceylon. From pink sunrise to pink sunset, Chichester is pressing on. Patch nodded in satisfaction.

One by one the Trojans finished the placards. *There,* Mick said. *I've done it,* lisped Helen in her little girl's voice. *Fuckin' finished me off,* said Kevin. *Done,* said Greg economically.

'Now colouring,' Richard said. 'What colours, Patch?'

'Red for me, mate. Let the others choose their own.'

The four elders chose yellow, green, purple and blue. Helen, who is a dab hand with colours, set to work.

While she was at her task, Richard asked the question that had evidently been puzzling him.

'But why Trojans, Patch? Why not Greeks? I mean, after all, the Greeks won.'

'Greeks? *Greeks*? You mean like that Achilles 'ittin' on that poor slave girl, an' then Agamemnon nickin' 'er off 'im an' 'ittin on 'er an' all, like she was... a thing? An' that Achilles hidin' amongst women and then up to I don' know what-all wiv 'is boyfriend? An' that Menelaus, couldn't even see to 'is own wife? You mean *those* Greeks, do you?'

But there was more to it than that, because then Patch added,

'Nah, they went down, din' they, the Trojans I mean.'

He meant they went down battling, all values intact, and so are admirable.

'By the way, mate…'

'Erm… yes… the play, you mean. Yes, coming on, coming on.'

Patch screwed up his piggy eyes and gave Richard a straight look. Richard looked a little sheepish.

And then like the king he is, Patch thought of me. He wagged his head at Richard.

'Now,' he began, 'about Gloriana…'

Richard came over and sat by my side and held my hand, which was nice. Patch said,

'You know what, mate, you know what Gloriana should do? After college an' that?'

'Ummm… well, she…'

'She should write poetry and stuff.'

Patch-like, Patch tossed this out and left it flopping without explanation for Richard to work out. It was like one of those oracles that Richard's read to us about, something some crazy woman comes out with and you can make of it what you like.

But after a bit Patch deigned to add,

'Like, wossname, Homer. They all got their drawbacks, don' they?'

Well! How did Patch know this? Because this is exactly what Monty says. Homer, and yes, Milton, and… Richard had just read me Monty's praise of blind and mad poets, of which there are apparently shedloads. Poets, it seems, were all blind, bonkers, cracked, barking or something. In the poetry line, it seems a drawback may be an advantage. So is there hope for me?

Richard was looking at me to see how I was taking this but I just smiled a not quite straightforward smile that navigated between seraphic and impenetrable. I knew Richard couldn't decrypt this smile, but then could I?

But it was, well, **something**. It had the appearance of an idea.

Ah Patch. Our Trojan leader. Our hero king. A poet. Who, I? Who, me?

But before we could study the question in depth, Helen gave a wobbly little cry and said she'd finished painting in the devices. Richard patted my hand and got up to start fixing them onto the electric chariots. This he did with twists of wire, attaching the boards to the back of the seats.

The Trojan elders looked a spiffy gang as they moved up to the House at the end of the school day. Their chariots whined in high-pitched unison. The warriors accompanied them and the whole cohort started to chant their ditty. *Hon hoi theoi…* Seeing them like this, the mottoes blazing on the backs of their chariots, the group packed close together, king and elders and warriors and nobles and heralds and all of them together, I could see what an enterprise it is. They're a band, a doughty band, distinct in all the world.

And best of all, as we moved into the Great Hall, with the Trojans shouting out their chorus *NEOS APOTH-NEISKEI!* there was the Rat carting an armful of bedpans through from the Sluice. Her mouth dropped open. I'm sure it was terror I spotted in her face.

And so, just now, here in the stippled shade of the lime, through its alternations of shadow and radiant light, I made up my mind. I discussed it with that little off-white butterfly. She was looking at me when I said Hallo and she spread her wings so daintily, just like a girl showing off her best new outfit.

It was at that moment, looking at that beautiful creature, that I knew I am going to be a poet.

I mean, it's pretty obvious, isn't it? As I said, I can't be a waitress or anything, can I?

I'm going to be a POET. Because I want my poetic soul to sing. I want to show the world my heroine heart.

20

Combing Homer again, Richard had still found nothing suitable for a school play. He had been to the Public Library and looked into *The Trojan War Did Not Happen*. He had even leafed through a synopsis of the plot of Berlioz's *Les Troiens*, which turned out not to actually have a plot to speak of. None of this had produced any material suitable for a play for the limited theatrical talent available.

So he had begun to ad lib a text in which a nasty Menelaus beats his pretty wife Helen who runs off to Troy for a second marriage with the handsome Paris (Act One). The former husband comes round with his big brother Agamemnon to beat up the Trojans. Paris' dad, Priam, defends a woman's right to get out of an abusive relationship, and Priam's ten burly sons chip in to protect their stunning new sister-in-law even if she is a divorcee (Act Two). King Priam then beats off the crafty Greeks (the Trojans never bought that wooden horse trick). When the war is over Priam introduces full employment, universal tertiary education, a national health service and pensions for all at fifty. At the close of Act Three, Priam is seen relaxing with his innumerable grandchildren who have been born in the baby boom after the end of the War.

But was that The End? Or should there be another Act? Ending the play with that comfortable 'family Troy' note of Act Three, Richard felt it somehow sagged. All that Beveridge and Butler and Bevan stuff was a bit old hat now. He felt the play should end more forward-looking. But how?

Priam's Act Three reforms seemed pretty much the end of things, everyone taken care of from the cradle to the grave. What else could happen in the world?

He decided to give the play a more contemporary feel. He toyed first with the idea that King Priam might renounce war and disband the Trojan military, or at least give up their heavy weapons, the new iron ones. However, that didn't seem very practical, given the continuing Greek threat to Trojan civilization.

Perhaps Priam might bring in advisers and push the economic reforms a bit further, another round of public investment, say, or collectivization of olive groves and presses, state control of fuel woodlots and so on and so forth. But that looked iffy – could you really get a Trojan consensus on a programme like that? And Richard's Priam was a consensus man if he was anything.

Finally, he decided on a dreamier, more Sixties ending. He was just putting pen to paper when Pete came hammering on the door.

'Fancy a pint, mate?'

'Oh, shit, look.'

Pete raised his honest face which was creasing into an unaccustomed frown and pointed with his chin.

Richard was treating on the strength of a £10 postal order from Bunter Hall. The reference had escaped Pete. However, as Richard was buying, Pete had repressed the scornful toff-deriding words that sprang to his democratic mind.

Richard looked where Pete was gesturing, across the stained bare boards of the Public Bar, up the step, through the arch and into the Lounge Bar where, seated uncertainly on a high stool, half-slumped across the zinc, looking generally more than half seas over, could be discerned a familiar dishevelled figure in a sagging tweed coat, tie awry, collar gone to the dogs, holding up his glass and pointing a finger into it.

'Crikey,' Richard said.

'Christ Almighty,' Pete agreed.

'Does he want a drink?'

'Nah, think he's offering.'

'What do we do?'

'There's one thing God cannot find it in his heart to forgive...'

Pete had early on taught Richard the Basics of Pub Mateship and this was about Number Three.

... when a man offers you a drink and you do not take it.

This was really irritating. They were already finishing off their fourth pint and Richard was enjoying a warm glow from having at last treated Pete and found that the treater actually does get a faint measure of respect. At least Pete had handled the discussion of the debacle with Debbie in the Sluice with slightly less larkish humour than he usually brought to this kind of post-review. And Pete had then provided a good breakdown of his progress with Angela Cudmore's bra strap – this section of the conversation had given Richard a pleasurable little kick as the progress was so very limited according to Pete's ingeniously detailed account which had focused on both the mechanical and the psycho-sexual aspects of the case. Then they'd gone over the Lizzie question, where Pete had rather scoffed at Richard's sentimentality and pushed for a more results-based approach. That was where they'd got to and it had all been most enjoyable. The evening was balmy and they had been looking forward to rounding off their talk during a pleasant walk back to Park House. Now factoring in the mournful problems of the lone and signalling figure at the bar looked like putting the lid on their innocent pleasure.

The Laws of Pub Mateship prevailed, of course, and they presented themselves like lambs. Mr. MacAskill greeted them a little groggily. His mahogany-coloured face had taken on a slanting, thwarted look, and there were blotches on the mahogany.

He at once ordered them each a pint and a whisky.

'Never a wham without a dram... and vice versa, come to that.'

The drinks came, set down by the publican himself, who gave Mr. MacAskill a not very favourable look.

'Ah, yes, lads,' Mr. MacAskill began, articulating carefully, 'yes... life lies before you... nothing defines you yet... time of change... on the cusp... peace... prosperity... travel... birth control... free love...'

Right away Pete had said they'd just have the one and he put away the pint and the dram in an incredibly short space of time and started making grunting sounds and rolling his eyes at Richard, meaning Let's go. But the less practiced Richard was still on his pint when Mr. MacAskill noticed Pete's empty glasses and swiftly ordered a fresh round.

The new pints and drams rapidly appeared, placed very carefully on the zinc bartop by the publican whose eyes swivelled meaningfully from Pete and Richard to Mr. MacAskill and back again.

Mr. MacAskill was now saying thickly,

'Of course, her face behind the specs... ha ha... intriguing embittered look, don't you think?... but then so shamelessly... repulsively really... repulsively unhappy. Struggling... such a negligible life...'

Richard, still not fully used to drink, had by now drunk the four pints with Pete and two whiskies and two more pints at Mr. MacAskill's expense... and now there was Mr.

MacAskill ordering a third round of whams and drams and the publican's eyes were swivelling even more meaningfully and he was setting the fresh glasses down even more carefully on the bar counter.

An obscuring fog began to descend on Richard when he was halfway through this latest pint and whisky, and he temporarily lost several faculties, including counting and seeing straight, a loss not much compensated by the new faculties he felt he had acquired, such as the knack of smoking about ten of Mr. MacAskill's full-strength Navy Cut gaspers in quick succession without coughing once.

He couldn't even put his finger exactly on the subject of Mr. MacAskill's conversation now. Before, he had the impression it had been Miss Ratcliffe, but now Mr. MacAskill had switched topic and he was saying dramatically,

'… changed… utterly changed… utterly utterly changed… Drambuie, After Eight Mints, Viyella blankets, king-sized cigarettes, fish fingers, meals out, prawn cocktail, chicken Maryland, Indian takeaways, lager, Nescafé, pasta, pizza, Chinese takeaways, sliced bread, alphabetti spaghetti…'

Richard suddenly had the impression that he might actually be smoking two cigarettes at the same time. At least, if he'd got his figures right, there were four of Mr. Mac-Askill's Navy Cut alight in the crammed ashtray between the three of them, so something plainly didn't add up.

'… aubergines, courgettes, broccoli, dolly birds, miniskirts, DIY, sunshine, jeans, Beatles, Mary Quant, Rolling Stones, The Pill, the Kinks, sex at Butlins…'

Richard noticed Pete was grasping the back of his quite short-cut hair in his fist and grunting at regular intervals, which Richard guessed was Pete's way of semaphoring Let's Go. But Mr. MacAskill never paused to leave that little leeway needed for the boys' adieux. Anyway even Pete – actually especially Pete who was after all Richard's mentor in this – Pete would acknowledge another iron law of pub mateship, you drink a pint a bloke has bought you and you smoke his smokes and then *you bloody well listen to his conversation*. Which was in Mr. MacAskill's case becoming more and more erratic.

'Yes, changed... unrecognizable... coming back... utterly, utterly changed... trendy, groovy, fab, swinging, smashing, with-it, kinky, whacky, square, I dig you, chat up birds, in-crowd, doing the ton, this gear cost a bundle... Avengers, Z-Cars, Ready Steady Go, Newcomers, Rin Tin Tin, Doctor Who, Steptoe and Son... purple hearts, Niersteiner Domtal...'

This virtuoso recital had by now attracted a good deal of attention in the Lounge Bar, most of it unfavourable, although a few louche types who crowded through from the Public Bar had clustered round Mr. MacAskill and were egging him on and even trying to buy him further drinks.

But by now the landlord's eyes were oscillating wildly and he was jerking his head towards the door.

The two boys grasped Mr. MacAskill as best they could, eased him off his stool and headed to the exit.

'... hanging, divorce, homosexuality, gambling, abortion, suicide, immigration, censorship, Sunday Observance... free love...'

21

I am in the Great Hall when Richard mooches in next afternoon. Oh boy, does he look in poor shape! Of course, he's desperately hung over from his jolly with Mr. MacAskill. And I bet he's still nursing dark thoughts about darling Debbie and the thing in the Sluice. I mean, what a double humiliation – Debbie's repulse **and** the worse shame of it being all round everywhere in no time. But then that's the way things go for silly boys. I mean, Debbie indeed. What was he thinking of?

As Richard slopes through the Hall, Mick helpfully calls out,

'Got it in yet, Richard?'

And Patch pipes up,

'Nah, toffs only like it up the arse.'

Richard puts on an offended look. You can see he's still struggling with Patch's way of working. One minute, Patch is all confiding 'Come on, mate, let's solve this or that or the other' and the next minute he's all coarse and abusive, like that thing he just said. But then Richard doesn't understand politics yet. He doesn't understand that like any politician, Patch needs his tough public persona.

At this point, Lizzie runs in and past Richard and calls back over her shoulder. 'That must 'ave been a good old splurge with Mr. MacAskill last night.'

To which young Richard feebly replies,

'Errr... Lizzie, I hope... I mean...'

She stops then and faces him and laughs her deep cackly dirty-sounding laugh, wretched girl.

'The less said the better, Rich. Anyhow, I managed to get it all cleared up.'

With that, she runs on, leaving Richard looking even more feeble and pained, and I'm quite sure Lizzie just made that up about the mess. Still, it's a good learning curve for him. When he leaves this place, he'll have a skin as thick as an armadillo's.

Richard goes wearily over to the piano and plonks himself down.

And then – in strolls Debbie, cool as a cat. She glances at him and then comes to me.

Richard's whole body manages to take on a bitter, affronted look. It's quite a feat, but he achieves it. Debbie capably ignores this, as she ignores everything that looks like it might spoil her fun or upset her equanimity. Instead she leans over me and whispers,

'Darling, I want to say I'm sorry to Richard but I'm terrified he might ask me out again.'

But of course she should say sorry.

The Trojans all now stream in from their tea and there's the usual hubbub and milling round until Patch declares a game of Blind Man's Buff. They crowd around him for the Dip which is as complicated as usual. Patch starts chanting,

> Paddy on the railway
> Picking up stones
> Along came an engine
> And broke Paddy's bones
> Oh, said Paddy
> That's not fair
> Pooh, said the engine driver
> I don't CARE.

The children all shout the last word, and Kevin is counted out.

'Fuck you, Patch, you motherfucker,' he comments mildly.

Richard is watching all this, so he doesn't notice Debbie until she is right beside him.

'Sorreee, Richard. Sorry, sorry, sorry.' Debbie puts her hand on his arm in a placatory confiding sort of way. 'It just somehow slipped out. I am soooooooooo sorry.' She is close up to him murmuring, and then she gives him a quick peck on the cheek. He looks like he has instantly forgiven her for everything. She's really got him purring, the little minx.

Debbie and Richard suddenly become aware that Patch has suspended the Dip so that everyone can watch this touching little tableau of reconciliation. With the peck on the cheek a fair amount of jeering starts up from the older Trojans who are deeply suspicious of anything resembling love relations or sexy attachments between our carers.

When the jeers have died down and Patch has started counting out again, Debbie says, as though suddenly thinking of something,

'Why don't you come up to our room tonight, maybe? And bring Pete. We can listen to Flick's fab new record and…' The rest of the sentence is obscured by the hubbub of the counting out.

> Eeenie, meenie, macca, racca
> Ie, rie, dumma racca
> Ticca racca, lollipop
> Rum, pum, PUSH!

***

Richard. Focus. I know you have a 'date' tonight, a 'double date' even, and I can see you're really worked up about it. But keep your peepers on the Main Idea – keep it constantly before your mind: *Gloriana goes to university and then becomes a Poet.* Although how exactly I'm going to get into university I don't think you've quite worked out yet. And as to what the Rat and Sallow Salter think about all that, well, that's quite another question.

Not to mention the others. Patch has bullied Mick into seeking his salvation in Araminta's bosom, but even that's looking pretty iffy now that Minty has written to propose July 30th, 1966. This may seem just a day like any other but in Mick's eyes it is the Day of Extraordinary Yearning, the day on which he (virtually alone amongst the population of this island) actually believes that ENGLAND ARE GOING TO WIN THE WORLD CUP. Anyway, on these grounds Mick is now refusing to go up to see Minty. Everyone else is trying to reassure him by saying we're sure to get knocked out in the game that's coming up against the Argies. This discussion does not have a soothing effect on Mick. A whole palaver ensues and nothing is getting organized.

And then there's Greg, our sweet dreamer, always so smart in his trendy gear which miraculously appears clean and folded at his bedside every morning thanks to some unannounced angel specialized in overnight washing and pressing. What else the angel can do for him in the way of escape from the Doom of the Bin is none too clear. He keeps dashing and scratching away in his rough old notebook but whether a Greg pop song will make his fortune I'm not so sure.

And Helen? At least she's out of bed these days and she's doing so well in the kitchen. Can she make a career from that? Maybe, but I caught the Rat looking sourly at her yesterday, and I'm sure that cow is up to something.

Patch, of course, has organized his own mythic eternity. But, Richard, you see our problem – we need facts on the ground, we need action – and Salter is rattling the Bin.

By the way, please don't waste too much time on Debbie – she's my super girl, but she's DEFINITELY not for you.

Anyway, in our lesson today you just read out that bit from Monty about poetry, that *Poetry awakens a full, new and intimate sense of things...* which I suppose is OK, and also *Style is the sense of oneself,* which sounds meaningful but perhaps isn't or vice versa, but you read it in a distracted voice and then without explaining these thoughts at all, you rushed off to change for your Big Date.

So all I can say is – enjoy yourself as best you can – and watch out for Flick, she's Debbie's bestest friend but she's a bit too clever by half and a sardonic puss.

And in the meantime – well, I think I will make up a poem.

'Cor,' Pete had said. 'Cor.'

They went the very long way round to the girls' room to avoid the Argus-eyed Trojan mob in the Great Hall and any cruising scouts of Patch's. The children's nasty little imaginations could spoil anything before it even started.

Pete was wearing a black PVC jacket and a pair of flared white trousers Richard hadn't seen before. Richard was in his tweed sports coat and tie. He didn't really have anything else.

Flick opened the door.

'Oh, you're on time,' she said, as though that were a

surprise. 'Debbie's just gone to boil the kettle. You'd better come in.'

Richard had never seen Flick in a dress before. It was tiny, just covering her middle parts, not even covering much of her back. Gold and pink bands ran across it and then, in the short section below the waist, the bands executed a complicated turn and started to go up and down. Just above her disappointingly flat chest, the dress stopped arrestingly, and two thin gold straps ran up over her bony white shoulders to hold the skimpy thing on.

'That's a nice frock,' Richard said gallantly.

'*Bazaar*,' she said, and when she saw Richard's puzzled face, she said, 'the boutique, you know. In the King's Road.'

'Yes, yes,' Richard lied.

It was a nice dress, Richard had meant it. It ended about a third of the way down her thigh, and her thin legs then continued on down to a pair of dazzling golden slip-on shoes. She had brushed her short black hair carefully across her brow to a sort of fringe that ran along above her right ear. The eye stuff she had on made her eyes huge and startling.

She really looked something but sadly skinny Flick, all angles and bones, just wasn't the boys' type at all. It seemed to be a mutual thing as when Pete lunged a polite kiss at her she ducked, leaving Pete kissing thin air and looking more than idiotic in Richard's view.

So when Debbie came in with the kettle, neither of them tried kissing her, they just said Hallo politely.

Debbie's outfit was even better. She had on a tiny yellow plastic mini-skirt held up by a broad black PVC belt and a black polo neck jumper. Her blonde hair flowed loose and luxurious down her shoulders almost to her waist. She had on those short white boots that were all the rage.

'You look like lovely dolly birds,' Pete said, trying to re-cover a bit of the initiative. Debbie smiled at this, but Flick scowled. Even Pete, Richard thought, even Pete, was having trouble settling in. Drink would help. Would there be drinks? But Debbie quashed that one.

'Coffee?' she said brightly. 'It's Maxwell House. Milk and sugar?'

Flick knelt down and cleared some stuff away from be-tween the two unpromisingly narrow beds. Amongst the clobber was a thick set of forms *Application for Training as a State Registered Nurse*. That looked to Richard like some-thing they could talk about but when he reached out to have a look, Flick whipped the papers away and shoved them into the bedside cupboard.

'Paws off, Pompey,' she said.

They settled down on cushions between the beds. Debbie brought over four mugs. There was a silence, during which they pretended to sip their scalding coffee.

'So what's the record, girls?' Pete asked.

Flick's record player was on the floor beside her. It was a little Dansette, the top in beige Bakelite and the case in a maroon crocodile-effect leatherette.

'Joan Baez,' Flick said. 'She's so lovely.'

Flick carefully took the sleeve out of the cover and then eased the big twelve-inch disc out of the sleeve, keeping the rim against her thumb and stretching with her forefinger to reach the middle. Then she carefully transferred the record to two hands and put it on the turntable, slotting it straight on to the pin so that there were no unsightly scrapings. She juggled the control and the disc started to revolve smoothly. She lifted the arm across and lowered the stylus with abso-lute precision onto the little neutral zone that ran around the rim. The record crackled a bit and then the music started.

Richard recognized *All My Trials*. He liked it. The boys sat uncertain whether to listen or to chat politely over it. Pete was anyway looking a bit sorry for himself because he'd spotted where Flick was settling down and then had sat on the other side so as to be next to Debbie but then Flick had wriggled over onto the cushion next to him because that was where the record player was. Richard had then sat on Flick's old cushion and Debbie had settled down comfortably next to him.

Richard could see Flick easily because she was sitting opposite him. She had a rapt expression on her face as Joan sang, so clearly she didn't want to be chatted to. Out of the corner of his eye he looked towards Debbie who, it turned out, was now sipping her coffee and looking at him over the top of her mug. She wasn't exactly smiling but she wasn't not smiling, it was a sort of benign kindly look. He wondered if he should try and put his arm around her but decided it might be better to wait a bit, until she got warmed up.

He looked around. The walls of the girls' room were covered with posters. There was a big one which was like a picture from a comic. A young man of about Richard's age, dressed in overalls, was putting petrol into a flashy red American sports car with huge tail fins. The car was driven by a perky looking blonde girl who was frowning at the boy. It was clearly set in America because, quite apart from the car and the idea of a girl driving like that, the petrol pump had a notice **GAS Ten Cents a Gallon**. There was a big balloon coming out of the boy's mouth and he was saying 'Jeez, lay off Peg. I'm lucky to *have* a job this summer.'

On the wall opposite was another poster showing a curvy sultry looking girl reclining half on and half off a bed. A pink silk sarong was vaguely draped over one of her pleasantly rounded thighs. Apart from that and a pink Pharaonic headdress, the girl was completely naked. Behind her on a shelf stood a range of pots of various sizes decorated with a motley of arabesques in gaudy colours.

Richard glanced at Debbie again to see if she was still paying attention to him, but she wasn't. She was smiling at Flick and silently mouthing the words to the song – by now Joan had moved on to *Fare Thee Well*. Richard knew this one too, so he also started mouthing the words until Flick noticed and gave him a severe look.

He glanced back towards Debbie. Behind her, on the bed, he noticed a weird soft toy, just a huge face really, no body, and a sort of Beatles fringe of hair. Debbie now saw him looking, and she smiled. She leaned over and mouthed,

'That's my Gonk. Flick made him for me. I love him to bits.'

All this was really strange to Richard and it made him nervous. Anyway, how did you move from sitting on cushions with all your clothes on listening to some demure old folk songs your mother wouldn't object to and with the girl a yard away, how did you move from that to, for example, lying on the bed together with all your clothes off, kissing and so on and so forth? This remained a mystery. Pete wasn't helping much either. He was actually looking a bit bored.

Suddenly Richard found that Debbie had moved forward and was kneeling up close to him. She moved her big friendly face toward him and started whispering in his ear. Was this it, he wondered. Was Debbie making her move?

Her soft breath went on pouring into his ear for a bit. Then she stopped and drew away and looked at him inquiringly. She looked very lovely to him, kindly and not too earnest, like she wanted to laugh if she got the chance.

This would have been very good, if only he'd been able to make out what she was saying. Her eyes were on him expectantly and he did a little shake of his head and a quiz-zical look. She put two fingers to her lips and did a sharp inhaling impression. He nodded and gestured that he hadn't any cigs. *And why the hell hadn't he got any cigs? An-other chance missed.*

But Debbie wasn't even paying any attention to him. She was opening a box that was on the floor beside her and get-ting out some things, half a packet of Old Holborn tobacco, and a blue packet of cigarette papers, and then what looked like a flat shoehorn or a massive tongue depressor except that it was made of some gooey-looking black or dark brown stuff. She held all this out to him, but he waved his palms at her to say *No* and gestured at her to do it, whatever it was.

At this point, Richard became aware that Pete was watching intently with a sort of hackles-raised look about him. Debbie now held the things out to Pete but he shook his head furiously.

At that moment *Fare Thee Well* ended and in the silence between tracks Flick said with a fair amount of scorn packed into her voice,

'Debbie, they don't know how to do it. You do it yourself. Or put it away.'

Whilst her would-be lover Pete is engaged with Debbie and Flick, Angela Cudmore helps Greg to bed. She talks to him of Bungay, their common home, because she knows he likes this (and so does she).

And tonight, in a way, they are celebrating. Because Greg really seriously *has* actually written a pop song. For weeks he has kept on scribbling the runes with his pencil in his old rough notebook, and Angela Cudmore has sat with him for many sessions whilst he explained that the scratches and marks weren't just squiggles but his song and at last she was able to write out the words and the music.

And tonight, after tea, she showed him the final version which she has typed up with laborious stabs of her stubby country girl's fingers on the old Remington Crown Imperial in the staff room. There are still some crossings out, which she has done with xxxxxxx. She has drawn staves with her old school ruler and has put in the notes under Greg's supervision.

'You'll send it off then?' Greg asks and Angela nods. Her golden mane clipped up on top of her head above her ruddy country face makes her look like a turnip.

Angela puts Greg to bed. She hangs up his little black waistcoat with its silver spangles. Then she folds up his pink tie-dyed shirt and slips it under her jumper. She is going to wash it out as she does every night, but she prefers to keep that a Bungay secret between her and Greg.

Meanwhile, Greg dozes off. He loves the dim light and the shadows and the colours and pictures which crowd in succession under his eyelids as soon as he closes them. As he goes off to sleep, which happens very quickly, he can still hear in his mind the harmonies of *Sunny Afternoon* by his favourite Kinks that he has been listening to on Gloriana's transistor.

Very soon he dreams:

I play the perfect chord. The music fills the room. Everybody is amazed. They all ask **Who is that?** *And a voice says,* **That's Greg.**

We go outside into the golden sun. Two girls are walking on the short grass. They are called Mandy and Ariana.

We see soft creatures in the trees.

Later we walk to the top where a policewoman is direct-ing the traffic. She holds up one finger. She means 'Are you one single?'

Greg goes over the parts of this dream very carefully, the happiness part and the policewoman part. Nothing can be had for nothing, he sees. There is always a wagging finger. But he is comforted by the 'we' of the dream. All through it is 'we', even if the dream leaves vague who is the 'we'. The 'we' seems to answer the policewoman's question. He is not one single. Struggles may come, he sees that clearly, but with 'we' he is not alone.

***

While Richard and Debbie and Flick and Pete are having their party, I lie in the shadows and I compose my very first poem. One day I'll write it down, but for now I'll just re-member it, and maybe soon I'll tell it to Richard and he can tell me what he thinks of it.

Escape
A poem by Gloriana Gillespie

Escape to easy hours
In the wood
Seeing all
All might be good

Escape to where the sun will shine
Or to the kiss of rain
Clay loosened
Lovers gain

Escape the fallen apples
Wasps have eaten them
With our eyes we love
And never will condemn

Escape the dogging of old dreams
We may not speak
But loving we are different
So it's love we seek

***

'Dirty tricksters. Double-dealing dagoes. Come on Kreitlein!'

Mick shouts this out, in direct contravention of the rule of silence he has set himself.

On this night of action and passion, the most action-filled, passionate scene is down in the school, where the television arrived yesterday and very space age it looks with its four slim legs that end in dainty little plastic shoes and its two antennae on top – one is a halo of coiled wire that you jiggle around to whatever you want and the other is two slender tubes that extend out quite high. They can be set to any angle according to the weather and where the signal is coming from and so on and so forth.

'That bastard Rattin,' Mick calls out loud, even though he is quite alone. 'Look how he's jabbing his finger in poor little Kreitlein's face. The Bald Tailor of Stuttgart, that's what they call Kreitlein. He's such a pipsqueak. And look at the way Rattin's bullying him.'

The urbane tones of Kenneth Wolstenholme come on. Mick cranes his neck to hear. He has the volume right down.

'I am very much afraid that our friend Señor Rattin the

Argentinian captain has a difficult lesson to learn, that Association Football is not a street battle.'

'Right!' Mick shouts riskily. This viewing is clandestine. It is against the express orders of Miss Ratcliffe. Horrible punishment will follow a discovery. Mick has even draped a towel around the television to keep the light down a bit.

Finally, the timid little ref Kreitlein snaps. The Bald Tailor of Stuttgart raises his arm and points to the tunnel. He's sent the languid bully Rattin off. Or so he thinks. But the Argies come crowding round, threatening the little tailor, who disappears amidst a sea of burly Latin arms and legs. For ten minutes, all is mayhem.

Kenneth Wolstenholme comments silkily, 'Anyone who has travelled to a football match in Latin America will be aware that arguing with the referee is considered a part of the game over there. In Argentina, I understand, it **always** takes five minutes to send a player off, and it is perhaps ten minutes if it is the captain.'

Meanwhile, our boys keep out of it. They jog up and down and look all innocent, especially Nobby Stiles who has got a bit of reputation after hacking down a fellow in the match against France.

The police come on, the chairman of the referees' committee comes on, the Little Tailor of Stuttgart keeps flicking his wrists at Rattin like a man driving a bug away. Our English boys take the opportunity to have a quick sponge down. At last, Rattin deigns to leave the pitch but with a cinema that drives the English crowd to distraction, a slow provocative walk to the touchline and then an imperious amble to the tunnel.

But when at last the tricky Argies consent to carry on, there suddenly is Geoff Hurst springing forward with a prodigious leap and heading the ball in for a clear winner and it is all over. England are through.

At that very moment, Jane Ratcliffe's telephone rang.

She had poured the scalding water from her massive old electric kettle into the brown teapot. 'Tea, yes, the cup that cheers,' she had said to herself for want of a better companion. 'Always best from a Brown Betty don't you think? But remember, boil the water to a rolling boil, then wait a little before pouring it on the leaves, otherwise you'll burn them. Milk? Sugar? Yes, a bit of both, I think.'

She was snug by the fire, nice and snug. Although the night was warm, she had both bars on, just for the comfort of it. She was in the very act of reaching to take a ginger nut from the jar when, quite unexpectedly, came the telephone call.

It was none other than Mr. Salter, telephoning through, and with excellent news. He had a vacancy!

'Yes, dearie,' he said, 'I won't be able to get away myself, but I'll send someone over in a few days to collect the little miscreant, whoseit? – the Scandizzi girl, the Helen.'

Jane could not thank him enough. In fact, Mr. Salter had hung up before she had quite finished thanking him, or perhaps the line had got disconnected again by that frightful woman at the exchange.

Some indefinable, extremely long time later, all four of them, Debbie and Flick, Richard and Pete, were lying on their backs on the floor, their heads resting on the cushions, looking up at the ceiling, which had turned out to be decorated with the moon and seven stars set in an inky night sky. The room was full of a smoke of indescribable and extreme sweetness. The music had changed radically and was now yielding elemental rhythms.

All this was so delicious to Richard that he felt he was in heaven, and that Debbie and Flick and Pete were forever his sisters and brothers.

Somebody seemed to be saying, he knew it was Flick, beautiful little Flick whom he had always loved and would love forever, dear Flick, yet somehow her voice was not coming from her but it was flowing out from the air where the blue smoke curled and coiled and any conceivable care was whisked away, the voice that was somehow also Flick's voice was saying,

When our lot take charge, things are going to be SO DIFFER-ENT.

This was so entirely true and so incontrovertible that Richard stared to laugh, and Flick started to laugh too. She was next to him on his left, lying against a huge green and purple cushion in her beautiful dress. She leaned forward, bending her beautiful child-like body and took off her golden shoes. She gave one to Pete and the other to Richard, saying 'For my friends'.

It is time, the voice began again, *for far-out visions.*

'That is certainly true,' Richard said in what he thought was his own voice, but it too seemed to be emanating from the thick air.

On his other side, beautiful beautiful Debbie was lying propped on her elbow, looking at him. Did he imagine it or did she lean over and whisper in his ear.

'*You* are my vision, Richard,' he thought she said.

Richard saw that Pete was now asleep. Flick lit up another of those funny cigarettes and leant over Debbie and blew smoke into her mouth.

'Open very wide,' she said, turning to Richard and, drawing on the cigarette, she breathed sweet smoke into his mouth too. The three of them lay on their backs again and gazed up at the moon and the seven stars.

Four minutes, the voice of Flick not-Flick said. *What will you do with your four minutes?*

There was a pause. Debbie sat up. In the sparse light her hair was dark. She turned her head and looked at Pete sleeping and then down at Richard. As she turned to him, her hair filled with amber light. She was smiling but Richard recognized misgiving in her smile.

'Flick,' she said, 'what do you mean, four minutes?'

'Oh, I thought you knew.' Flick's voice was far off, languid, like an echo from a further shore. 'Four minutes early warning, before the bomb strikes.'

'Such crap,' Debbie said in a definite voice.

'Ah,' Richard said dreamily, 'but at least we have the music.'

'Yes, Richard,' the girls cried, clapping their hands together. 'Yes, we have the music.'

22

Richard and Mick emerged from Liverpool Street Station into London's strange air. They were on their way to the rendezvous with Minty. They felt straightaway the exuberant mood. In spite of the light rain that was falling, crowds thronged the streets.

Jane Ratcliffe had floated them for a fiver and Pete had helped Richard plan out where expenses could be trimmed so they could build up the war chest they would need for later. Relying on Pete's projections, Richard splashed out on twenty Capstan (recommended by Pete as a 'man's smoke') for 4/3d at a shabby tobacconist's beside the station. The old geezer behind the counter winked at them and gestured at a high shelf from which a row of dominant-looking Penthouse Pets gazed down as stonily as icons.

'Lovely girls,' the gaffer wheezed, 'Lovely. Nah? Well, never mind. Yer'll get yerself a real girl today, and for nuffink neither. Like VE Day, it is, today. Cor, lumme, that day...'

Mercifully the old gaffer's Capstan cough cut short the reminiscence.

While they waited in the queue for the bus, Richard smoked, pulling strings of tobacco out of his mouth from time to time. 'Cancer sticks,' Mick commented. He furiously resented the 4/3d out of their war chest.

When the bus came, the cockney conductor refused the wheelchair.

'You can't bring that thing on here, mate,' he said and rang the bell. The bus moved off smartly.

When the next bus came, the kindly Sikh conductor helped Mick on board and expertly stowed his chair in the luggage cubby hole.

'Where to, guv?' he asked. 'I'll make that two halves, shall I? Going' to the game, are you? Cor, wish I was.' He rolled off their fourpenny fares with a flourish.

Richard pushed Mick over Trafalgar Square, scattering pigeons. An old pigeon-fancier distributing crusts to the eager birds yelled at them 'Leave God's creatures alone.'

Crowds crossed and recrossed the square. The English seemed to have thrown off their habitual pessimism and their inhibitions and become for the day an uninhibited, heedless people. **THIS IS THE DAY WE FINALLY WIN THE WAR** the newspaper hoarding said – and then there was Mick in his big jeans, going up the steps of the National Gallery on his backside while Richard heaved the wheelchair up.

The rain had now stopped and the cloud had broken into big pulpy masses that were driving rapidly across a background of blue. The sun shone briefly through.

But what on earth was Minty Cavendish thinking as she taxi-ed in from Paddington – a story of atonement, a revised history, new departures?

She felt a pulse of terror. What if the boy was a monster or had horrid, disillusioning traits? And why, she thought irrelevantly, looking out of the window at the gay crowds around Marble Arch, were all these people in the streets? Hadn't they got homes to go to?

She had written that letter on a wave of sadness driven by the break-up of her ten-year marriage. It had long been clear to Minty and to her husband Jack Cavendish that it hadn't worked out. He was five years her junior, a big friendly Welshman and a consistently vigorous lover but he had wanted children and they hadn't come. The marriage had always felt incomplete, and they turned out not to like each other enough to make the effort.

Down Park Lane Minty's taxi got stuck behind a coach. THRIPPS OF DAVENTRY it read on its grubby rump and a stuck-on placard said WEMBLEY OR BUST. Minty sighed. It was the little things which had begun to loom large. It really had been the smeared toothpaste in the sink and the shoddily stacked dishes, his reluctance to do a proper deep pruning of the clematis. These tiny venial things swelled unaccountably to become intolerable causes of rift between them. Even his once welcome uxoriousness came to look to her like a form of control, almost like he was checking up on her. He was always picking her up from Townswomen's Guild meetings or coming to the station to fetch her in the car when she got back from visiting her mother in Littlehampton. She knew her suspicions of Jack's motives were ridiculous but there it was, and what might have stuck a more satisfied couple together ended up just irritating her.

In the end, he got a plump girl in his office pregnant. Chloe had been quite plain, as Minty found out with small satisfaction by lurking outside Jack's office, but she was a younger model altogether, ten years younger than Minty, and Jack had happily bunked off with her, leaving Minty at the age of forty-two with a semi in Hammersmith, a good income and a terror that the door of motherhood was closing forever.

No wonder, she thought – they were still stuck behind Thripps of Daventry and she was finding the cheerful bawdy gestures of the fans inside rather wearing, and now the taxi driver had begun an endless story that he'd driven his petrol cab on diesel for a whole day after a mix-up at the pumps, or was it the other way round – no wonder she had written that letter and left it a whole week on the hall table. The moment she finally slipped it into the mouth of the big red pillar box on the corner of Fairview Road, she had immediately felt stinging regret.

Thripps moved and her taxi moved and they rounded Hyde Park Corner and edged slowly down Piccadilly and at length the driver's story ended – had he been going slowly on purpose so that he could complete his tale? The National Gallery came into view through a mist of Minty's tears. What was she doing? Changing her life forever, and not for the better?

She gave the driver a threepenny bit for a tip and he said sarcastically 'Easy to see you've got into the mood, love'. She bought a newspaper from the stand and read the headline: **We've beaten them twice at their national game – now we'll beat them at ours too**. Was that sort of comment really needed, she wondered.

She knew, of course, that she could never love this child, perhaps she could never love anybody but certainly not this child, conceived a hundred ages ago in a completely forgotten mood. Was it anger, or despair? She had no idea. She had been another person altogether. And what begins badly ends badly, she thought.

Now she clacked across the foyer of the gallery, a lonely unsteady woman looking hopelessly for her younger self, tears of regret for what might have been filling her eyes.

Richard and Mick were keeping the appointed vigil on a bench in front of Uccello's *Rout of San Romano*.

The picture had been proposed by Minty as it was the only one she could recall from her sparse visits to the Gallery many years ago. She'd once met her first boyfriend

Steven there and she remembered the chubby horses.

'So where is the silly old cow?' Mick demanded sulkily, slumping down. People rushed past them, the gallery was emptying, everyone was making for a television set. And these people rushing by were irritating Mick a lot. They either looked abruptly away which was annoying, or assumed brief, put-on charitable expressions of high solicitousness, which was *really* annoying.

Richard, meanwhile, was in a much better place. He was watching all the untouchable girl art students showing off their endless legs as they paraded by with glamorous self-consciousness in their mini-skirts, their blackened houri eyes darting mischievously from side to side. They were like the colourful but risky nymphs in the Claudes and Poussins that Richard had glanced at as they came in through the galleries.

Mick was doing some wheelchair push-ups. He asked,

'What's madder, toffee nose?'

'I think it's a pigment.'

'Oh, what? Never mind. 'n what's coition?' Mick said it like *coy-tee-on*

'What? Oh, *co-ishun*,' Richard pronounced it correctly and a dazzling girl in a shimmering blue sequined dress that barely covered her modesty whipped round. He lowered his voice. 'It's sex,' he whispered into Mick's ear.

'And Titti-Ann? That's a painter, right?'

Richard nodded.

'Tishun.'

'Oh, OK, great, do you want to hear a poem about art?'

'OK.'

'Titian was mixing some madder

With his model quite nude up a ladder
To Titian her position
Suggested coition
So he nipped up the ladder and 'ad 'er.'

Two blonde girls with racehorse legs in skirts the length of narrow friezes who had been peering at Uccello turned round. A tall weedy man with whitening hair and a droopy moustache put his hand over his mouth. The old geezer in uniform dozing on a chair at the end of the room dozed on.

Richard wondered whether he might approach the race-horse girls but the moment they registered Mick in his wheelchair they moved off, their long slim legs carrying them swiftly from the room.

The fatal hour had come and gone. It was ten past when Richard looked up from his discreet and ravenous study of a black-haired girl whose sleeveless white top and tiny skirt were rendering him literally unable to breathe, amazed at the licence that 1966 gave him to see practically all of a girl's body. Then he saw, craning in the doorway, a respectable-looking middle-aged woman in a light summer coat and a straw hat and sporting sensationally unfashionable button-over shoes. When she saw him looking at her, the woman looked away and disappeared so sharply that he knew at once that it was her, the Minty Cavendish. He jumped up and said to Mick,

'Hold the fort, I'm going to the bog.'

'Typical,' Mick said, eyeing the pastel-coloured rumps of Uccello's horses for the hundredth time.

Richard caught up with Minty as she stepped rapidly across the foyer towards the exit. He put his hand on her arm and she looked up at him with a driven, bitter grimace.

Her eyes were blue. Her face seemed vaguely familiar with its milky look and the pale freckles that her powder did not quite disguise.

'No, don't,' she said. 'I can't, you see. I just can't.'

'I just want to ask something,' Richard stammered, still holding her arm. He could see her reddish hair beneath the straw hat. She pulled away but he clung on. Through the linen sleeve he felt her body shaking. She looked terrified now.

'Yes, what is it?'

Richard hesitated. Everything was going so wrong.

'I mean...' he stuttered, 'I mean... was it... love?'

She started. Her eyes were wide and bright with tears.

'Whatever do you mean?'

'I mean... was Mick born... conceived, I mean... were you...?'

She looked at him, bitterly now, and pitiful, as though she was regarding her own sadness anew. A thin black trail of mascara started from the corner of her eye.

'Good Lord, no. No, it wasn't love... but...'

Now her eyes brimmed and her pale freckled cheeks flushed beneath her powder. Her face took on a sad, pleading look.

'Please don't tell. Don't tell him I was here.'

She pulled away from him and clacked on across the big black and white tiles, walking more slowly now. He watched her shoulders sink as she made her way down the steps and into St Martin's Lane. At length she hailed a taxi from the pavement and disappeared inside.

Back in the gallery, Mick said to Richard,

'Typical. Come on, quick, let's go.'

***

Wow wow wow wow wow wow.

Mick's jaw dropped a mile as he saw the ocean of Union Jacks and heard close-up the thunderous clamour of the crowd.

'Get off with yer, 'op it,' the usual short-arse officious bloke in the peaked cap had said when Richard broached the subject, 'an get that wheel chair out of the road, it's against fire regs that is'. He didn't warm when he probably heard Mick mutter *'Little tit'* under his breath. But then they'd nipped round the back of the toilets where a spiv in a shiny suit was touting and he said 'How much you got then, mate?' and he took the four oncers they had left in their war chest because the game was already starting.

The short-arse in the peaked cap was mellower when he saw they had tickets. Anyway, he wanted to close the gate and get up to see the game, so they nipped in sharpish and he parked them by the boxes where Mick could stay in his chair.

The atmosphere was thick with the excitement of it. A hundred thousand people were hopping from foot to foot in the pale sun and smiling nervously, jostling against each other in anxious camaraderie. There was a big bloke next to Mick in a Union Jack cap who said to him, 'Three Hammers, three goals, you'll see, son.' Richard offered him a Capstan which he took. 'Ta, mate.' Everywhere there were these brief alliances, people laughing too loudly with complete strangers.

Then the roar really went up as a hundred thousand voices, precious few of them German, bayed and bellowed. Our boys were on the pitch. They were in red and white, the colours of England. And gone were the flapping Eighth Army-type bags of yesteryear. Our lads were in trim white shorts. Hurst's superb thighs gleamed in the yellow light.

They got off to a smashing start, four shots in as many minutes, and Peters let fly from a cross from Jackie Charlton and sent the German goalie really diving for it. Ten minutes in, the German half headed the ball nicely out to Bobby Charlton, who took it on Beckenbauer's blind side and lofted it to Hurst coming in like an angel from out deep. But the German goalie dashed out to punch it literally off Hurst's eyebrows.

Then somehow, horribly, the Germans were away, passing deftly amongst themselves, and Ray Wilson only bloody muffed a clearance with a marshmallow header. The ball was at Haller's feet, he scuffed it, Jackie Charlton blinded Gordon Banks, and the ball slouched into the corner of the England net.

'Oh, crikey, no,' Mick cried, covering his eyes. Around them, a great groan went up and then an awful silence fell. Everyone was fidgeting nervily, glancing at their neighbour.

'That's brilliant for a start off,' Mick said despairingly, but the big fellow beside him in the Union Jack cap said, 'Don't worry, sonny, the Hammers'll sort it out.'

And pretty quick they did. The England boys refused to take this as a set-back. They almost seemed freed up by it and swept forward in attack. Moore of West Ham, lightly fouled, dipped a speedy free kick towards the left post. His fellow Hammer Hurst, disastrously unmarked, glided smoothly from right to left, picked up the cross and nodded it cleanly into the corner of the net. The German goalie was left standing motionless. One all.

'Square, did you see,' Peak Cap shouted to Mick hoarsely through the roars of the crowd, 'Hurst caught the defence square. Poor old Hans didn't know whether he was comin' or goin'. Ha ha.'

England now took real control, pressing forward wave after wave in attack. But always there was the German defence, their back four screening the goalie Hans against Hunt and Hurst who harried and shot and were all the time probing and seeking out the cracks.

The ref blew for half time. 'Oh, wow wow wow,' Mick kept muttering.

'Blimey, you look more done in than our boys do,' old Union Jack Cap said and bought him an ice cream.

'What do you think's going to happen?'

'Hurst'll score a couple more.'

Others joined in the debate.

'He never will.'

'Nah, never been done. Hat trick in the World Cup final? Nah, never.'

'You wait and see,' said Union Jack Cap. 'Alf's giving them all a pep talk right now. You wait and see.'

Rain was now slanting across the pitch but our boys came out looking fresh as daisies and began to press forward straight away. They'd got real control now, sweeping, probing, trying every angle.

'Come on, lads, come on!' Mick was leaning forward and shouting out. The rain stopped and the clouds cleared. And then, ten minutes from time came the miracle. Ball lofted the corner, it was headed out to Hurst, a German defender got his leg to it, the ball went loose, and there was Martin Peters hurtling out of the sun to sock it in. The German goalie went one way, his full back darted the other way, and Peters' brilliant smash went straight down the middle between them and landed thwack plump in the back of the net. Two one to England.

'Ha ha! That's it! That's the winner! We won the flaming World Cup! Oh, England, England!' The crowd began to sing **'E-i-addio WE WON THE CUP!'** Mick was rising out of his seat and waving his arms and shouting 'We won the flaming cup'.

The Germans were punctured, you could see the air going out of them. England pressed to make it three. Hurst went for goal but snatched it wide. Toothless Nobby Stiles efficiently cut down the German centre-forward when he looked a bit dangerous. It was in the bag and all around Mick and Richard the crowd were ecstatically singing *Rule Britannia*. The Germans held scrappily on but with a deflated air. Only Beckenbauer was covering the ground, smothering Bobby Charlton.

There were seconds to go, the crowd were already on their feet to acclaim the English victory. Then a German obstructed Jackie Charlton and the bloody ref gave an unfair free kick. Our boys rushed to form the wall, gap-toothed Nobby Stiles dragged the lads hither and thither to get them into place. It was all shouting and calling and nobody marking. The Germans threw every last man into it, crowding forward. Their striker Emmerich booted the kick poorly, it was heading out. But then the ball glanced off their own man, slowed and traversed lazily across and in a long moment of horror there was little Weber nipping round the back of the wall and before you could gasp, he'd lunged and scooped the ball and slotted it home past Banks.

'No no no. No, I don't believe it.'

Our boys didn't believe it either. A hundred thousand at the stadium, thirty million at home, four hundred million around the world, everybody had thought it was in the bag and then a scrabby scruffy rubbishy little goal and it was all back to Square One. Our boys stood a long moment in disbelief, turned away, and began the trudge back up to the centre circle to take the kick-off. But before they got there, the ref blew for full time.

Mick was in tears and he wasn't the only one. 'No no no.' Richard put his arm around the boy's shoulders. 'No, I can't stand it. Let's go, Rich, let's go.'

But the bloke next to them, old Union Jack cap, said, 'No, son, you hold on. There's extra time, an' that belongs to us. Look, there's Alf Ramsay going out to talk to the boys now. And you know what he'll say? He'll say, You've won the cup once, lads. *Now go out and flaming well win it again!*'

Everyone was chipping in, working up the mood. 'Yes, look at the Krauts now. They're knackered. Just look at them, they've rolled down their socks. They can dish it out but they can't take it. Can't take our turf, you see, it's that spongey. And Ball, look at little ginger Ball, bouncing up and down like he can't wait to have a good old crack at Willi and Wolfgang out there.'

'Anyway,' summed up Union Jack cap, 'three Hammers on the team, can't lose. Hat trick for Hurst, you'll see.'

The ragged Germans kicked off. Soon Ball took the corner, it dropped to Bobby Charlton, he shot, the German goalie sprawled and scrambled a scrappy save. The English swept forward in wave after wave, the late sun throwing their shadows before them so they looked a hundred feet tall. Stiles lofted to Ball, who turned it to Hurst, who feinted, swivelled, hooked and slammed it up against the cross bar. The ball bounced down on the line.

'Yes yes yes!'

The ref looked doubtful, shook his head.

'Oh no!

The ref consulted the linesman, and pointed to the centre circle. He'd given the goal.

'Hurray. HURRAY!' Mick grabbed at Richard and hauled himself up. He was really out of his seat. Everybody was out of their seat. It was like they'd won the Pools. Better. It was like they'd gone to heaven.

Now the Germans had a desperate look to them. Even Beckenbauer was clearly spent. Only their centre forward, the quicksilver Held, kept running, working, probing. But it seemed too late. The England fans were clapping rhythmically and whistling and shouting 'Time! Come on, ref, it's TIME!' It was time, seemed time. The ref put the whistle to his lips. Down below Mick and Richard, fans were already scrambling over the barrier and streaming onto the pitch.

'Nah, come off it,' Union Jack cap shouted, 'the lads aren't done yet.'

And too right, there was Bobby Moore lofting a pass to his fellow Hammer Hurst, and Hurst turned and ran with it and the beleaguered, exhausted German defence just fell away before him. He reached the edge of the penalty area and there was only the German goalie between him and his hat-trick. Hurst didn't pause, he didn't blink, he just kicked the ball perfectly to the top left-hand corner of the net. The poor old German goalie launched himself towards the ball, it flew inches beyond his fingertips, and the stadium erupted with noise.

'He's slotted it!' Mick cried. 'That's four! We've won! We've won the World Cup!'

PART THREE: AFTER THE CUP

23

E-I-ADDIO, WE WON THE CUP!' Mick shouted. Bertie licked Mick's hand. The bright green bird perched beside them looked at the boy and the dog as though they were eccentric fellow creature of the forest.

That thunderous song which had surged from a hundred thousand throats was now hallowed in Mick's soul forever. Since The Game it had throbbed through his head day and night, waking, sleeping, dreaming. It was running on permanent loop, dinning constantly in his mind. From time to time he couldn't help himself, he had to let it out.

Because Mick couldn't stop thinking about England's victory. His mind was now forever painted with its gaudy hues. They'd sipped champagne and old Union Jack cap had said *That's champagne for us – and real pain for old Hermann*. Ever since The Game, Mick had felt released into a permanent heaven of victory, a world of tumultuous celebration that would go on for ever and ever and never die.

Even these lustrous birds – for Mick and Bertie were actually in the bird cage which Pete had finished while Mick and Richard were away in London and he had gone into the local town and bought the tropical birds as a treat for Mick – even these jungle birds looked like a celebration.

The bright green job – it was a turaco with a funny red splash on its head – was sitting on a low perch beside them.

Two guinea fowl, dumb and pretty, were clucking in the corner like oversized ladies gossiping in their flowing spotted frocks and turquoise scarves.

The three parakeets were sitting on a far perch. Since

they'd arrived, they'd scarcely budged. They were spending their time looking at each other, preening like neglectful pretty girls.

The turaco edged along its perch in the direction of Mick and Bertie, turning towards them and then angling its head in a coy gesture. Was it having a stab at some sort of a relationship?

Maybe it was trust. Because Mick was thinking you probably could trust a turaco, like you could trust Bertie. But beyond that, Mick's circle of trust, forged from his almost sixteen years of experience was small, pretty, pretty small. In fact, at that moment it held, in addition to Bertie, just Patch and Gloriana and Greg, and then on the outer fringes were possibly the helpers. Newly top amongst these fringe-dwellers was Richard. He'd got them into The Game! How brilliant was that! Yes, Richard was definitely top amongst the fringe, and then a little further out came Lizzie and Debbie, perhaps, but no one else. Not for example Debbie's friend Flick who was definitely unreliable. Or busty old Angela who really only cared for Greg, which was fine for Greg but didn't help anybody else.

In any case, Mick had a problem with all that lot, the nurses, the helpers, because really they only appeared to help, or only helped a bit. What they were really all thinking about all the time was not how to help but love and sex and stuff and all this thinking about themselves and love and sex made them permanently unreliable, so in the end you just had Patch and Gloriana to rely on, and Greg as a mate.

And Helen? Wouldn't she be in the circle of trust? Of course, Mick trusted Helen. Absolutely. But she wasn't in a circle at all. She was in his heart, where she had always been.

All at once, the birds set up the most awful squawking

and Bertie peered round at them with an ambiguous air. To him as a dog they fell somewhere between competition and lunch and on both grounds his instinct was to eat them up on the spot if he got the chance. But the birds were clearly Mick's, and Bertie's love for Mick was marginally the stronger instinct so he held off and sat with an air of assumed docility that masked for now his burning inner dilemma.

As for the 'Minty', the so-called 'Mother', well, frankly Mick wasn't giving the old bag a thought. She didn't care for him, he didn't care for her. That's even Stevens, thank you very much.

Anyway, if he must have a parent, he'd go for a Dad. Someone like old Union Jack cap who would ruffle your hair and take you to see the Hammers of a Saturday afternoon.

'Oi, posh boy, made a bugger's muddle of that one, din you?'

Richard knew better than to protest at this stunningly unfair assessment. Patch, who had buzzed up to where Richard was sitting at the piano, regarded him though mordant eyes.

''ave to think of something else for Mick, now, won't we. Anyhow, where's our play?'

'Coming on,' Richard said guardedly, 'coming on.'

In fact, he had finished writing the play – *The Triumph of the Trojans*, it was called – the previous week. In the end, he had opted for that dreamier, more Sixties ending. He had reasoned that if Beveridge and Butler and Bevan and so on really was the End, what was there left for young people to do? So he had sketched out a sort of light-hearted ending, more like a masque rather than another 'political' Act.

He had some young people discussing how, because there was no war and no want, it was perhaps time to move on from the old collective efforts to something more individual, a sort of liberation of the self.

These young men and women started wearing their hair short and not dressing it much, and the girls started cutting their chitons shorter and shorter and showing off their pretty legs, and they developed a new 'big' lute that was extremely hard to play but which made a lot of noise. At the end of the play, the young people said farewell to Priam and sailed away to Djerba in search of the sacred herb called *moly*.

There! How was that for a contemporary feel?

The problem was, how would Patch take it? Confronted now with Patch's challenging regard, he decided to temporize.

'I'm still working on the dialogue,' he muttered. 'I'll show you in a few days.'

'Well, get on with it, mate. We gotta start rehearsing.'

But then there was Kevin shambling towards them, his face illuminated by news.

'Your girlfriend...' he gasped, panting from the effort.

Richard waited.

'On the fuckin' phone, mate.'

'Who is it, Kevin?'

'Told you, you motherfucker. It's your girlfriend.'

Richard went to the telephone room. The heavy black Bakelite receiver was on its cradle. He waited a minute and then Kevin shambled in.

'I thought you said there was a phone call.'

'There was. She wants you to call her back. Callin' from the fuckin' pub.'

'Oh. Did she give you the number?'

'Yes. Errr… it's… ummm… yan sethera methera sethera…'

Christ. It would take both Ventris and Chadwick to unravel this one. But Richard had a brainwave.

'Just write it down for me, will you please, Kevin?'

Kevin looked at Richard as though he were a lunatic, but when Richard pulled out his notebook and a stub of pencil, Kevin wrote down quite amenably **1646**.

After the usual ritual humiliations, the old bag at the exchange consented to patch Richard through to the pub. The receiver was immediately picked up at the other end and a loud, distracted female voice shouted,

'Richard! I'm at the pub!'

'Errr…'

'Can you get up here right away?'

He at least had something to go on by now, as he had recognized the bossy tones of Miss Payne, the swimming teacher.

'Ummm… well… I'm with the children… and I haven't got any money…'

'Don't play silly buggers, young Richard. Just get up here. I need you. And bring Pete. I need him too.'

'Ummm… but…'

'It's MacAskill, you ninny. And bring some transport.'

'What… why…?'

'Oh, come off it, Richard, do I have to spell it out? We're supposed to be on a date. MacAskill is pissed. He's passed out. The landlord wants to call the police but I said you'd take care of it.'

Pete was watching television in the staff room. When he heard the story, he said 'T'riffic' and at once agreed to nip round and get the big blue school bus out of the stables and drive it up.

When they got to The Dog, they found Miss Payne sitting up in the Lounge Bar enjoying an Advocaat and chatting with the publican, who jerked his thumb towards the door of the Public Bar.

Mr. MacAskill was lying on the grubby floor. His head was pillowed on his right forearm, and his left hand was on his chest. His posture recalled, at least to Richard, the sort of rather romantic attitude that he imagined Steerforth to have adopted when lying dead on the beach after being drowned by the author as penalty for tampering with Lil' Em'ly. Mr. MacAskill's tweed jacket was neatly arranged – Miss Payne had done at least that much for him. The scene was spoiled only by a trickle of something yellowish that ran from Mr. MacAskill's mouth down his mahogany cheek.

'Right, let's get him into the bus,' Pete said, and the two boys picked Mr. MacAskill up, Pete taking the head and shoulders, and Richard the legs.

The wheelchair section at the back of the bus provided ample space to stretch MacAskill out.

Miss Payne followed them out of the pub.

'So, thanks, boys. I'll be off. Ray will be home soon.'

With this, Miss Payne vaulted over the door of a largish sports car which was parked nearby, gunned the engine, and shot off quite noisily.

'Cor,' Pete said, 'Cor!'

'What?'

'TR3. "A" reg. With the two litre straight-four overhead valve engine. Cor! By the sound of her, she's got overdrive, too.'

Richard was more interested in the human aspects of the

situation, such as what Mr. MacAskill and Miss Payne had actually been doing together at the pub? Could it really be a 'date'? How did this 'date' square with Miss Payne's intimate relations with the used car dealer Ray, especially given that gentleman's reputation for robust defence of his interests? And why – or even *how* – had a problem created by two adult moral agents, namely Mr. MacAskill and Miss Payne, suddenly become the problem of two entirely different people i.e. Pete and Richard? And, thirdly, what were they going to do now? He consulted Pete, who was rounding off a panegyric on the TR3's 'high-port cylinder head' and its 'enlarged manifold'.

'Don't worry, mate,' Pete said confidently, 'I've dealt with loads of drunks in my time.'

So Mr. MacAskill had joined a whole new class. *Drunks.* It had a nasty sound to it, and Richard immediately wondered, beyond the immediate business of the night, how on earth to move Mr. MacAskill out of that class.

Richard had no idea where Mr. MacAskill lived, but Pete said he did, and after arduously but more or less accurately piloting the big blue bus along some narrow lanes, Pete soon turned into what proved to be a field of cabbages in which the only visible object in the half-light of the rising moon was a small caravan.

'Home Sweet Home,' Pete said. Apparently Mr. MacAskill actually lived in this caravan.

They manhandled him out of the back of the bus and into the caravan and laid him on a narrowish bunk which seemed to be the only place in the caravan where he might conceivably sleep. The rest of it was given over to domestic purposes and to an enormous number of books.

'Turn him on his front,' Pete said, and they heaved Mr.

MacAskill over.

'Cor, what a dump,' Pete commented, looking around, but Richard couldn't think of a place containing perhaps a thousand books as a complete dump, even if the way the books were piled here, there and everywhere did lend a certain dump-like aspect to Mr. MacAskill's little nest.

While Pete was making Mr. MacAskill a bit more comfortable, Richard inspected a few titles – Nietzsche, Mannoni's *Prospero and Caliban*, Camus' *The Myth of Sisyphus*, Fanon's *The Wretched of the Earth*. There was even a well-thumbed copy of Sartre's *Nausea*. Seeing that, Richard felt a minute tinge of regret for his forgotten past self. Since his arrival at Park House, he had got no further than page seven.

He opened Mr. MacAskill's copy at random. The margins were covered in hard-to-read squiggles, presumably Mr. MacAskill's, and the occasional majuscule YES!!!! He glanced at the other books, the Fanon, the Camus, all had their greater or lesser squiggles and an assortment of YES!!!!, and the occasional laconic NO.

On a small Formica-topped table, which evidence suggested doubled for dining and for some fairly heavy arm-lifting activities, lay a pile of papers, stiff, old-fashioned folios, perhaps a hundred leaves, covered in close writing in pencil in Mr. MacAskill's distinctive uncial hand. In a chipped china mug next to the papers stood, point up, about a dozen extremely well-sharpened, mottled-green HB pencils.

Beside the table, a wicker wastepaper basket contained, in addition to two empty whisky bottles (Haig), a crumpled-up paper. Richard hooked it out and uncrumpled it. It was a working title, apparently rejected, for Mr. MacAskill's manuscript: *EXISTENTIALISM & EMPIRE*. In the bottom right-hand corner, Mr. MacAskill had done an elaborate doodle of arabesques and serpentine flowers around the gothically-calligraphed words,

Published by the Casaubon Press

'I think we can leave him,' Pete was saying. 'I'll run over in the morning and check on him.'

Propped up against the wall at the back end of the table were two postcards. One was clearly a Degas. The right-hand side of the picture showed young girls practicing ballet in rather random postures. In the near ground, filling the left-hand side of the picture, slumped a young girl in a striking orange top, head in her hands, weeping. Her tutu billowed out like a pigeon's fantail.

The other picture, which Richard recognized at once from a family visit to Florence a couple of years previously, was of a chunky naked Adam, covering his face but not his ample virilia, and at his side a plumpish weeping Eve, also stark naked, her hands covering her pudenda, the First Couple, on their way out of Eden. Yes, Richard thought, that would be Masaccio.

24

Gloriana has heard about Mr. MacAskill's big night out.

Mr. MacAskill! How could you do that to poor battling Miss Payne? She may be tough-looking and tough-sounding but her thing with Ray is hanging by a thread. And getting stuccoed like that. I don't call that a date at all. It's just self-pity. Pity yourself if you must, but please don't drag our Miss Payne down with you.

But still... **Something Definitely Happened To Mr. MacAskill In Africa**. And if Mr. MacAskill is going down down down, I suppose we must do something for him. Pete and Richard saw the place where he is squatting – a caravan in a field of cabbages. And him an Oxford man! He didn't come to school again today, presumably sleeping it off. Richard had to hold the fort yet again, which he did rather charmingly. We watched telly much of the time, a most interesting documentary about people in Africa who eat snakes to make them cunning. Then he read to us from *Gulliver's Travels*. It was quite entrancing, how to extract sunbeams from cucumbers.

Then Richard said he'd write down my poem for me. This took a very long time as he kept making some quite elementary mistakes in understanding my signing. But in the end, he got it down right, and then he sat for an age reading it, running his finger along the lines and all sorts of theatre like that. I was on a rack of worry all this time. In the end, he said,

'Mmm... I like it very much... I like the theme, and the

way you've put the metaphysical and the ordinary side by side... *Seeing all, all might be good...* that's excellent... And the wasps and the apple... sort of rejecting Eden, plumping for love... making no judgements... super. And that last couplet *But loving we are different/So it's love we seek...* that's quite beautiful. It's... it's, well, Audenesque.'

Which is nice of him.

After that, we continued Our Quest for the Symptoms of Literature. Here's Monty's lesson for today:

> *And I will show you something different from either*
> *Your shadow at morning striding behind you*
> *Or your shadow at evening rising to meet you*
> *I will show you fear in a handful of dust*

Erk. This poet knows how to make you feel afraid. Afraid of your own shadow, being shadowed... This is so strange, really disturbing...

Richard reads out Monty's stately take on this. *We may strongly be tempted to feel as we read this that here is literature.* Strongly be tempted? Or is that *be strongly tempted*? I fear Monty is here the prisoner of some old grammar thing from about last century. Doesn't it sound funny? Anyway, this is what he says:

All life in the raw is heterogeneous. It is only by effecting *associations* amid the welter of impressions that we establish any order in our experience. The New Poetry by its new associations establishes a *new and further order*. New Poetry picks a scene of everyday and persuades the reader that *the real strangeness and magic of the world are lurking and are busy.*

Well. Just now we've got some new associations right here at the House. There's Mick who nearly had a mother and got the World Cup instead. There's Helen who is cooking up a storm. There's Patch who's become King of the Trojans. There's me hunting for the Symptoms of Literature. And there's Greg – apparently Angela has come up trumps there and transcribed the dreamy runes he's been scratching in his old rough notebook – she's even 'sent off' the results to somebody somewhere.

So, Richard, lots of stuff going on that you could at a pinch call *strangeness* and *magic*. Mick is certainly enchanted, and so I suppose am I, in quite a different way. And Helen wears a beatific smile as she puts her dainty dish before her king (who unfortunately seems to be you, Richard, for the time being). Patch is living out his myth. And even Greg has the look of someone who is not only intent on his dream but has had it transcribed **and** 'sent off'.

But but but but but…

Establishing a new and further order? How grand that sounds! A new and further order. Just the ticket. But is that what's coming up here? *I don't think so*. Because what does it all amount to, Richard? You prod these things and they wobble like Young Win's jellies. And they're just about as nourishing (i.e. NOT).

Aren't they *all* just dreams, Richard?

And all the time what is it that is really lurking? What is it that is really busy?

Why, it's Mr. Salter.

Whilst we've been making good progress with these dreams of ours, Sallow Salter has been establishing our new and further order without any help from us. Yes, he's been prepping the Bin, ready for our transfer. It's just a matter of weeks now, and I have to say, dear Richard, for all your charm and your nice shaving (which is anyway for Lizzie, I know, and not for us), for all these lovely dreams and myths about university and scrummy dinners and World Cup victories and seductive poetry and Greg's pop hit singles, we have made **No Progress Whatever**. There is not one single fact that has been established that will save us from the Bin.

Come on, Monty. Come on, Richard. Strangeness and magic, OK. But we need FACTS ON THE GROUND if we're really going to have a new and further order other than the Bin.

Days are rushing by, these numbered days of ours. There is Binstead – looming. Mr. Salter – looming.

At the end of our lesson, Lizzie looks in. Richard perks up at once.

'Oh, you here?' Lizzie says in his general direction.

'You coming to the birds thing later?' Richard asks.

There is a Ceremony this afternoon for Pete and Mick's bird cage.

'Maybe,' Lizzie says. 'How's the forty inch chest coming on?'

And then to me,

'Look, darling, letter from Robbie. Shall I hold it for you?'

Richard feels he is dismissed and trails out.

***

Binstead Village
Surrey-on-the-Styx
Hell

Day 25 of the 12,410 days I am now certain to spend in The Bin

Darling Glor, Soul Mate Patch,

Poo poo poo.

The Clinical Review Board met this morning in the Boardroom. It was a lovely room with a carpet so thick my wheelchair got stuck and Steve had to give me an extra shove through it. Well, it's nice to know there's at least one comfy room in The Bin.

Inside, three sombre geezers in dark suits were sitting behind a long table. We sat in a row before them. There was Norma, there was me, and there, like our nemesis, was Mr. Salter, acting as advocate for the Asylum.

It all started so well. Two doctors came on and said that Norma was, well, normal. She has, apparently, an IQ of about 90 which is below 100 – but then half the population has an IQ below 100. They said there was no reason why, with some re-education, Norma should not lead a full and satisfying life on the outside. The Chairman asked mildly,

'Are you saying there was no reason for her original committal in... my goodness... 1935?'

To which the doctor sagely replied,

'In 1935, I was a schoolboy. I have no knowledge of Miss Cummings at that time. There is nothing on file. All I can say is based on her condition since I began to observe her...'

So it was in the bag. Then Nemesis Salter got up and fixed old Norma with his beady eye and jaundiced look and, well, she quailed.

'Do you really, really want to leave us, Norma?' he said, advancing impressively towards her. 'Do you really in your heart of hearts think that you want to live all alone out in the big bad world?'

The Chairman intervened and said 'Please, Mr. Salter,

this is a Clinical Review Board, not a forensic exercise.'

But the damage was done. The Chairman asked Norma to speak on her own behalf. What did she really want? And she said, of course, that she wanted to stay at Binstead for ever and ever.

So Norma withdrew her case.

Curtains. Norma's been put straight back into Specials – Salter's not taking any more risks. And I feel that immense and brooding presence has something up his sleeve for me too. Because he muttered to me as we trailed out at the end of the meeting, 'You're so full of shit, Willis, aren't you. But fortunately we know what to do about that, don't we?'

Love from your dispirited friend,

'Hamilton Burger' Willis

25

Fighting sleep, Richard settles in his room to study. Today's lunch was exceptionally heavy – a vaporous *bollito misto*, beef that melted on the tongue, pieces of buttery chicken, a satiny shin, and plump rosy sausages soft as cream. Helen served the dish as she does every day, as if it were a mystery, holding it up like the Host. She always serves Richard first. When she has served everybody she stands shyly by the door for a minute, watching him eat. Nobody is objecting. Everyone is growing fat and glossy.

The pages of the scrawled-over palimpsest of *The Triumph of the Trojans* lie scattered on the bed. However, it is not yet another rewrite of the troublesome Act Four that Richard is about to work on. And the gentle Helen, whom he intends to cast as the controversial runaway Princess of Troy, is also far from his thoughts. He does, however, have a girl in mind.

In truth it is not really study to which Richard now settles down, but revision, because he has already made a very close study indeed of *A Doctor's Marital Guide for Patients: Regular and Rhythm Edition*. The *Marital Guide* is an 86-page booklet, plus a most useful two-page glossary, and an extremely helpful *Coital Posture Diagram Supplement (To be Dispensed at the Discretion of Doctors)*, which is a sort of wall chart showing pretty well everything you need to know.

Richard particularly likes Diagram (B) Man Above – Weight Supported, and (H) Wife Above – Between the Thighs, and also (J) – Sitting Position. In fact, all the diagrams are very good indeed. They are very clear and beautifully drawn, although for one or two of them – such as (D) – Full Weight or the one (E) where the wife is on a table, he has to check the full written text to get the drift.

He reads the entire booklet again twice (including Chapter XII *Obstacles to Sexual Satisfaction*, and Chapter XIII *Sex Anomalies and Abnormalities*), and then he runs back over the key Chapter IX *Principles and Techniques of Intercourse*.

It all seems very straightforward, although he is surprised by the emphasis on the man's duty to give first place to the pleasure of the woman (usually referred to as 'the wife' whereas for some reason the word 'husband' is barely mentioned, it is all 'the male', 'the man'). For example, in the section on *Intromission: When to proceed to the first climactic step*, he reads 'Keeping in mind that the main objective for the man is to assure the wife's climax, we can see that sexual contact is a matter of individual programme.'

But all through there is a wonderful generosity to the booklet. He particularly likes the passage on *al fresco* sex:

'The beauty of nature is often a potent force in arousing sexual appetite. No sound scruple forbids responding spontaneously between the earth and sky, or anywhere the couple thinks fit and friendly.'

All this is very sexy and exciting, but also rather liberating and fine. In the diagrams there is a sort of happy abandon to the bodies of the slim fit young couple who work their way through the chart (their faces are not shown, but Richard presumes something ecstatic playing there). He reads in the booklet that 'couples in their late teens have sex seven or more times a week', so that with a bit of a push one could run through the entire chart in a week and then start again at the beginning.

He also reads that 12.6% of middle-class women have two or more orgasms in a single sexual experience.

But what is all this study for, delightful though it is in itself? It has to do with Richard's absolute determination to move from the theory of lovemaking to the practical. And very soon indeed.

'Watch it, toffee-nose.'

Today is a sort of state occasion so Patch, King of the Trojans, has reverted to his 'political' manner and he is dealing with Richard with all his old scorn. As the Armstead 302 can't handle the cobbles in the stable yard, Richard has to heft Patch across in an old mechanical chair. The weight is stupendous. Since he became King of the Trojans, Patch seems to be putting on the pounds on a daily basis and to be glowing ever brighter and hotter.

Richard sets Patch down amongst his Trojans and turns to look for Lizzie.

Coincidentally, she is looking for him.

Because Lizzie has her struggles and her complications and Richard seems somehow to be a simpler proposition.

She comes and stands beside him.

Because it's a half-holiday which brings its own atmosphere, her idea, if she has one which is not necessarily the case, is to embark on a little flirting exchange with Richard and, to be honest, to see where it might not lead. For even if Richard is not so on her mind as she is aware she is on his, she quite likes him really. And still there is that snapshot in her mind that pops up from time to time, of his smooth, shining chest she'd seen that first day.

'Ummm...'

Oh, come on, Richard. Ummm?

Richard can easily see there are some hidden codes to do

with flirting that he hasn't yet quite mastered. His eye rests stupidly on Lizzie and he shifts from foot to foot.

'Come on England,' she says encouragingly, shaking her head in a rough circle so her tousled locks flop about.

Suddenly, on a faint breeze, he catches her scent – she must have slapped it on for the occasion – and his whole being quickens. He feels a deep thrill which is certainly connected to what he has been studying in the *Marital Guide* and the *Posture Diagram Supplement*.

But how on earth can he move from here to there? This thought leads to a further pause in his dialogue with Lizzie and her eyes are rolling about in an exasperated way when the whole thing is interrupted by the most almighty shout.

Hon hoi theoi philousin…
…neos apothneiskei!

The Trojans have clustered round Patch and the elders and are doing a kind of special ceremonial antiphony, with a lot of waving of their arms and drumming on their chariots.

Lizzie now smiles at Richard, crinkling her nose good-naturedly. His whole body had been like a young boy's, but then there had been that dark V and the slim untried virile part.

For a moment, the pall of the afternoon lifts. The clouds part and a weak sun shines slantwise across the courtyard, touching the sombre buildings with a dab of gloss. The sunshine falls also on Lizzie and lights up her sensationally tousled hair.

'You're alright, Richard, you know,' she shouts above the continuing racket of the Trojan's cacophony. 'Who you got your eye on then?'

Her gratey Essex voice is music.

She is thinking – It would be so easy, he so eager, so young. So unlike her present trials.

'Well, you, Lizzie'

She just laughs, but with a cloudy look about her eyes.

Mick is in place by the cage, raptly gazing on his birds which flutter uncertainly before him. They seem to him somehow to carry on the spirit of The Game, that blazing triumph.

The three parakeets are lined up on a single dowel. They grip on tight, nodding their outsize heads to each other and touching up their blue-grey feathers with their scimitar-like beaks. Suddenly, with a screech they fly with short, hard wing-beats the length of the cage and back again, and line up on the dowel in the exact same order. On the ground, the guinea fowl fuss away amongst the litter, clucking softly.

The turaco perches in the branches of a small tree which Mick has cut from the copse and stuck in the corner of the cage. The bird looks sprightly if confused, a splash of malachite green and a bandit's hood of black and red.

***

Gloriana has been wheeled out to the state occasion.

Eventually Patch's Trojans stop their racket. I think the grown-ups don't quite get it. The Vicar is definitely looking askance. He is probably alarmed that polytheistic ritual is on the rise again in his parish.

Who cares anyway? The grown-ups then start on some emptier rituals of their own. They make some speeches, bla bla bla, even the grown-ups themselves don't bother to listen to them. Then they drink some ritual tea. The noble old biddy who's on the board of the school passes round and patronizes us all like mad. The sun goes in again, the stables assume their old grey hue, the damp begins to rise.

At this point, the birds seem to realize that they are stopping here. They take on an alarmed look. They start clucking disconsolately to each other and ducking their heads beneath their wings as if they are trying to make it all go away.

Lizzie sits by me and feeds me fairy cake. Then I drain my lemonade. I close my eyes, for I am tired. Do I doze off for a moment or is it a day-dream? I see Richard as a man, in a suit of white linen and a pale blue shirt, sculling Lizzie on a jewelled lake. She, shaded by a parasol, trails her hand in the flickering waters. They regard each other with delighted eyes as a lambent, gentle sun dips towards the far horizon…

'Oi.'

I open my eyes. Lizzie, the ever-alert girl, has jumped up. She bounds off and grabs Helen who has sidled up to where Richard is talking dutifully to the Vicar. Helen has begun to wriggle out of her rather tight top. Underneath she seems to have not much else on. Lizzie firmly tugs the top back down. Flick comes over. She takes Helen by the hand and goes back with her towards the House.

The afternoon now seems to be failing at its own speed but quite quickly. The visitors begin to make their excuses and leave. Then all of a sudden there is Pete standing on a chair and shouting,

'Nurses booze up tonight. Seven o'clock start. Meet in the Great Hall.'

Wow. Only Pete can do that sort of thing.

The nurses all cry, **Oh yes**.

The Rat's mouth purses to its pruney *moue*, but it is a half-holiday and the word is out and she cannot call it back, at least not without a big fuss and right in front of the Vicar and the noble old biddy.

So she enters no opposition on this one.

And then the clouds part and the sun shines through.

26

Gloriana watches the preparations for the night.

Our nurses gather in the Great Hall. Most are wearing jeans and odd tops, covering up the arms and legs and tummies they all think are too fat or too thin. Only big bold Debbie wears a skirt. It's her tiny red mini-skirt which she tugs down so that it just about covers the fork between her plump dimpled thighs. Beside her, slim, flat Flick stands attentive, erect in smart tartan trews.

We children brood over by the piano. Spirit is draining from us in the exact measure that it is enlivening our nurses. Mick plays a desultory bar of *Heart and Soul* and then thumps down the piano lid. King Patch sits apart, scowling, resting his big head on the stick of his Armstead 302. Only Kevin is showing any spirit, going round and flailing his sticks at the nurses' legs. 'Go on, 'op it, fuckin' nosepickers,' he grumbles as they skip nimbly away.

The sky is now pure azure and the declining sun shines through the vast windows of the Great Hall, throwing obliques of gold across the tiles. The nurses seem enchanted as they move between the warm light and the shadows, the air about them full of glistering dust. All this makes the Trojans feel even more earth-bound and despondent.

Suddenly in dashes Pete, all energy, calling out *Come on, birds* and *Let's get going, all my little pets*. Pete today shows this extraordinary flair for youth and all its dalliances. There seems nothing he cannot do. His self seems fully formed and hard-wearing and he gets our little community of nurses going, full of playful tussle and feigned reproach. They laugh and preen. I think most of them are half in love with Pete anyway, man-starved as they are. And he knows the steps, he knows the language, all that primrose itinerary from flirt to touch to kiss and on.

But Pete, who clearly knows the secrets of the teenage heart, is scanning the eager girls for just one. It is Angela Cudmore – I know because Mick never stops ribbing Pete about his 'hots' for this country lass. In fact, I bet the whole outing has been thought up as a mechanism for Pete's continued pressing desire to conjugate with Miss Angela Cudmore.

Yet while the girls crowd round Pete and flirt with him, there is Angela hanging back by the old sideboard, working some moves with her compact and lipstick.

And Richard? And my Lizzie? Where oh where are they?

When Lizzie doesn't show up in the Great Hall at the appointed hour, Richard goes hunting for her. He runs to her room and knocks. When there is no reply, he opens the door to find her lying asleep on her narrow bed, still in her old green jersey and jeans. She opens her eyes and peers at Richard.

'Are you coming, Lizzie?'

'What?'

'Pete's drinks.'

An expression that could be disdain flickers across her pale face. At any rate she looks dopey and still half asleep.

'Do come, Lizzie.'

'Maybe I've got plans.'

'Please.'

Lizzie, covering a yawn with her fingers, nods slowly.

'Is that a yes?'

She nods again.

'Gimme five minutes, Richard.'

Richard comes back looking apprehensive and excited. He's put on his best shirt (fortunately not his best tie, in fact no tie at all). As he goes past me, he smiles nervously. I catch the faintly antiseptic smell of *Arrid Roll-On Extra Dry*.

Pete says, 'Come on mate. The kids are going bananas.'

Because a deep sense of betrayal is festering in the Trojans. They are growing crosser and crosser. Mick is now wheeling about crazily, round and round the knot of nurses. Patch mutters something to the Trojan elders and their electric chariots advance in a line four abreast towards the nurses.

'They're going to get plastered,' Mick calls out, spinning his chair at breakneck speed straight at the nurses, then thudding to a halt at the last moment.

'And they're going to start snoggin'',' Patch cackles, making his Armstead 302 whine with distaste.

'And Pete's going to grope that fat tart Angela.'

'And Richard's going to try to stick his face in Lizzie's titties.'

'And what are the rest of them going to do?'

'Yeah, what are the rest of them going to do?'

'Fuckin' motherfuckers,' Kevin adds with satisfaction from a safe distance.

The Trojans are not malicious, they just see the party for what it plainly is, a betrayal, exclusive. They hate this going out and they are punishing the nurses – *their* nurses – with the only weapon they have – the truth on a sharp tongue.

'Let's go,' Pete says. I can tell he feels the mood slipping away, but Richard begs for another minute.

'Lizzie's coming,' he says, and Pete throws him a sharp look.

But then suddenly here is my Lizzie strolling in, cool as a cat. She is still in her jeans and green jersey, she's really not making much effort here. Her wavy black hair is wild and tousled. But she has put on a touch of make-up – her eyes are lined in an arabesque of black with a little Egyptian tail in the corner. Richard looks stunned and ecstatic and extremely nervous. I can just feel his whole being straining towards my girl.

Lizzie spots the problem with the restive Trojans and jumps straight in.

'Shut up will you, you lot. We're just going to have a bit of fun for a change.'

'Oh well, if that's all…' Patch says sourly.

'May we go now, your kingship?'

'You may, panda-face. But I'd keep your 'and on your halfpenny if I was you.'

Lizzie bridles. A tell-tale reddish flush flares up along her cheek bones and she eyeballs Patch fiercely.

'Don't be disgusting, Patch.'

King Patch does look suddenly abashed. He hesitates a moment and then his noble nature kicks in.

'Sorry, Lizzie, really sorry.'

'Alright. And keep this lot in order while we're gone. Do a game, Patch, do a game.'

Patch nods slowly and turns his Armsworth 302 away. His elders and the other Trojans follow and in a minute he has the Trojan girls on one side of the Great Hall, the Trojan boys on the other and they are advancing and retreating in line abreast and chanting,

Who do you want to marry

To marry, to marry
Who do you want to marry
Alla balla kiss-me-toe.

We want to marry Bacon Face
Bacon Face. Bacon Face
We want to marry Bacon Face
Alla balla kiss-me-toe.

Lizzie clearly thinks this slightly rude mating game is a fair compromise on which to finish, so she shouts out,

'Alright then. Ta-ra, kids. Don't go giving Miss Ratcliffe any trouble now.'

For yes, the Rat is being left to hold the fort.

Lizzie comes and gives me a kiss and says 'Goodnight, darling'. She's dabbed on some really nice scent. Then she walks up to Richard and links her arm through his.

'Come along,' she says, leading off past Pete, who can clearly be heard to mutter *Jammy devil* in Richard's direction.

And over in the dark corner of the Great Hall, I spot Helen – she has not joined the game, she is just looking on, watching Lizzie and Richard as they waltz off. I see that tears are falling on her starched white chef's jacket.

Through the unblemished evening they make their way in knots of twos and threes across the meadow and through the giant lime's long black shadow. The warm air moves rhythmically around their heads. Debbie is telling jokes and riddles.

'What's the best thing to put in a pie? Your teeth.'

'Why does your dog always go round and round before he lies down? Because he's a watch dog and he's trying to wind himself up.'

Pete flourishes a quarter bottle of whisky and passes it round. The girls refuse until Lizzie grasps it and takes a good swig, and then Debbie follows suit. Angela is keeping clear of Pete, fringing round the edges of the group.

At The Dog, Pete buys a round of drinks. All the girls ask for Snowballs and his lip curls. But he gets them all the same, and a pint of bitter and a whisky mac each for Richard and himself.

'There you are, girls,' he says. 'Drink it slowly now. It cost me bloody nearly three quid, that lot.'

Pete tosses back his whisky mac and bolts a gulp of beer to wash it down. The girls laugh, turning their shining faces to him and calling out 'Cheers, Pete. Cheers, everyone.'

'Hey, Pete, what's yellow and sings?' Debbie calls out.

'A Snowball as it goes down your throat.'

'No, silly. It's Banana Mouskouri.'

The girls shriek with laughter, and the blokes at the next table look round grinning. One smirking overweight lad in a purple flowered shirt and a red military tunic calls out to Pete.

'Nice balance you got there, mate. Six to one, eh?'

'We're all just good friends.'

'Well, let me know if you need a hand.'

'You keep yer bleedin' 'ands to yerself, matey,' Lizzie calls out, turning on her grating Essex voice. 'Anyway, you look like a bleedin' Chelsea Pensioner in that gear.'

'All right, love. I know when I'm not wanted.'

The pub grows darker and nobody wants to break the spell by turning on the lights. They sit in the gathering shadows, warm and slightly drunk and talking amongst friends as the earth bowls unhurriedly away from the sun and the embrace of night approaches. To Richard, warm with the whisky, Lizzie at his side, everything seems clearer and more straightforward. Flick kisses Debbie full on the lips, tugging down Debbie's scarlet mini-skirt so that her startlingly white panties no longer show.

But then comes the time for dividing. Pete puts out his hand to Angela Cudmore but she pouts and refuses. Does she put out her tongue at him? Richard thinks she does, a wicked snakey dart, but maybe he is mistaken, as he is looking at Lizzie beside him. Her Egyptian eyes are brighter now. She threads her arm through his.

Pete, brazening out Angela's brush off, calls out,

'Now, girls, walkies.'

'What do you mean, Pete?' they chorus.

'A little walk up by Abbott's Hill, a quick snog if anyone's willing, and then back home. Everybody has to come.'

'We're coming,' Debbie and Flick call out.

'And me.'

'And me.'

'Well, I'm not going on any bloody walk,' Angela says darkly, tossing her curls and looking curmudgeonly.

There is a long pause during which everyone looks at Angela, and then at Pete.

Nobody has much clue what is in the mind of the pouting Angela at that moment. She's not a very communicative type and she hasn't really made any friends, so no one really knows what lies behind her placid milkmaid-complexioned face which only her violet eyes and copious skeins of wavy blonde hair enliven.

Some of the girls are thinking it's a pity because they like Pete and wouldn't mind a snog or heavy pet with him, or even going all the way, although they wouldn't let on about this. Others reckon Angela's in the right to keep Pete at bay, as he plainly only wants one thing. A third party see in

Angela the sly schemer out to net her man through snares of layered resistance.

As to what Angela herself thinks, like the Song the Sirens sang, it is not beyond all conjecture. She sums it up to herself in her plain country way. She actually doesn't much fancy Pete and she has a horror of his slick suburban ways. And for all that she might be bursting out of her bra and looks like she is really panting for it, she has her own position on all this question. She is going to keep herself nice for the farming man she is going to marry and who will be the father to her many babies.

'Oh, come on, Angie,' Pete says, and Angela's smooth cowgirl face tightens alarmingly. *Angie* she hates with a deep hatred. Her mother has named her for the angels, after all. Angie is *common*, and it sounds a little dirty.

'Yeah, come on, do yer good,' Lizzie says, hamming up the Essex. Richard, who she is keeping tightly linked at her side, can feel Lizzie's breast against his arm. It's like there's a pulse running between them.

'I won't.' The beleaguered Angela takes on a petulant and sulky look.

'Like heck you won't,' Pete says, although even he must know that this hectoring will not get him very far. 'Don't want to spoil the nice evening, do you, Angie.' He seizes Angela by the arm. She doesn't clobber him as Richard half-expects but lets herself be carried along by the group as they surge tipsily out of the pub. The lads at the next table applaud raucously. What Angela's attitude is at this stage is not very clear. She isn't exactly resisting but she is certainly not cooperating either.

The lights outside the pub cast a brassy glare on the night and a car races by much too fast. Pete leads off and in a minute he is squiring them into a narrow lane where the uncut hedgerows arch above them. The only light now is from the stars, which throng above their heads, although a pale light on the horizon promises the rising of the moon. *Shhh,* Pete says and they stop and listen. In the banks, small creatures are ferreting noisily about.

A vehicle can be heard ahead. Pete calls out *Single file* and everybody hugs the bank. Pete has released Angela and she can be dimly seen walking ahead of him. *Ow, there's stinging nettles,* squawks some weedy element. Richard is in front of Lizzie who gives him a pat on the bottom from time to time.

The noise of the vehicle grows louder, a grumbling unsure sound as though all the individual parts are finding it a struggle to line up their contributions. Flashes of light shoot into the lower sky as headlamps flutter up and down on the small hills and bumps of the lane. Anticipating, the nurses crush into the hedgerow, squealing at the brambles and nettles and putting the noses of the busy hedgelife creatures out of joint. And then the vehicle speeds around the corner in a blaze of blinding light.

Pete leaps to the front of the group, calling *Whoa up there,* and putting up his hand policeman-fashion. The vehicle, which practically fills the width of the lane, slows and stops and the lights dip. It is an old truck, dented and scarred, its engine sticking out like a giant dog's snout. Ranged in the cab a knot of youths can be seen, eagerly staring at the girls like Adam at the first woman.

The driver sticks his head out of the window. His uncombed mat of hair falls down like a dish mop.

''allo 'allo 'allo,' he says. 'What have we here? Out for a little bedtime walk, are we?'

Pete moves towards the lorry. It is a Bedford three tonner, in poor shape. No discriminating letter on the number plate to denote the year, Pete sees, so older than '62, quite a bit older in fact, by the looks of her. Pete stands in front of the lorry and calls out,

'It's you that needs to take a walk, mate. Move along now.'

The uncombed youth is still hanging out of the window.

'Temper, temper. Well, we're going into town, to the Pally. There's a dance on. Anybody coming, seeing as we've got room in the back and you've got a bit of spare there, mate?'

And all at once there is Angela running past Pete with surprising acceleration so that almost before he sees what is happening she is already slipping down the side of the truck. Two of the lads jump down from the cab and run round to help her up into the back of the lorry. They swing up behind her.

Pete starts to go after her but the lorry is already moving forward with a crash of unsynchromeshed gears and a throaty sound of protesting tappets.

Pete shouts 'Angie' but then he has to jump aside as the big truck starts to move towards him.

Toot, toot, pip pip, the lank-haired driver calls down as he steers past Pete, who is pressed against a very thorny bramble. The girls too all have to press against the bank as the truck moves slowly past them and then they stand in the road as it edges away and starts to accelerate. Through the cloud of exhaust, Angela can be clearly seen, as in a still from a romantic film, embracing a youth in a surprisingly poised and artful way.

And then suddenly Pete is running past them all, up behind the truck, shouting up to Angela. The girl pays not the slightest attention to him and continues with her clever tableau. The truck accelerates and begins to disappear around the bend. Pete runs on behind.

***

Lizzie lies on the warm ground, her limbs flicking as if an electrical current were passing through her.

'Tonic and clonic,' she says, her right forearm and her left calf jerking. She is showing Richard what Kevin's fits are like. To Richard, standing over her, she looks suddenly dear and vulnerable. He kneels down and darts in to try to kiss her. She clobbers him with a sudden convulsive movement of her arm.

'You're supposed to put me in the recovery position. Like this.'

She rolls on her side with her arm above her head. He lies down bedside her.

Snatches of song waft up. '... *Harry Hawk, Old Uncle Tom Cobleigh and all...*' Richard and Lizzie have fallen behind the gaggle which in the light of the now risen moon can still be seen below them, high-spiritedly making their way back down the grassy slopes of Abbot's Hill towards the squares of light in the House. Now Richard kisses Lizzie.

'Here? In the bleedin' open?'

'Well, no sound scruple forbids it...'

'*What*? What are you talkin' about, Richard?'

Rather than answer on this point, he thinks he'd better kiss her again. This seems to go well, and he slips his hand unopposed up her jersey.

This also seems to go well and so he begins moving his hands around experimentally.

'Richard...'

'Yes, Lizzie?'

'If we're going to do it, don't you think we should take off our clothes?'

'Errr...'

'You have to. It's not the same otherwise.'
'Alright.'

'Have you got a thingy?'
   'Ummm... what?'
   'Typical! You know...'
   'Oh... yes. Here.'
   'Lumme, let me see... where did you get *that*?'
   'My Dad's drawer, actually. Under his socks.'
   'When? Last century?'
   'Well, maybe... you know... they may not have done it in a while...'
   'Cor blimey. Well, go on then, pop it on.'
   'Errr...'
   'No, not like that. Like this.'
   'Ahhh...'
Lizzie does it with her deft nurse's hands and then lies back on the jewelled sward. The warm night air wafts its balm about their naked bodies. The risen moon shines on the girl's glistering breast and on her spangled hair.

   'That's it!' Richard cries, leaping into a brave new world.

   After a long uncertain pause, Lizzie says,

   'You can get off now, Richard.'

   He kneels beside her, conscious of her gaze upon him. Her Egyptian eyes are smudged and he kisses them both. He wants to worship her – or perhaps eat her up or lick her all over. He is surprised at how close sex feels to eating.

   He wonders now what words of love shall he and Lizzie speak.

   'Do you have another?' she asks him.

   'Another what?'

   'Another... thingy.'

   'Well... no.'

'Typical.'

'How do you mean?'

'Well... nice for you was it?'

'Errr... rather.'

'Rather?'

'Yes, rather nice.'

'But there's me too, yer know.' She is slipping into Essex. He wants to know why and when she does this. He wants to know everything.

'Well, yes, you were... in it too.'

'Typical. Come on, don't be a thicky, Richard. You know... a girl needs to... you need to...'

'... assure the woman's climax.'

'Yeah, well, you could put it like that.'

'You mean... we should do it again?'

'Rather. And a bit more... well... let me show you...'

'But... the thing...'

'Never mind about that now.'

I see them coming back across the park, my Lizzie and her Richard. I have my bed by the big window and each night I look out and see the creatures playing. And tonight, the best of nights, this young couple, best of creatures. How fine they look, strolling hand in hand through the silvered night, his jaunty stride, her swanky step.

How simple life can be, a boy and girl in love – and more. For love is present, yes, but also youth and folly and glorious risk and all the possible dazzling provinces and kingdoms shining with quivering light that are to come.

And yet. And yet.

Stupid stupid me. Oh Richard. Oh Lizzie. If only I...

I thrust away the thought. I force myself to smile my peaceful smile.

27

Coming in after midnight from the portico into the Great Hall by way of the high French doors, through which the full moon was shining its silver light, Richard (who had just made love to a girl for the first time in his life) and Lizzie (for whom this pleasant al fresco event didn't have quite the same *grande première* status but who was all the same very pleased with her evening) had hoped to escape any prying eye. Richard was prouder than at any time in his life, even prouder than at that moment of ecstasy when Ken Bell had announced his colours after the Donhead game. He wouldn't have minded the entire household being assembled to welcome them back in triumph, but he understood that some things are best kept quiet about, at least until he could let something drop at The Dog and hear Pete say, *You and Lizzie. You jammy little devil.*

But this discreet stratagem failed immediately when Richard fell over a body that was lying on the floor right inside the doors. The body was stretched out across the big black and white tiles like an Agatha Christie victim.

'Fuck,' Richard said, emboldened to say it out loud for the first time ever, while Lizzie more usefully dropped to her knees and held up the head of the person lying supine on the floor. In the light of the moon, she quickly identified this as the pretty stoat Dan, the gangling walking haemo guy. Dan, spotting through one half-open eye that it was Lizzie and thinking there was some chance of sympathy, started tuning up with a low moan and saying, *Me leg, me fucking leg.* Dan, like the other kids, felt no need of any special enfranchisement to say words like fuck.

Lizzie fussed suitably over Dan's leg. The boy, sensing that he was in a zone of sympathy, tuned up some more, letting out an agonizing howl.

Lights came on, and soon the entire household was gathered. The children assembled in their night things with pale faces, discussing Dan negligently. The reeking Bertie pushed in through the open French doors and licked the recumbent boy on the face. It was not at all the sort of triumphal gathering Richard had had in mind. He was a bit put out too that Lizzie was now cradling the Dan, who had always seemed to him rather an evil kid.

'Fuck you, Richard,' Kevin said, prodding at the whimpering Dan with his stick, 'you fuckin' killed him.'

But where was the Rat? She had, after all, agreed to take over night duty. Where was she indeed at this moment of high crisis? She was in fact slumbering in the over-heated staffroom, where she had dozed off while watching *Crossroads*.

It was only because everybody was out that Ratcliffe's stern conscience had slipped into a temporary remission and another, more lenient department had taken over. This more accommodating segment was one that apparently admitted guilty, trashy pleasures like watching commercial television, even *Crossroads*.

Dan, prowling about, had spotted Helen crying in the Sluice. She had gone there to wash out the bright red briefs that were her pride, and to weep over the end of her affair with Richard. She had seen Lizzie linking her arm through his and she had known at once that all was over. How could she compare with Lizzie?

All the other children bar one had been asleep. Only King

Patch was awake. Only he saw Dan creeping out.

In a minute, Helen was fleeing down the corridor. Her hand-me-down winceyette nightgown was ripped at the shoulder and she was gripping the torn cloth in her fist. Behind her ran Dan, panting.

Helen careered round the corner into the Great Hall, heading for the safety of her dorm. Dan, following, pulled up abruptly as Mick's great bulk heaved out of the boys' dormitory and filled the corridor. Unusually, Mick was on crutches. He kept them by the bed and they had been the quickest way to carry out Patch's urgent instruction to *Wake up. Follow that fucker Dan.*

Later, while the Ratcliffe dozed on in front of commercial TV – she slept through *Criss-Cross Quiz*, and then *Emergency Ward 10* – Patch consulted his Trojans. Helen, it had been ascertained by an embassy to the girls' side, was asleep, curled up in Gloriana's bed, her body fitted round Gloriana's like a spoon. Dan was now on his knees on the floor by Patch's bed. Mick was in his chair. He was leaning forward, his beefy right arm round the throat of the frightened Dan. Patch conducted the interrogation from his bed. His plump red face looked very grim and fiery against the white pillows. In his high voice, he asked,

'What the fuck, Dan?'

'I didn't mean nothing, Patch. Honest.'

'Ha. Han't I told you to leave them girls alone.'

'I did. I do.'

'If you want to fuck someone, you can fuck that tit Jane Ratcliffe. She needs a good seeing-to.'

'I never touched Helen.'

'Liar!'

'She was… you know how she… you know…'

'You little prick. You blamin' that poor girl?'

'I'm sorry, Patch. I'm really really sorry. Please don't do anything.'

Patch, whose face seemed to have swollen to gigantic wrathful proportions, motioned to Mick who adroitly bent his ear to the bulky king whilst keeping a tight grip on the neck of Dan. That unfortunate, bent double, his brow touching the floor, was now letting out low dismal moans. As Mick swivelled to hear Patch, he must have tightened the screw a bit on his prisoner as an unhealthy cracking sound came from Dan's neck and the boy's mouth dropped open.

''ere, careful Mick, don't want to top him – yet.'

Mick eased his grip a fraction. In the gloomy light Dan's face had acquired a more gashly paleness.

'You look like sick, Dan,' Patch commented. He whispered something into Mick's ear and then pronounced his judgement.

'I told you a thousand times, Dan, no muckin' about wiv the girls. Now you had a go at poor Helen, and you know she's a kid who's not quite wiv it an' vulnerable an' all. We Trojans respect our women. That's a evil thing you done. So...'

Dan moaned. The Trojans craned forward to hear his sentence.

'If you won't stay away from the girls, I'll have to make you stay away, won't I?'

'No, Patch, no.'

'Oh, take the fucker away, Mick. Just do it.'

Out in the Great Hall, by the French doors, stood Dan, trembling. Mick, who was soft-hearted, nonetheless muttered *E-i-addio* and gave him a kick Hurst would have been proud of. With luck, the little stoat would avoid hospital. A couple of months of bed rest should see him right.

28

Do you think I am lying here this morning waiting for Lizzie (who is late late late) and dreaming pastoral love, Richard on pipes and spouting eclogues and Lizzie in scanty kit beside the brook coyly ranged for love beneath a bending willow?

Pah! Fat chance. This is such a catastrophe. Ructions in the night. Ag-ag-aieee!

Patch is here. He's in a real state. He's quite laconic but he's watching me closely for my views.

'If this gets out,' he says, 'they'll send Helen to the Bin straight off. Sexually precocious an' that. They'll dose her up. It'll be curtains on her life. An' Mick, if they get to know it's him that did it, it's Young Offenders at the least, maybe even Borstal. So…' – Patch's face has that flat emotionless look it takes on when he's thinking and then he goes on,

'I gotta manage this. Keep the Stoat quiet. Keep Helen safe. 'n keep all you lot out of the Bin.'

I give him my wondering, admiring, assenting look.

'Erm…' he says, '… erm… can Helen go on bunking in with you for now?'

I sign to him Yes! Yes!

He grimaces, which with him is an acknowledgement of my support, and then he buzzes off without a word. I mean, would a king say Thank you?

I know he's made up his mind what to do. But can he do it, our Trojan king?

Richard is late for breakfast, of course. The nurses all stare at him.

'Do you notice any changes about Richard?' Debbie asks, peering at him.

'Yes, I think he may have dried behind his ears this morning,' says Flick.

'He does look different somehow. Sort of knowing, if you see what I mean,' Debbie goes on. 'When are you getting married, Richard?'

'Can I be flower girl?' Flick asks.

'Matron of honour, more like,' says Debbie.

Richard flees. He has no appetite anyway.

In the Great Hall he encounters Mick who is staring morosely at the piano keys. Richard sits down on the long piano stool.

'*Heart and Soul*?'

'Sod off,' Mick says.

A sudden tingling memory of Lizzie's soft flesh pressed against his strikes Richard and he lets out a small involuntary moan.

'Fuck off will you, mate,' Mick says and wheels briskly away.

But where is she? The eager boy runs to his lover's room, but she is not there. Not quite clean sheets lie in a heap on the narrow bed. An unappealing grey teddy bear, short of one of its black button eyes, lies on the floor like the victim of a natural disaster. Its pelt is rubbed bare and black on its chest through somebody's childish clutchings – presumably Lizzie's, although the thing has the moth-eaten antiqued look of something her granny might have clutched in the Victorian era. He gives the thing a kick to knock out any remaining sentimental power. Lizzie shouldn't be cuddling teddy bears, she should be cuddling him.

He bends over the chest of drawers, scanning for something of his lover amongst the random pots and tubes of obscure feminine application scattered there but they remain obstinately unreadable.

Suddenly, Debbie is at the door, shaking her head like a dratted auntie, and Richard snaps up to his full height. Debbie is back in her big comfortable pink pants. She has a superior-looking grin on her handsome face. She starts shaking her head in very small but knowing motions, as if she has understood the secrets of Richard's heart and perhaps found them not very special after all.

'Lizzie stepped out,' she informs him blankly.

'Where…?'

'Dunno. Don't ask.'

Richard thinks that if Debbie is going to go on like an aunt, she might at least be a useful one, like a whatsit, a duenna. But Debbie just smiles an irritating smile in such a superior way that Richard takes it almost for a sneer and no longer feels friendly to the girl. He pushes out past her.

Back in his room he quickly writes a note, does a calculation, alters the note – scratching out **one gross** and writing in **two dozen** above it, then he scratches that out and writes **one gross** again – makes out a cheque for One pound five and six, addresses the rather hairy buff envelope which he considers appropriate for this communication, sticks on a twopenny halfpenny stamp, and rushes off down towards the school where he is overdue and the class is probably rioting. On the way he drops the stamped and addressed envelope on the marble-topped table in the hall.

Patch gets to the stricken pretty boy Dan well before the Ratcliffe and it turns out not too bad. Dan after all knows the Trojan code and observes the Iron Law – *Don't tell.* So when Miss Ratcliffe interviews him, he lets it be known that his leg, which swelled in the night to the dimensions of a small tree trunk, has been 'done for' by somebody or some-bodies. But he 'ain't tellin' who.'

Miss Ratcliffe has been caught on the back foot. She had woken in the stuffy staffroom aware that somewhere in the House all was not quite well. She had quickly snapped off the television and, peering out, had seen the gathering in the Great Hall – the injured Dan, the chattering children, that stinking mongrel, Richard looking too perky for words, Elizabeth bowed over the groaning boy.

She has already been sensing her power guttering away and she is not at all prepared for a crisis. Ill-advisedly (but no one was giving her any advice anyway), she decides to Make a Stand. At mid-morning break, a House meeting is announced for after tea. All are summoned to the Great Hall, all sixty of the children, all twenty of the nurses, the teachers, Pete, Richard.

As the Great Hall fills up, Richard starts to edge along in a manoeuvre designed to get him across to where Lizzie and Debbie have appeared, steering Gloriana's massive bed. Lizzie is evidently back from wherever she 'stepped out' to. Richard hasn't seen her all day, in fact not since they stum-bled over the inconvenient Dan. But Lizzie is making a great show of helping Debbie to get Gloriana's bed into a position where the girl can see proceedings. As she heaves the bed around, she glances at Richard and ghosts him a pretty smile, but then she flicks her hand, which he takes to mean *Stay where you are.*

The Ratcliffe's speech proves brief but memorable.

'I want to know,' she says in a gloomy, hopeless tone, pushing with her forefinger at her heavy spectacles which forever threaten to slide down her shiny nose, 'who kicked Dan, and why. No need to say anything now. I want to see each of you one by one in my office afterwards.'

Richard is focusing on Lizzie, trying to get her to look at him again. She is leaning against Gloriana's bed, whispering to the girl, laughing about some feminine solidarity thing, or pretending to. Then she stands up and yawns, not covering her mouth. Richard's whole being leaps towards her, even though today, objectively, he admits to himself she is looking rather used up and super pallid, almost plain really.

Richard's encounter last night has created vast new perspectives, and he is desperately keen to fill those perspectives with as many repetitions as is conceivably possible – starting now, today. He signals to Lizzie again, waving his hand. Surely his wild yearning will hook a response from her. But she is always obtusely looking elsewhere, even down at her feet or talking to Gloriana, and his little semaphores seem to go unremarked. He feels a twang of terror. Is she ignoring him?

Standing beside Richard and looking at him with a leery eye, Pete suddenly administers a swift kick to Richard's calf.

'Come off it, mate,' Pete mutters, and Richard becomes aware that he has sighed out loud. And did he imagine it or have his hips been gently undulating?

Meanwhile the Ratcliffe has progressed to her peroration.

'If,' she says, and here her hand creeps nervily to the huge safety pin that keeps her plaid skirt together, 'if no child has told me the truth by six o'clock tonight, then...'

Clearly the Ratcliffe has been trained in the classical school, because here she pauses before delivering her damning apodosis.

'… then – *all swimming will be cancelled until further notice.*'

The Ratcliffe's pronouncement falls on the children like a sudden fog.

Into the shocked silence, one high, firm, discerning voice of protest drops like a pebble in a well.

'That's not ruddy fair,' says Patch.

Patch's intervention seems to provoke the Ratcliffe to yet more strenuous injustice. She cries,

'And I saw that filthy mongrel in here last night…'

Did she? Where *was* she exactly last night? How come the Dan thing happened on her watch? But nobody dares to ask.

Miss Ratcliffe fixes Pete with an imperative eye.

'Kindly run the creature down to the vet straight away.'

'Why? I mean, he isn't sick or anything, is he?'

'Have it put down. It's a hazard to the children's health.'

The children cry out, but the Ratcliffe turns harshly on her heel and strides away.

***

Pete runs the big blue bus round to the gravelled yard and lets down the ramp. Angela Cudmore brings Bertie out, drawing him by the collar. The children are all watching from the windows of the Great Hall. The dog digs in, resisting, you can see the muscles tensed beneath his greasy coat.

Angela, the country girl, does not brook stubborn animals. She drags the dog through the thick gravel and up the ramp. Bertie's eyes bulge and show all white. Pete then takes him by the collar and heaves him in. Pete and Angela exchange a glance of which the tone and meaning are unclear.

Pete closes up the ramp and moves forward to start up the bus. Bertie's head appears at a window. He presses his doleful muzzle against the glass, making a gummy patch.

The big bus moves off, scrunching through the gravel. The children turn away in disbelief.

29

Parcel for you, Richard.'
'Yes, brown paper and sellotape.'
'No return address.'
'Very discreet. Very tactful.'
'It's in the hall.'
'Not a very big parcel.'
'Will it be enough?'
'Too much, the way it's going.'

Richard left his breakfast egg, which he had been enjoying till then, and got up.

In the hall, Patch and Mick were positioned next to the marble topped table. The post was piled on a brass dish.

'Letter for Mr. MacAskill,' Patch said in his annoying high-pitched voice. 'That'll be about the divorce. Letter for Helen from the Mario Lanza fan club. A bill for the Ratcliffe. Stamp approvals for me, lovely...'

Patch was silent a moment and then his piggy eyes swivelled to Richard and back to the brass dish.

'Oh... and a brown paper parcel for... ahh...'

Patch affected to peer at the name and address, which was written in a sloppy hand and with two misspellings in the address.

'Good job it got here.' Patch commented.

'Buy me and stop one,' Mick said.

In his room, Richard opened the package carefully on his bed, slicing through the sellotape with his nail scissors and unfolding the brown paper until the package lay open like a flower. He flipped back the top of the carton and there they lay – one gross, exactly as ordered.

He picked one up and ran his finger over the cool smooth surface of the shiny packet, feeling the ribbed circumference within. He was tempted to open it and have a look, but he was afraid the erotic charge might seep away.

He closed the carton and slipped it into his drawer, under the socks. He felt excited. He'd gone one better than his Dad. Because these were gossamer. This was 1966.

Of course, the Rat's no-swim threat kicks in. No one would break the Trojans' Iron Law. No one would run to Ratcliffe telling tales. We would have become a tribe without honour. But the punishment is heavy indeed. The Rat is soon spotted striding down to see Miss Payne, the echoes of a brief, high temperature exchange reverberate around the House, and when the Rat clacks back up, slightly flushed, the deed is sealed. The pool which floats away our cares and limits is closed forthwith, without the slightest ceremony.

It only takes a day and then you can see the Trojans' spirit wilting visibly. The piano falls silent. Nobody dips, no game is played. The children mope and talk in undertones. Even Kevin's famous rage damps down and he sits morosely on the horsehair sofa picking out the stuffing, his sticks thrown down.

Our king has to act and pretty quick. After tea one evening he summons us all to a Trojan assembly in the Great Hall.

'Lean me back, Debbie,' he says in his commanding way, and dear Debbie helps him back from the stick of his gleaming Armsworth 302 and sets him carefully against the cushion in the rear of the seat behind him. His head lolls slightly to one side. Debbie asks,

'Shall I move you out of the sun, Patch?' but he shakes

his head a fraction.

'Nah, fanks, Deb. I need the sun.'

Patterns of evening sunshine slope on the floor around him and splash gold across his assembled Trojans. Debbie wipes a little something from his nose and excuses herself. Patch's keen eye follows her out of the Hall. It's her big pink elasticated pants he's noticing, I just know it is. And sure enough he says,

'Good girl, that. Looks after me. I keep meaning to tell her about them romper pants. Don't half make her bum look big.'

He chuckles. I suppose he thinks kingly figures such as he can pass comments on girls' bums. It's like his own harem rule.

But I'm sorry, Patch, you can't. In another life I'll tell you, and I'll tell you why. But for now, we have bigger complications, so let's get on with it.

Patch faces his Trojans. He looks massive, red, the picture of Oriental power.

'So,' he says, 'Mick, after the meeting you go and check on Pretty Boy in the San. Make sure he'll go on keeping 'is gob buttoned. If not, you know what to do. And now, Ratcliffe…'

All eyes are on Patch, expectations are high that he's going to deal the Ratcliffe a knock-out blow. After all, the woman has struck out most cruelly – and a double blow. It is true, Bertie was disgustingly smelly, he was old, decrepit and a nest of fleas – but also he was a trusting, living creature and the loyallest dog in the world – inconvenient but family. In our view, you don't run family down to the vet.

And with that swimming ban, by chance or, worse still, design, the Ratcliffe's hit spot-on the one thing that gives us all delight, the thing I always say that makes us the *unbound, unbounded beings that were intended all along.*

Patch glances about him. The sun has now moved around some tiny fraction and plays around his head in a radiant halo. It's like a stage set or a film – even the sun seems to be playing a role, like it's enduing Patch with power. I look at the faces of the Trojans. They are staring rapt at Patch. They can feel this charge gathering about him.

He has decided on his course of action. He has reviewed relevant precedent, he has consulted, he has ranked the options. The trick is, he says, to find the enemy's weakest spot and attack.

The sinking sun is spilling all around. Patch now assembles his words and begins to set out before the Trojans his stratagem.

'You see,' he says, 'I seen in the *Daily Express* 'bout the London dock strikes, what they done... withdraw their labour an' that...'

Then he says simply,

'So... we won't go to church no more.'

Wow! I have to say that this idea does seem pretty enormous, and everybody there is looking at Patch like he's some sort of genius.

'You see,' he goes on, 'it's fair-dos, it's like... proportional. She's cancelled what we like, so we'll cancel what **she** likes.'

And in doing this, of course, Patch menaces the Ratcliffe's authority at its weakest point: the way she's bullying the frail kids, especially Patch and the short-perspective Trojan elders whose days are already racing to their close.

And above all, it's something we can actually do. Yes, we can definitely not go to church. No way can the Ratcliffe make us go to church.

Or so we think.

After the meeting, Mick and Patch come to see me and show me the letter that came from dear Robbie this morning.

> Binstead Village
> Surrey-on-the-Styx
> Hell

Day 29 of the 12,410 days I am now certain to spend in The Bin

Dear Gloriana, dear Patch,

I wrote four days go about the debacle at Norma's Review Board. It was bad but the aftermath was worse. When she got out of Specials yesterday, she'd turned a bit crazy. She chucked her lunch on the floor and smashed her plate. In the afternoon, she attacked Mr. Salter as he was walking along the corridor, gave him quite a nasty scratch on his sallow cheek. They put her in the Slammer after that. That, for your information, is about three notches up from Specials. In the Slammer, they use the straitjacket. Big Bev had to do it, strap her up. Now they're just shoving her food in. Big Bev told me Norma only has one way to express herself now and that's not in the bucket provided for the purpose.

Poor Norma. Her spirit is at war with itself. She hates to be here. She fears the idea of not being here. It is because she has been taught to hate herself. That's the wickedness.

I sped round to Salter's to protest. There in the outer office, like a cooling stream to a panting hart, was Dawn, her beehive piled high, her lips and finger nails a beautiful pale lavender shade.

I didn't say anything but just burst into Salter's sanc-
tum. He said,

'Willis, this is entirely your meddling fault. You have
landed that dimwit in the shit and now she's covered in
it.'

Oh, God! Is he right? Have I done the wrong thing?

I scooted out of Salter's office as quick as I could.

'Robbie, hang on a mo,' Dawn said.

I let my eye rest on her. I needed some beauty at that
moment. She swivelled in her chair and faced me.

'Look, Robbie,' she said, 'just take a look at this.'

And she showed me a letter. An extraordinary letter
about Norma. From her daughter.

Your friend in despair and a glimmer of hope.

Robert *De Profundis* Willis

30

R ichard's amorous adventure may have been all very well for him, but he's finding his stock as teacher and guide and friend of us children on the slide. Patch is incredibly cross with him and keeps calling him a 'useless git', especially after Richard finally reads out to Patch the play he's written, *The Triumph of the Trojans*. At first, Patch nods thoughtfully and says 'Yeah, OK. Good title, mate'.

Patch likes the theme of Helen escaping from a loveless marriage and he admires how Priam and his sons defend the pretty girl against the sleazy Greeks.

'S'good,' he mutters when Richard reads out how the Trojans trounce the Greeks, after twigging that patently obvious wooden horse stunt. Priam's ten burly sons simply shove the thing back into the Greek lines whilst keeping up a stream of ribald commentary about Achilles' doubtful parentage and the size of Odysseus' private parts. Patch loves all the post-War settlement – the Baby Boom, the free orange juice and cod liver oil and the bottles of free milk each day for the little kids, the magnificent theatre that adorns the centre of Troy where compelling Trojan dramas and comedies are played every day and where on a nightly basis recitations of the brilliant new epic poem *The Myceniad* are given by a blind bard with the most incredible memory. Not to mention the public libraries full of scrolls of Trojan history and philosophy, the free education for all up to the age of twenty-five…

It's only at the end of Act Three that Patch starts to look

uneasy. There is a scene where Priam decides it's time to scale down the Trojan Empire. A few of the more advanced of the Black Sea colonies like Trebizond and Colchis get Home Rule. It is probably a mistake of Richard's to let the colonists, who are a rough lot on the whole, issue their own stamps without the head of King Priam on.

'Pfoo,' Patch says.

Richard reads on. It's when he starts on Act Four that Patch's colour rises and his eyes shrink to menacing little dots.

'Right!' he says in his piping voice, 'Right! Stop right there!'

Richard pauses and looks up anxiously.

'You stupid git,' Patch says. 'Woss that rubbish? Hector's son, wossname, Astyanax, says to his gaffer Priam *You can bag the whole deal, man, we're gonna split and head out for Djerba*! Come off it.'

So it's back to the drawing board for old Richard.

That day, Mr. MacAskill doesn't turn up for class **again**. That's the third time in a week and it's only Wednesday. So Richard has to improvise as usual but he can't get the telly going, and there is a fretful feeling going round which means he has trouble keeping the class quiet. So he starts scanning the Francis Chichester map. Apparently the master mariner has got to the Sandwich Islands, but Richard can't find them on the map and Patch, who certainly knows, is not helping.

Mick is bored and he calls out,

'Have you heard the good news about Francis Chichester?'

'No,' everybody choruses. We are all expecting a good joke.

'He's been drowned. Have you heard the bad news?'

'No.'

'We're following the body home on the map.'

Everybody laughs. Except Patch, of course, who buzzes his Armsworth 302 up next to Mick.

'Shut your bleedin' cakehole, Mick. Don't talk about Francis Chichester like that.'

Mick scowls but takes it on the chin. Patch is the king, after all.

'Don't forget, Mick, that 'e's a Plymouth boy like meself.'

'Oh, get the fuckin' telly workin', Richard,' Kevin calls out gruffly.

We watch as Richard kneels like a votary before the set and starts to adjust things. Actually, it needs a space engineer to figure out how the thing works anyway. The dials and knobs on the front give little away. For some reason you turn a knob to 9 for BBC and to 10 for ITV, presumably slots 1 to 8 have been left vacant for some unimaginably far-off future when another eight channels might be added, but why on earth would you want so many? This is just one of the very many obscure technological puzzles of the TV.

Anyway, Richard now clicks the set on, fiddles again with the dials and knobs, the valves at the back light up encouragingly, and after a couple of minutes a rather fuzzy picture forms on the screen. It actually does turn out to be school television, which is fine by me – I'm learning loads. Today, it's a very neat film about Greek peasants in Kalamata in the Peloponnese who seem to subsist entirely on soft fruits – olives and grapes and tomatoes.

Towards the end of the film, just as the industrious peasantry are preparing to consume the lion's share of the fruits of their labours in a massive post-harvest knees-up, for which they are donning frocks (both men and women, it seems, the men in minis and the ladies in the new maxis, ankle-length affairs), Mr. MacAskill wanders in. This breaks the mood. His face looks quite blotchy and highly coloured in a palette of reds and purples and altogether he looks the worse for wear. He sits down heavily just behind me, at Helen's empty desk. There is an atmosphere about him.

We try to recover our mood and the film ends happily, with the Kalamata peasantry tucking up for the winter, the olive oil and wine that are to see them through the lean season all nicely stored away in massive earthenware flasks.

But then quite against the spirit of the thing, Mr. MacAskill starts making sarky comments.

'They have gone down, those Greeks, I mean since Homer and so on. Must be all that soft fruit, frightfully bad for the bowels.'

Mr. MacAskill then gets up and comes to the front. He looks very miserable, I must say. These days his personality seems to be a real problem to him, he's so morose and un-believing and self-regarding, so loveless, really. It's a shame. Anyway, he now announces that he is going to take Poetry. Uh-oh.

Last time he was actually here, sometime last week I think it was, he set us to learn a few lines from *The Lady of Shalott*, which was OK. I could get quite fond of Tennyson, I suspect.

Patch goes first in his piping voice.

> *'On either side of the river lie,*
> *Fields of barley and of rye'*

But then Mr. MacAskill calls on Mick. Big mistake. I think since his World Cup glory Mick has been living in the clouds. He just goes down and talks to his lovely birds and goes over The Game with them. Again and again, they must know The Game off by heart, shot by fulminating shot. I bet if there's a talking one amongst the birds it can say *Nobby Stiles* by now. Anyway... of course Mick has not learned his lines, so he recites the only rhyme other than *E-i-addio* that he has in his head at present which goes,

> *'My friend Billy had a ten-foot willy*
> *He showed it to the girl next door*
> *She thought it was a snake and hit it with a rake*
> *And now it's only five foot four!'*

During this performance, a disturbing change comes over Mr. MacAskill. The colouring of his face turns incredibly bright and sort of livid, and his whole body begins to quiver. His mouth opens very wide, he is really gaping, and out comes a strange cry, a sort of Aaaaaaaaaaaaaaa, like an animal in the night. He begins pacing wildly up and down, waving his arms. This fury gets him in its grip, but it is not nice, it's sort of ugly and empty and it goes on for ages. It does include some more entertaining sections such as hurling of chalk and books and a few other things that come to hand, and there is even a bit of dodgy rocking of the telly. 'Careful!' Richard cries out, 'It's rented!' and this logic does seem to get through to Mr. MacAskill because he then switches to some less risky but even more theatrical stamping up and down and gripping of the fists, all of this with a horrid contorted face.

At last he seems to run out of steam. His colouring goes down by a few shades, his pacing gets slower, his whole body quietens down. He then starts to mumble, he seems to be conducting a conversation with himself, but rather indistinctly. You can just catch snatches which are kind of remote and a bit frightening, like ... *if existence has ceased to retain significance... confronted with the fragmented and meaningless reality of the human condition... what then should prevent... suicide...*

It is at this point that Patch finally takes control. He beckons to Richard.

'C'm here, mate.' Richard slips over to where Patch's Armstead 302 is parked.

'Get 'im out of here. This is not right for the kids...'

But in fact it doesn't come to that as Mr. MacAskill is already heading for the door.

'Take over, Richard', he mutters and stumps out.

Richard was hoping to see Lizzie at lunch and as he wandered up to the staff dining room, there she was. He spotted her through the windows of the children's cafeteria. She was feeding a little kid. Something about her shoulders told him she knew he was there, but she didn't look up.

Mr. MacAskill did not come to lunch. Richard poked listlessly at the tripes and cabbage which Helen had shoved at him through the hatch. What *had* happened to her cooking? Then Mick's chair nosed around the door of the dining room and he said, 'Richard, you'd better come.'

Down at the stables, Mr. MacAskill is sitting in the corner of the bird cage. The affronted birds have all migrated to the other end, although not before depositing something sticky-looking and white on Mr. MacAskill's shoulder. The birds are now sitting in a row, solid in the face of this violation, stonily regarding Mr. MacAskill's slumped form.

'I don't know what happened to me,' Mr. MacAskill says as Richard settles down beside him. 'I feel quite worn out.' Mick makes himself scarce.

But Joe MacAskill does know in his heart what has happened to him. His whole life has been razed to nothing by shame, by the shame of what he did, and now he is condemned to live in the cracks, unregarded and prone to frenzies. Every memory seems to be a focus of regret for his one calamitous choice.

The girl. The girl dusky and erotic, there on the ground, on the grubby mat, coupling doggy fashion.

The light snaps on. Margot staring at the dirty pair as the filthy type thunderously ejaculates into the brown native girl.

About five minutes did it, bar some earlier discussion, five minutes in which his life exploded beyond repair.

Every minute of every day, this picture floats before his mind. The memory doesn't even knock but just strolls in and takes up residence.

Rushing out of the class that morning, MacAskill had run down to the stables, to the birds, where waves of horror and sadness felled him. Now he slumps there, a shrunken, dejected man, with no truth or hope left in him.

For a reason he cannot understand, Joe MacAskill now spills his story to Richard. Richard doesn't say anything and MacAskill realizes too late that the raw boy can have no understanding of such a thing or its consequences, of how one disastrous choice can change everything, not only the future but the past, of how Joe's entire history has had to be rewritten or rather blotted out. Everything now pivoted around that one hideous event, all the other events of his life were now doing a spectral dance around that one central fact.

'Margot loved turacos,' he said absent-mindedly, and Richard looked politely questioning.

Joe longed to conjure up the memory of Margot as she

was soon after she came out to him in Africa. He let the picture of her then breathe through his mind, her sun-burned legs in her white pleated tennis skirt as she ran in from the court to embrace him and he smelled the sweat and the last lingering fragrance from the scent she had smoothed on her breast with a light motion of her hand as she dressed for the game. Or at least this is what Joe tells himself.

Maybe it was the place, he thought, that fag-end of Empire place. It was the tyranny of the specific. Too much old worn-out story there, our hands dirty from too many old crimes. *The colonists not only mystify the natives, they mystify themselves.* We lost the sense of wholeness in which it might all have made sense. We lost that sense of continuity that would have allowed us to clutch at our own identity.

The funny thing was, coming back to Blighty, he just couldn't get used to the white faces of the children. He longed for black faces, exuberant black faces, the intense velvety black of the children's bodies, such a restful colour. He dreamed all the time now of black, of the comfortable black he had in mind, a black so black it absorbed all light, and there was no evidence of an intruding sun anywhere. The only place you could ever be truly alone and at peace...

Richard, coupied down beside old MacAskill, was wondering what to do. How could his rapturous surging youth speak to such disappointment? What solicitude could help this melancholy, begging figure?

MacAskill himself was exhausted by the staying power of his misery. Already he regretted confessing the trials of his life to Richard, as though a boy could somehow bring him benediction. All his life now was clustered around that one great crime, five minutes wantoning with the native girl.

And all such unsmiling absorption in his own great fat

self. What of Margot, what of her hurts? And the native girl – what had been her name even? – what about her hurts, her dignity?

Memory! The light had snapped on, and now he could never be free of its glare. His life would draw out until he joined the prostate-dead, the mindless, memory-less guys, fading and fading until life just stopped. Maybe he should just do away with himself, right now, on the spot.

'Mr. MacAskill, Richard, look, I brought you a nice cuppa.'

And there was Lizzie, full of beans, bearing a tray of tea before her, her pallid face bending over Mr. MacAskill as she helped him up out of the straw.

'Eaugh,' she tutted, rubbing the bird shit off Mr. MacAskill's jacket with a grubby handkerchief. 'Now, what have you two been talking about?'

31

Joe MacAskill went down to the doctor in the village and got a range of pills, some to soothe him, some to knock him out at night. They appear to do the trick as the next day, he actually turns up at school and he stays eerily calm in class.

Miss Payne the swimming teacher pops her head round the classroom door and says A word, Mr. MacAskill, a word. And gloomy doomed Mr. MacAskill files out and can be seen by the children through the glass light in the door locked in brief conclave with Miss Payne, shaking the head, then straining the ear, then finally nodding. It seems that Miss Payne has set aside memories of their catastrophic date and is advising Mr. MacAskill professionally. He comes back in and announces to the children,

'Swimming this afternoon. Miss Payne tells me that swimming is vital to your physical and mental health.'

A cheer goes up. Mick asks,

'What about Miss Ratcliffe?'

'She is off today, I believe, visiting her mother.'

'But she said…'

'I don't give a damn what Miss Ratcliffe said.'

'Cor!' Patch comments admiringly.

Richard goes to help with the swimming. He hopes Lizzie will be there, which is quite likely, as she is a good swimmer and often helps. He is desperate to speak to her. He hasn't really spoken to her since The Night, which is already interminable days ago.

At first, everything had been altered forever, or so he had thought. He had felt a cool and erotic touch in even the most trivial tasks of his day. But now Lizzie, skipping past him in the corridor with a smile or a nod or Lizzie briefly waving from the girls' dorm as she changed a bag or most of all Lizzie absent all the time – from lunch, from tea, from her room even – this is taking it out of him.

However, Lizzie doesn't come to swimming. Debbie is there, but although Debbie's embonpoint is impressive in a pretty rainbow-striped costume, this is not what Richard is after.

Nearly at the end of swimming, there is a gurgling sound from the filter and some murky-looking stuff washes back into the pool. Miss Payne orders everybody out and asks Richard to fix it and then thinks better of it and tells him to get Pete, but Pete is off, so she says to get John Fry at Home Farm, he is good with machinery.

John Fry lives in a brick and flint cottage down past the stables. His door is locked but from inside Fry can easily hear Richard's steps approaching up the gravel path and then the polite knock on the door, and then the pause, and then the louder knock, and a further scrunching on the path as Richard moves back to scan the windows, noticing that the curtains on one upstairs window are drawn to. John Fry correctly believes that Richard will tut tut that the curtains were not drawn back this morning, because a lad raised in the town where neighbours have more eyes than Argus and every twitch of a curtain is parsed would never believe that a man would draw the curtains in the afternoon and go to bed with his girlfriend.

For in bed with his girlfriend is where John Fry is, and sadly for Richard the girlfriend is Lizzie, and at the exact moment when Richard is knocking at the door, the lovers are in fact making love.

At another time Lizzie might have felt the stirrings of conflict in her soft breast but there is no stopping John Fry and, while Richard is scrunching around, the girl gives way to her nature.

John Fry has been Lizzie's secret lover for seven months now. Secrecy has been essential as John Fry has a wife and two children, and the secrecy has in fact turned out to add an adventurous edge to their affair and even a certain piquancy to their love making.

Fry is a handsome fellow (in Lizzie's view) of twenty-eight with a long flop of shiny jet-black hair that he constantly sweeps back. He is clean-shaven but his beard shoots out by noon each day. Lizzie complains of the roughness. Occasionally he shaves again before they meet – usually they have sex in the barn down by the home field, although today they are taking advantage of Fry's wife absence, out visiting with the children – but when he doesn't shave again, he shuts her up by saying that it is the sex makes it start out like that. His chest has prominent sculpted pectorals and a mat of straight black hair which tapers to a single line of fuzz running all the way to the thicket at his crotch. His limbs are large and startlingly white and hairless. They look soft but Lizzie knows there is steel inside.

He is Lizzie's third lover and much her best so far. Not that John Fry does anything much different, positions or anything, but he is so hard and big and she lies pinned down by his power as though in a trance.

John comes off her now and she rolls towards the window. Richard has long since scrunched away – a minute ago, five minutes, half an hour, she has no clear idea. She feels sorry. He is a pest, but a very sweet one.

'Your lover called,' John Fry says. She had mentioned

that night to him. He had asked her how it was and she had said that word 'Sweet', at which John Fry had laughed a lot and given her a glass of the rough-edged potato wine he fermented in the bath.

'So what now, Liz? Swap a man for a boy? Or you like it too much for that.'

'Dunno,' Lizzie mutters absently.

Richard still comes to read with me and talk about my set books but now he reads in a mechanical-sounding voice, and today he says,

'University without A Levels, I dunno…'

Richard, gloomy. Too gloomy. Instead of this gloomy stuff we need answers to all our questions. We need solutions to all our difficulties. We need more love (and less complicated love).

Because this is getting out of hand. Now we need solutions not just for Helen and Mick and Greg and me, but for Mr. MacAskill too. And now for Richard and for Lizzie too, I suppose.

Help! Difficulties are multiplying, solutions are absent. Come on, Richard! Just two weeks until the end of term, and still NOTHING HAS BEEN DECIDED. Our world is upside down.

Yet, according to one of Richard's poems, first came Chaos, and then divinely-ordered Cosmos.

So maybe Richard's not to be our redeemer. Maybe our futures are being formed somewhere in this turmoil. Maybe Chaos has its uses.

But hurry up, Chaos! Come on, Cosmos! The end of term is rushing upon us. Salter looms. He's readying the Bin.

***

And with all these troubles swirling around us, no one has had the sense to **cancel the Annual Theatre Trip**.

Ye gods, as if we didn't have enough trouble on our plates. Every year the Trip is a fiasco, except last year when it was a disaster. We are always put on Best Behaviour and so naturally we behave very badly indeed. Last year, in the middle of the deathbed scene, Mick shouted out *Oh get on with it* and Kevin took his sticks and set about an elderly lady who made the big mistake of trying to befriend him.

So please Ratcliffe, cancel. Please please Mr. MacAskill, call it off. Summon what dregs of common sense remain and CALL IT OFF!

Later I am looking through my window, a little disconsolate and puzzled about where all this is going, and I spot Angela wheeling Greg across the stone flags. Angela, that generally lethargic girl, is talking in a spirited way, and as she comes to a halt Greg slowly draws a paper from his pocket. Angela stops and reads the paper. Then Pete appears carrying a bag and he and Angela chat for a moment. Pete gives the bag to Angela who heads off up towards the Tower. Pete then takes over Greg's wheelchair and pushes him smartly back to the house. Such mystery! What are these young people up to?

Trying to show she was in charge, nervily uncertain what to do, the Ratcliffe plumped for the hardest line. She fired Mr. MacAskill.

The interview was brief but poignant. Jane was sitting behind her desk when Joe came in but she at once stood up and moved awkwardly to greet him. The desk was a large antique construction and she bumped her thigh on an over-decorated corner. They sat down warily on the two most challengingly upright of the chairs that were dotted around the room. Jane Ratcliffe checked the hemline of her plaid skirt with a deft tug that brought it virtually to the middle of her strongly formed calves.

'Mr. MacAskill… ah.'

'Ummm.'

'You had better… ummm…'

'Of course.'

'But…'

'Mmm?'

'… would you… stay until the end of term?'

'If it would be a help.'

Jane's nose was always glossy, but today exceptionally so, and her specs now slid down and right off into her lap and thence to the floor.

'Oh,' she said, apparently unable to move, and MacAskill, driven by old-fashioned courtesies, ducked down and plucked the spectacles from the Axminster, where they had fallen on a particularly worn-out patch.

'They're rather misty,' he said, and gave them a little polish on his clean handkerchief.

'Thank you,' she said, taking them from his hand and restoring them to their place.

They were both dreadfully aware that the scene was muddled beyond retrieval. Jane, in particular, had so totally missed the stern reasoned redemptive tone she had had in mind. In fact, as she jabbed her glasses back onto her nose, she felt a strange pricking in her eye that in a lesser woman might have been taken for a sympathetic tear. For his part, Joe MacAskill had cast this as a tragic scene and had gone in with eyes down, all woebegone and doomed, ready to thrash around in misery.

But in the end there was a nagging humanity about it

that caught them both, so that the encounter was strangely stirring. MacAskill even felt somehow better, as illnesses can be cured just by the doctor's cool hands palpating an organ and his murmured 'It's nothing much to worry about'.

'This is absurd,' Richard exclaimed. 'We'll fight.'

But Joe MacAskill continued to feel strangely better and later that day he was spotted wearing a fugitive smile not previously seen. He had touched bottom, and the only way was up.

'I feel sealed, you know,' he replied to Richard, 'sealed against any more disappointments. A bit numb, of course, but I expect feeling will return at some point.'

The world had gone mad anyway, in Joe MacAskill's view. He had left England for Africa in the Age of Duty – and returned to the Sixties. The day he landed back he had read in the newspaper that a footballer had transferred to another club for *fifty thousand pounds* – and the man was now drawing wages of £200 *a week*!

As the world was mad, Joe considered he might as well go mad with it. He had nothing to lose.

Even the memory spasms began to ease. The lurid doggy moment on the mat still flushed up a hundred times a day. But now it was set in a slightly larger production, like seeing the whole movie and not just a loop of that one drastic rush. His loss still loomed, but other losses now remembered seemed to counterbalance it, and the various threadbare trials of his life seemed to be cancelling each other out. Perhaps, behind the eclipse of his heart, a new sun was forming.

***

'

'You know, even before,' he said to Richard, 'it was one carnal bloody fight. We hadn't slept together in years. She said there was no point. I'd had mumps as a child and couldn't give her children. And she wasn't interested in sex *per se* at all, you see. More in mulling over her own disappointments.'

And this slowly inflating buoyancy of Mr. MacAskill's was not the only thing he took away from his meeting with the Ratcliffe. Because when the specs were off, he'd spotted, just next to the ruddy indents where her glasses clasped the bridge of her nose, that glistening in the corner of the eye, and she had been suddenly recognizably human in a way that she never had been before.

And she had felt it too, and although she jabbed the specs back smartly into place and the interview had ended, there had been a cool, almost pleasurable feeling left wafting in the space between them.

32

This slight swerve from the narrow and stony path Jane had set herself was soon corrected. She decided to take the afternoon off. The weather was fine. She would walk in the beechwoods and then perhaps go into town to buy herself something nice as a treat. She called Debbie in to tell her she was being left in charge.

So it was that Jane missed the arrival of the Furies she had unloosed. Or at least she missed the arrival of Alan Hopcraft who came over around the middle of the afternoon from Binstead in the Vehicle of Doom and demanded of Debbie where Her Nibs was. Told Miss Ratcliffe was out, Alan showed Debbie a pink sheet headed Movement Order which was his authority to collect one female minor Helen Scandizzi and to convey her to Binstead Asylum. Whilst Debbie was reading the form, Alan looked her up and down with some pleasure.

'Oh yes,' said Debbie, 'come in, Alan, and have a cuppa and I'll just go and fetch her. You pop in here. It's Miss Ratcliffe's office.'

Whilst Alan Hopcraft was helping himself to one of Jane Ratcliffe's ginger nuts, Lizzie came in with a pot of tea on a tray. Alan eyed her too, as he had Debbie, and she stopped and flirted with him in a very low-key way.

After a few minutes, Debbie came back and said she couldn't find Helen just now. Lizzie said that she would go and look, so Debbie stopped and sat down behind Miss Ratcliffe's desk and asked Alan about himself and his family and his hopes and dreams. Alan was flattered by the attention of this big handsome blonde girl and he talked quite happily about all these things for quite some time.

Eventually Angela Cudmore came in with a fresh pot of tea, and Debbie went out to look for Helen. Angela was not such a one for flirting or small talk or family history but she was easy on Alan's eye and she knew a lot about bovine artificial insemination. Her account of how she would put on a very long rubber glove right up to her armpit and reach into the very centre of the cow, and of how the cow got seriously pleasured by this operation and cooperated with great alacrity, especially as the risks involved were so much less than when she had a three ton bull up on her – this account kept Alan spellbound until Debbie reappeared and admitted that Helen seemed actually to be missing.

Alan was not fussed by the news. He had in any case been uncertain about the mission. Normally it would be a two-handed job, with a female partner for the proprieties and in case the patient needed restraint or anything as they often did. But Mr. Salter had marked it Urgent, so even though Julie was off today, he had agreed to come over.

'Can I... err... phone the boss?' he asked. Debbie got him the number and he explained the situation to Mr. Salter. The conversation was brief. Alan was ordered back to base.

Debbie, Lizzie and Angela Cudmore came out on the steps to say goodbye. Alan returned their cheery waves and drove off. From the Girls Dorm upstairs, Flick watched, her arm around the weeping Helen.

'Never mind, my darling,' Flick said, stroking Helen's hair and dabbing at her damp cheeks with a tiny scented handkerchief. 'Never ever mind. We'll think of something.'

So it was very unfortunate that Jane Ratcliffe, her head full of the joyous song of nesting yellowhammers and in her bag the little purchase with which she had sought to soothe herself, the most perfect fawn she had ever seen, long-limbed and sweet faced and with the dearest pricked up ears in green – the rest of the little glass animal was tastefully transparent – had alighted from the red 213 bus which stopped at the end of the drive to Park House just two minutes before Alan Hopcraft's rousing send-off.

Jane met Alan and the Vehicle of Doom half-way up the drive, and as the drive was too narrow for the van to pass her, Alan pulled up whilst Jane stepped onto the grassy verge. He rolled down the window.

'Miss Ratcliffe, I presume.'

Jane's eyes narrowed almost imperceptibly at what sounded like impertinence. She nonetheless admitted her identity.

'I was sent over by Mr. Salter at the Bin to collect one young lady. Helen by name.'

'Oh... but... is she in the back?' Jane tilted her head slightly towards the windowless back of the Vehicle.

Alan laughed, coarsely in Jane's view.

'Blimey, no. No, we don't lock 'em up in the back. We just restrain 'em with this gear here.' He indicated the sturdy leather straps.

'So... umm... where is she then?'

As Alan Hopcraft explained what had happened, Jane's previously tranquillized mood quite fell away and was replaced by strong feelings of anger.

'Wait here,' she ordered Alan and strode on up the drive.

'I will deal with you three later,' Jane Ratcliffe said.

Debbie, Lizzie and Flick stood in a line by Helen's bed. An old blue suitcase with the initials E.G.A.D. of some long-dead previous owner stamped on its front lay open on the rumpled coverlet. Some shabby frocks had been stuffed inside, clearly in haste. On top of the frocks lay the bright red briefs that were Helen's pride.

Helen herself was not to be seen but her sobs could be clearly heard from the nearby Girls' Toilet where she had locked herself in.

'Where is that man?' Jane asked crossly, looking at her watch. She had dispatched Angela Cudmore over ten minutes ago to fetch Pete, who was after all the handyman, or failing him, to summon John Fry from the Home Farm 'with a big crowbar or something.'

Eventually it was John Fry who came, a bit sheepish-looking, but carrying the requested crowbar. He cast a glance at Lizzie who would have spat in his face if he had not kept his distance.

John applied the crowbar to the door. From inside, Helen's sobs became louder and more frantic.

There was a cracking sound.

'Mind!' Jane exclaimed and John Fry looked at her contemptuously.

'You want me to jemmy 'er open or not?'

'Proceed,' Jane said, and John Fry applied the crowbar more vigorously.

The door splintered and sprang open. There was Helen crouching on the floor by the toilet. She had messed herself.

'Now get her out.'

After a moment's hesitation, John advanced and Helen cowered. In the end he grabbed her by the ankles and yanked her out. Once she was clear of the toilet, he bent to pick her up, but a little gingerly due to the mess and also because he thought she might scratch his eyes out. However, Helen's terror had clearly overcome her. Although the mess did get on John, on his arms and right down his front, she let herself be picked up without a murmur.

'Now take her down the drive,' Jane ordered. 'The van is waiting there.'

'No!' Flick cried out.

'The less we hear from you, the better,' Jane said.

'She can't go like that. Let me wash her.'

Jane's instinct for hygiene kicked in.

'Alright, but be quick about it.'

John Fry laid the girl on the bed and went into the Girls' Toilet.

'I'll just clean meself up a bit,' he said. Lizzie shouted after him, 'Leave it on. It suits you.'

Flick, with the help of Debbie, took off Helen's soiled clothes. Lizzie went into the Girls' Toilet to get a bowl of warm water and a pile of clean flannels from the cupboard. While she was there, she gave John Fry a painful kick on the shin.

'It's me job, Liz,' he muttered, 'the wife an'…'

Lizzie kicked him again, much harder this time, and went out.

Helen was now naked on the bed. Jane Ratcliffe turned away. She couldn't bear the way the nurses were washing the girl with the flannels, with discreet careful motions, dabbing and smoothing. Jane felt this gentle way of doing it was somehow a wrong act, too much like something else that couldn't or shouldn't be connected. So she went out and stood in the corridor, like one standing guard.

After a minute, Patch came by, buzzing down the corridor. He appeared not to notice Jane until the very last moment when his heavy Armstead 302 suddenly veered at her and rammed quite painfully into her right calf. She yelped.

'Whatever do you think…' she began but then she saw

Patch's face horribly red and distorted in a look of utter loathing. He said,

'That's a evil evil thing you're doin', Ratcliffe, and you will go to Hell for sure.'

He buzzed on, leaving Jane Ratcliffe to nurse her calf and ponder this further affront.

Almost at once, somebody hit her quite hard from behind, between the shoulder blades. She spun round angrily. It was Lizzie.

'Alright, you can look now,' Lizzie said and turned away.

There was Helen sitting up on the bed, still naked but for the bright red briefs that Jane had earlier seen in the suitcase. Jane had reprobated these briefs then and she especially reprobated them now that the nurses had slipped them up over the girl's smooth young hips. They were like a horrible suggestion of something. She called after Lizzie who was heading back towards the others.

'What am I supposed to be looking at?' Lizzie didn't reply but waved her fingers in a disgusting V sign.

Flick had a little glass bottle in her hand and was smoothing something onto Helen's breasts and tummy. Debbie fished a clean white bra out of E.G.A.D.'s old blue suitcase, and then a whiteish frock, and she and Lizzie put these on the girl.

'Try these,' Flick said, holding out a pair of old white satin dancing shoes that she had found in the rummage of the shoe hamper. They fitted Helen perfectly.

'Take her down now,' Jane called out to John Fry who was just emerging from the Girls' Toilet.

To carry Helen out of the door, John Fry had to walk past Lizzie. As he came level with her, Lizzie landed a vicious slap on his exposed cheek. He looked away and carried on at a faster pace.

John Fry walked past Jane. Helen's eyes were closed, her thick raven hair falling down over John's arm, almost to his waist. The air around Helen was full of the scent of lily of the valley.

'You'll find the van down the drive,' Jane said to John Fry as he went past her. 'And... errr... don't forget to... umm... get a docket... and a signature...'

Greg lay as usual, eyes closed, awaiting sleep.

A pensive Angela had just put him down and whisked away his colourful shirt to the wash. He asked Angela if Helen would be coming back but she shook her head and murmured 'Shouldn't think so.' She let him touch the shiny blonde curls which fell about her ruddy features.

Strange distorted monstrous faces played before Greg's eyes. He didn't mind. These demons were of many colours, in bands and stripes. They often did this cinema, then fled when true sleep flowed in, sleep and dreams.

There was a noise. Greg opened his eyes. It was Mick, getting into bed. Mick's bed was next to Greg's.

Greg had been beside Mick, watching, when John Fry carried Helen out. Helen had looked like she was dead, flopped like that in John's arms.

There was no time that Greg could remember when he and Helen and Mick and Patch and Gloriana had not been together. Now John had taken Helen away and put her in a van. He and Mick had gone behind them down the drive. Mick was shouting. John Fry waved his fist at him. They saw John Fry and the man put Helen in the van. They tied her up with straps. Greg had looked at Mick and saw his face was wet. Then Mick scooted off. He was away for hours and hours. He came back just now.

Greg said 'Mick'. He wanted to tell him about the new song he was going to write. It was called *Helen's Return*. But Mick was already under the blankets, turned the other way.

Greg closed his eyes and the colourful demons came back and did their dance. After some minutes, they moved on and Greg's sleep came, gathering dreams behind.

I help a girl to chase wrongdoers. We get on a barge to cross a river and she nearly falls through a big hole in the bottom. She says 'That is where the other girl fell through.'

When we reach the other side, we see a tiger. We try to get a lift from a man on a bike. There are some backpacker girls hacking meat off old bones to make a small stew.

Miss Ratcliffe takes a blood sample from me. She pricks me with a pin near my willy. The blood spills out.

The police chief takes us to his station. It is a dormitory with a lot of children. I push past one bed and the leg breaks off. The boy sitting in the bed doing his homework says it doesn't matter.

The dream was very bright. When Greg went over it, he wanted to know why the boy doing his homework said that it didn't matter. With all the bad things, Greg was sure that it did matter. He wanted to ask Mick but he couldn't.

PART FOUR: DOWNHILL

33

Aaaah. Helen's gone, and in a horrible horrible way. And the rest of us shan't be far behind.

Last night Patch paraded his Trojans in the Great Hall and they raised their Greek shout of *Whom the gods love…* But they looked as glum as anything and Patch's little pep talk didn't quite come off. 'We'll fight her on the landings, we'll fight her in the school' was quite good, I suppose, but sadly no one got the reference but me and Richard. The Trojans just looked sad and puzzled, and after a couple more rounds of *Hon hoi theoi* they broke up. They didn't even grumble when Debbie said it was time for bed.

Since yesterday afternoon my girls have been spitting with anger. And today, the Rat piled it on further. She docked Lizzie and Debbie and Flick two pounds each off their weekly wages. I heard Lizzie shouting, using the C word and some others.

Even Angela's had a pound taken off as the Rat got the driver chap Alan to describe the girl who'd kept him talking about AI and she recognized Angela straight away from the wordless gesture Alan made with his hands.

Last night Patch came to talk to me. For once even he seemed stumped.

'I just dunno what to do, Gloriana. Nothing's working out. I'm gonna get Richard to phone to Mrs. Noble tomorrow but I dunno…'

To cheer him up, I explained the theory of Chaos and he perked up right away.

'OK,' he said. 'She's asked for it. Chaos it is.'

But I'm in mourning. I miss dear Helen snuggled up against me at night. She's gone, and as far as I can see we're all about to follow.

Come on, Chaos.

'Oi, posh boy,' Patch said, 'I thought I told you to get rid of the Rat.'

'I wrote to Mrs. Noble. You know I did.'

'Yeah, well, that's not enough, mate. Send 'er a telegram. Phone 'er up.'

Richard tried to telephone from the old black Bakelite instrument at the House but the high-handed lady at the exchange refused to place the call to California. She said it was 'against regs' or some such, or perhaps she just couldn't be bothered, or maybe she was an agent of the Rat.

Richard borrowed a fiver off Pete. Pete asked what it was for and when Richard told him, he said it wasn't a loan, he could have it. So down at the Main Post Office in town Richard paid over £3/11/9d for the three-minute minimum and then he waited from nine o'clock up to eleven o'clock on a bench and then until twelve noon in a booth until at last the telephone in front of him a gave a desultory dring and he saw the lady at the counter waving at him to pick up.

'Hallo,' he cried, 'Hallo. This is Richard from Park House. The children are desperate. The House is falling apart. Please can you come back at once?'

In the period of time that Richard then allowed for Mrs. Noble's response, there came first a long silent pause followed by a hard to interpret noise like the surge of the sea on pebbles, rhythmically advancing and then retreating. This was followed by a second period of silence which had an almost devotional quality to it, it was so silent. This was equally hard to interpret. Then a distinct human female

278

English voice came on as clear as if in the next room.

'Hallo,' it said.

'Oh, Mrs. Noble, can you hear me? This is Richard...'

The tidal surge again swept in a stochastic wave through the earpiece.

'Richard!' he bellowed, and then, clear and loud, the English voice said from the other side of the world,

'Hallo, hallo, who is this calling please?'

Richard began speaking rapidly.

'... Park House falling apart... Miss Ratcliffe... children wretched... Helen carted off to Binstead... Gloriana wants to go to university... please come back...'

About halfway through this speech, Richard became aware of a lengthy passage of static which started with an impression of the purring of a deep-throated cat and transfigured wonderfully into a Stockhausen variation on the *Telstar* theme by the Tornados. At the end, a silence of a particularly profound and meaningless quality gathered in the earpiece.

Into the utter void of this silence came the rasping tones of the lady at the Post Office counter.

'Sorry, love, your three minutes is up.'

The call had been a complete waste of money. Richard went to the counter to mention this poor value and to see if he couldn't get a refund.

'Frankly, love,' the lady said, 'I'd have advised against a telephone call if you'd asked me. They hardly ever gets through satisfactory. Especially to the West Coast of America at four in the morning their time. There's not many of them up over there just then and those that is tend to be not at their best if you get my meaning.'

'So what can I do? It's life and death.'

'No, it isn't,' the lady said. 'It's them cripples up at the

279

'Ouse, isn't it? My advice is, don't get mixed up in their dirty little business.'

Rather than enter into an argy-bargy with the telephone lady, Richard decided to try to save something from the mess. He pressed her and, relenting slightly, she agreed that for the £1/8/3d left from Pete's gift money and a few shillings he had left over from his weekly thirty bob pocket money, he could send a five-word telegram to California.

For an hour, Richard played with formulations of epigrammatic brevity. It was like the six-word novel George Orwell wrote. In Latin you could do it. In Latin there was that one-word telegraph from General Napier when he'd conquered Sindh – *Peccavi*! I have sinned. But could he count on Eleanor Noble as a Latinist. He knew so little about her. And what was the Latin for *Balls Up* anyway?

In the end he settled for PARK HOUSE UTTER RUIN RETURN.

The Post Office lady read it through, bristling with censure.

'I told you there's no good meddling with that lot.'

Richard pushed the money over the counter.

'Please just send the telegram,' he said.

With Mr. MacAskill sacked and Richard off on his telephoning mission, school was sort of suspended today. We just sat in our classroom and watched telly. Then about mid-morning, in stumps the Rat. She looks really nervy. Her nose is extra shiny and she practically has to keep her finger on her goggles full time to stop them slithering down. Everybody glares at her.

'There has been,' she says, 'an unparalleled breach of discipline…'

Well, that's one way to describe sending an innocent

young girl to a lifetime's Doom at the Bin.

'… and sadly both staff and, I suspect, senior pupils have lost sight in recent days of the ethic of Park House…'

Oh? Which ethic would that be? The one that stamps on joy and condemns us all to the Bin?

'The basic tenets by which we live our lives…'

Bla bla bla. Anyway, the long and short of it is that she says she's cancelling the theatre trip.

Two days ago, I'd have said Yippee, but Patch spots an opportunity to create a right bit of chaos.

'Oh, but Miss, that wouldn't be right,' he says.

The Rat stops in mid-sentence, alerted by these unusual grounds of opposition to her will. After all, rightness is *her* prerogative.

'Whatever do you mean?'

'Miss, you must know in your heart of hearts it wouldn't be right to cancel the theatre trip.'

'Heart of hearts' is very good indeed, as this organ un-known to science has somehow been revealed to the Rat as the seat of incontrovertible conscience.

'Pardon?… sorry, I mean, What?'

Patch does one of his pregnant pauses. It lasts so long that I suspect from her absent look that the Rat thinks he's lost the thread. She says *Pardon*? again, and then *What*? She's looking really cross by this stage. Clearly, she can dish stuff out but she can't take it.

'I mean,' Patch at last goes on, 'wouldn't be right, would it, Goddard Bequest, innit?'

The Rat bridles. She's just not used to being called out on righteousness questions. I spot moral conflict in her brow which takes the form of some extra lateral furrowing above the spectacles. This is the field on which two conflicting principles battle it out, the urge to impose discipline struggling with duty to our maiden lady founders. The Misses Goddard, the spinsters who left Park House to our charity many years ago, also left a bequest of money to pay for our Cultural Advancement in the shape of the Annual Theatre Trip.

'Mmm,' the Rat says. 'Mmm. Perhaps you have a point, Patrick. Perhaps in view of the character of our obligation… I mean, to our founders… perhaps I might exercise leniency in this one case…'

But Miss Ratcliffe is not one to be turned without her Parthian shaft. She goes on,

'But it should not be an occasion for licence or unruly behaviour as it was last year. In fact, my decision is… that only selected children may go…'

Later, in her office, Ratcliffe wrestled with her behaviour during that difficult meeting with the children. Had she lost face? She felt she had – in her own reckoning at least. The crux of it was stumbling over those stupid words, the stupid Pardon? and the stupid What? Just which of these two formulations was the one to avoid, the lower middle class one, was always such a puzzle. She is pretty sure it is 'Pardon?', but then 'What?' sounded distinctly… well… coarse. She always saw this crux arriving and she always ended up like today just blurting them both out, but then that meant she was sure to be wrong. It was the same with toilet and lavatory… and that new 'loo'. How on earth did that fit in…?

34

The Bin
Binstead Village
Surrey-on-the-Styx
Hell

Day 33 of the 12,410 days of the rest of my life in The Bin

Dear Gloria, dear Pat,
What the heck? This is crazy. They brought Helen here today. Here! The girl belongs with Jean Shrimpton on a catwalk, not with the Loopy Ladies of Binstead. Of all the life-denying, cruddy things to do, to send that poor dear girl here. I can take The Bin (just) but our lovely Helen, who we cuddled all our childhood? She deserves a life of adulation, not The Bin. She will never survive for a minute here.

I saw Alan Hopcraft bring her in. The Loopy Ladies were all agog, massed in the hall. It's not often they get a new arrival these days. Alan, who's not a bad bloke at heart, tried to whisk her in sharpish but the Ladies came flocking down the big stairs, reaching out and touching her dress and feeling her hair until Norma (yes, Norma! See below) pushed them back, saying 'Leave her, poor pretty thing, the poor little dear.'

Mercifully Helen just stayed slumped like she was in a swoon. She never opened her eyes. One of the female charge nurses, the nice-ish one called Big Bev, took her from Alan and carried her up to her dorm. She's in *Elizabeth Fry*. Nuff said.

So, what about Norma? That was our good news until poor Helen was brought in. Because Salter saw the letter from Norma's daughter and immediately let her out of the Slammer on parole. She's back in the dorm, subdued but OK-ish. I read her the letter from her daughter. Dawn copied it for me, as she says that Salter had just marked it File Up. He wasn't even going to reply. He wasn't even going to tell Norma that her daughter was looking for her.

Of course, Norma can't take it in yet. It's just too enormous. But for sure some good will come of it.

I'll write more when I know more. But we've got to get Helen out of here as soon as possible. Ideas please on a postcard to

Your true friend,

Ivan Robertovich

35

After a rapid risk assessment, Jane Ratcliffe chooses the children to go on the Annual Theatre Trip that she considers least likely to cause trouble. This flawed procedure ends up with Mick, Patch, Greg, Kevin (almost certainly the biggest of her mistakes) and nine or ten others.

Patch, the new adherent to Chaos Theory, has nothing planned as his understanding is that you don't plan for Chaos. You just set up the conditions and it sort of happens.

It begins well as preparations take all day and by the time the big blue bus is nosing down the drive at six o'clock, the children are fractious and their nurses are worn out.

Overseeing the outing are Jane Ratcliffe herself and Mr. MacAskill who surprisingly has required no persuading to take on the responsibility despite being sacked.

Lizzie and Richard are on board, but at either ends of the bus. There is, however, a general expectation that in the excitement of the outing there will be some definite move between them. Certainly this is Richard's intention as, on Pete's advice, he has invested 12/6d – practically half of his weekly money – in a quarter bottle of Johnny Walker whisky. The bottle is in his trouser pocket, where it feels heavy and dangerous. In his other pocket he has not one little packet but two selected from his precious store.

Pete is driving and after an eventful five-mile journey to the nearby town, they arrive outside the theatre with only a small abrasion to the front mudguard that Pete confidently says 'will rub up OK so it won't notice'.

The trouble starts when a figure of authority in a navy-blue uniform and a peaked cap comes up and shouts to Pete just as he is beginning the tricky process of letting down the ramp, 'You can't park there, sonny.'

Pete says back, 'Says who, mate?' and they have a bit of a set-to.

The uniform gives little clue to what powers have been conferred on the authority-figure – he could be a park keeper or a chauffeur or even a handler at the zoo – but he confidently orders Pete to *Move on, 'op it, pipe down* etc. The altercation continues for about five minutes until Pete gives him ten bob and the fellow grudgingly gives way.

Jane Ratcliffe calls out that she has arranged for the children to be let in by the side door so that they can be wheeled easily to their places at the rear of the stalls. However, this compact proves unimplementable. Nobody at the theatre is aware of it. The manager is off. The uniformed figure says darkly that it is 'against regs'. Anyway, the key to the door in question cannot be found. Jane Ratcliffe bristles and mutters something sour which sets the situation back even further.

Meanwhile, people – regular people – are beginning to crowd into the foyer. They all cast hostile glances at the big blue bus. A guy in a duffel coat says loudly 'Oh, Christ, here we go.'

At last, Miss Ratcliffe just orders everybody off the bus and a confused log jam of chairs and walkers and nurses makes its way through the appalled crowd. Mick wheels ahead shouting Gangway! Patch, who has been transhipped to his mechanical wheelchair for the occasion, calls out in his high voice:

'Out of the way, you silly old moo.'

Kevin carves his own passage with his sticks.

The first half of the play goes off without incident. In fact, the children are interested and laugh a lot. It is *Billy Liar*, which turns out to be quite naughty and subversive. Why Jane Ratcliffe had not known this in advance is not clear. Probably she had too many other preoccupations. Mr. MacAskill, by contrast, had good advance knowledge from having read a scathing critique in the *Daily Express*, and this was amongst his reasons for agreeing so readily to come on the trip. The children all make sure to laugh very loudly and coarsely whenever Billy nips down to Foley Bottoms with one of his three girlfriends.

Richard only half attends to the play. He is waiting for the interval. The minute the curtain comes down, he dashes out and goes into the cloakroom where he takes a good swig of Johnny Walker. Then he sets off to hunt for Lizzie. When he spots her, she is in a cramped phone box in the foyer where, through the glass panels in the heavy wooden door, she can be seen with the receiver clamped to her ear and her finger poised on Button A as she waits for her call to go through. He taps on the glass and she glares at him and mouths something that looks pretty much like *Bugger off*.

He hangs around for a bit but she is watching him and makes a V sign, so he slips back to the cloakroom for another strengthening swig. As he returns, Lizzie is just hanging up. He opens the door and squeezes in between her and the phone.

'Cor, you reek, Richard.'

'Night out,' he mutters, suddenly awkward, turning away so that his whisky breath will not be all over her.

They are tightly wedged in there, her head comes up just to his chin. He lays his face against her wild black hair but she pulls away and angles her head back to look up at him. He has never been so close up to her in the light and it is a thrilling experience. He is keeping his lips tight shut to contain the whisky breath. He can see little flecks of brown and violet showing in her ash grey eyes. She has put on her Egyptian eye stuff again, but more carefully this time. She looks like a harem beauty. Her lips are a pale pink.

'Give us a swig then,' she says unexpectedly and Richard slips the Johnny Walker out of his pocket and unscrews the cap with one hand. The cap drops to the floor. He wriggles the bottle up and puts it to Lizzie's lips. She gulps at it like a greedy child. Richard keckhandedly moves the bottle away and a trickle of the raw liquor starts from her mouth and runs down her chin. Richard licks at it. Mingled with the whisky, he can taste the faintly spicy smack of her skin. Then, being so close, there's nothing to stop their lips joining easily in a delicious big wet kiss in which whisky and their most intimate secretions mingle in an explosion of unexpectedly luscious flavours. Richard can feel her breasts against him and perhaps her beating heart – or maybe it's his own.

It is a completely thrilling moment which risks lasting much longer until an old biddy in a red beret raps angrily on the glass and hisses 'I'm going to report you', although for what and to whom remains unclear.

Lizzie pushes Richard back and there is a clattering behind him.

'You just pressed Button B, Rich. Now gimme me pennies back.'

What follows next in matters of the heart? Drinks, a snog, and so to bed was the sequence Pete had sketched out for Richard. But nothing could have prepared him for what actually happened next.

Lizzie was at his side, like they were an actual couple. He was floating along on a big cushion of pride and expectation. Lizzie, for her part, was reflecting that it was probably OK that no one had answered the phone at John Fry's cottage, better really. The idea she'd vaguely had of buggering up John Fry by telling Mrs. Fry about the affair was pretty crap really...

... and then there was Mick bowling his chair at top speed down the corridor towards them, calling out. From behind the boy, through the open doors to the theatre hall, an uproar could be heard, as though the entire audience had taken to bawling at the tops of their voices, and a certain amount of confusion could be seen of people running and waving their arms and all kinds of hullabaloo.

'Richard, Lizzie, come quick, it's Kevin.'

The aura had begun in the usual way, brought on perhaps by the lights flashing and flickering and by all the colourful goings-on onstage. There was the feeling of weightlessness, his sticks dropping away and his body floating up like one of those helium-filled balloons until he was high above, amongst the mouldings and the flecks of gold and the weird paintings of fat women. He was flying with no sticks, and then his feet swelled to enormous size, bigger than footballs, and there was a tiny Ratcliffe far below, wagging a finger at him, and he floated down and gave her a whacking great kick. Then he fell unconscious.

They ran to the auditorium and there was little Kevin flailing on the floor.

'Oh my Gawd, he's fitting,' Lizzie cried and pushed through the crowd to where the Ratcliffe was craning uncertainly over the boy. Lizzie shoved her aside and knelt down. Kevin's arms and legs were beating about in spasms, dangerously close to the iron seat stands. Lizzie turned the unconscious boy on his side and checked his jaw to make sure he was not biting his tongue.

All around was chaos. People were clambering over seats to get away from Kevin as though he were a rabid dog about to bite. Agitated women were rushing up the aisle, the uniformed type was shouting incoherently, people in other parts of the theatre were standing on their seats to get a view of what was happening.

Lizzie jerked her head at Richard and he pushed through the crowd towards her.

'Get them to sit down,' Lizzie shouted. Richard looked over to Mr. MacAskill who was standing helplessly nearby, but Lizzie shouted 'Rich!' and she made an intense angry face at him. Kevin's limbs were still flailing wildly. Tonic and clonic, Richard remembered. He bent over Lizzie.

'Not MacAskill,' she shouted, seeing where Richard was looking. 'He'll flip. You do it. Get up on the stage and make an announcement.'

Richard glanced up at Mr. MacAskill and it was true. The man was dithering fatally.

Richard hesitated. Kevin's thrashing had subsided and he seemed to have fallen into a trance-like state. Lizzie was now stroking his Harpo Marx hair. She had taken off his National Health specs and undone his tie and collar. She turned her Egyptian eyes up to Richard.

'Go on, Rich. You get up on stage and make an announcement.'

This, in fact, turned out to be easier than Richard had expected. One of the actors gave him a microphone, and even while he was tapping it to see if it was working, the crowd began to quieten down, as though all they wanted was someone to stand up and acknowledge that something out of the ordinary had happened.

'Sorry, ladies and gentlemen, sorry,' Richard said, too loudly. 'Sorry. Kevin's... err... had a fit. He's... err... prone to them from time to time and... errr... well... he just had one. Laughing too much maybe...'

This at least raised a titter. Richard was almost but not quite beginning to enjoy the sound of his own voice.

'Now, could you all please just sit down... and... the show will go on.'

People milled about uncertainly. A few could be seen heading for the exits but eventually most people made their way back to their seats and sat down. Richard could see Lizzie in the aisle, now bent over Kevin, cradling him, wiping his nose. The boy lay quite still, a crumpled little heap.

'We will just need... one minute to take little Kevin out of here.'

Lizzie, he saw, was now scooping Kevin up and giving him to Mr. MacAskill to carry. The boy stirred and came to. He remembered nothing. Lizzie slipped his glasses back on and he looked around in puzzlement. And then all at once he recollected – floating weightlessly, flying through the air, that wonderful release – and then the oblivion of the fit closing down his reverie. He began to sob. A woman with earnest polished round cheeks and wearing a beige coat darted up to him and tousled his hair.

'Poor dear,' she muttered, touching his cheek.

'Fuck off, you motherfucker!' Kevin shouted and lunged to bite at the woman's finger. Mr. MacAskill and Lizzie whisked him up the aisle. A voice called out,

'And you can take the rest of them, too, darling.'

'Yeah, get the lot of them out of here.'

Richard, still on the stage, shouted angrily through the microphone,

'Stand up and say that!' His face was burning with embarrassment at their lack of shame, and a grudging kind of shame did seem to fall on the proceedings. At least, nobody stood up. Then somebody shouted,

'Oh, get on with the bloody play.'

And all the while Jane Ratcliffe was standing helplessly by, not knowing what to do.

In the big blue bus going back, there was a strange celebratory mood. The children had exhausted the entire compass of their emotions and now only wanted to sing. Mick's booming tenor led them in *Ten Green Bottles...* Jane Ratcliffe and Mr. MacAskill sat in silence at the front, not intervening. At the back, Lizzie and Richard sat hand in hand, alongside Patch in his wheelchair. Kevin lay stretched out fast asleep across their laps.

Patch turned his big red moon face to Lizzie and Richard. It had an unusual look to it that turned out to be satisfaction with the evening, because he said,

'That was really really good.'

36

Indifferent to the couple coiled in love below, Sir Roper Smytheson gazed out, dreaming stonily of Discipline Established and Settlements Extended, of Armies Defeated and Peace Concluded, if not – as Mr. MacAskill had recently stencilled on in large capitals in paints he'd filched out of the Art Cupboard – of Ill-Gotten Fortunes Greedily Amassed.

Cushioned beside the Saviour of the Indies' sandalled foot, Richard and Lizzie lay on quilts, quite nude, and sipped at wine. In the pale moonlight that fell on her from the narrow slitted windows, Lizzie looked to Richard mysterious and full of fun, endless pleasure, no end of love.

Since their rapprochement at the play, Lizzie had turned out the Tower. First, she had shut the cats in for a day to drive away the furry, scurrying creatures, then locked the moggies out for good. Deft work with a broom handle had persuaded the bats to move to a better place. Then she had cleaned the place out entirely, swept and scrubbed the floor, set out a low table, popped in candles, put down mats and strewn some quilts she pilfered from the laundry closet.

'Ow.'

Lizzie now sat up, fending off a damp muzzle that was pressing urgently against her thigh.

'Just bugger off, will you, Bertie.'

Bertie made a lunge at Lizzie and tried to lick her cheek but she shoved him away.

'Richard, kick that bleedin' dog out.'

For Bertie never had been 'run down to the vets', never

had been 'put down' at all. The artful, good-hearted Pete had driven him around for an hour or so and then brought back a mournful blanket wrapped over newspapers and loosened earth. He had buried that with a little ceremony the children had attended.

But what to do with the still-living Bertie? At first, Pete had left him at the pub, and then at night he popped him in the Tower with a box of Bonios pro tem. And then – a brain-wave – he had asked Angela Cudmore for help. Here he had some good luck because the girl's farm breeding told her you may kill an animal to eat it but you never kill a dog who has served you.

So Pete's luck was to get Angela's help with Bertie. She did a no-questions-asked deal with Helen on kitchen scraps and leftovers which the dog wolfed down indiscriminately, avoiding the odd piece of cutlery that had fallen in the mix. It was Pete's good luck, too, to spend time plotting with the girl he fancied, sharing secrets. At first this seemed to Pete like children's playground stuff and well inferior to fum-bling with her bra strap as an approach to the main idea. Strangely, though, this plotting together over Bertie began to move Pete's relations with Angela along in a way that the fumbling never had. Definitely she was looking at him in a new way.

Richard now dragged the reluctant Bertie by his collar and put him out of the door.

So for the hours till dawn, while Richard and Lizzie are couched together on their quilts, sprawled against the plinth on which Sir Roper Smytheson soars, the blameless dog sits guard outside, moving his muzzle from side to side, sniffing at the scented air and listening to the calls of birds and the furtive movements of the creatures of the under-wood.

**

'Right, lover boy, about our play,' Patch calls out rudely to Richard as Mr. MacAskill slips out.

Actually, **was** that Mr. MacAskill? He bore some close resemblances to Mr. MacAskill, but there were some biggish discrepancies too that create doubts in my mind.

First there's his signature bog brush hair which through months of neglect has been silently growing ever longer and suddenly we see that it's an Afro look. And the antique tweed jacket has disappeared and in its place Mr. MacAskill is now wearing a pale blue short-sleeved shirt not tucked into his trousers, and it's open at the neck. The shirt is hugely big on him. He looks like a mahogany bell with his legs as the clappers.

The other big change is that Mr. MacAskill's personality has completely altered. Gone is the old gloom and in its place a startlingly debonair Mr. MacAskill has sprung up. He's still not here most of the time, so Richard's mostly having to take charge, but Mr. MacAskill no longer nips up to The Dog at all hours. Instead he is to be seen strolling the grounds in thought, or sometimes going swimming down at the pool. Often now you can see him chatting with Debbie and Flick who have taken him up. In fact, several times Mr. MacAskill has been spotted heading out somewhere in the park with Debbie and Flick and coming back an hour or two later looking dreamy.

Well! At least we don't have to worry about Mr. MacAskill anymore.

And in Mr. MacAskill's constant absences from class, Patch has called rehearsals of our play. Richard has made the changes that Patch required. The Trojan Empire, it seems, does not contract. Instead it expands to cover the whole of the Mediterranean basin. Britain, too, is incorporated in the Trojans' civilizing mission. A fleet commanded by a general called Brutus sails up the River Dart and lands at Totnes to begin the process of constructing governance institutions on the Trojan model and educating the rude Britons in civilized Trojan values.

Patch did ask for the landing to be switched to his own home town of Plymouth but here Richard for once put his foot down and insisted on historical accuracy, and in the end Patch accepted that if the play was to be credible it must stick to the facts.

So now, every day, we rehearse in class. Only Helen, disputed princess of Troy, is missing. Richard asks if he should cut her part. Mick, who is playing Paris, shouts *No*. Patch says to Mick,

'Don't worry mate, we'll get her back somehow.'

And of course, rehearsals are absolutely and utterly chaotic. But then that's Patch's idea.

With all the House against her, children and nurses alike, Jane Ratcliffe's star appears on the wane. Her limp performance at the play has pushed her right down. For several days there is a strange vacuum. During this time, Jane does not come out of her office. Instead she calls in Debbie and issues instructions which Debbie passes on or not as she sees most fit.

In our view, this is just fine. Patch keeps saying that Mrs. Noble will be returning soon, although to be honest nobody can understand why this should help, as Mrs. Noble is no pushover either. But we kind of trust in Patch and we wait. With the riotous rehearsals of our play, we are all easier, even having fun.

But then Jane learns that the new bishop will be

preaching this coming Sunday. She has long awaited this event. And so she decides to Make Another Stand.

Debbie refused point blank, and so of course did Flick, for which they were both disciplined on the spot, a quid docked off their weekly wages.

Lizzie's response was so rude she lost two pounds docked off. And when the Ratcliffe put out feelers to the other nurses, they all said no. Even Pete said no, he wouldn't drive the bus. That was when the Ratcliffe brought in John Fry again.

Lizzie was incandescent. She accosted Fry in the Great Hall and gave him a great smack on the face right in front of everybody. 'You turd!' she cried, but he just came back in his country way,

'Look, Lizzie, maybe you can afford to lose your job. But I got me wife and kiddies.' The brick and flint cottage was tied and Mrs. Fry valued clothes on children's backs and bread on the table over siding with Patch in his religious wars. Lizzie smacked him again.

Chaos, did I say? Well, certainly, everything is falling apart quite rapidly and we are more and more embattled.

We are in the Great Hall, prepped for church. It's a complete capitulation. The Trojans' mood is very sombre. And it's cold. The wind has come up in the night and is blowing from the north-east, from the Arctic across the North Sea, over the marshes and it is now battering the front of the House.

Lizzie and Debbie and Flick have volunteered to come with us after all, out of solidarity. They still got their money docked, though. Richard's coming too. Lizzie asked him. They're all busy wrapping us up in swaddling blankets, except Debbie who has gone to have a word with the Rat in her office. She wants to ask the Rat to postpone church parade as the temperature is still dropping and the wind is veering easterly out of a steely sky and blowing half a gale.

Debbie's back in a tick, shaking her head.

'Nope,' she says.

'Sorry, old boy,' John Fry says as he single-handedly hefts the heavily swaddled Patch from his Armsworth 302 into a manual chair. Patch lets him off with an absolving nod and John wheels him away.

They say that in Arabia the religious police drive you to your prayers with whips – but here in old England? And that vulnerable boy, in that tomb-like church, on so cold a day?

At the ramp stands the Rat, her arms folded. She says,

'I am sorry, Patrick. It didn't have to be like this.'

Patch says nothing, but his eyes stay on her and his head moves a fraction up and down. Debbie runs out of the house with another blanket and a scarf.

John Fry tips the chair back and gets the front wheels onto the ramp, and then races King Priam up into the big blue bus.

The vast church is black from the ground up.

A century of coal smoke from the twenty thousand domestic chimneys of the town plus the soot coughed from the smoke stacks of the town's brewery and from the local treacle factory have worked their way beneath the skin of the stone and stained it through and through.

High up on the front of the church, some grubby saints look down. Half have lost their heads to spirited iconoclasts, the rest are still whole but bear little resemblance to what the sculptor intended. Centuries of bracing weather have worn them down and they have lost their contours. They look like used-up bath soap.

The bishop is saying something but the words glance off Patch. He can feel the peculiar cold inside this church working its way beneath his skin and into the texture of his body. It seeps towards his slowly beating heart.

He drives it away with noble images from his stamp collection. George V's disembodied Roman head, 1912 Barbados definitive, 3s. violet and green. Magenta on sepia, Griqualand West 20 cents. Nigeria 1953 2d definitive, black and ochre 'Tin' – hatched and dashed and printed by Thomas de la Rue – dispatched to Lagos and then up country – licked and stuck on by perhaps a black man's tongue flicking over the sticky side – perhaps a love letter or a request to attend a college.

Debbie wheels Patch up to where the bishop, who is oddly called 'Ted Barking', lays on his hands.

Patch is thinking of something that could be known but wasn't quite, like a black man touching that square of paper and what was in his mind and what he wanted to do or say by that, what were the projects that he was moving forward.

Was it by any chance to do with 'Tin' or was it just totally impossible that the stamp should match the project?

The priest was now fitting a silver goblet to Patch's lips but the fit was poor and the man said Sorry and wiped away the trickle of wine that ran down Patch's plump cheek. Patch ran his tongue over his lips. The wine was sweet. He was thinking again of the Nigerian's tongue passing over the bitter adhesive of the 2d definitive.

One fact among the billion trillion facts, only a few of which he knew.

But it was something that could be known, not like the wine and the meaning of the wine which were as obscure to

Patch now as when the vicar had explained it all in Confirmation Class.

The stamp had value, 2d when the man had stuck it on. Then the stamp had another value (3d once franked, 5d if the man had just hung on to it, kept it 'mint', according to *Stanley Gibbons Elizabethan Stamp Catalogue 1961*. These facts were clear.

And even beyond that, stamps meant something, Empire for instance. One hundred and three territories coloured red, each with their definitive series and their special commemorative issues, and each definitive series renewed reign by reign, or even twice in the case of a longer reign:

Queen Vic 1840-1901
Edward VII 1901-1910
George V 1910-1935
Edward VIII 1936
George VI 1936-1952
Queen Elizabeth II 1952 up to now

There was length in all these monarchs reigning from the first stamp in 1840 right up to 1966 – and breadth, breadth of Empire. And never once had the name Great Britain appeared on any stamp. It wasn't needed. Everybody knew. Britain was the first.

Patch felt the cold drawing closer to his heart. There were facts that could be known and other things like the wine that never could. And others still which wobbled when you pressed them. Even Empire wobbled now as new countries sprang up overnight that were simply not on Patch's map, and the world became bigger and more hopeless.

There was a dark corner to the big church and the

draught flew out of it and gathered about Patch.

He sneezed and Debbie started forward. He flapped his eyes at her and she darted her big stupid handkerchief at his nose, white polka dots on corn yellow, dabbing expertly and when he muttered *Get me out of here* she at once whizzed him out into a pale sunshine, where he sneezed again.

'God wears me out,' he said.

37

The Unplumbed
Depths
of Hell

Last but one (or two) days of my life in The Bin

Dearly beloved,
From the Depths. I can scarcely describe my anger. Norma woke me up this morning and told me to come quick. I nipped over to *Elizabeth Fry* and there was Big Bev warming a pan of milk on the stove. On the draining board I spotted the big bulb syringe they use.

'What's up?' I asked all casual like.

'Oh just the Bulb for the New Girl. She was naughty in the night. Sheets were sopping this morning.'

Big Bev reached down the big tin of treacle they mix in with the milk. I said, 'Bevy, please,' so she put her hands on her hips and stared me out. 'Standin' orders,' she said, 'wet the bed, you get the Bulb in the morning.'

'Bev, please. Please just don't do it and say you did. Just this once. Please.'

She pursed her lips into what for Big Bev passes for a thoughtful look and said,

'Hmm, she your girlfriend or somethin'?'

'She is my oldest friend.'

Bev did a bit more considering and then she said,

'Well, just this once. But you change the sheets then.' So Norma and I went in and there was Helen sitting on a chair

302

in a dressing gown. She had her legs up under her chin and she was hugging and rocking like a little child.

'Come on, darling,' Norma said, and took Helen off for a nice hot bath. Now Norma's starting to understand about the letter, she's quite changed.

I pulled the sopping sheets off and then Big Bev came and helped me make the bed after all. She said,

'You know, Robbie, I don' agree with them enemas neither. They get the bloat and cramps something awful. But Salter's orders...'

Enough! I wanted to cry. We've stoodsed enough and we can't stands no more!

But craftily I murmured something soothing to keep Big Bev onside. And I began to hatch my plan. I'm going to become a Top Lawyer, lock up Sallow Salter in the Gulag, and blow this dump up with a hydrogen bomb.

No, actually my plan is a bit more short-term. It starts right now with Dawn in Salter's office. And it ends within forty-eight hours. And the long and short of it is – we are coming to you. Expect us in a day, or two at the most.

And if all comes out right, the plan includes Norma.

With my serious love and in the certainty of your warmest welcome,

I am sincerely yours,

Robbie 'Colditz' Willis

38

Jane Ratcliffe sat at her desk, tormented by the bites of regret. How could she have been so stupid, so heartless, so unthinking, so inconsiderate of the vulnerable children in her care that she had not just taken them to church but forced them to go, and then this had to happen? It was perhaps the lowest moment in what Jane saw as her pastoral mission for those poor benighted limited children.

What had that wretched Ted Barking got up and said? And him the new bishop! Jane had been so very keen to hear his sermon, the first after his inauguration. They had been promised a new spiritual force – and what did they hear? 'To the twentieth century, the old man in the sky and the whole supernaturalist scheme seem as fanciful as the man in the moon.'

The new bishop was practically an atheist! He'd said 'We may have to give up using the word God for a generation… God is not another Being at all but the depths of our life…'

Jane's torment was interrupted by a loud rapping at the door. It was Debbie.

'Come in, Deborah.' Although Jane had growing reservations about Debbie, especially after her disgraceful performance over Helen's transfer to Binstead, she was at that moment glad of some respite from her spiritual reflections.

'Miss Ratcliffe…' Debbie was hovering by the door. Jane beckoned to her.

'Deborah, tell me truthfully, do you think the children came to any harm last Sunday in church…?'

'Oh, yes,' Debbie said fervently, 'that's what I've come about.'

Jane's heart leapt. Sometimes she felt so alone in her spiritual views. She wanted urgently now to share with Debbie.

'Yes,' Debbie repeated, 'Patch caught a dreadful cold.'

'Oh!' Jane winced in her exasperation. 'No, Deborah, I meant the effect of that dreadful, wicked sermon.'

'The sermon? Oh, I dunno, I never listen. I'm too busy looking out for the kids.'

'So you don't think the children...'

'Listen to the sermon? That lot listen to a sermon? Come off it! But look, Miss Ratcliffe, I've got Patch waiting outside. There's something he wants to say to you.'

'Oh, very well. I'll see him now.'

'OK, I'll be back in a tick.'

It turned out to be quite a long tick as Patch had got bored waiting and buzzed off somewhere. While Debbie was rounding him up, Jane first recalled those days of ordered discrimination when she had felt able to dock the nurses sixpence when they used that dreadful Americanism. Those days, it seemed, were ended. Now no one quite respected her rules any more...

This glum reflection was driven out by a sudden return of memory about the end of Ted Barking's frightful sermon, the last few words which he had spoken with an extraordinary gentleness... what was it?... 'the only imperative is to follow the path of love... the only intrinsic evil is lack of love...'

There had been a dangerous appeal in the man's voice. But he was practically an atheist... he should be prosecuted for heresy...

Suddenly, Jane's office door was flung back and there, lolling like a great red pasha in his gleaming Armsworth

302, was Patch, King of the Trojans. Debbie stood behind Patch but she did not come in. She stepped back and closed the door behind Patch who buzzed right up to Jane Ratcliffe's desk.

'I've come to confess,' Patch says in his high, squeaky voice. Jane at once detected impertinence.

She waits.

'Yeah, if it's OK with you, I'd like to confess. It's me that done for Dan.'

Patch's motive is to get the swimming ban finally lifted so the children, who are pretty miserable at present, can slide back down into those regenerating waters. There is also the question of Mr. MacAskill, for whom Patch has a surprisingly soft spot. Patch thinks that if swimming is re-instated, the Rat could give Mr. MacAskill his job back.

Patch also has a slightly less high-minded motive. As he has caught a cold in the big church, he wants to show the Rat the results of her spiritual and disciplinary dispensations. This motive is less worthy as it comes under the class of 'I told you so' and 'you'll be sorry when...'. Patch knows that this class of motive is childish and beneath a king. However, he has concluded that as his bigger motives are well in the public interest and are directed towards the good of his people, he can indulge this subsidiary motive without shame or impairment of his overall kingliness.

'Oh my goodness,' Jane exclaims. In the swirl of things recently she has practically forgotten Dan and the swimming interdict. Nonetheless, she summons up her wits and starts to ponderously reply to Patch's absurd confession. Does Jane pause to reflect on whether Patch actually could be the culprit? Does she imagine that a dystrophy Stage Five, as Patch now is, could even move his foot to crush a flea let alone give a nimble haemo a kicking? Or is she so versed in the spirit of sacrifice that she suspends disbelief and accepts the ram in the thicket? Who knows? Because while the Rat gathers the fair breeze of propitiation behind her and is sailing through a gracious speech towards the safe harbour of forgiveness, Patch gives the most almighty sneeze. Infectious particles fly out across Jane's desk and some generous matter appears below Patch's red pug nose. The Ratcliffe's hand flies to cover her mouth and nose. She moves nimbly around her desk whilst tugging out her hanky to wipe Patch off and calling for Debbie.

Jane pops the handkerchief straight into the Sani-Bin. She won't use it again now, even though it's from the initialled set her mother gave her two Christmases ago. She moves well away from Patch and calls more loudly for Debbie.

Debbie comes running in.

'Sorry, I just popped upstairs a mo to change.'

Patch gazes at Debbie appreciatively.

'Not them elastic pants again, Debbie!'

'Sorry, I know my...'

'Yup,' Patch says, with satisfaction. But Debbie is already rummaging in the medicine cabinet and gathering into her arms a bunch of pills and potions. Then she follows Patch out and they head together for the San.

Angela Cudmore wheels Greg into the telephone room next to the Sluice. It is getting dark, so Angela switches on the light. A singe unshaded 40-watt bulb comes on and Angela parks Greg next to the deal table. The bareness of the room doesn't worry Angela as she's used to scrubbed down venues at the farm. Nor does it worry Greg whose mind is full of the colour of his dreams.

The lady at the Exchange barks 'Has the Warden author-ized a Trunk Call?' and Angela, whose childhood was full of the incredible lies her father told the panicked cows as he prodded them into the abattoir lorry, just says Yes without any hesitation whatsoever.

''allo, Angie darlin,' Trev says. 'Thanks for callin'.'

Trev is the manager of The Grief. Both Trev and all the four lads who make up The Grief come from Greg and Angela's home town. Bungay it's called, a settlement that has sat since Saxon times on a patch of heavy clay located precisely in a part of deepest Suffolk to which nobody ever travels, and which people generally leave never to return.

'Yes, Trev, have you got some news for us? Greg's right here with me.'

'Oh, yes, hi Greg.' Greg can just hear him and he nods. Angela briefly holds the receiver up to Greg.

'Hallo Trev,' Greg says.

'Hi Greg. How you doin'?'

Angela puts the receiver to her own ear again.

'Well?' she demands.

'Angie, Angie,' Trev purrs, 'sweet talkin' as ever.'

Angela grunts. She has been defending her virtue against Trev since she was twelve.

'Well, Angie, it's good news. Like I said in me telegram, the lads 'ave 'ad a look at Greg's song and they think they can make something of it.'

It was to The Grief that Angela 'sent off' Greg's song – and Trev now informs Angela that they're going to play it. Next week at Felixstowe. And Greg and Angela are to go up.

'So, err, Angie, what about it? When you come up... you 'n' me...? Seeing as how...'

'Thanks, Trev, I'll bear it in mind.'

Trev correctly takes this for a No but he cares less about Angela's refusal than he used to in the old days as he is now in London and on the scene and his horizons are extremely wide.

That night Greg dreams:

> *We want to go to the town on the hill to go swimming in the pool. At the bottom of the hill are some still shallows. Then we climb fast up the track, up the green hillside. It is very steep but I have seen the way and I know we can do it.*
>
> *Near the pool are some pretty girls in short skirts. They say the pool may be open or it may not.*

For Greg, the dream is very good. He knows the way from the still water to the pool. The pretty girls are full of life. The pool may be open. He is full of hope.

Jane Ratcliffe stood in the yard outside the San. She was reluctant to go in. Through the window, she could see Patch's bulk in the bed. His eyes were closed but still she felt his presence.

Since Debbie had taken Patch to the San, Jane had become scared. She was scared because she had sent him to church, and scared because he had then caught cold. Bitterly she regretted what she had done, and not just the church but more than that, all that harping on rules when what she had meant was *love*. Why could she not express the love she felt?

Even St. Paul had said it. It had been in the epistle in the church that day, just when Debbie had wheeled Patch out and she had heard it:

He forgave us all our sins, having cancelled the written code, with its regulations, that was against us and that stood opposed to us – he took it away.

Colossians, it was. *Cancelled the written code.* Was that possible?

Patch stirred and turned his head and opened his eyes and looked straight at Jane. In shame she ducked down and ran, bent double to avoid his look.

It was the cruellest moment to choose, that first drifty moment after sex. The only moment of a grown-up life that is really of the moment, with no past and no projects, that motiveless moment of just being, raptured and content in the loved one's embrace.

Flick and Debbie, in the room they shared, were intricately entwined on Debbie's slightly bigger bed in a complex of limbs and lips that had emerged from their playful love-making. The door swung open to reveal the Ratcliffe's skirted form and the Ratcliffe's hard and affectless face which then reconfigured on the spot into an image of shock and awe that could have served as a model for a Norwegian painter's grimmer visions, bar the specs.

Now the playful girls, although disturbed, were not without resources. The outgoing, cheerful Debbie uncoiled her body from her lover's and slid easily from the bed and stood confronting the Ratcliffe. Faced by the big, fit, starkly naked girl, Jane took a step back, where she collided with the tray of soup and soldiers that Lizzie was carrying along the corridor for Patch in the San.

The skinny, petite Flick, meanwhile, reached for the rumpled sheet that lay on the floor between their austere iron bedsteads. With a quick motion of her lean, sinewy body she pulled the sheet from the floor and arranged it deftly over her front, drawing it up to her neck, all the while

310

staring at the discomfited Ratcliffe, who was now mopping soup from her cardigan.

'I... I... just wanted to ask you something, Deborah...'

'Thanks, Miss Ratcliffe,' Debbie said firmly. 'I'll be down in a tick.'

But when Debbie approached Jane Ratcliffe half an hour later, Jane did not ask her anything. She found it was too hard to frame the question, or perhaps it was too late to put it. And as the question had to do with love, and as she seemed now to be presented with a bewildering variety of different possible loves, it all seemed too complicated. Probably even Debbie, whom Jane had chosen as the nurse least likely to misunderstand, would be puzzled and would not give any sensible reply.

So Jane Ratcliffe kept her peace and tried to concentrate on humdrum things, while waiting for news from the San.

Class is a desolate place without our great leader, our kingly Patch. Everyone looks around and all we feel is a great emptiness. It's like soul has drained from us. Richard limply suggests we rehearse the new Act Four he has agreed with Patch in which King Priam sets out on an expedition to conquer Persia and India and beyond. But as Mick points out, without our King Priam, it doesn't make a lot of sense.

'an' without Helen, too.'

So Richard, evidently dredging up some lesson he has suffered in an ancient kindergarten, decides we should do geography. He tells everyone to draw pictures of Warsaw-on-the Vistula in their Rough Note Books.

The effort of imagining Warsaw-on the-Vistula keeps everyone unusually quiet, as no one has any idea about it. I can't do it anyway, so I just lie and look at everyone and think about Robbie's letter. Whatever does he mean? *My plan is a bit more short term... within forty-eight hours, we are coming to you.* Well, Robbie, time is up! Where are you?

And the plan includes Norma? What on earth?

There is a noise as Mick throws his Rough Note Book on the floor. He has been colouring in the Vistula with violent jerky strokes. Now the city lies there on the floor, the Vistula a turbulent, improbable cobalt blue.

I look at Greg. He is staring out of the window. Warsaw is on the desk before him, many-towered.

Oh Patch, come back to us!

39

They'd had a couple of pints of Adnams, at Richard's expense because he had a huge deficit with Pete and was momentarily flush with a fresh postal order from Bunter Hall that he'd wangled from his mother.

Pete helped himself to a fifth gasper from the packet of Embassy Richard had got out of the cigarette machine.

They were discussing the arrangements for Felixstowe.

'It should be quite an outing,' Pete was saying. 'I'm going to drive the bus. And you know Angela's arranged it all, she's mates with The Grief and everything...'

Pete had a faraway look in his eye. Richard said,

'You know I've seen you chatting to Angela quite a bit recently. Going well?'

'Ummm... no, not really. No, we were chatting about... well, Bertie, if you must know.'

'You mean, you haven't been out with her or anything?'

'No, not really.'

It was a puzzle to Richard, and a relief. He had been expecting an update on Pete's grappling with Angela's dicky bra strap and frankly these days such gropings seemed to Richard, well – childish.

Pete was looking embarrassed but he quickly recovered. '... anyway, I think this concert thing will do the trick. We're staying overnight. So here's how we'll do it, mate. You and Lizzie come too, and we'll book two rooms, so say one for me and you and the other one for the girls, and then you nip in with Lizzie, and Angela will have to come in with me. Sorted.'

This scaled up version of the bra strap grapplings seemed to Richard a bit of a shabby plan, cornering Angela like that. But Pete was insistent and Richard let it go. Anything might happen on the night, and Angela seemed quite capable of defending her own interests. In fact, Richard was actually developing rather an admiration for the powers of resistance of this sturdy country girl, although he had not yet shared this view with Pete due to mateship reasons.

Richard had a thought.

'How exactly are we going to get there? Don't we need a... errr...?'

Richard couldn't offhand think what the English for an *exeat* might be.

'We'll take the bus, won't we? I tanked her up today on purpose. The old bat'll never know.'

'But Greg'll need some... err... chitty, won't he?'

'Bollocks, mate. That Ratcliffe's too busy disappearing up her own backside these days to even notice. 'N' Debbie said it'd be OK.'

They had another couple of pints until the proceeds of Richard's postal order – sadly a smallish one, Bunter Hall having stepped on the sumptuary brake – ran out and Pete had smoked the last of the Embassy. Then just as they were getting up to leave, Pete's face took on a furtive look and he grasped Richard's sleeve.

'You know... that book you were telling me about...?'

'What book?' – Richard and Pete didn't discuss literature much – '*The Love Machine*?' This was Richard's current reading. Lizzie had lent it to him

'Come again?

'The *Love Machine*... it's quite a good novel about...'

'Nah, not that one.'

'Erm... not *Nausea*...?'

'Nah.'

'Oh… *A Doctor's Guide to…*'

'Shhhh! Well… could you let me have a quick dekko?'

'Why?'

'Errr…'

'But I thought…'

'Look, Rich, just gimme the book will you?'

Greg, unfortified by pints of Adnams ale, lay quietly in his bed and full of fears. When Angela had put him down, she had said to him over and over that it would be alright, *The Grief* were nice Bungay boys and they would do it right. She stroked his head and gave him a kiss. With her trailing mop of golden locks she looked like an unruly corn goddess. But all the same, Greg tossed from side to side, fretting, and when at last he slid into a shallow sleep, he dreamed:

> *We are doing well in the war in the air and the girls fly many sorties. But they are always arguing. Somebody lets loose a mouse. The girls scream and run about. The girl pilot chokes on her oxygen pipe and the plane crashes.*

Greg woke up very afraid. It was still early, the middle of the night really. He knew the girls were not really girls, they were *him*, parts of Greg, *his* ideas and *his* hopes. He was trying to get up high but he needed oxygen up there. His hopes were frail and they came apart when just a tiny mouse came out. The whole thing crashed down.

Later Greg dreamed again:

> *We are going in muddy lanes. The countryside is wet and sad. I see two brightly coloured birds in a tree but Angela can't see them.*

Greg knows he is a pilgrim and that Angela is his Little Mother. But she can't see the lovely birds. Maybe they're not really there at all.

'Bugger off, Richard. I'm trying to get some kip here.'

Lizzie's tousled head could just be seen, framed by the window she had flung open.

'Won't you come down, Lizzie?'

'I told you, Richard, bugger off.'

'Oh come on. Juliet would have.'

'Well, you can get off with her then, can't you. Anyway, you're pissed.'

'No I'm not.'

'Yes you are. And don't go throwing stones at my window like that. You'll break the bleeding thing.'

'Come down. I've got something to tell you.'

'So what is it then?'

'What?'

'What you're going to tell me?'

'Oh… we're going to Felixstowe with Greg. You and me and Pete and Angela. Pete's going to drive us in the bus.'

'Hmm. I dunno.'

'Come on, it'll be a treat.'

'And the Rat?'

'Oh… we're not bothering about her.'

So Lizzie said yes.

'And won't you come up to the Tower tonight?'

Again she said yes.

Lying on cushions and quilts against Sir Roper's plinth, Lizzie has just dozed off and is snoring lightly. Richard, on whose arm Lizzie's head is lying quite heavily and delightfully, is wondering why lovers do not spend their entire life making love. Just then Bertie, who is on guard outside, starts a big barrage of barking.

Richard eases his arm out from under Lizzie's head and gets up from the quilts, which Lizzie then pulls luxuriously over her. Quite naked, Richard runs to the door, opens it and makes a grab for Bertie.

With his hand on Bertie's collar he looks up and is astounded to see a small crowd assembled, each of whom, except for Helen, takes one look at Richard's skinny naked form and bursts out laughing.

Most raucous of them is a short plump lady wearing high heels and an extremely tight skirt and top. Her hair, which is piled high on her head, quivers with her laughter and she covers her purple lips with a podgy hand on which the fingernails, in matching purple, have been sharpened into what look like talons.

This lady stands behind a wheelchair boy, a Mec who looks vaguely familiar to Richard. The third of this crazy group is a ragged unkempt soul of uncertain age whose grey frizzy hair shoots out in wild wisps. Dressed in a soiled green coat tied round with sisal string, she looks like a bag lady.

And then there's Helen, who is not laughing at him but who steps forward and gives him a sisterly hug. Closer up, he sees that she is in fact crying in a gentle fashion.

'Oh, hallo, you're that brilliant bloke that broke Salter's cane,' the Mec kid says.

Lizzie now appears at the door behind Richard, wrapped in quilts. She's brought one for Richard which he quickly pulls around him.

'Oh, hallo, Robbie,' she says cheerfully. 'I thought we got shot of you.'

'Hallo, Lizzie. No, absence makes the heart grow fonder. You see I even brought my friends.'

'I do see.' Lizzie looks around at the little group and, spotting Helen, steps forward and hugs her tight.

'Darling! But, Robbie, what on earth…?'

'Didn't Gloriana and Patch tell you we were coming?'

'Nope.'

'I did write.'

'Yeah, well. What's up?'

'Helen and I have run away. We thought we could stay here until…'

'Oh, yeah? And your chums?'

'Oh, Dawn and Norma, don't worry about them. They just came to drop us off.'

'Yes,' says the short plump lady, who is in fact Dawn, 'we're going to Liphook.'

'Liphook,' the ragged greying soul repeats uncertainly.

40

On the big day Greg looks like a massive pensive hero, resting his head on his hands, elbows on the arm rest of his wheelchair.

All dressed in black leather, their greasy brown hair hanging down to their shoulders, *The Grief* shamble on to the stage of the Felixstowe Winter Gardens. They are the biggest thing to come out of Bungay since the Peasants' Revolt. Their leather trousers cling to their plump country thighs and calves. They are accompanied by their girlfriends who are dreamy, indolent-seeming dolly birds with pretty faces and long, clean hair. All these girls are blonde and they all have very long legs and very short mini-skirts.

The dolly birds disperse below the stage. Two of them come up and hug Greg and stay by him.

The lead singer struts and swaggers like a peasant Byron. The noise is cataclysmic, like all-out battle on the plains of Megiddo. You can't hear the words, of course, but Richard has a handout with the lyrics. He is surprised because these are full of a great deal of hate but are also actually quite subtle. One of the songs is in French, by Rimbaud.

The dolly birds stick by Greg. They don't speak because the music is much too loud but they dance continually, very well indeed, and they whirl Greg around a lot.

Lizzie reads the words too and shouts in Richard's ear that it is all CRAP, but she is moving with the music, getting nicely hot.

At last they sing Greg's song. The dolly birds bring Greg up on stage and he plays the drums. Nobody has a clue what this song is about except Richard who has the handout, according to which it goes as follows:

BUNGAY GIRL

Listen!
I'll get lucky
In my head
Escaping
Not yet dead
    I'm gonna escape escape escape
    In my head. Yeah!

Yeah!
Cos I love you
Bungay girl
I'm escaping
Give us a swirl
    I'm gonna escape escape escape
    In my head. Yeah!

Yeah!
Know I'm dreamin'
Coming right
Escaping
From the night
    I'm gonna escape escape escape
    In my head. Yeah!

Yeah!
Thing is, Bungay girl
I try my best
Escaping

Fuck the rest
I'm gonna escape escape escape
In my head. Yeah!

The Grief give it a thick impasto treatment, very very loud, with plangent bass and they have brought on a sitar, the first that has been seen in England up till then. The song is a huge success and Greg is hoisted up on his chair and danced around above people's heads. His face wears a transcendent, blissful look.

This is probably the first pop song to have the word *fuck* in it, so it gets a Lady Chatterley kind of notoriety and sells 100,000 singles in a week. But this is later. Tonight, the dolly birds take Greg off to their hotel, where he will have a late supper with them and then sleep over – they have reserved a room for him. Angela gives the dolly birds a small bag containing Greg's neediments and the girls swing off, trundling Greg along the promenade at a fantastic pace.

Richard and Lizzie, and Pete and Angela go off to their own hotel. Richard and Lizzie walk arm in arm, and so do Pete and Angela.

That night, Greg falls asleep at once after his very long day. He is completely, blissfully happy. His dreams try to make sense of so much happiness:

We are going to the concert. I am sitting at a table in the kitchen. Suddenly it is time and Angela comes in to dress me. She wheels me out but I have only one sock on. Angela is very calm. We are late but we are only going to miss the back-up band.

Then Angela is driving quite fast on a big road in London. A huge crowd of people are coming down the church steps and into the road. The women are smart. They stand very tall with their shoulders back. They are brown from the sun. Angela puts on the brake and we go past slowly. We have clean white dogs in the back.

We get there and go round shaking hands with people. In a room there are decorations and about five dolly birds.

Then outside some children come. They are dressed up as fairies. They begin to dance and we all link in to the circle. We go round and round like we are running, all in time with each other. We dance and dance and everybody is very happy.

In the morning, Pete drives them back in the big blue bus without a word. Angela sits in a seat in the middle of the bus looking out of the window. Richard and Lizzie sit at the back on the double seat next to where Greg's wheelchair is parked with both brakes on. Greg is physically present in the wheelchair but plainly his eternal spirit is somewhere else entirely, lofted high on strong young arms amidst the music and the dolly birds. Richard and Lizzie are holding hands until Lizzie says 'Sticky' and pulls her hand away.

They skirt Bungay, which is a low flat settlement with a rash of pebble-dashed council houses on a low rise above the town. Apart from that, fields stretch out, mostly ploughed-up brown ones, flecked with white gulls. Angela stares at her native earth without any particular expression.

And then, bowling down the drive to the House and swinging the big bus into the courtyard, Pete exclaims,

'Strewth! A DS 19!'

Without a herald, the sleek old Citroën swings round on the crunching gravel before the front door which one alone enters by. The elegant car eases down on its haunches like a gazelle sinking to its rest. Eleanor Noble steps out, enters the house by the front door that only she may use, and resumes control.

PART FIVE: LAST WEEKS

41

So give me one good reason why I shouldn't sack the lot of you on the spot.'

Eleanor Noble was a far cry from what Richard had been expecting.

First of all, she was quite cross at being called back from her stint in California, which had been most enjoyable. Then on her arrival back she had been confronted by mess on top of mess. After consulting with poor Jane Ratcliffe, she had given the woman two weeks' leave and hoped she would absent herself as her presence seemed to be putting everybody's back up. Jane in fact had seemed on the verge of some kind of breakdown, chattering on about 'the man *is* in the sky', whatever that might mean, and 'the only intrinsic evil is love' (although that couldn't be right, Eleanor felt she must have misheard Jane's outburst).

Eleanor decided to round up the apparent ringleaders and deal with them first. So she hauled in Debbie, of whom she had had great hopes as future management material, and the Richard, the New Man who, whatever his part in all this, should have known better, with all his good upbringing and education and whatnot. As an afterthought, she'd hauled Lizzie in too as she seemed to be implicated. The others – Angela, Flick and co – well, she'd come to them later.

So Debbie and Richard were on the carpet, literally, in front of what Richard had assumed to be Jane Ratcliffe's desk but which now turned out to be Eleanor Noble's. Lizzie was there too, standing a little to one side of Richard, looking dreamy.

'Well?'

It was Lizzie who opened the case for the defence.

'The Rat's just an old cow.'

'Yes, Lizzie, I see you expressed yourself there. Miss Ratcliffe tells me you punched her. Quite hard, too.'

'She bloody well deserved it.'

On Eleanor's desk lay a yellow pad on which she had made a list of the points she had been able to winnow from Jane's ramblings.

'Miss Ratcliffe has been quite erratic,' Debbie said diplomatically.

'Alright, Debbie – and you've helped her out, have you?'

Debbie nodded guardedly.

Mrs. Noble's finger brushed up and down the yellow pad.

'Trying to hide Helen when she was due for her transfer. Allowing the school bus to be practically hi-jacked and driven across two counties. Allowing Greg to go to some wild pop concert...'

'Ummm...' Richard said.

Everybody looked at him. He glanced at Lizzie for moral support but she was clearly a world away. The last few days she seemed to Richard to have undergone a change. She was looking really seriously pretty.

'Ah yes, the New Man, the Richard. Yes, well, speak up.'

'Errr...'

Richard was wondering why Patch considered Mrs. Noble such a superior item to the dreaded Rat. So far she seemed just a tougher, cleverer version of the same.

'Yes? Did you really think,' Eleanor asked, 'that it was kind to get Gloriana keyed up like that? University indeed. She hasn't got a single O level...'

Richard now felt Lizzie's eyes upon him. He also felt a shameful red flush sweeping up his cheeks.

'Well may you fly the red flag, young man. Working Gloriana up was shameful indeed.'

'We… umm… we felt things were generally not quite right.' Richard knew his voice was quavering. What a weed. He had to rally.

'She…'

'Who is she? The cat's mother?'

This was completely hopeless.

Richard struggled to remember all the things Patch had suggested when he had gone to see him in the San, and what Gloriana had said, and what Robbie, who was hiding in the Tower with Helen, had said. If only Patch and Gloriana and Robbie were here!

'Miss Ratcliffe sent a minor to an adult institution.' That was one of Robbie's. 'And she had her taken forcibly.' Robbie'd got something on that from the law book Richard had sent off to him.

Mrs. Noble stared very hard at Richard and Richard looked down.

In fact, Eleanor Noble had indeed been wondering what all that had been about. She knew Helen as a fragile child, and Binstead, for all its undoubted virtues as a shelter, was not perhaps the most suitable environment for a sensitive adolescent girl.

Nonetheless, it was not up to this Richard to lecture her on what was or was not correct care for Park House children. That was up to trained professionals.

Debbie now chipped in.

'Yes, and she was trying to dose her up with bromides.'

Mrs. Noble's head jerked up very slightly. She wrote one word, very small indeed, on the yellow pad. She had heard all about the circumstances of Helen's transfer to Binstead, but this bromide thing was quite new to her. She'd gone over the Daily Reports carefully and she'd seen nothing about that. She'd read the Prescription Log and there was nothing untoward there. There had been no mention of a change in medicaments in Helen's own case file.

'Nonsense,' she said.

'No, it's not,' Debbie said. 'Flick tried the emulsion. She came over all queer. She had to stop it.'

'What? Felicity stopped a patient's medicine against instructions? If that's the case, I'll be having a serious word with her about that. In fact...'

Mrs. Noble picked up a form that lay on her desk and looked briefly at it. Debbie recognized it as Flick's application to enrol in nursing training.

Richard now recalled another of Robbie's points.

'And she sacked Mr. MacAskill without proper process...'

'That is no concern of yours.'

'And she cancelled swimming, even though the children love it...'

'... and they need it,' Debbie put in. 'Miss Payne said so.'

'That was a disciplinary sanction. And swimming at Park House is a privilege, not a right.'

'And she used church parade as a punishment. She forced the children to go, even Patch. And it was a chilly day.'

'I understand they were well wrapped up.'

'It's all... it's all a failure of the duty of care.'

At this, Eleanor Noble showed signs of anger.

'You watch your words, young man. It's not your place to tell me my duty. Now clear out the lot of you before I throw you out.'

Lizzie, who had been largely looking out of the window during all this, suddenly spoke up.

'Well?' she said.

'Well what, Elizabeth?'

'Have we got the sack or not?'

'We will see about that, my girl. But right now, get back to work. This place is falling apart. Oh, and errr… you' – she pointed at Richard – 'you come and see me, today after lunch.'

They moved towards the door. As they were about to leave, Mrs. Noble called out,

'By the way, I had a phone call from Mr. Salter at Binstead. He told me that Robbie and Helen were missing, as well as some other older woman whom Robbie had befriended. Do you lot know anything about that?'

They shook their heads.

'Because if I find out that you've been involved, I really will come down on you like a ton of bricks.'

'Nah, you just don't get it, do you mate?'

Patch was propped up in bed. His generally red colour seemed inflamed further by his cold and he made a very technicolour picture against the starched white pillowcases.

'I mean,' he went on, 'you didn't seriously think she was gonna come along like a whatsit – fairy godmother – and sprinkle a bit of stardust?'

Sadly, it was indeed true that in Richard's imagination the longed-for return of Mrs. Noble had featured rather like that last minute intervention of Pallas Athene in the Greek play they had done for A Level. The goddess had come down and in twenty lines settled all the tangled affairs of the house of Atreus – not, admittedly, very fairly, but at least she had sorted them all out.

'Nah, mate, life's not like that.'

'So what's the use?'

'What's the use?'

'Yes, what was the use of me calling Mrs. Noble and getting her back? She's just as bad as Miss Ratcliffe.'

'Oh, 'ere we go… givin' up, are we? You toffs are all the same. You just haven't got it, have you?'

Richard wagged his head about a bit, stung by Patch's critique but not knowing what to say.

'Thing is, mate, what you got to understand is – the Rat's weak. She's got no power. She can dish it out but she can't change anything. But old Ma Noble… she can do stuff… she's got real power.'

'But she doesn't want to change anything. It's just going to be Binstead, after all. And as for Gloriana going to university…'

'Yeah, well. Maybe you did go a bit far there, getting' 'er 'opes up an' that.'

'Cripes. So what do we do now? And what are we going to do about Helen and Robbie?'

Patch snorted.

'You really don't get it, do you? Ma Noble back, and Helen and Robbie done a bunk with that old biddy – it's all fitting into place.'

'I don't see how.'

'Course you don't. You been educated beyond what your poor brain will stand. Just get Gloriana and Robbie over here. I need to talk to them.'

Jane Ratcliffe read Joe MacAskill's letter carefully, all through, twice. She was sitting in her pleasant bed-sitting room with its view of the sunlit Italian Garden fringed with hydrangeas whose whitening heads were nodding in the breeze. Beyond, through the small herd of transparent and coloured glass animals given to her by her mother that were dotted spiritlessly along her windowsill, she could see the copse on its rise and, on the top, the ugly Tower where some people, she suspected, got up to filthy things. (This low rise did, she acknowledged to herself, have a suggestive swell, it was just like a bosom, and the Tower – well!)

She sighed. Just as she had been looking forward to the two weeks' rest that Mrs. Noble had so kindly suggested, Mr. MacAskill's letter had strangely come by post that morning in a buff envelope – she appreciated, at least, his old-fashioned instinct of economy. But he could have saved the twopence halfpenny altogether. It was not as though he did not see her twenty times a day but lived instead in some far-off district whence only a posted letter could carry his thoughts.

And what thoughts! She sighed again. She worked so hard at trying to be good, yet that effortless flow of good-ness she had anticipated in herself seemed to be so sluggish, as though clogged up at some moral narrows so far up-stream that she had never been able to work out what or where the blockage was or how it could have occurred, still less how to loosen it.

As now, for instance. For there was the distinct figure of Elizabeth – Lizzie – moving on the path in the dappled leop-ard shade beyond the billowing hydrangeas and then Richard just behind, and in a minute they could be seen emerging from the trees and walking up the hill arm in arm towards the Tower like those pastoral lovers in the feathery Watteau painting Jane had once seen in the Wallace Collec-tion on her school trip to London.

The scene confused Jane Ratcliffe profoundly, because it was so plainly wrong and yet somehow not wrong at all really. But she put this moral debate aside for later. She was too taken up with the more violent conflicts aroused by Mr. MacAskill's love letter. She sighed and reached for the letter and read it for the third time.

He had written,

> Dear Jane,
> I just want you in a quite simple desperate human way. For everything you love, you have to pay a price. Name your price.
> Joe

Jane considered that although Mr. MacAskill was quite possibly deep down a good man, his intemperate character often seemed to be an obstacle to him, and this outrageous letter was a flagrant example of this intemperance of his. Mr. MacAskill was, she felt, so terribly consumed by his obscure struggles that even his victories were Pyrrhic and cost him too dearly, leaving him used up and unavailable for the main paths of righteousness.

He seemed burned like his tanned face had been burned. And the dark face suggested something exotic, even dangerous about him, like he had been living altogether too close to the sun and it had deranged him.

But then she was so opposite to him, not burned at all but cold, frozen even. Sometimes, as time flashed by and changes rushed upon her, she felt she was on a planet further off, like Uranus, where the sun looks 300 times smaller, just a dot, and no heat comes from it at all.

The letter seemed wild, almost desperate in its message but the language was strangely controlled. In fact, Jane, who amongst other things had studied English Literature at one of the new universities, was almost sure she recognized the phrases. A quick hunt in her trusty Oxford Dictionary of Quotations revealed nothing, however, and she gave Mr. MacAskill the benefit of the doubt as a stylist. But not on content, there she could not be budged.

She decided that all the ambient folly had gone to the man's head and she wrote briskly,

Dear Mr. MacAskill,
I have to return your letter. You will, as a good man, understand my reasons and will not write again.
Yours truly,
J. Ratcliffe

***

What madness had seized Joe MacAskill? What impish power was thrusting him towards the hard rock of Ratcliffe?

He himself had no idea. The notion had just come to him when he saw that tear in her eye and suddenly she had been revealed to him as human in a way she never could have been by any amount of talk or thought.

The shocks he had suffered were leading Joe to some pretty radical readjustments. The perfection of life for which he had yearned had not yet appeared, and he was by now pretty sure it never would. Life was proving in practice mixed, dreadfully mixed, and he had decided he would embrace its mixed-ness, all the confused tangle, the elegiac along with the ecstatic and the plain old business of living. He would stop dreaming of paradises, because by now he was sure they were all lost anyway.

And in view of the surge of change that was being endlessly and self-consciously discussed on all sides, he would join in. He would love and redeem a good woman. He would *join the Sixties.*

But first he must heal his back. Carrying Kevin out of the theatre had really done for it. He needed a massage, and he had an idea who he might ask.

That afternoon, after lunch, Richard was at the rendezvous. He put his head round the door but Mrs. Noble waved him away and made him cool his heels outside in the corridor for a good quarter of an hour, just like that brute Jeff Abbott used to do at school before he made you drop your trousers and caned the hell out of you.

The interview began on a discouraging note.

'I am extremely angry with you. I've a good mind to send you packing right away. Or put you in the kitchens.'

Young Win had been persuaded to return temporarily but the meals were of the direst. So far Turkey Twizzlers with watery cabbage and Spaghetti Hoops on burned toast had been her finest outputs.

'In fact, as soon as I can persuade Mr. MacAskill to come back, I think you can ship out.' Eleanor was smiling to herself as she used this nicely Californian phrase.

Richard found he was trembling before the onslaught. Feeling that this was unworthy, and glad only that Lizzie was not there this time to see his humiliation, he determined to make an effort. He glanced at Mrs. Noble's face. The light from the desk lamp caught one side and showed up some heavy lining, while the other side was quite hard to see. Overall, the aspect was pretty grim. She had these brows that came right out over her eyes like a sort of ledge, and from under that the eyes looked steely and unremitting.

'... look to you to keep up standards... maintain the tough love which the children need... avoid indulging them in fancies...'

336

His eye moved to the elegant fall of her silver-grey hair that came right down to her shoulders. How many women of his mother's age would have the daring to leave their greying hair undyed and loose like that, with not a Kirby grip or Alice band to be seen? He looked away, down at her silk blouse and the beautiful folds in…

Overall, Patch was right, she looked… well, authoritative. But where was the use in that? How on earth was that authority going to get them out of the mess they were in? In fact, now Mrs. Noble was uncovering new depths of mess.

'… poor dear helpless Gloriana… really led her up the garden path… severe disabilities… deluded into thinking…'

Richard spoke up, interrupting.

'Have you ever talked to her?'

'What? The poor dear can't talk.'

'Because she's really really bright. We've been reading together…'

'Oh, reading.'

'… and often her ideas are really brilliant.'

Eleanor Noble paused to consider this.

'Well,' she said at length, 'that's very nice for her, a nice little interest to keep her chirpy. But you of all people know what getting into university entails… writing exams, getting good O Levels, three good A Levels, interviews… How are you expecting a girl who can't even talk or write to do all these things? And then the idea that she could follow a university course, even were she to get in… seminars and what not. How would she even get to lectures…?'

During this just tirade, Richard felt red shame surging through his entire body. Of course, Mrs. Noble was right. Of course, it was all impossible. He'd peddled poor Gloriana an empty dream. He'd set her up just for her to tumble down. Her disappointment would crush her. And he, Richard, was responsible. Culpable.

Richard was so taken up by these remorseful feelings that he didn't notice that Mrs. Noble had moved on to a new class of critique entirely.

'... and here I blame you one hundred per cent. You're supposed to be educated and responsible. Didn't they teach you anything practical at that school of yours? Now what's the girl to do? She'll have to leave, of course. Miss Ratcliffe told me about that new place the Council opened. I'll have to try to get her in there, I suppose. She won't like it... but you should both have thought of that before you...'

By the end of this speech, Eleanor Noble was surprised to find she was talking to the empty air. Richard was already heading out of the door. This particularly annoyed her, because she had really wanted to question him about the missing Robbie and Helen. She had a strong suspicion that Richard knew something about that.

Ignoring Mick's invitation as he ran through the Great Hall to play *Heart and Soul* and side-stepping Kevin who was waving a stick at him as he raced past the Sluice, bumping past Debbie and Flick as the two girls adroitly wheeled Gloriana in her heavy bed down for afternoon school, calling out 'Talk later,' to Gloriana, and then almost cannoning into a patently subdued, eyes-lowered version of Jane Ratcliffe as she came out of her room, shoulders slightly hunched, Richard ran, in two minutes flat, from Mrs. Noble's office up to Lizzie's room.

Lizzie was lying on her back, her mouth open, snoring gently. How young and undefended she looked! How his heart beat with pride and fierce male protective longings!

The panting thoughtless boy fell on his sleeping lover

and started to kiss her on her cheeks and lips.

'Gerroff,' she said pushing him away by the shoulders and turning on her side.

Richard slipped under the covers and made a spooning S with Lizzie's back and started to stroke her thigh which was bare below her pleasantly abbreviated nightie. He wanted to touch her tummy.

'Gerroff,' she said again. 'Stop pawing me, Richard. Go to your own bleedin' room.'

'But Lizzie, Lizzie, I heard. I heard your news.'

He thought, I'm going to die of pride and love and now he did quickly slip his hand onto Lizzie's tummy which seemed very warm and ample and capable of breeding life. At once he felt Lizzie's whole body wake and then tauten like a guy rope after rain, and then a surge of what felt like an electric current but which turned out to be an incandescent rage. In an instant she was leaping out of bed, her hair wilder than a maenad's. She danced round in a trice and hit him very hard on the face with the flat of her hand.

'What?'

'*Fuck off.*'

'But...'

Lizzie's hand darted to her bedside lamp which was a very substantial square-bottomed brass-effect affair with its top part in the general shape of a candlestick and some very heavy fluting around its sturdy base. Her grip was firmly on the candlestick bit and she was upending the thing in a dangerous looking move – her eyes were vast, he noted, huge and volcanic, she looked like a wild beast about to spring. He scooted to the door and nipped out. The brass-effect candlestick came hurtling after and fell with a loud crash in the corridor behind him.

He ran down the nurses' corridor, slowing when he saw

Pete up a ladder. Pete was cleaning the transom window above the door of Angela Cudmore's room.

'Spot of bother?' Pete asked helpfully as Richard squeezed past. Richard kicked at the ladder and went to his room and wept.

42

Joe MacAskill's body, stripped naked to the waist, lay prone, his chin pressed awkwardly on the table's edge.

When he had taken off his shirt, Jane Ratcliffe had drawn in her breath, without of course meaning to. It was not the sudden nakedness of Joe's top half although the sheer, well, nudeness of it was indeed striking, nor the strong look of his torso, although that also had been unexpected. It was the whiteness of him, a startling white, like alabaster. The deep mahogany brown which she had thought was the colour of MacAskill all over turned out to be just a very deep sunburned veneer effect that covered only his face and neck and forearms. The look of deeply stained wood halted abruptly at his elbows and the heavy leather finish on his face ended in a little V below his Adam's apple.

It was all a bit disconcerting. He looked like those particoloured shoes that cads used to wear in films.

Tentatively she put her hand on his back, at the side, what was it called, that bit? For some reason, the word *chine* came into her mind, but that couldn't be right. *Flank*? But that, too, sounded, well – rather meaty. MacAskill gave a little start, like a shiver. Were her hands too cold? It was actually the first time that Jane had touched a man's body other than to change a male patient's dressing or to put him on a bedpan. Apart from laying out her father all those years ago, when she was a student nurse and she herself had asked to do that, out of duty.

Now she began to work the muscles, pressing and

kneading MacAskill's sinewy, lean back. He grunted and moved slightly and the surprising muscles rippled like lava flowing beneath the taut skin.

Joe began to relax. He talked to Jane in his mind, telling her about his mahogany colour and the white, because he had seen her start of surprise as he took off his shirt. He told her how his wife Margot had been censorious in her usual way, suntan was so 'common', only artisans removed their coats or rolled up their shirtsleeves. But he also told Jane that it was on mahogany that his life's compact had been made, on mahogany that Sir Ralph Furse had stretched out between the silver and the crystal and had laid a confirming hand on his forearm, like a pledge......

He told this to Jane. He said it was like the dyer's hand...

But silently. He let her work away. He fell into a deep sleep. He began to snore.

Wow. I can only say Wow. And Double wow with knobs on.

A baby! We had never reckoned on that. It is so wonderful – and such a complication. Lizzie an unmarried mother. Richard a father at seventeen. This is truly Chaos. What happens next? Search me.

But a baby has to be a blessing, doesn't it?

Richard is super-agitated about the baby and about Lizzie and – bless him! – about me and the university thing. He is in tears, saying over and over 'It's impossible. I am so sorry.'

I sign to him that it'll be OK, that Patch and Robbie and I have a plan. And not just about me, but about Helen and Mick too, and even for the others, for Robbie and Greg as well.

He strokes my hair and looks at me all bleary and disbe-lieving. He is a mass of self-pity.

Richard, tears are unprofitable. And don't go to pieces now of all times. You are part of the plan. We can't do it without you.

He starts to push his stupid red sopping face against mine and to hug me, like I was his mummy or something. I can't wait for him to pull away.

Richard, focus. Patch'll tell you what to do. Now read me a poem, please. Something lyrical and ecstatic. A poem for Lizzie.

At that, he looks all sentimental and dries his childish tears and starts hunting through our books. Finally he lies down beside me on my bed and strokes my hair and reads out this.

> *Lay your sleeping head, my love,*
> *Human on my faithless arm…*
> *Time and fevers burn away*
> *Individual beauty from*
> *Thoughtful children, and the grave*
> *Proves the child ephemeral:*
> *But in my arms till break of day*
> *Let the living creature lie*
> *Mortal, guilty, but to me*
> *The entirely beautiful.*
>
> *Soul and body have no bounds:*
> *To lovers as they lie upon*
> *Her tolerant enchanted slope*
> *In their ordinary swoon,*
> *Grave the vision Venus sends*
> *Of supernatural sympathy,*
> *Universal love and hope.*

Beauty, vision, midnight dies:
Let the winds of dawn that blow
Softly round your dreaming head
Such a day of sweetness show
Eye and knocking heart may bless,
Find the mortal world enough;
Noons of dryness see you fed
By the involuntary powers,
Nights of insult let you pass
Watched by every human love.

***

'Women!' Pete said morosely in the general direction of a small flotilla of empty tankards and thoroughly drained whisky glasses. They were drowning their sorrows in The Dog.

As Richard's thirty bob pocket money had been spent the previous week on the large spree to Felixstowe and as Bunter Hall had put a stop to further postal orders, the drowning was proceeding at the pace of Pete's misery. Fortunately for Richard this seemed to be as deep as his own. It involved some obscure matters arising from Pete's part in the Felixstowe trip and what had passed or not passed between Pete and Angela Cudmore.

Pete had four quid left from his wages and he had calculated at the outset of the evening that if they had eight pints each that would be two quid and, say, four whisky macs each at three and six, they should be able to get very satisfactorily trolleyed within budget. And so it was proving. They had reached a profoundly philosophic stage well before closing time where they understood everything, forgave everything, had almost forgotten everything.

Surprisingly, Pete was not forthcoming about the origins of his own gloom, although they were clearly Angela Cudmore-derived. Instead he advised Richard.

'You can't go through with it, Rich. Christ, you're only seventeen.' The landlord, with whom they had remained over all the months on only transactional terms, looked alarmed at this juncture, but the pub was otherwise empty and Pete and Richard were just about his best customers these days, now that Mr. MacAskill no longer came in, so he looked the other way.

Richard listened politely. After all Pete was buying the drinks. He nodded vaguely and said nothing when Pete called him a stupid romantic idiot and said he'd regret it for the rest of his life. But Richard kept coming back to the question that dogged him,

'Why do you think she hit me?'

'Because she knows what a stupid git you are. Because she's bright, unlike some, and she can work out just how long thirty shillings a week would last when you've got a baby and that's about half an hour max. Because you know absolutely sod all about sod all, can't even change a light bulb. Stupid toffee-nosed git is right. Look, you're on benefit in a council flat if you're lucky with a baby tuning up and Lizzie putting on weight and too tired for anything at night and there's not even half a crown for a pint. Then you'll soon see how long love lasts – about six fucking hours, I should think.'

Later that night, at just after eleven, lying flat on his bed with arms crossed, his eyes closed and the room spinning round him, Richard was thinking what a good friend old Pete was because he would listen to you all night long and talk back all night long and then when you took not the slightest notice of what he said, he would not mind one little jot.

This generous reflection was interrupted by the sound of purposeful steps proceeding down the corridor and then by Richard's door being wrenched open and thrown back roughly to reveal a rather frenzied-looking Lizzie. She was in her usual green jumper and jeans but her hair was splayed out and her face was white like parchment. Her eyes were ringed with black, where she had erratically slapped on her eye liner like war paint.

Did she look a bit puffy in the face? Were her jeans hugging her tighter because her tummy was swelling with precious leaven? Richard had only a moment to regard Lizzie eagerly, if a little blearily, through these thoughtful lenses. She was already marching past his bed and reaching behind his chipped and scratched old wardrobe.

'Ahhh, here we are,' she said and yanked out Richard's Bullworker. 'Let me show you how this thing really works.'

She held the Bullworker by the wire on the side and swung it round with surprising accuracy against Richard's chest of drawers. With the momentum she got from her half turn, the blow proved a heavy one that splintered the top drawer of the chest, revealing the sorry rummage of Richard's largely odd socks, as well as a brown paper packet that slid gracefully to the floor. Lizzie then grasped the Bullworker with both hands, raised it above her head, and brought it down with considerable power on the top of the chest. Some major structural thing snapped and the chest collapsed inwards. Richard's monastic collection of toiletries imploded within the broken chest and the glass in his only picture shattered into bits. The shards of glass sliced through the snap of Lizzie that he had stuck in the frame, and the studio portrait of his mother and father was again revealed, against a rustic background with his father's pipe at the jaunty 'manly' angle the photographer had suggested. Lizzie, however, didn't pause to consider symbolic meanings here. She was now too busy attacking the wardrobe, against which the Bullworker proved a remarkably effective instrument. The mirror in its front shattered and slid to the floor like a waterfall. The thin wood sides of the wardrobe cracked under a rain of Lizzie's blows.

At that, Lizzie, panting, her face now an endearing pink, her pretty bosom rising and falling with a particular allure, paused and looked at Richard fiercely. God, how he loved her at that moment! He wanted it to go on forever.

'Not bad for someone up the bleedin' spout, is it, Richard?' She was ramping up the rasping edge of her gratey Essex accent. It seemed to come over her at these emotional, emphatic times. It was one of the myriad things he felt he loved in her.

Lizzie was now engaged in a more methodical pattern of destruction, pulling open the remaining drawers and scattering clothes and papers all across the floor. She grabbed *Nausea*, still barely started on. She looked as though she was about to tear the paperback to shreds but she glanced at the title and instead threw the book at Richard, hitting him in the groin.

Then she was wrestling the wreckage of the chest onto its side and bashing in the panels. She took Richard's light wooden chair to the window and used it to smash all the panes. The cold night air rushed in. She tried to shove the chair out of the fractured window but it stuck in the struts and she left it wedged there.

In a last magnificent move, she picked up the brown paper packet, held it over Richard on his bed and shook out a confetti of condoms.

'Won't be needing those now,' she commented tranquilly.

Festooned with condoms, *Nausea* in his hand, Richard gazed in wonder at the now fully dishevelled Lizzie, whose raging eyes and fantastic flush gave her a batty look. A huge surge of love for her rose up in him. He started to get up from the bed.

'Lizzie, darling...'

'Goodbye, Richard,' she said, and turned and quickly left the room.

43

S	trewth, mate.'
	'Wow.'
	'Bloody hell.'
'This is comprehensive, Richard.'
'Proper job.'
'Looks like after an Arsenal match.'

Everyone was gazing appreciatively into Richard's room. He felt a dash of pride. The wreckage was untouched since last night but looked more definite today, an altogether bigger fact, like reading in the paper the next day about an epic game whose significance was veiled at the time.

'Looks like true love, mate,' Pete said. Pete seemed cheerier today, no doubt helped by this dramatic evidence of Richard's troubles.

'How exactly?'

'Don't want to be exact, Rich. I'd say it's approximately love. Wouldn't you, girls?'

Everybody agreed except Jane Ratcliffe who was at the back. Over the heads of the others, she could see the smashed-up wardrobe and the ruined chest and the chair stuck in the window frame like a surrealist assembly. Jane wasn't disagreeing, only puzzled and wondering what Pete and these young women knew, and how on earth they had come to know it.

'Better tidy up your confetti, though,' Pete said and all the girls laughed, except Jane who craned but still couldn't see the bed and so missed seeing the condoms which littered it.

'What is it?' she asked. 'Why is there confetti?'

'Tell you what, Rich,' Pete said. 'I'll nip down and bring the pick-up round. You lot can chuck the stuff out of the window, and we'll run it down to the dump.'

The wildness of chucking the furniture out of the window matched the wildness the girls felt drifting in the room. It was still present like an electric charge in the heap of smashed-up objects.

Debbie and Flick and a few other girls took part, carting the broken doors and smashed panels to the open window and hurling the debris out. Their aim was poor and a lot of it missed the pick-up and smashed onto the gravel. Stationed down below, Pete laughed and gathered it all together and heaped it into the truck. Across the courtyard, the children were watching from the windows of the Great Hall. Richard, meanwhile, packed his few surviving things into a couple of cardboard boxes.

'Here, give us a hand, Rich.' Richard helped the strong and limber Debbie manhandle the broken frame of the chest of drawers to the window and slot it through. Like wreckers, they watched in satisfaction as the chest splintered into fragments on the gravel below. Then Richard saw the front door open and Mrs. Noble coming out, followed at once by Lizzie, who shut the door behind her. His heart began to race and he felt dizzy. Lizzie was still in her old jeans and jumper, but she had brushed her hair and tied it back with a blue ribbon. He thought his heart would stop.

At that distance – about twenty yards, across the court-yard – he could not easily tell her mood. Her shoulders were back and she was stepping steadily in her old flat plimsolls behind Mrs. Noble's confident stride. He felt a stab of terror. They were headed for the big Citroën.

'Wait, Lizzie, wait,' he shouted from the window and Pete looked up, grinning stupidly. But Lizzie strode on towards the car. Richard dashed from the room, bumping against Debbie who was holding up his Bullworker.

'Finish the job,' she called out, but he was already far away down the corridor.

As Richard pelted headlong through the Great Hall and into the corridor, he careered into Mick who was in the doorway, blocking his path. He squeezed past the boy's bulky chair and heard him say,

'Leave it now, Richard. Let her go.'

Outside, the old grey Citroën rises expectantly on its springs like a girl rising for the dance, and as Richard runs headlong towards it, the car glides smoothly away, unhurried at first, at a speed that equals Richard's, but then noiselessly gathers pace until it disappears around the bend in the drive and Richard is left panting on the gravel.

Jane Ratcliffe watched this scene from the window of Richard's now deserted room. It was, of course, right that Lizzie should be sent to that Council home in town. She would be properly cared for all through her pregnancy. She would be in with all those other 'unmarried mothers' and everybody would be saved a lot of embarrassment and shame. And then the baby could go to probably quite a good home and after a bit Lizzie could get another job in a different place, or she might even get married if she went far enough away from all who knew her story, and if the girl herself could keep her peace.

And yet. And yet. As Jane watched the car containing Lizzie move off and that silly Richard running after it so fruitlessly, there seemed to be something in the boy and the girl and whatever it was that bound them together that was signally absent from the solution to the stupid girl's plight which Jane had so carefully thought up and presented to Mrs. Noble.

Jane sighed and drew back quickly from the window. Richard was now returning panting and hangdog-looking up the drive. She didn't want him to spot her if he looked up, although that didn't seem very likely. He was studying the gravel on the drive closely and kicking it up as he trudged towards the house.

Jane returned to her own room and as she slipped along the corridor, trying to avoid meeting any of the nurses, she reflected on something she had learned in her devotional studies. Jane had learned that in *koine* Greek, the language Christ is represented as speaking in the Gospels although of course he never did any such thing but spoke in old Aramaic, there are three words for love. There was *Eros*, the carnal bit, which so often seemed to Jane the source of all the trouble in the word. There was *Philia*, the bonds of friendship, which was fine in its way, she supposed. And then there was *Agape*, which was like spiritual love, the one her pastor sometimes called the love of God.

Now what had always puzzled Jane in her studies of the basic texts of her faith, and what was puzzling her particularly now and was becoming quite a preoccupation of hers, was *Why in English there was just the one word*? Why exactly was it that English, so abounding in words, such a plenitude of synonyms, had just one word for love? Her Roget's Thesaurus was the fattest book on her shelf. And yet for this concept of love, there was just that one little word.

The thought that just maybe in this singular case, the exuberant English language had just one word because there was only one thing referred to was lying in some vestibule

of Jane Ratcliffe's mind like a letter she was fearful of opening.

'You know,' Richard is saying, 'in the future an expanding
red sun will engulf us.'

He's sitting on my bed. Lessons seem to be suspended
for today. In fact, they've been pretty much suspended for
the last few days unless these mournful thoughts he tosses
out from time to time from his brooding inner depths are
supposed to be part of a new curriculum.

I think you could say that Richard's mind has not been
on the job. And you know, with that expanding red sun, I
believe he's torn between longing for it to come and believ-
ing that it has already happened. With Lizzie gone, he has
the air of a man to whom everything seems torrid and dry
and burned, a man preoccupied with his own doom.

He even tried to cancel the play. But we weren't having
any of that. Mick talked to Patch about it, and the kingly
command came back from the San that The Show Must Go
On. And that absolutely definitely he, Patch, would be out
of the San to play his role of King Priam.

And all the most unlikely people popped up and said
yes, the Show Must Go On.

Mr. MacAskill, interrogated whilst he was painting sets
with – guess who? Jane Ratcliffe! and not just Jane Ratcliffe
but a revised, possibly updated, version that was sporting
quite grubby overalls and continually asking with a shy
eagerness *How can I help?* – Mr. MacAskill said The Show
Must Go On, and the New Model Ratcliffe nodded in a subdued kind of way which showed correctly that she knew
nobody cared what her opinion was any more but that she
was siding with Mr. MacAskill anyway, whose opinion we
do sort of still consider a bit.

Mick too is of this Show Must Go On way of thinking. He's to be Paris, who carried off Helen from her husband Menelaus. Now Richard's always held that Paris has had a bad press as a bit of a philanderer and pincher of other men's wives. Whereas Richard's deeper psychological insight is that Helen was in a loveless marriage, actually an abusive one, and that she sees in Paris the man she's always had in mind, the one that she was already praying for at the age of fourteen, and all the other lovers and husbands and whatever were just approximations to this real Love of Her Life. And Paris too, wearied of arbitrating competitions amongst vain girls who claim they want World Peace when what they really want is to own the world, is far from being a callow adulterer and beauty contest judge – Paris too sees in Helen the life partner he's been seeking, and one he's prepared to go into bat for, even to the extent of provoking a ten year international war.

So Richard's Paris (played by Mick) is transformed into a tender wooing husband who holds the hand of Helen and breathes sweet nothings into her ear and it's not *E-i-addio* either.

The only hitch in this, as Richard points out, is that there is no Helen. In fact, Helen is still secreted up at the Tower and how she is to be reintroduced to the world is a conundrum, at least for Richard. But he has written the Helen part with no actual lines at all, just a great deal of posing and pouting, so her absence from rehearsals does little to disturb the in any case rather uneven flow of the run-throughs.

Greg is also up for it, because there's now a big musical section where he conducts the massed bands and choir of Troy and they do a rendition of the Trojans' sacred ditty. They've even brought in some extra features to pep it up. Mick's carted some tambourines and triangles up from school for the little kids and Pete's found an old drum kit for Greg, so he can conduct and play the drums at the same time which seems to pose him no insuperable problems. Some of the girls have got recorders and they all blow and bang away in an astonishing din.

And as for me, I am definitely up for it. Cos why?

Because it's complete absolute utter Chaos here.

And from Chaos comes Cosmos, a *further and new order*.

Yes, it's the Trojans' Last Stand – against the forces of the Bin. And we've got a plan. A plan that will sort everything out once and for all. It will even get your Lizzie back, Richard.

44

Eleanor Noble sweeps her hand through her beautiful silver hair. The Chairman of the Board of Governors that Park House shares with Binstead is on the line and he is extremely cross.

'... marked personal, private and confidential, mind you... I've had to ask Salter to take leave. And it looks bad for your Ratcliffe woman too.'

Eleanor knows the reason for the panicky sounds Alderman Sir James Cossins is emitting. After a lifetime of public service, he believes that he has finally brought the balance of his interests in his retirement into the equilibrium he yearns for. This is predominantly golf, and then his grandchildren, and then, in last and diminishing place, the chairmanship of the trust which runs these two charitable houses. This chairmanship is the sole survivor of many. A dozen others have been divested in recent years so that he can bring his life onto a new, more restful plane. And now an intrusive letter is threatening to knock everything seriously out of kilter.

Understanding this, Eleanor immediately recognizes Sir James's tactic. He has received a letter containing some inconvenient truths that look likely to create problems for the Board. So he is ringing her up to offload these problems onto her.

Well, first she must hear what these truths might be, and then she will decide how far to go along with Sir James's little scheme.

Sir James explains briefly. In his time he has been accustomed to getting to the main idea promptly. He says that a letter has been sent to him and – so far – to him alone, making allegations against the management of both Binstead and Park House. The letter is signed by a Patrick Beer, a Robert Willis and (p.p.) a Gloriana Gillespie.

The allegations concern a Helen Scandizzi, formerly at Park House and now transferred to Binstead. There are also allegations concerning a Norma Cummings, a long-term patient at Binstead.

'I understand from Salter that these two – your girl Helen and the Cummings woman – have actually… absconded, if that's the word. Along with another one of yours, well ex-yours, the very Robert Willis who's a signatory to this letter. Although Salter hasn't reported anything about these absconders to me. Or indeed to anyone as far as I know, so that's a big black mark for him, I'm afraid. Were you aware, my dear?'

Eleanor murmured non-commitally. She wanted to see where this was going before she said anything.

'So what are the allegations?'

'Let me read them out to you, my dear. Tum tum… "circumstances under which Helen Scandizzi, a minor, was forcibly restrained and transferred without appropriate order and unaccompanied by a female guardian to Binstead, an adult institution, contrary to Cap 46 Section 17 of the Protection of Minors Act of 1947…" … tum tum tum… "Norma Cummings… inappropriate representations to the Clinical Review Board…" tum tum tum… "Cap 88 Section 143 of the Mental Health Act of 1933…" tum tum tum…'

'That's it?'

'In brief. There are a few more Caps and Sections but that's the nub of it.'

'And are all the legal references in order?'

'Frankly, my dear, I haven't the foggiest. Not my department. But I will tell you one thing – I am not running to the lawyers with this until you've had a good look into it. If this gets out and the lawyers get their hands on it, we are done for, as they used to say in the films.'

'Hmm. I see what you mean. And so far you are the only one to receive this letter?'

'Yes, so it seems. But there the plot thickens. It says at the bottom cc Chairman of the Clinical Review Board – that's Dr. Gilfillan, who as you know is a bit of a maverick – and cc the Chief Constable. I haven't heard from either of them, so I presume that the copies have not yet been dispatched.'

'I see.'

'In my experience, sending a letter like this and keeping back the third-party copies is a prelude to some pretty serious arm-twisting.'

'Blackmail?'

'Well, at least a negotiation. Now, Eleanor, tell me about these three who've signed. Do you think they're trying to pull a stunt on us? What do they want from us?'

'I have no idea. It's all very odd. The first signatory, for example, Patrick Beer, is at present in the Sanatorium with suspected pneumonia. As he's dystrophy Stage Five, he might not even emerge from the San.'

'So what on earth could he be after? And the others? The Robert is the one that's miked off from Binstead. So as he's plotting with two of yours, I suspect he must be back with you somewhere.'

'I'm honestly not aware.'

'Well, be aware, my dear. Become aware. We must all be on our toes here. And the Gloriana? My God, what a name! Fit for a queen.'

'Gloriana's going over to Binstead at the end of this

term.'

'And why the p.p.?'

'She's a tetraplegic.'

'And a dissident.'

Eleanor Noble agreed.

'So, Eleanor, I think this needs a bit of looking into from your side. And the sooner the better.'

'Let me do some digging. I'll ring you back when I have anything definite.'

'She'll never agree,' Richard says feebly. He's super-glum and pining for poor Lizzie who's down in the Unmarried Mother's Home in town. But he has agreed to come to the San and hear what we've decided. Because Patch has appointed Richard his messenger.

'Like wossname,' Patch says. Against the plump white pillows on which he reclines, Patch's redness looks extreme.

'Hermes, I think you mean' Richard says, not putting much energy into it.

'Yuss, messenger of the gods, that's you, Richard. Say you'll do it.'

Richard was not too enfolded in gloom to notice that this was the first time that Patch had ever called him by his Christian name.

'I dunno.'

I sign to him, Dear Richard, just listen. You'll see.'

Patch says,

'Go ahead, Robbie.'

Debbie has fetched Robbie down from the Tower by the back route through the hydrangeas and smuggled him in through the kitchens past a wheezing Young Win who was much too busy boiling a vat of noisome Brussels sprouts to within an inch of their life to notice. Robbie gives Richard a run-down on our plan. Richard listens to it all with a pretty sceptical air until Robbie comes to the part about me going to university, and then Richard looks really distressed and starts to shed tears.

'Oh crikey,' Patch says. 'That's right, start blubbing.'

'I dunno, Patch, I just dunno.'

I know how bad he has been feeling about my university prospects since Mrs. Noble poured cold water on them.

'Follow through, you stupid git,' Patch says crossly. Like the king he is, he knows how to use a dab of righteous anger.

'But how? Without A Levels? It's impossible.'

'Nothing is impossible.' Patch says this with such certainty that Richard stops blubbing and pulls out a very grubby handkerchief to wipe away the tears.

'Now,' Patch goes on, 'Robbie's going to read you something.'

Robbie has open on his lap a big thing like a newspaper. It is the *Oxford University Gazette*. Robbie reads:

> 'A college will not ordinarily admit to matriculation any student who has not obtained two passes in the General Certificate of Education at the Advanced Level...'

'You see...'

'Button up, mate,' Patch says. 'Let 'im finish.'

> 'Notwithstanding the foregoing provisions, a college may admit any student to matriculation if the award of an Open Scholarship shall have been made.'

'So there,' Patch says. 'Sorted.'

'Pfff,' Richard says. 'And as for the rest of it…'

He looks at me. I smile and sign to him.

'Just try, Richard.'

'An' if you do it, we'll see you right. We'll get Lizzie back for you.'

'And on those terms they'll withdraw the letter?'

Sir James was pleased at this prospect of an easy closure.

'No,' Eleanor replied, 'no, suspend. They'll suspend the letter. Not action it for now. Not send the copies out. I understand Mr. Salter's secretary has the copies ready to be posted off to the Chairman of the Clinical Review Board and the Chief Constable.'

'You mean that painted lady in Salter's office? The mutton dressed as lamb woman? So she's in on this, is she? It really is blackmail.'

'It's not all downside.'

'Really?'

'Taking Helen back into the kitchens *pro tem* will actually be a plus as I understand she's a top-notch little cook. And letting Robbie back here until the end of term isn't really a problem.'

'But I presume that's not all they want, is it?'

'Of course not. They want a new arrangement for the leavers. They say they're still working out the details.'

'Oh, any idea what they've got in mind?'

'Not yet. Or only for one of them. They want Gloriana to go to university. To Oxford, in fact.'

'My goodness. How are you going to swing that?'

'I was hoping you might do it. As an old Oxford man.'

'Nope. I'm afraid she's your responsibility, Eleanor. You're going to have to think of something there. And do we know the whereabouts of the other escapee? The older woman, the Norma Cummings? Any word on her?'

'The story is a bit cryptic there. But I believe she is alright.'

In fact Richard, in his meeting with Eleanor, had relayed the message 'She's gone to a better place', which sounded alarming but Eleanor suspected it was somebody's little joke.

'So, Sir James, shall I go ahead?'

'We're over a barrel here, so yes, please proceed. Tell them it's a go, but we want the final terms – this "new arrangement for the leavers" – ASAP. In the meantime, I'll try and work out something for Salter. He's clearly not the right man for the job.'

What Eleanor did not mention to Sir James, because it all seemed just too much and not really relevant, was the strange demand that had been passed on through Miss Ratcliffe, that Lizzie should be allowed back. Jane had been to see her earlier in the day.

'For goodness' sake, Jane, why don't you just go home? I've given you two full weeks off. Go home to your mother's and get some rest.'

Jane Ratcliffe removed her spectacles and rubbed her eyes. She was in Mrs. Noble's office, which had so recently been hers. Her electric kettle was still there, and the Brown Betty, and the ginger nuts, although people had clearly been helping themselves. The jar was practically empty. But recovering her tea things was not what had brought Jane hastening here.

'And what on earth possesses you to bring this up now? I mean I've just taken the girl there precisely as you yourself suggested.'

'I just thought it would be… somehow kinder.'

'And why did you not think like that before, Jane? I mean, only two days ago you practically made me take her there as though she had the lurgy, and now you come to me with this. Whatever has got into you, Jane? I really do suggest you take those two weeks and get right away from here.'

Eleanor's tone was uncharacteristically peevish. She had, after all, a lot on her plate and Jane Ratcliffe's temperamental about-turns were the least of her worries. Anyway, she wanted Jane out of the way for everyone's good. The children bristled and cowered in turns when she was around. If Jane would only just go away, there was a better chance of protecting her – and Park House – from some of the repercussions of The Letter. And Eleanor could use the time to reverse some of Jane's more disastrous decisions, starting with the un-sacking of Joe MacAskill.

So why would Jane not go away? And what exactly had got into her regarding Lizzie?

In truth, she couldn't properly account for it herself. All she knew was that Mr. MacAskill had requested another massage. He had also asked her if, in addition to scene painting, she would help with the costumes for the play.

But most significant of all was the way he had looked at her when she had proudly told him what arrangements she had suggested for young Elizabeth. She had wanted to impress him with her efficiency, and even with her thoughtfulness for Lizzie's welfare, and she had been astonished when he had muttered 'Badly done, Jane, badly done indeed.' And the fact that she had recognized the quotation, could even locate it precisely on the slopes of Box Hill at the end of an exhausting day out, seemed to give it a force of truth that went beyond the words themselves.

So without thinking anything through at all properly, she had decided not to use this unexpected leave to fly to her mother's bosom – in any case an adamantine feature harder than flint – but rather to stay and give Mr. MacAskill a further massage and to help out with the play.

And for Lizzie? There Jane had devised a fresh solution which had impressed even Mr. MacAskill with its positive Sixties-ness when she had sketched it out to him.

'Well, I give up, Jane,' Mrs. Noble said, standing up to end this bothersome meeting. 'You do what you like regarding the girl. Just take care of it and don't harass me any more.'

'Oh, thank you, thank you. There is just one little thing more…'

'Yes?'

'My Brown Betty and…'

'What? Oh, Jane, for God's sake.'

When Jane had left clutching her tea things, Eleanor Noble let her mind turn to a more generous reflection – Tigger Monteith.

Tigger. She hadn't seen him since UNRRA days, just after the War, '46-'47, he just newly married, she engaged, life embarked upon.

But Eleanor's real memory of Tigger was pre-embarkation, before the War, '37, when they were undergraduates, Young Ambassadors at the League of Nations. The trips to Locarno to swim in the lake, the dancing nightly to the gramophone at their digs, the cards, *bataille tous les deux*, what was that silly game where no one ever got knocked out, you could 'slap in' endlessly, *bataille tous les deux*, slap slap, and Hutch purring, the same record over and over

There's danger in the waltz when I'm waltzing with you and on the other side *Bare arms shining something something*, sailing on the lake and the silver shadow of the storm coming off the mountain and we regained the land just in the nick, the two of us, and *bataille tous les deux* right there on the shore in the rain. Blimey, you said.

Well, no doubt Tigger would be his generous self still. And if anyone would even listen to a request on behalf of a tetraplegic mute sans A Levels, sans voice, sans everything that would normally qualify you to get a scholarship to Oxford, it would be Tigger. Monteith of Balliol.

45

Preparations for *The Triumph of the Trojans* continue apace. Helen is back and working wonders in the *cuccina* but she takes time off to pose and pout as Helen, opposite her Paris, played by Mick. Robbie takes on a write-in part as the wily Odysseus.

Even Patch declares his cold better and insists on getting up for the dress rehearsal. So Debbie and Flick bring up the regalia of King Priam from the Great Hall to the San and dress him up. Debbie gives him huge majestic eyes with an eye pencil as thick as a stick of Blackpool rock. Then Patch buzzes off in his Armstead 302.

Richard comes across Patch down in the schoolroom. In his full Priamic regalia, the boy looks very royal with his stupendous body and fiery red cheeks and ermine and scarlet robe and golden cardboard crown. Patch is gazing up at Mr. MacAskill's old pink map of the world. The way he is sitting, there is even perhaps a touch of a king's loneliness about him.

'Time for the dress rehearsal to start,' Richard says.

'He's nearly there,' Patch says, still looking up at the map. 'He's nearly round the world. Practically home, Chichester.'

F. Chichester has sailed out from that small pink island where the postage stamp has been invented, sailed out from Patch's beloved Plymouth even, and passed those useful pink Atlantic rocks (St Helena, Tristan da Cunha, Ascension, stamp issuers all) and then round the pink Cape and past pink Mauritius and Seychelles and the pink Maldives, below the big pink Indian triangle and then past pink Australia to slalom amongst the pink islands of the Pacific and then to face the tremendous winds about the pink Falklands and the pink Falklands Islands Dependencies (Graham Land, South Georgia, South Orkneys, South Shetlands) and so back to the useful pink rocks and now he is Practically Home, back from all those lands where stamps have been graced by the monarch's head to the homeland of the stamp and the monarch.

'Ascension Island,' Patch says. 'An island in the South Atlantic. A dependency of St Helena.' He is quoting from his stamp album, which he has learned by heart. 'It's not far now, Chichester.'

The boy sneezes and Richard ducks forward with his handkerchief.

'No, you stupid git, do it properly.'

Richard knows that Patch speaks to him like this to break the elegiac mood, but then Patch asks,

'How long will it be now, Richard?'

It is not the wistful character of the question that strikes Richard but that Patch has again called him by his Christian name.

'About two weeks, Patch, I should say. If the wind is with him.'

'About two weeks, if the wind is with him. He'll be home for his birthday then.'

'Yes, I suppose so. Come on now, time to hit the boards.'

On the whole, the dress rehearsal went according to expectations. In the words of Mr. MacAskill, at the height of his post-performance critique, it was a 'complete bloody shambles'.

Everybody forgot their lines but they made them up as

they went along in the spirit of the thing. *Stupid git* was far and away the favourite way of addressing both enemy and friend.

Strangely, the Rat, who had slipped in unexpectedly to watch, demurred from the general opinion and said the play was 'quite good, really'. She even volunteered to patch up Helen's frock where Menelaus had ripped it during a marital dispute in Act One.

On the whole, the children too felt things went off quite well. Even Patch said to Richard as they went up to the house for tea,

'It'll be alright on the night – now you got rid of that crap ending.'

Then he sneezed.

The Ratcliffe's appearance at the dress rehearsal, and her unexpected pliancy, had two causes. One was the despondency that had followed the ticking-off Mrs. Noble had given her, which had deepened the unusual degree of self-doubt she was experiencing. The other was that she was intrigued – rather than repelled – by Joe MacAskill's second love letter, strange though it was.

For this was what Mr. MacAskill, impelled by a renewed surge of Sixties-ness, had contrived to write:

My dear Jane,

David Hume says that desire and imagination are prior to reason, and so perhaps you will listen to me without too much thought darkening your dear mind.

I have lived a hackneyed life and have often been at fault but I have won a certain self-acceptance and I have concluded, with Camus, that there are more things to admire in men – and especially women – than to despise.

Love is the great imaginative act, and even if we can never hear the poetry of everlasting love, we can approximate it. If we imagine well, we will love well.

You bow to God, but remember it is the rebel who is disloyal to God who has advanced the cause of man. Prometheus stole the fire, earning the wrath of Zeus who wanted to hold man back. Moses struck the rock to bring water to his people in direct contravention of God's command.

I am not young. I fear the direction of my travel has been fixed – and the cul-de-sacs along the way have been too many. It is late but it is not too late. Won't you join me on the road?

I do still desire you in that quite simple, desperate, human way.

    With my love,
      Joe

Again, she detected a certain *hommage*, even *collage*, in this screed, and Joe had frankly acknowledged a couple of them. She knew the Camus thing, of course, from A Level – they had 'done' *L'Etranger* in the days when people still actually read their set books. The Hume was new to her though – *desire and imagination are prior to reason* – it was one of those things that you could say, just as you could say exactly the opposite if the mood took you.

Yet there was a seduction in the letter. Not the words but the energy, the evident desire.

Her sewing had become absent-minded and she pricked her unprotected finger. A spot of blood fell on the old white sheet that was serving as Helen's frock, and there at once was Joe MacAskill bounding over, all concern, proffering Savlon and Elastoplast, like the doctor coming to heal her.

'There,' he said. 'There.'

After tea the ambulance comes.

The idea was to get the ambulance round to the San directly so the children would not see, but the thicko driver has scooted to a handbrake turn on the gravel outside the Great Hall and now he is coming into the Hall, leaving the engine running and a rotating light which rakes the courtyard and eerily fills the Hall with waves of electric blue.

Debbie runs up and has a word with him but you can see the ambulance man is not really listening at first but gazing at Debbie's breasts. They look particularly rounded and fruity in her tight-fitting top with the garish hoops which has recently shrunk below her size in the wash. But in the end he gets his mind on the topic and drives off round to the San.

However, by this time all the Trojans have scooted down and as Patch is wheeled out by a now tearful Debbie and the ambulance man, the shout goes up.

Hon hoi theoi philousin…

Patch acknowledges his people with a small motion of his hand and then the doors of the ambulance close on him.

Neos apothneiskei!

For a long time after the ambulance has disappeared down the drive, the Trojans continue chanting their ditty, staring into the evening until their eyes grow blank.

46

His rather dismal script for The Trojans now looked to Richard too upbeat. He toyed with the idea of darkening it, but let it go. He himself stands in for Patch in the role of Priam.

On the Big Night, they laboured through Act 1 and Act 2. Mick and Helen gave a rousing performance including some quite realistic embracing of each other that drew considerable applause. Richard gave a competent if listless performance as Priam which quite dominated the show as he was the only actor who knew more than a handful of his lines. However, much of the audience's appreciation was drowned out by resounding *tutti* from the massed bands and choir of Troy that Greg's baton skilfully brought in at quite unexpected points in an interesting medley of their native Lydian and the new 12-tone Aeolian modes. Some needle negotiations between Paris and Odysseus over who'd actually won a skirmish and therefore had the right to put up a trophy had to be aborted when the massed bands and choir of Troy marched across the stage playing and singing at full pitch:

Hon hoi theoi philousin, neos apothneskei

'This is absolute chaos,' Richard said to Gloriana in the interval and he was puzzled by the sweet smile she gave him.

Probably the best bit was the big fight when the Trojans saw off the Greeks at the end of Act 2, although it did get a bit ragged after ten minutes or so and Mrs. Noble had to signal to Richard to bring the curtain down even before Priam could make his speech claiming Final Victory and setting out his terms for the armistice.

Richard quickly considered going out on a high note, ending the whole thing there while the going was still relatively good. The children were tired, anyway. The mood of the audience was hard to gauge – attendance was sparse – at least three of the local worthies from the Rotary who were supposed to be there had been spotted by Pete up at The Dog instead. And those who *were* there seemed puzzled, not only by the ambiguities in Richard's rather elaborate text, but also by the free-form method acting and 100% ad-libbing that the children brought to their parts.

Under the circumstances, would Act 3's apotheosis of the Butler/Beveridge/Bevan Settlement really come across as compelling drama? And Richard felt that the new Act Four with its vast tableau of Priam returning victorious from the Indies, a host of enslaved nizams and akonds in his train and the Indian emperor grovelling in a cage, might not quite come off as he had intended.

They pressed on with Act 3 anyway and then suddenly, with a lover's keen antennae, Richard picked up her presence, even before his raking eye spotted her, at the back. He saw her raise her hand and smile her pretty smile. She was in a sparkling green dress, obviously new, and her hair was back in a bunch and she was wearing her Egyptian eyes. All this was quite swoony for him, but Richard ploughed on.

But then further decisions were taken out of the hands of the *auteur* because halfway through the Act, at the very moment when the Aneurin Bevan figure was explaining exactly how he was going to get the disciples of Aesculapius to heal slaves free at the point of treatment, the lights went out.

On the stroke of eleven by the old stable clock, when Richard was sitting up in bed rereading *The Love Machine* by the light of a tilly lamp, she slipped into his room without knocking. Her dress was a shiny emerald green, and satisfyingly short enough to show off her rounded thighs. In the challenging light of the lamp, her skin looked startlingly white, almost translucent.

'Cor, bright in here, isn't it?'

'Lizzie, sit down, sit on the bed with me.'

She sat down beside him on the edge of the bed. He took her hand which was warm and slightly damp and then ducked his head down to her tummy. She didn't object but started laughing, so Richard sat up and put his arm around her and started laughing too.

'What's so funny, Lizzie?'

'That cardboard don't half look stupid.' Pete had tacked up old cardboard across the smashed up window.

'Oh. I thought you were laughing at me.'

'I was.'

He kissed her on the cheek.

'Can you turn that bleedin' light down, Rich?'

The darkened room took on a more private atmosphere.

'Tell me, Lizzie, what you want to do. I'm your man, you know.'

She laughed again. She was really in high spirits.

'New Man,' she said.

'I mean, will you… you won't do anything… to the baby, I mean?'

'Nah. They asked me about that at the home. I told them where to get off.'

'I can't believe you've come back. And the Rat…'

'Buggered if I know what that was all about. One minute, Ma Noble's marching me off to the House of Shame, next thing I know is the Rat coming in all humble and begging me to come back.'

'Weird.'

'Bloody weird, if you ask me. She even took me into town and bought me this dress.'

'Mmm, nice.' Richard slipped his hand onto Lizzie's thigh. She let him.

'So, Lizzie… what now?'

She pulled away from him and perched on the end of the bed.

'Rich, look, there's something…'

Then she told Richard the truth, which made the boy jump up and pace about and prise a bit of Pete's cardboard away and peer out of the window. Chilly air rushed in from the dark night. The sky was crammed with stars.

At last he sat down again next to Lizzie, but carefully, not touching her at any point.

'So,' he said, 'the story is…'

'Not a story, Richard. It's the truth.'

'The truth is that you slept with me and John Fry in the same week…'

'Not slept, Richard, not slept. I never did that with John.'

Richard couldn't see the difference but he ploughed on.

'So… you had sex with me and John Fry in the same week and he didn't use any…'

Why couldn't he say *condom*? It was just a stupid town in France. Anyway, he gestured loosely towards the shelf Pete had run up for him. Lizzie, who was sitting very demurely but showing no particular signs of unease at this conversation, looked up at the four stacks of condoms that Richard had piled near the edge of the shelf. She smiled faintly.

'Why? I mean with me I know why – but with him?'

'He fancied it that way, and I thought it was my safe time of the month.'

As she said that, Richard became suddenly aware of Lizzie in a completely physical way. It was the scent she'd put on, and the new smell of her dress and the freshness of her hair and the way she was sitting up straight on the bed. Her supple nurse's hands were folded in her lap, lying on where new life was planted in the wall of her womb. The green dress crossed her in a V, leaving bare her throat and the bit under the throat and the top of her breasts, which really did look bigger already. He felt a heave of desire.

And other newer feelings came crowding in, mixed, muddled ones, which felt gloriously adult, intimations that the dull, unclouded choices of childhood were behind him and that life was opening up in many dimensions and he would be challenged by choices and consequences, open to life, always on his toes, alert to risks, understanding that there might be more than one good choice – or no good choice at all…

'Richard!'

She was looking at him, her eyes narrowed in an amused, irritated way.

'Mmm?'

'Stop day-dreaming. I want to tell you what I'm going to do.'

Straightaway Richard felt exactly the opposite of his day-dream. He now felt the overwhelming luxury of letting a woman tell him what to do.

And the fact that one thing seemed to be true – that he should be a sovereign chooser – and the opposite also true at the same time – that his girl should make choices for him – suddenly seemed part of that world of many dimensions that now lay close to his hand.

Lizzie sketched out her plan.

'So you leave here now and...'

'Go up.'

'...yes, that. And I'll stay on here and have the baby.'

'But who'll look after... it... her...?'

'Richard, there's twenty nurses here. Twenty little mothers, Debbie and Flick and all that lot. Don't you worry about that.'

'But will Mrs. Noble agree?'

'She has agreed. She went to see Patch and he asked her and she said yes.'

'Extraordinary. But she's been saying yes to a lot of things recently. Helen and Robbie and...'

Richard told Lizzie about all this and of his part in it. She listened and then laughed.

'So that'll be it. Patch must have got her to agree to me coming back. Or maybe it was the Rat.'

'Who cares? You're back. So Lizzie... what about us? Me and you?'

'Depends. If you want, you can come and see me in your... wossit... holidays...'

'Vacation. But then...?'

'Oh, depends...whatever we decide. I mean, when you...'

'Come down.'

'... yeah, when you've got a job. Oh, and by the way, I got this in town for you...'

It was a silver Ronson cigarette lighter.

'Look, Rich, your initials.'

'Wow. Thanks. Shall we have a ciggy then?'

'Yeah, go on.'

***

Richard was spooning Lizzie. It could have been a super-sexy thing, and in Richard's mind it was, loving youth and beloved girl curled in a rapturous S on his narrow cot, he with his hand on the gentle convexity of her fertile tummy. The snag was the huge amount of clobber Lizzie had put on, including a hideous quilted car-coat in slithery brown nylon.

In the night a cold front had swept across the marshes from the east and thrust through the smashed window and the bit of corrugated cardboard Pete had tacked up. The room had taken on a chilled character that Lizzie said did not make for nudie spooning. She had agreed to stay with him but only with every single stitch on. Richard had put on several layers too and they were lying like puffed-up blimps as the cold easterly poked and ferreted around them.

When Richard suddenly wakened, he thought at first it was a beast of the night, it was like the eerie reasonless cry of an animal – *ah ah ah…* – and then a low moaning sound, like protracted sobs. There was surely a lot of pain in it, like an animal that has despaired of life. But then he heard the scrunch of wheels on gravel and he leaped up from the bed and, prising the cardboard away from the window frame, looked out.

A flat grey dawn was forming. The sky was spread out in a featureless sheet, except for a knot of lower darker clouds moving like dirigibles along the horizon. A cold rain now began to fall in large drops on the windowsill. In the reluctant light, he spotted the elegant lines of Mrs. Noble's Citroën slumbering comfortably before her door, and then beyond, trailing up from the direction of the stables with disconsolate heavy thrusts at the wheels of his tungsten

Lavington, was the figure of Mick, bundled up in a swathe of jerseys and scarves. There was something desolate and angry about the way he was jerking at the runners, and once again he opened his mouth and gave that desolating animal howl.

'Mick, what's up?' Richard called down. The boy stopped beside the sleek Citroën and looked up. Seeing Richard at the window, he scooted over.

'They're dead,' he said, 'they're forking dead, the whole forking lot of them.'

'What?'

'Forking birds. Dead. The lot of them. Typical!'

When the lights went out, nobody had thought of those heat-seeking tropic dwellers. Their electric heaters went off, and when the Boreal chill blew in during the night, it froze the blood in their veins. They had soon dropped off their dowelling perches onto the floor. When Mick went in the early morning to top up their food and water as he always did, he had found them lying in their own litter.

'I'll be down,' Richard called.

Lizzie had turned on her back. Her mouth was open and she was snoring gently. Richard shaped his lips into a rough O which he tried to plant on Lizzie's mouth in a symmetrical kiss, but the move didn't come off as she shifted slightly and his lips fell on her nose. She pushed at him irritably.

'Bugger off, Richard, I'm trying to have a lie-in.'

Richard had never been at a deathbed before. He supposed it *was* a deathbed, it certainly appeared like one, with Patch looking absolutely ghastly, propped up on pillows, his face bright puce and horribly swollen, his breathing coming with a terrible gurgling effect. As it was his first time,

Richard had no idea of the form. He muttered,

'I'm so sorry.'

Patch looked at him scornfully and said distinctly, if a little hoarsely,

'We all 'ave our difficulties, mate.'

For Patch, from the very outset, time has always been defined and therefore infinitely precious. He was never going to spend it in scared anticipation of sickness and death, and certainly not now. He had stuff to do.

Richard felt Patch's shrivelled eyes fixed on him. The boy king was so incredibly red. The heat in his face was tremendous, as though he was burning up. Richard stupidly thought of 'burning up on re-entry' like that Russian spaceman, but was Patch re-entering somewhere? Or was he only just setting out? Nobody had any idea about this, as far as Richard knew.

'C'm 'ere, Richard,' and Richard bent over the boy's huge plump face. Patch looked like a red planet, or a reddened moon with his Man-in-the-Moon features. He looked like the red face on the Raspberry Cremola Foam tin.

Richard couldn't help smiling at the Cremola Foam thing, and Patch gave him what Richard tried to interpret as an indulgent look.

By now, Patch's mouth had almost closed up with the fantastic swelling of his face. He looked like he was about to explode.

Yet Patch, despite his shrunken eyes, could see the cooling mist that was gathering in the corners of the room. He knew he should make haste. He had chosen Richard on the grounds that Richard was the least stupid git available and the most likely to do what he was told. So with Richard's ear pressed close, Patch began to run over a few things. His high pitched, squeaky voice was muffled and rather dim, but still distinct enough for Richard to hear.

'Mick marries Helen, 'appy ever after.'

'*What!*'

'You'll get it, mate, give it time. 'e's always loved 'er. She's an Eyetie, all their marriages is arranged. She'll love it. Then Gloriana goes to Oxford... OK? And then after that, what-not...'

'What-not?'

'Yup. Po'try 'n stuff... An' Mick gets qualified and earns a bundle...'

'As what? A carpenter?'

'Come off it, you stupid git. What carpenter ever earned a bundle?'

Patch paused to wheeze a bit.

'... nah, something' with a bit o' money in it but what a thick bloke like Mick can do. Like, chartered accountant, fr' instance... Get your Dad to fix that up.'

'Wow!'

'An' Robbie becomes a lawyer. Get someone to fix that up too. Your Dad or someone.'

'Errr...'

'An' Helen goes on with the Eyetie scoff. And... and...'

'Yes?'

'They all live together an' 'elp each other. An' until Mick's made his pile... Sir James forks out. Gets 'em a flat and that.'

'Err... I don't know about that.'

'He will. You'll see. We all gotta help each other, 'an't we? 'E'll get some points doin' that. An' don't tell me he can't afford it.'

Patch's tiny eyes rested on Richard, until at last Richard said,

'OK. OK, Patch, I'll try.'

'Just ask Ma Noble. She'll fix it up.'

That seemed to be it. Patch's ballooning face took on a more restful look as he watched the mist billowing out from the corners of the room and folding gently over him. He closed his eyes.

Then he murmured, or seemed to murmur,

'... oh, an' give me *Marital Guide* to...'

47

Eleanor Noble put down the heavy black Bakelite receiver. She heard the line cut off with a ping.

She thought, here the phone is black because it has to bear so much bad news. That is why I avoid answering it if I can. Yet, that morning she had lifted the receiver almost hopefully when she heard the sketchy trill that the fearsome telephonist at the exchange raised as she plugged in to ring you up. She had been hoping to hear from her old chum Monteith of Balliol. However, it proved to be the hospital and she took the news. For a moment, she considered trying to telephone through to Patch's parents in Plymouth, but they were rare visitors whom she scarcely knew. She decided instead to tell the children first. She would telephone to the parents later.

It took an age to gather the children into the Great Hall. They were reluctant, sensing a doom that didn't go well with the make-believe look of all the stuff for the play which was still in place, the cheerful decorations, the colourful costumes still draped around, the towers of Troy that Pete and Mick had constructed on the stage. Once gathered, the children shifted awkwardly.

Mrs. Noble drew the children close around her, she wanted a ceremonial atmosphere but still an intimate one. The children formed a close half circle around where she sat on an orange plastic seat. The nurses and Pete and Richard stood behind the children.

'Our dear Patch died peacefully in the night. I am so sorry. We will all miss his great spirit and his great authority. But he will live on in our memories.'

Nobody spoke or cried or even moved.

Priam's Trojan elders all closed their eyes, thinking for just one second of their future. Then they began to murmur the *Hon hoi theoi* ditty and the others all joined in.

Something more was needed, and Mrs. Noble said 'We should have a good old send-off. Richard, what can we do for a Trojan king?'

'Well, a pyre was usual, I think. A big bonfire.'

'Oh, yes,' Mick shouted.

'Bonfire! Fuckin' marvellous,' Kevin chipped in. 'Let's fuckin' burn Patch up.'

'We want a bonfire, a bonfire, a bonfire.'

Again Mrs. Noble addressed the big black telephone. She spoke to Alderman Sir James Cossins.

'Well, I've heard their terms.'

'And?'

'It really depends on you.'

'Oh Lord.'

'They want a flat. The leavers who are left, that is…'

'What does that cryptic phrase signify, Eleanor?'

'Well, Patrick Beer died.'

'Oh, dear. I'm so sorry.'

'And…'

'Hmmm.'

There was a pause.

'I have to say that Patrick passing away does change things a bit.'

'Hmmm.'

'Makes it more somehow more… serious…'

'Humph, yes, I suppose you must be right. At any rate, you could look at it that way. So tell me, Eleanor, what's the big idea with this flat?'

'The three of them want to live together in the flat. Mick...'

'Remind me again, Eleanor... Mick?'

'The bifida... he wants to be a Chartered Accountant.'

'An FCA? Mmm. Is he up to it?'

'I wouldn't know myself. They claim anybody can do accountancy.'

'There could be something in that. But he'd need five-year articles.'

'They say that can be arranged. Their ambassador, the young man who's been carrying the messages, he says he'll ask his father. And the girl Helen, the one that got sent over to Binstead, she'll keep house. And she and Mick will marry.'

'Err... is that alright? I mean, isn't she...'

'I think it will be fine. She'll need her parents' consent as they'll both be only sixteen. But otherwise, why not? They seem very happy together. As I recall, that's the general idea of these things.'

There was a short pause.

'I suppose it is. And the other girl, the one that wants to go to Oxford?'

'Gloriana? I've asked an old friend if he can help. In any case, their idea is she'll live with the other two in the flat. They'll look after her. Oxford or not, she says she's going to be a poet.'

Sir James whistled.

'Aiming low, I see. And the other boy? Our absconder.'

'Robert? They're not asking for anything. I think he may have something arranged. He apparently wants to be a solicitor.'

There was compete silence for a minute at the other end

of the line. At length, Sir James said,

'I am astonished, Eleanor. Is any of this possible?'

'They say so.'

'And your view?'

'My honest view?'

'Of course.'

'I would like to see them succeed. And to think that we could support them.'

'I see. And if we go along with all this, find them a flat and cetera…'

'… then the letter will be withdrawn.'

'Hmmm.'

'But I'm beginning to think that's not the point.'

'You mean?'

'I'm beginning to think this might be a good solution for them anyway. Compared to Binstead…'

'My goodness, Eleanor, you absolutely astound me. You've quite gone over to the side of the dissidents.'

Eleanor laughed. When Sir James fell into his urbane manner, he could be good company.

'So the essence of it is that we back this harebrained scheme for the troublesome trio? And my own bit is that somehow I raise the wind for a flat for them?'

'Yes, that's it.'

'Hmm. Well, my dear, let me do some telephoning. And when this is all over, we must have a drink together.'

As soon as Eleanor had replaced the receiver, the telephone rang again.

'Eleanor.' She recognized the voice at once, even after twenty years.

'Tigger.'

'I got your note, my dear. Just one question. Is this

Gloriana a goody-goody sort of girl?'

'No, not at all.'

'More your type?'

Eleanor laughed.

'Right. I'll try to pop over in a day or two to have a look at her then.'

Of course everything is suspended. Nobody has the heart for anything. Every day we troop down to school but there's no teaching or anything like that. To keep us busy and keep our minds off things, Richard lets us watch telly all day in class. There was a programme the other day about the Merina tribe of Madagascar (oh Patch, don't you see you should be here. Where on earth is Madagascar?)

Anyway, the Merina have loads of odd customs as these tribes generally do. This particular lot wrap their dead in silk shrouds – spider's silk if the family is really rich – and pop them in the family tomb. Then every so often, when they've some spare cash or have come into a bit of money, they splash out on new silk shrouds and get the ancestors out and rewrap them all over again.

The rewrapped ones they keep out overnight and put them in the biggest bed in the house and all the small children have to get into bed with granny or great-grandpa or whoever as the case may be. Then in the night, the spirit of the ancestors enters into the little ones. All this we saw on the telly.

The little kids didn't seem to mind one bit being in bed with the ancestors. Actually, the only really scary bit was when the bull was sacrificed for the funeral bash and the big cutlass effort the men used was none too sharp and they took a fair time hacking at the poor beast's neck... erk...

Another odd custom these people have is, if they respect

you, or they depend on you, whoever you are, family or not, they call you *our mother and our father*.

So now I'm thinking about these two points very hard. Because Patch, you were *our mother and our father* and you still are – deep inside us somewhere.

I'm thinking about you as the king you were, living out your kingly story to the end, sort of debating and deciding in a kingly way on vital matters like peace and war and crime and punishment and so on and so forth. And of you as the founder of our new Troy, our just leader, bringing us all under the rule of law. And then there was your sort of – well, your enlightenment – no mumbo jumbo, no oracles or omens, we just had your fair mind solving all our problems. And then – and this is the terrible wonderful thing – you, Patch, at the end of your story, you were our sacrifice. Yes, you were. Standing up to the Rat when she broke the code, struggling to keep us together in all the mess that followed, catching that cold and everything that came after that. It was a sacrifice – and that's how you finally undermined and discredited the Rat.

You see Patch how I'm boosting you up, like a myth. Because now the hard part starts. We need you for the next bit – and the bit after that and after that. But you are in us, your spirit's in us. Patch within us, *our mother and our father*, within us, forever in our hearts and souls, Patch wrapped in silk.

48

It's raining hard when Lizzie and Richard bring me down to where the Trojans are watching from the windows. Pete and Mick are out in it, building a monster pyre out of broken farm gates, and timbers that have been lying about for years, and whole saplings and round woods that John Fry brings up from the Home Farm coppice.

In the event, even Kevin's bent for lurid happenings does not stretch to imagining that Patch's actual remains are going to be popped on this bonfire. Kevin's next suggestion is to 'put Patch's fuckin' electric jobby on' but Mrs. Noble sensibly says that the Armstead 302 should go to the senior Trojan elder. This is a lugubrious boy with big brown eyes called Martin Coade. Not that Martin's a successor or anything in any big sense, but he is now the senior Trojan elder. Anyway, we all know the Armstead cost well over £100 and we're definitely not going to burn up a perfectly good bit of equipment like that.

'What about 'is old mechanical?' Lizzie says helpfully.

So the Trojans accept Patch's old manual wheelchair as a proxy for Patch. It's a symbolical bit of Patch's kit which, like a Norse longboat, we can ceremonially burn up and there's a vague feeling amongst the more thoughtful children that this will be a way of somehow releasing Patch's spirit and sharing it out and perhaps reincorporating it. Which, if you think about it, is a notion that the Merina tribe of Madagascar might well recognize.

So there are Pete and Mick out in the rain, splashing about in the stable yard and we're all watching from the warmth of the House. But they're boys and they look like they're loving it. They construct the pyre cleverly, like a wigwam, starting with a framework of four of the long beams they've found in the barn. They cross and tie these four beams at the apex, and then fill up the body of the bonfire with the old gates and saplings and some other stuff, old pallets and wooden crates.

Then John Fry appears driving the big JCB – it's a ginormous mechanical shovel thing he uses down on the farm. John Fry lowers the shovel bit and Mick clambers out of his chair and sits in the shovel, and Pete hefts Patch's old wheelchair in beside him.

The two boys look like drowned ducks by this stage. Mick is sitting in the shovel and Pete's leaning up against it. They have a little exchange of views and then Pete nips into the old bird house and comes out with four brown paper packets. They're sellotaped up and tied with different coloured ribbons.

I know what this is – it's Mick's imaginative contribution to the protocols of death. He's going to put his dead birds on the pyre. It's like another proxy really. The little beggars must have died at about the same time as Patch.

Debbie, who gave Mick the ribbons, told me this morning that Mick's colour-coded them – the red ribbon for the lonely turaco, yellow ribbons for each of the three parakeets.

And the guinea fowl? Apparently that's a surprise for later. Suffice to say that Helen has claimed them and Mick has agreed.

John Fry is now powering up the big JCB engine. There's a lot of throaty roaring and clouds of bluish smoke pump from the back of the machine.

'Looks like it's fuckin' fartin',' Kevin says with satisfaction.

The hydraulic rods ease out, glistening like silver, and Mick and Patch's chair and the four brown paper packets are hoisted aloft. There's a bit of jockeying and jostling, with John Fry manfully pulling on levers and then the huge yellow machine is at full stretch and there is Mick high above, at the very top of the cone of wood.

He grabs hold of Patch's wheelchair from beside him in the shovel and lofts it above his head. The rain is really sheeting down now. Rivers are running down the wheelchair's tubular frame. With his strong arms, Mick moves the chair across and flips it atop the pyre, slotting it so that one of the poles slides up through the undercarriage and keeps it steady. Then he leans out and places the four sodden brown paper packets one by one on the canvas seat of the chair.

Everybody watching claps and drums on the window panes and Mick gives us a triumphant smirk and two thumbs up. You can see him but not hear him calling down to John Fry. John Fry returns him back to earth.

All this time, Lizzie and Richard have been by me, Lizzie sitting on the edge of my bed stroking my hair and Richard leaning against the end. They don't say anything but they are obviously communicating with each other in lovers' semaphore. I watch Lizzie particularly when John Fry is in the picture, because I know she had a thing with him. But nothing shows on her pale face. She just looks at Richard and ghosts him the tiniest of smiles and does something complicated and colluding with her eyes.

I am, to be honest, in love with them, in love with the idea of them.

By nightfall, all is ready. But a big problem has arisen. It's practically freezing out there. The rain slackened but a cold drizzle has been falling. It's now stopped but the cobbles are all slick and slippery.

Mrs. Noble says we all have to stay inside and watch from the windows. The Trojans greet this with cries of protest. They want to honour Patch whatever the risk. Martin Coade, the senior Trojan elder, rolls his big brown eyes in his gaunt face and smiles at Mrs. Noble a little helplessly.

Mrs. Noble consults with Debbie and Lizzie and Flick. The Rat is there, lurking at the back, but no one is about to consult with her.

Eventually, it's agreed that Pete and Mick and Richard – 'the men' they're being called now – it's agreed that 'the men' should go out and get the pyre blazing and toasty hot, and then the rest of us will nip out well bundled up.

The men seem happy to do as they're told, so they pull on some manly looking clobber – even Richard's got a thick, dirty-looking donkey jacket from somewhere – and out they go.

'That fucker'll never burn,' Kevin says happily. 'Wood's too fuckin' wet.'

But Pete can now be seen pouring paraffin all over the wood at the bottom of the pyre. Mick and Richard are holding up two long poles. Mick has previously packed twigs around the ends of these poles and bound them up with surgical bandages and tape. Pete nips over and douses these makeshift brands with loads of the paraffin.

'That'll never fuckin' work either,' Kevin says. He's really in his element tonight.

Pete now throws a match on Mick's brand which flames up immediately. He does the same to Richard's. All the watching children cry out Aaaaah! and Mick and Richard thrust their burning brands into the base of the fire and flames leap up, shooting at once almost to the very top.

Lizzie slips out and has a word with Richard, and then comes back in and gives Mrs. Noble the nod. And then we all troop out. Debbie and Lizzie take care of me and park me right by the pyre. And it's ROASTING. No, really, it's absolutely toasty hot.

Richard is going round poking his brand here and there in the bonfire and flames are bursting out all over. Kevin shouts ecstatically 'Stick it up yer fuckin' arse, Richard.'

Now the pyre is flaming on all sides. Richard and Mick toss on their brands and retire to a safer distance. Lizzie whispers in my ear 'Won't be a minute, darling' and she goes right up in front of everyone and stands beside Richard and links her arm comfortably through his. Noticing this, a couple of the kids start up the usual catcalling, but then someone – and it's Mick – starts clapping and soon they're all clapping, and my heart does a flutter.

By now, the fire is reaching towards the top of the pyre, up to where Patch's chair is fixed. All eyes are on the chair. A flurry of wind whirls up from a far corner of the yard and there is a whooshing sound. All at once the flames billow up and envelop Patch's chair.

Now the air about us is full of sparks and moving shadows. Everything that is burning is rising up. The bright scintillas of burning matter, canvas, wood, the roasting birds, the rubber and the plastic from Patch's chair, fragments of burning paint – all spin like spangles through the boiling air. It's like a purging, it's an ending and a beginning. We feel the sacramental power of fire. I experience a sudden exultation and with it a deep content.

The children in their chairs are canted forward, eager for the spectacle and blessing of the pyre. Even Kevin sits speechless for almost a minute, the round orbs of his spectacles are filled with twin fires, but then suddenly he shouts out,

'Fuck me. Look, look! It's fuckin' Bertie. He's come back from the fuckin' dead.'

And there he is. It's Bertie back from the dead. And he seems completely unaware of the sensation he's causing. He's just wandering carelessly through the yard like he's never been away. He's checking the smells, just like he never died.

'Bertie, Bertie, c'm here,' Mick calls and Bertie lumbers over.

'Fuckin 'ell,' Kevin cries, 'it'll be fuckin' Patch comin' back next!'

'So you will?' Richard murmurs in Lizzie's ear. He means 'Marry me.' Lizzie's face is a bright puce. Richard thinks her blood must be super-hot and so she must say Yes.

But she just laughs and says,

'Come off it. I told you what we're gonna do.'

Strangely Richard takes this for a sort of yes, because she is hugging his arm and pulling him back from the scorching heat, and he feels there is nothing that can separate them now.

'Treacle toffee, treacle toffee. Stick your jaws together.'

Mick is going round with a tray of treacle toffee Pete has made that afternoon. Bertie is trailing him closely.

'Come on, lovebirds,' he says, eyeing Richard and Lizzie severely. They look complete dafties holding hands and whispering like that. In fact, Mick feels he may have gone too far in leading that round of applause. He shoves the tray at Richard.

'Get on with it,' he says, 'Have your snog, eat your toffee, stick your jaws together.'

Eleanor Noble is standing alongside the Trojan elders.

The nurses are standing behind. A little apart, in the shadows away from the pyre, a middle-aged couple cling together, grey, exhausted, full of dread. Patch's parents, clearly. Mrs. Noble goes over and speaks to them. They both shake their heads.

Then Mrs. Noble steps forward, claps her hands and begins to speak in a high, ringing emotional voice.

'So, dear Patch, our King Priam, we mark your passing. We show our respect.

'We have sent you into the great world to new frontiers with fire and love, and we all share in your spirit. As we prepare ourselves for the long project of life, each of us carries you in our heart, and our best memories of you will become our true memories. You're still with us, Patch. Love to you.'

The Trojans, Martin Coade leading, chant *Patch! Still with us, Patch!*

Martin Coade gestures to Richard to move him closer to the fire. In his hands he has Patch's device, from his Armstead 302 – *hon hoi theoi…*

'Chuck it on, would you, mate…' So Richard takes the sign from Martin Coade's fingers and throws it into the fire.

The Trojans start their antiphony.

Hon hoi theoi philousin…

Neos apothneskei!

***

'Hey, gerroff, Richard!'

Lizzie's wriggling. Richard has his arm around her, feeling the heat on her body and he's trying to kiss her flaming cheek. She's about to let him when suddenly she jerks back and points her head for Richard to look.

'Hey, Rich, just look at that.'

It is Joe MacAskill standing next to Jane Ratcliffe. They are *holding hands*.

And there on her bed, illuminated by flames and heated to ecstasy, smiling her sweetest smile, the lovely Gloriana. And beside her an unknown visitor in a dark and formal suit, an elderly man with flowing silver hair and a face on him like Bertrand Russell, full of clarity and understanding.

'Who is that talking to Gloriana?' Richard asks Lizzie.

'Dunno. I let him in earlier. Monteith of Balliol, he said, whoever that is.'

'Monteith of Balliol,' he said to me, suddenly appearing. 'Sorry to burst in on you like this but I was motoring over from Oxford to see my sister and her family at Aldeburgh and I thought I'd just drop in and have a look at you.'

His face was so brown and his nose so big like a beak and his eyes so twinkly and his manner so gentlemanly that I just smiled and smiled and he smiled back. This lovely Brownlow moment went on for a bit but then I got scared that whatever it was that was about to happen would be disappointing to us both.

'Shall we just talk here?' he asked. 'This big bonfire has a nice pagan feel to it, don't you think?'

I was so nervous I was shaking. I wanted Richard to come and hold my hand but of course he was off necking with Lizzie. So I signed yes and tried to smile again and he smiled back.

'You like a chair?' Debbie asked, bringing one over.

'Mmm, thank you my dear.'

'Errr... do you need me for anything?'

'No, thank you. Gloriana and I will just stay here and have a talk. Thank you so very much.'

Monteith settled on his chair. How on earth were we to have a talk? He was looking at me all the time, so I looked back at him as steadily as I could manage. His face was quite unlined although he looked extremely old with his long silver hair.

'Very good,' he said at last and took my hand and stroked it.

'What would you say was the greatest difference between Virginia Woolf and Richmal Crompton as writers?'

Wow. Is this an interview? Is that my first question? Whatever does he mean? What is R. Crompton doing in a sentence with V. Woolf?

I had no choice but to try to answer, so I began to sign to him,

'Both are good writers. Their books have an essential humanity. But the significance of what they write depends on your own point of view.'

These are extremely hard things to sign but what else could I do? And at least with signing the fact that you are quaking with fear tends not to come across so much. But signing – what was the point? I watched him for signs of puzzlement. I expected him to shake his head, but I saw that he was watching me with great attention and when I had finished, he said calmly in his gentle voice,

'Go on, my dear. About significance.'

Monteith understood my language! He understood signing! He even grasped my paltry little thought. I must have shown my astonishment because he said,

'Don't be surprised, Gloriana. My sister in Aldeburgh went to a dinner party when she was pregnant and caught the measles. Her daughter Flora was born deaf. She is a most charming, clever girl. We are preparing her for Cambridge. I learned to communicate with her when she was just a little child. Signing is not so difficult to learn when, for example, you have had to learn Ancient Norse. And it is such an articulate form of communication, so conceptual. And wonderfully soothing, so much more so than all that talk talk talk…'

'So,' he went on, 'tell me what you mean by significance.'

I did my best.

'I think the William stories are well organized and well-proportioned and their language and expression are perfectly adapted to the subject. But perhaps their significance is limited by a conventional psychology.'

'Ah. How would you characterize that psychology? Childish?'

'Not childish, but it doesn't go very deep. It's not a very developed psychology. The motives are all very simple.'

'Do not most people have simple motives for things?'

'Well, yes and no. They may account for their reasons for doing things in simple terms. Like *I stole the loaf because I was hungry*. But why I had become the sort of person who would steal a loaf because I was hungry would be a deeper question.'

'And you feel that Virginia gives a more profound account of that than Richmal?'

'Yes.'

'And does that make her a better writer?'

'No. Just different. Everything Richmal Crompton writes is absorbing and beautifully structured. All her stories achieve the effect she intended.'

I was watching Monteith to make sure he could follow my signing. He clearly could but I also noticed a look come over him that was hard for me to interpret. If I got it right, it was like a faint humorous recognition of something.

'My dear, have you ever seen a little book called *Reading for Profit*?'

The most dreadful flush of shame shot through my body. I am sure my cheeks were on fire. Somehow, Monteith had spotted that everything I'd said had been practically parroting Monty Belgion.

But he was already changing the subject.

'So, my dear, what classics have you read? Anything eighteenth-century, for example?'

I admitted to *Gulliver's Travels*. He said at once,

'Ah, spot on. The University Press is just bringing out my new edition. You must tell me your thoughts.'

That he should care about my thoughts was the most wonderful thing. So I did my best and he listened, saying nothing.

By now the fire was dying down and Lizzie and Debbie came over and hovered.

'Erm, Sir,' Debbie said. Monteith stood up at once. He was half a foot taller than Debbie, who's no midget.

'Excuse me, ladies. Of course, of course. Gloriana must not catch cold. Please, wheel her in.'

'Would you like a warm spot inside, Sir?' Debbie asked.

'No, no, my dear, thank you so much. Gloriana and I have had a lovely chat. I'll just nip in and have a word with dear Eleanor and then I must be getting on for Aldeburgh. Well, goodbye, my dear.'

He shook my hand and left.

The nurses wheeled the chairs back towards the House. Lights came on. The children went to their tea, a special meat tea Helen made, an *ossobuco*, which they thought was alright with plenty of brown sauce on it.

Richard went to help Pete and Mick arrange the remains of the fire. The flames had burned down. The cold filled the yard. The shadows vanished, night came in. Bertie nosed around and found the treacle toffee tray which he licked ardently for more than half an hour.

49

S ally Moreton has a nice house in Liphook, just south of Guildford. The house has a huge salon that gives onto a terrace, below which the hill falls away so that Sally can look down over the paddocks, where she keeps her four-year-old gelding Breeze, to the strip of woodland which also belongs to the house. The dining room, the kitchen and three of the five bedrooms as well as three of the five bathrooms also have this view. Sally has a nice husband called Euan and two nice children. She has all the other things that go with the big income that Euan earns in the City, and she has her own income from her Interior Design practice which she has kept going part-time since the birth of Julian, now four, and Emma, now two.

This satisfying accumulation has made Sally very happy, so that it was odd that she did not mind a rather derelict woman of forty-six but who looked much older than that and who had escaped from an asylum moving in. Odd, too, that she didn't mind taking this worn-out creature into Casa Magnolia in Guildford and buying her four, five, six of everything, nor introducing her to Amanda, her hair stylist and to Paula, her manicurist. Nor to taking her four times in a week to Peter Withers-Jones, her dentist. Least of all did she seem to mind spending day after day in conversation with this used-up old soul, nor did she mind when Julian and Emma took to the old girl and soon began to call her Granny.

'Lord, Sal, are you sure you know what you're doing here?' Euan reasonably asked. Sally, who had come to know

Euan very well indeed during the three years they had lived together in Little Venice before they were married and in the six years since they had settled in the nice house in Liphook, understood that this was a big question. What Euan meant was that Sally should know the weight she assigned to the even comfort and deep pleasure of her (and his) present steady life before she voluntarily drove a wedge right into the heart of it.

Euan's initial thought was that it would probably be a mistake. From his own point of view, it had suited him very well to marry this slim stylish girl from nowhere, whose adoptive parents had been killed together in a car crash while she was at university and who claimed no other relatives either of her adoptive or of her blood family. That she was a girl from nowhere and without origins meant that she was completely herself. That she came without a trail of embarrassing relations who might make Euan's own parents sniff was an added bonus. To his father's question 'But who are her people?', Euan's 'She has none' had seemed an excellent response.

Because he loves his pretty wife, and because he loves his comfortable life, Euan pressed the question, although in a sense it was fait accompli. Having discovered this batty old mother, Sally could hardly undiscover her. The woman could go into a home, of course, but that didn't seem on the cards.

Actually, once spruced up, the old bird didn't look so bad. She had beautiful grey eyes, just like Sally, and the same fine-boned face. In fact, side by side, in their smart clothes, the two women strangely resembled mother and daughter. The posture was a problem, and the gait. Perhaps some re-education was possible. The speech was odd. But she could pass easily enough amongst the resident Liphook eccentrics.

In the end, two things proved decisive. Sally plainly wanted a mother, which was fair enough. And the children loved this granny figure who had parachuted onto them like Mary Poppins. With Stella, stiff old Stella, his own mother, the children cried when she tried to pick them up, but they seemed to recognize something in Sal's old Ma that was hidden from Euan.

So when Sally stood close to Euan one evening and murmured *Why not buy Lilac Cottage in the village*, one of those quaint timbered places, and put it against tax as a company thing, and let Norma stay there, he was inclined to agree. And to let the disabled boy she had befriended at the asylum stay with her, and for him and Norma to mess together – this also seemed fine. Getting the boy articles at their solicitors in Guildford would take a bit of finagling but he seemed a bright kid and all that gobbledygook with the bogus statutes that he'd pulled off to hoodwink the people at Binstead had been totally brilliant. He seemed to have a good legal mind and Pat Meadowes, the senior partner at the Guildford firm, had already said he'd be happy to take a look at him. Pat had a disabled younger brother who was doing well in insurance over in Leatherhead.

And, Sally said, on Sunday afternoons we'll send the children up to Lilac Cottage and have time for us like we used to. So Euan agreed and it was all settled.

Helen ran her finger along the breast until she found the opening between the two muscles. Her fingertip slid in. She took the sharp knife and severed the larger muscle from the side of the breast, then cut it loose from the breastbone. Then she did the same with the smaller muscle. She repeated the procedure for the other side of the breast.

She laid the four pieces on her block, two large pieces, flat and triangular, two smaller, rounded and tapering. Deftly she drew out the white tendons that poked from the end of the two smaller pieces. Then she put her palm on one of the two larger flat pieces and carefully sliced through it horizontally. Then she did the same to the other large piece. Now her guinea fowl fillets were ready.

For this special dinner, she would abandon her mother's exuberant Bolognese *cuccina*, which stuffed rich ingredients into rich ingredients and coated them in shaved white truffles. She would do it simply, in the sparer style of Siena, so that her lover's birds would sing for themselves.

She popped oil and butter into a cold skillet and warmed it. When the butter ceased to foam, she slid in the fillets and cooked them half a minute on either side, then removed them and, setting them on a warm dish, sprinkled on salt and pepper. She now added lemon juice to the skillet and briefly simmered the juices, running the wooden spoon round the sides to scrape off every last bit of goodness. She added chopped parsley and a little more butter and briefly stirred, then reduced the heat and slid her fillets back in. She turned them in the juice three times, then took them out and put them back on the warm platter. She garnished them with thin lemon slices. They were ready. They were perfect. She carried them through to her man.

***

Oh deary me
Mother's caught a flea
Put it in the kettle
To make a cup of tea
The flea jumped out
And bit mother's snout

In comes daddy
With his shirt hanging OUT

The Trojans were playing Chain He in the Great Hall.
Martin Coade had organized it. At first he'd had a commemorative, tribute-to-Patch thought in mind, and that *was*
in the children's minds. This might have had a palling,
morose-making effect but as soon as they started the Dip,
the spirit of the game asserted itself and they dipped and
played as cheerfully as ever.

Now the chain was a fearsome twelve abreast and it
came thundering down the Great Hall towards Martin
Coade, who deftly whizzed the Armstead 302 around the
piano. It was a tight squeeze and he wasn't used to handling
such a big chariot, especially with Patch's old saddlebag
strapped on the back but he managed it. The Chain would
have a real job squeezing in after him.

We are fifteen for the Leavers' Dinner at the big round table
in the staff dining room. Let me go round the table – Mrs.
Noble, Richard and Lizzie, Mr. MacAskill and Jane Ratcliffe,
Debbie and Flick, me, Mick and Helen, Greg, and Angela
and Pete, and Robbie. Oh, and Bertie, our Lazarus dog.

We are eating the most delicious guinea fowl. Those
clucking ladies, those pretty pearly queens gave up the
ghost in a good cause, even if their demise was an accident.
Helen serves the dish very fast, straight from the kitchen,
her nimble brown fingers working the big spoon so deftly,
and then she settles herself happily next to Mick. They smile
at each other nervously, and Mick gruffly announces what
we have all come to know already anyway – that they are
getting married as soon as they are sixteen which is actually
next week. But we cheer and cheer as if we didn't know.

Mick says he has spoken to Helen's father who is happy with it, and to Helen's mother who chattered in Italian but who was reported by Helen to be already imagining babies.

Then a lovely thing happens. Helen goes out and comes back with a huge wooden bowl, very flat and wide, made of some beautiful old-looking wood like walnut wood or something and in it are a huge number of salad leaves and shoots and beans. She brings it right up to me and she holds it there, and she says in her sing-song voice,

'At home it is the lady with the most beautiful hands who must mix the salad.'

I plunge my hands in and they go round and round and the leaves become all glistening and shiny and the salad starts to have a living look about it. Helen puts the bowl on the table and then she pulls out a soft, soft cloth of the purest white and gently, very gently she rubs my hands and between my fingers and all around my wrists and she says 'There!' And my hands are glowing with the last of the golden oil.

Everybody takes salad from the bowl, using two huge wooden implements that Helen has produced, a huge fork and a gigantic spoon. Only Pete doesn't take any. In fact, Pete seems altogether rather subdued. He and Angela came in holding hands, but now he's just sitting quietly alongside her, saying nothing. It is hard to read the expression on his face. He clearly wants to be here, and to be next to Angela, but he looks puzzled and altogether not very bouncy.

As for Angela, she sits looking very much in charge of herself – and perhaps of Pete too. The truth is – Lizzie told me, because she and Angela have been chumming up – that Angela says she is 'considering' Pete, she thinks she may be able to make something of him.

Richard and Lizzie mostly just sit there laughing, and

Mr. MacAskill embarks on a long thing about guinea fowl in Africa. He says he once read Donkin's groundbreaking monograph on the guinea fowl. Apparently the bird is called *Meleagris* because Meleager's sisters, weeping for his death, got turned into guinea fowl, hence the pearly spots which are really tears. Hah!

But there are no tears tonight. We are all a little awkward, of course, but also full of certain joy, all apprehensive and excited because we are all on the threshold of a new life, all going forward, yet no step beyond the next step is clear, nothing is finally decided, all is glorious choice and chance.

At about a quarter to eight there is a commotion outside and in burst three long-legged young women in very short skirts. Everybody brightens up. They say they have come for Greg. It turns out they are the girlfriends of The Grief, and they certainly don't come from Bungay, The Grief having moved well up from there. In fact the latest Grief album actually has on its cover a picture of Greg being chaired above the heads of the crowd at Felixstowe. Now this record has sold a billion copies or something and The Grief have received a special Golden Disc in consequence, as well as these nice posh girlfriends.

As Greg's song is on the record, royalties are rolling in, and Greg has been called to London where he will be the patron of The Grief Fan Club and honorary editor of The Grief Fan Club Magazine. How exactly he will live remains clothed in glamorous vagueness, but Angela as a Bungay girl says she will keep an eye out for him. Bungay boys and girls, it seems, don't return to their native earth but like Bungay clay they stick together. Anyway, for now, these good-hearted, spirited, beautiful dolly birds have the appearance of loving Greg already. Greg himself looks quite ecstatic as they wheel him away to his future.

The Rat and Mr. MacAskill are side by side. She has a new, doe-like look to her, the main component of which is the absence of those massive binocular lamps which formerly filled half of the Ratcliffe countenance. From the fact that she came into the room unaided and has eaten up her dinner more or less accurately, I deduce that she can see perfectly well and therefore she must be wearing – contact lenses. And now that I look more closely I do see a swimmy look in her eyes and a lot of blinking, as of one adapting to having hard, round little glass windows stuck on her eye ball.

Ratcliffe's uncovered eyes turn out to be rather shiny and they have a moist look about them as though tears are, if not imminent, at least a constant possibility. This newly softened Ratcliffe is on the whole well-behaved with looks of modesty and deference predominating, and subsidiary notes of elegy and regret. All of which is fine and most appropriate. She barely talks. In fact, she doesn't pronounce any general opinion to the table at large at all but murmurs things Mr. MacAskill-wards and also chats a little to Debbie who is on her other side, dear ebullient Debbie.

And we have wine. Mr. MacAskill has brought a bottle of red wine. I have the tiniest sip and it is like sunshine. Robbie drinks off an entire glass. Debbie has two big glasses and then puts her arm around Flick and kisses her smack on the lips. Then Flick's lips are also red with wine. Then they kiss again. It is the most charming thing. I love it, as do the others, except perhaps that old-fashioned moralist Pete, but at least Pete has the good grace to pretend he doesn't mind.

Richard then gets up and reads out a telegram that has come from Monteith of Balliol this afternoon. Mrs. Noble showed it to me an hour ago, and my entire being flooded with happiness. Richard reads it in his new, deep voice.

Dear Gloriana, Doing honour to Monty Belgion who also gave me my start – as a young officer, I sat at his feet in Stalag 15 – we are offering you a scholarship for next academic year – or the year after if you wish to take more time to read before you come up. Sadly, Balliol cannot (yet) take girls but I have arranged with my colleague Dame Diana Jackson at Somerville to take you on. My heartiest personal congratulations. Sincerely. Monteith, Balliol College, Oxford.

And how did all this come about? Richard says it – he got it from Auden, of course: *Because we saw and were indignant.*

So we are all together for the last time. Richard gets up and says Raise our glasses to Patch and we all say *Hon hoi theoi philousin, neos apothneiskei.* Then Richard reads out a poem. He smoothes his floppy hair with his hand and says, in a gruffish, apologetic voice, This is for Patch, and then he reads quite well,

> *Surely Shakespeare is wicked, the map a bad example*
> *With ships and sun and love tempting*
> *For lives that slyly turn in their cramped holes*
> *From fog to endless night?*
>
> *Unless...*
> *This map becomes their window and these windows*
> *That open on their lives, break, O break open*
> *And show the children to the fields and all their world*
> *Azure on their sands, to let their tongues*
> *Run naked into books, the white and green leaves open*
> *The history theirs whose language is the sun.*

The Author

Christopher Ward is an author who writes both fiction and non-fiction. He has written about the natural world and has published four books on the environment and the consequences of scarcity and climate change. He has also written half a dozen novels that deal with themes of life and love and responsibility, including three books that take up themes about humanity and the ends of life mooted by JM Keynes. The first of these, *The Resistance of Anna and Magdalena*, was published by Minos in 2024. He lives on Dartmoor amidst family and friends, mourning the passing of his beloved, Isabelle Ruth, the artist, and hoping ever for new projects.

Thanks

Great thanks are due to everybody who helped in the writing and publishing of this book and especially to dear Isabelle Ruth who always believed in it and read many drafts, to my brother Philip Ward who read drafts and has worked tirelessly for its publication, and to Ed McGown who gave extraordinary support to the creative process.

CW

www.ingramcontent.com/pod-product-compliance
Lightning Source LLC
Chambersburg PA
CBHW021214260626
47172CB00002B/416